LOVER'S LIES

Justin sought her lips, savoring them, devouring their fullness. His arms encircled her, gathering her against him so that she felt the heat of his passion.

His hand played along the narrow length of her back, defying her to make him stop. Desire knifed through her as she arched against him, beyond thought, beyond reason. Only a moment ago she was hating him for taking away her freedom, yet now she wanted nothing more than to clasp him to her, to beg him to quench the flames of her desire. Wave after wave of aching engulfed her, sapped her legs of their strength to stand.

Justin lifted her passion-weak body, staring hotly down at her. His flint-dark eyes bore into hers.

"Say you were lying about not wanting me."

"I—"

"Say it, Shiloh."

The night breeze cooled her flushed cheeks and left her longing for him to continue his caresses. Her faint whisper was nearly drowned out by the buzzing of the cicadas.

"I lied, Justin. Damn you."

MORE HISTORICAL ROMANCES
from Zebra Books

PASSION'S FLAME   (1716, $3.95)
by Casey Stuart
Kathleen was playing with fire when she infiltrated Union circles
to spy for the Confederacy. Then she met handsome Captain
Matthew Donovan and had to choose between succumbing to his
sensuous magic or using him to avenge the South!

MOONLIGHT ANGEL   (1599, $3.75)
by Casey Stuart
When voluptuous Angelique answered the door, Captain Damian
Legare was surprised at how the skinny girl he remembered had
grown into a passionate woman—one who had worshipped him
as a child and would surrender to him as a woman.

WAVES OF PASSION   (1322, $3.50)
by Casey Stuart
Falling in love with a pirate was Alaina's last thought after being
accused of killing her father. But once Justin caressed her lus-
cious curves, there was no turning back from desire. They were
swept into the endless WAVES OF PASSION.

SURRENDER TO ECSTASY   (1307, $3.95)
by Rochelle Wayne
A tall, handsome Confederate came into Amelia's unhappy life,
stole her heart and would find a way to make her his own. She
had no idea that he was her enemy. James Henry longed to reveal
his identity. Would the truth destroy their love?

RECKLESS PASSION   (1601, $3.75)
by Rochelle Wayne
No one hated Yankees as much as Leanna Weston. But as she met
the Major kiss for kiss and touch for touch, Leanna forgot the
war that made them enemies and surrendered to breathless
RECKLESS PASSION.

*Available wherever paperbacks are sold, or order direct from the
Publisher. Send cover price plus 50¢ per copy for mailing and
handling to Zebra Books, Dept. 2054, 475 Park Avenue South,
New York, N.Y. 10016. Residents of New York, New Jersey and
Pennsylvania must include sales tax. DO NOT SEND CASH.*

Texas Wildflower
Susan Wiggs

ZEBRA BOOKS
KENSINGTON PUBLISHING CORP.

For Jay

Prologue

Salado, Mexico
March 1843

Isabella's huge, liquid brown eyes blinked twice, very slowly. The incredibly long black lashes grazed her tawny cheeks. Her lovely face was immobile, but her lush, ample bosom rose and fell quickly.

Looking up from where he knelt in the dust, Justin McCord was struck—not for the first time—by her sultry beauty. She had the face of an angel and a body straight from heaven. Justin's gut tightened as he remembered the long, breezy nights he'd spent in her arms.

"You bitch." His voice was a soft snarl in the dusty afternoon quiet.

"Justin, *caro*, you do not understand—"

"Oh, I understand everything now, Isabella. 'Just one more night'—wasn't that what you asked me for? How sweet you were when you claimed my wound still needed your care, yet all along you were waiting, weren't you? Waiting for Huerto and the reward he'd

7

give you for my capture."

"That is not true! Your shoulder has not healed properly—"

Justin laughed harshly. "I guess that doesn't matter much now, does it? Now that you've delivered me into the hands of Huerto, his men will see to it that I die well before the wound has a chance to fester."

"You will not be killed. Domingo promised." She moistened her generous red lips. "You'll be questioned, and then you can come back to me." She bent down and leaned close to him. Her small tongue darted artfully into his ear. "You will come back, won't you, *caro*? We were happy together, were we not? No man has ever made love to me like—"

He pushed her into the dust. "Get out of my sight."

One of the guards stepped forward quickly, outraged at the Texan's actions toward a Mexican woman. The butt of his rifle swung out, knocking Justin on the side of the head.

"*Diablo tejano!*" the soldier spat. "To your feet. I think it is time you joined your *compadres sangrientes.*"

Heat shimmered on the dusty white plains of Salado. The air was still, silent but for the incessant buzzing of flies. Justin was taken amid the other Texans, most of them even worse off than himself, having been marched from where they had been captured in the border town of Mier. Sweat coursed down Justin's face and drenched his shirt as he was shackled to the line. His shoulder throbbed and oozed wetness from the bullet he'd taken. Through a haze of pain, he looked around at the walls of the Hacienda del Salado, which bristled with the tiny black eyes of dozens of muskets.

Colonel Domingo Huerto, the ranking Mexican

officer, strode forward smartly to explain the fate of the Texans with obvious relish. His hard, cruel eyes flickered over the group.

"Your sins against my people are many," he said loudly. "For the taking of Mier and the capture of its *alcalde*, you deserve to die like dogs."

Around him, the soldiers and subalterns nodded in agreement and nudged one another. Huerto continued. "However, I am told that British and American envoys in Mexico City have been begging for your miserable lives. Do not ask me why. You are a disgrace, storming villages and stealing from innocent people. But you will not all die. One in ten will face the firing squad. That is the Latino way, but I am told you Anglos have a fondness for gambling, too. So that is what we shall do. Gamble for your lives."

He threw back his head and laughed, his even white teeth glinting in the sunlight. At his gesture, a subaltern scurried forward with an earthen crock. Over the opening was a folded scarf.

Huerto held the jug high. "There are one hundred seventy-six beans in here—one for each of you. Seventeen are black; the rest are white. Those who draw the black beans will die."

"Sweet Jesus," someone muttered. Justin looked to his left and saw that it was Edmund Katz, whose pockmarked face and trembling lip betrayed his adolescence. He couldn't have been more than sixteen.

On Justin's right was Thaddeus Stripling, who swayed and almost fainted from a gaping saber wound in his side. Discreetly, Justin put his arm around the man to hold him steady, and wondered why Stripling, a political appointee, was among the scruffy men of the Mier expedition.

"You should've listened to me back in San Antone," Stripling wheezed, leaning heavily against Justin.

Justin looked at him sharply. "What do you mean by that?"

Stripling wiped the beads of sweat from his upper lip. "The Hernandez woman—Isabella. Isn't that where you first met her? I told you she wasn't just an ordinary whore. She's with the Accord, but I guess you know about that by now."

Justin drew in his breath with a soft hiss. How had Stripling known about the Accord?

Before he could ask, the crock of beans was put before him. He stared coldly at Huerto's avid face.

"Is this your idea of a game, colonel?" he drawled.

"It is better than you deserve," snarled the Mexican officer. He looked over his shoulder at Isabella. "Well done," he told her. "We could not have afforded to let this one go."

Isabella only nodded, refusing to look up.

Huerto thrust the crock at Justin. "Draw."

With deliberate slowness, Justin reached in. His hand closed around a bean and he pulled it out. His eyes never left Huerto. The Texans around him were laughing and joking, characteristically full of bravado in the face of danger.

"Beats rafflin' all to hell," one of them said.

"Tallest gamblin' scrape I've ever been in," said another.

Finally Huerto grew impatient. "What are you waiting for, *tejano*? Show us your hand."

Justin held out his clenched fist and opened it slowly. The sunlight glinted across his palm. The bean sat there, deadly as a lead ball.

Isabella gasped aloud. "No—"

Huerto grinned. "Sorry, my friend. It is the luck of the draw, as they say."

Justin made no reply. As a cold feeling gripped him, so did an overwhelming hatred of Huerto and his kind.

10

Texas had won its independence seven years before, but the defeated Mexicans persisted, trying to eat away at the borders, taking all the little villages and hamlets that would succumb. Justin was surprisingly calm about his fate; he only regretted that his passing would leave a lot of unfinished government business.

The lottery went on until all the black beans had been drawn. Cries of outrage, pleas for mercy, and curses of defiant bravado sounded among the Texans. Justin remained silent, refusing to think of what was to come, more angry at the bungled expedition than distraught about the firing squad.

Stripling swayed against Justin and pressed a white bean into his hand. "Give me the black bean," he rasped. "I'm going in your place."

Justin drew away. "I can't let you do that, Thad—"

"Just shut up and listen. There's not much time. I'm dying anyway, Justin. I wouldn't last the night."

"Thad—"

"Now look, I'm not doing this out of any sense of brotherly love, although I'd be obliged if the Maker would believe that." He coughed and grinned crookedly, his dry lips cracking. "After all, we had that fight back in San Antone. . . ." He grew serious. For a moment, his eyes cleared and his speech became completely lucid.

"I wasn't along on this raid as a regular, and I happen to know you weren't either. I'm a special agent of the government, like you. I've been charged with investigating The Accord, a group of Texans and British who mean to overthrow the government and sabotage plans for statehood. The ringleader is Harmon West, a Houston judge. You'll want to watch that one." He pushed a set of keys into Jusin's back pocket. "I've got a farm near Houston. There's a strongbox in the library that has all the information you'll need. Use

11

it, Justin."

Justin looked at Stripling for a long moment. "Damn it, Thad, I—"

"You've got a job to do, and I aim to see it gets done. Now, don't wait around for the Mexicans to set you free," Stripling rasped. "They'll kill the seventeen as promised, but the rest will be marched to Mexico City—"

The doomed Texans were unshackled. A soldier came along and prodded Justin with his bayonet. "Let's go," he said.

Stripling staggered forward. "I'm going in his place."

The soldier looked suspiciously at the two of them. But then he shrugged and stepped aside for Stripling to pass. Thaddeus turned and stared intently at Justin, his pain-filled eyes placing all of his trust in him.

"Don't fail us," he whispered, and reeled ahead to the makeshift execution gallery.

Justin's heart pounded, with relief, with dread, with agonizing wonder at the nobility of Thad Stripling's last act. All eyes were riveted on the spectacle. The Texans were lined up and seated on a log some distance away. Blindfolds were given to those who requested them. The Mexican Red Cap company assembled, their muskets loaded.

There was no time to think. Justin took a step back, then another. He heard Huerto's shouted command.

"Ready . . ."

Two more steps. Justin was now behind the line of silent, appalled Texans.

"Aim . . ."

Suddenly Justin felt the tingle of someone's gaze. Isabella was watching him with her sharp, bright eyes. His heart grew cold as her lips parted to cry out.

But she didn't. Giving him a look that begged forgiveness, she closed her mouth and looked away.

Justin ran, the dust flying under his boots. It was just a few steps to the crumbling wall of the hacienda where a few horses were tethered to a rail. Hands flying, Justin unlashed a pair of reins.

"Fire!"

The discharge of forty guns masked the sound of hooves thundering off to the north.

One

Shiloh Mulvane slapped at a lazy fly that buzzed about her neck. She shifted her position slightly and lifted the hem of her scratchy wool serape to let in a small breath of hot, dry air. Sweat rolled in rivulets down the sides of her face, which was concealed by a wide-brimmed sombrero.

The waiting seemed interminable. Afternoon had lengthened into evening. Dust motes spun amid the amber shafts of light that slanted in through the window of Hatfield's saloon. A scruffy assortment of men, the members of Congress indistinguishable from the outlaws and gamblers, lounged at the bar, laughing raucously at coarse jokes and downing the sharp-edged whiskey that was served by an aging barman.

Shiloh ignored the jokes and gossip of the dusty frontier capital. Her shaded eyes were trained relentlessly on one man, who leaned easily against the back wall of the saloon. By now, she'd memorized the shape of his black hat and the shock of straight blond hair that fell across his brow. For hours she'd watched that

15

hard, angular face, the eyes of flint that flicked watchfully about the room. She knew every fold in his snug-fitting trousers, every dust-lined crease in his boots. She gazed with interest at the man's hands. Tanned and rough, one of them held a cheroot and the other, which had a curious little ring on the fourth finger, rested with studied nonchalance on the polished handle of his Texas-model Colt's. Overall, Justin McCord had the look of a dangerous man: strong, capable, and tense as a tightly coiled spring.

Judge West had warned her about him. McCord wouldn't be an easy one to take; only the element of surprise would give Shiloh an edge. She smiled to herself. She was sure he hadn't noticed her. For all he or anyone else knew, she was a sleepy Mexican napping away the afternoon in a corner of the saloon.

With studied casualness, McCord checked the gold watch from his vest pocket, and frowned slightly. Obviously the person he'd come to meet hadn't shown. Finally, as if in sudden decision, he tossed back the last of his whiskey and stood to his full height. He was well over six feet tall, Shiloh noted, tensing a little. With swift, easy movements he tossed some silver coins onto the bar, lifted his hat, and strode out, leaving the doors swinging lazily behind him.

Unremarked by anyone, Shiloh rose from her position on the unswept wooden floor and followed discreetly. Her stiff legs screamed in protest as she crept along the planks of the walkway, her soft knee-high moccasins making no sound. Main Street, so primitive that numerous stumps still marred it, was deserted. After his triumphant meeting with Indian tribal leaders in the spring, Sam Houstin and his entourage had left Washington, taking the better part of the population with them. Grateful for the isolation, Shiloh advanced silently on her quarry. She was inches from

16

McCord. Her heart pounded wildly as her hand closed around her six-gun. As she drew it out, a bead of sweat collected on the tip of her nose. McCord had reached his bay horse and was untying it.

Shiloh seized on the moment. She cocked her gun with a metallic click and shoved it hard into his back.

McCord froze.

Shiloh pressed harder, her eyes riveted to his hands. The fingers of his right hand twitched slightly, a sure sign that he was going for his gun.

But he didn't. With shocking speed, he spun about and swung his doubled fist into Shiloh's middle. She grunted, fell back against the building. Her sombrero fell askew, revealing a mass of tight, red-gold curls. Yet her well-trained hands hadn't betrayed her. She still held the gun fast and was ready for him when he lunged at her.

Quicker than McCord by a split second, she leveled the barrel at his face.

"You make me nervous," she said simply, with more composure than she felt. Her finger tightened meaningfully around the trigger. "I'd feel a whole lot better if you got rid of that gun."

McCord was practically smiling as he looked at her. A dimple showed in his tanned cheek and his eyes crinkled at the corners.

"Aren't you a little young to be playing with a grown-up weapon?" he asked.

Incensed, Shiloh put still more pressure on the trigger and silently prayed that her nervousness didn't show. "I'm not playing," she replied calmly. "Now, drop the gun."

It fell with a thud onto the planks. Eyes never leaving him, Shiloh stooped and picked it up, and shoved it into her belt.

McCord eyed her, more with curiosity than with

fear. The flinty eyes swept over her.

"Who the hell—"

Shiloh smiled coldly. "I'll explain everything on the way to Houston." She jerked her head toward the street. "Get in the wagon. And put those handcuffs on."

McCord's mouth tightened. "Now look—"

Shiloh thrust the gun closer. "Get in, McCord."

He studied her for a long, deliberating moment, as if wondering how far Shiloh would carry her threat.

Reading his thoughts, she said, "No, Mr. McCord, I won't kill you. But if you don't cooperate, it could cost you some vital part of your anatomy."

She heard him swear under his breath, but he swung himself up into the wagon and fastened the cuff around his right wrist. The other ring of the cuffs was secured to an iron bolt on the wagon's side.

Shiloh nodded, satisfied, and holstered her gun. With a sigh of relief, she stripped off the stifling, musty serape and untied the oversized sombrero from where it hung about her neck. She felt McCord's eyes on her tight-fitting doeskin breeches and sweat-drenched cotton shirt. Despite the heat, a shiver went through her. This McCord, with his lazily appraising eyes, might be dangerous in more than one way.

She reined his bay to the back of the cart and settled herself next to him, checking that the handcuffs were secure. They left the tiny frontier town of Washington-on-the-Brazos in a cloud of dust, their departure remarked only by a large armadillo that scuttled out of the wagon's path.

McCord seemed surprisingly—maddeningly—unruffled by his capture. He even joked with the ferryman who took them across the river. As they turned eastward, he lounged against the side of the wagon and watched Shiloh's carrot-colored hair as the hot evening wind lifted it from her shoulders.

"So tell me," he drawled, "to what do I owe this ride with a girl who masquerades as a Mexican?"

Shiloh glanced at him, bristling slightly at his mocking tone, and a little surprised at the barely disguised overtones of culture in his speech.

"Not that it's any of your business, but I'm a grown woman of twenty. And to answer your question, you've got an appointment to keep, Mr. McCord. With Miss Jessamine West."

"Jessamine—" For the first time, a line of concern deepened Justin's brow. "What the hell does she want with me?"

Shiloh laughed humorlessly. "You would know that better than I, Mr. McCord. Although I suspect it has something to do with marriage."

McCord gave a low whistle. "I'm not in any position to oblige."

"You should have thought of that when you—compromised the young lady." Shiloh made no effort to conceal her distaste. She had no respect for men who used women.

The flinty eyes narrowed. "So that's what this is all about." He chuckled. "A good old-fashioned shotgun wedding. But I must say, I always thought it was the offended damsel's daddy who brought the reluctant groom to the altar, and not some child playing at dress-up games."

Shiloh was tired of his snide references to her slight stature and childish looks. But she stifled a retort, knowing that he would try his best to get her to lose control.

"I'm sure Judge West fully intends to deal with you when we reach Houston."

McCord nodded. An unpleasant look had crossed his face at the mention of Judge Harmon West. It was clear to Shiloh that he wanted nothing to do with the

19

man or his daughter, although she wondered why he'd gotten involved with Jessamine in the first place. Apparently McCord was like most men, allowing his head to be turned by the young lady's yellow ringlets and teasing, pouting red mouth. She shrugged. Jessamine's conquests were well known in Houston. She'd always wondered who the girl would finally settle down with, and wasn't surprised by the choice. McCord was more than merely handsome; he was an awesome specimen of masculinity, and appeared to be educated. If Jessamine could put up with his utterly irritating manner, Shiloh supposed they'd make a likely pair.

They rode along in silence for a while. The sun sank low behind them, gilding the gentle rises of pasture and the stands of post oak in the distance. A lone hawk wheeled overhead and dove for its prey. Somewhere far away, a wolf howled plaintively.

At length Justin asked, "Is she—Jessamine—with child?"

Shiloh shrugged. "It didn't occur to me to ask. But no mention was made of it."

McCord settled back then, seeming to grow more relaxed with each passing moment. Clearly, being captured by a woman in disguise didn't cause him any undue alarm. He rested his free arm on his drawn-up knee and looked over at Shiloh.

"At this rate, it's three days to Houston."

Shiloh nodded and stared ahead.

"Don't you think I should know your name?"

Shiloh glanced at him, wondering if he was honestly trying to be friendly, and then doubting it.

"All you need to know about me is that I was sent to do a job, and I intend to see it through. To be honest, Mr. McCord, I find this whole business as distasteful as you seem to, but I wasn't in a position to turn it down." Anxiety tightened her throat as she had a

20

sudden image of her father, sweating and feverish, abed with a dangerously festering leg.

She swallowed hard and forced herself to sound nonchalant. "I'm a reasonable person, Mr. McCord. There's no reason why you shouldn't know my name. I'm Shiloh Mulvane."

She saw him tense slightly. He let out another of his low whistles. "Nate Mulvane's daughter? Damn, I should've recognized that carroty hair, those moss-green eyes, the freckles—"

"You know my father?"

"Anyone who's been in Texas for the past ten years has heard of Nate Mulvane. His reputation as a frontier detective is known pretty well in these parts."

Shiloh lifted her chin slightly. She was proud of her father's accomplishments, even though his personal traits were something again. After distinguishing himself as a scout in the Texas Revolution, he'd gone into private service, bringing down criminals from every class: from cattle rustlers to murderers, bigamists to robbers. It was said that Nate Mulvane had brought more lawbreakers to justice than anyone else in Houston.

Because her father was a master of his trade, Shiloh was able to live with his faults. Although he drank heavily and seemed to lack affection for his daughter, that had never interfered with his work. And if he managed his money with total ineptness, that didn't matter. Mulvane had little sense for anything other than his work. That was why this job was so important to Shiloh. If he couldn't love her as a daughter, at least she might win his respect by proving herself capable in his profession.

She drove on, aware of her prisoner's eyes on her, and somehow discomfited by his stare. Justin McCord was as wily as they came: smart, cautious, and self-

21

assured. She knew the next few days would not be easy.

She chose a sheltered coppice in a quiet meander of a deep creek to pass the night. There was a wealth of salt grass for the team and a thick covering of long, reddish-brown pine needles to cushion their bedrolls. Jumping down from the wagon, Shiloh drew out a heavy length of chain and locked it around the base of a pine tree. The other end she clamped around McCord's ankle.

"Leg irons?" he questioned mildly. "How imaginative."

Shiloh shrugged, freed him from the handcuffs, and drew the wagon away. "I can't afford to take any chances with you, Mr. McCord—oh!"

She gasped as his hand closed around her wrist. His other arm encircled her waist and pulled her against him so that she was forced to look up at his angry face.

"Let's get this straight, Miss Mulvane. I'm not real happy about being dragged around by a money-grubbing female bounty hunter. I could break your neck right now with only the slightest effort—"

She squirmed against him, equally angry. "A whole lot of good that would do you, McCord. You'd still be chained to this tree, and everything—guns, keys, team, and wagon—is out of your reach. No one is likely to pass this way for days. You'd die of exposure, if you didn't starve first."

He grinned, his teeth glinting white in the starlight. He brought his face very close to Shiloh's and held her wrapped against him. His mouth began a slow, deliberate descent to hers. With a startled cry, Shiloh turned her head away, eyes snapping in anger. He might use his attractiveness to get what he wanted from some women, but not from her.

With an abrupt laugh, he relaxed his hold on her, so quickly that she stumbled back.

22

"You've thought of everything, Miss Mulvane," he said, raising his hat in mock salute. A dimple deepened as he smiled. "I concede to your superior wiles. I'm at your mercy."

Shiloh sniffed, more shaken by the encounter than she cared to admit, and went to unhitch the team and McCord's big bay, tethering them near the water. As McCord watched with almost patronizing amusement, she laid out two bedrolls. From the wagon she brought a hamper of bread, hard cheese, jerky, and a pair of soft, ripe peaches. For all his blustering and dickering over fees, Judge West had equipped her generously.

Both ate sparingly, sitting on the soft bed of pine needles. McCord watched her thoughtfully as he chewed on a piece of jerky.

"So tell me," he said, with an annoying mixture of friendliness and mockery, "how is it that you're in the business of pursuing hardened criminals? Hasn't your mother taught you that women don't do things like that?"

"My mother died when I was five. Left to my own devices, I guess I never had a natural inclination for domestic chores. Father sent me East to a school for young ladies, but I never took to practicing inane conversation while pouring tea and fluttering a fan in front of my face."

McCord laughed, his voice rich with amusement. "I don't guess you would. I didn't think there was much of the woman in you."

Shiloh had bitten into a peach and was about to wipe away a trickle of juice with her sleeve. She stopped in midmotion, changing her mind, and delicately dabbed at her lips with a napkin from the hamper.

"I don't give a damn what you think of me," she said sharply. "But I'm not a complete oaf. I can behave properly if necessary."

"Touchy, aren't you?"

She turned away and tossed the peach into the creek, having lost her appetite for it. Without looking at McCord again, she went to rub down the horses. She spoke softly to them as she worked.

"Damned outlaw," she muttered, pulling the curry brush down a sweat-dampened flank. "What would Jessamine West ever want with such a man? She must be more a fool than I thought to be taken in by his handsome looks. Lord knows, he doesn't have anything else to recommend him." The horse bobbed its head and snorted as if in agreement. Shiloh worked on with a satisfied air. This was the first job she'd done on her own, and it had gone without a hitch. It had been almost too easy. Unaware that he was being pursued, McCord had been simple to find. He seemed a cooperative captive, but Shiloh knew better than to let down her guard. She gave each horse a sack of oats and returned to the campsite.

McCord had fallen asleep on his bedroll, his long, lithe frame relaxed and his hat pulled down over his eyes. Still, Shiloh didn't trust him.

"McCord . . . ?"

No response. For a man being forcibly dragged to the altar, he was amazingly unperturbed. Shrugging, Shiloh went to her own bedroll some yards away. One by one, she removed her high moccasins and loosened the top buttons of her cotton shirt. Grimacing, she noted that nightfall had brought scant relief from the hot, dry heat of summer. She felt gritty and sticky with dust and sweat.

One glance at the slow, eddying waters of the creek convinced her to put off bedding down for the night. She gave one last look at McCord. He hadn't moved. Shiloh left her clothes in a heap and stepped soundlessly down to the creek's edge.

She waded in, sighing softly at the cool, silken feel of the water as it swirled about her thighs, her boyishly slim hips. She went deeper, the flesh of her small, high breasts tightening as the creek closed over them. Finally Shiloh sank beneath the surface, glorying shamelessly in the cleansing, cooling sensations.

For a quarter of an hour she floated and bobbed, feeling better than she had in days. Stars sprayed across the night sky, silvering the tops of the pines. The sliver of a new moon cast an otherworldly, enchanting glow upon the water. Cicadas buzzed their endless night song. Shiloh's heart filled with love for the country called Texas, the country her father had fought for, the one that had given her the freedom to do as she pleased. Nowhere else could she pursue her career, and she was thankful for it. Its rugged beauty daunted some, but Shiloh felt completely at home.

She went to the sandy edge and took up a cake of honeysuckle-scented soap, one of the few indulgences she'd brought along. Standing hip-deep, she lathered herself slowly, soaping her torso and arms, her tightly curling red hair. Then she plunged in for a last rinse.

Justin stared sleeplessly into the black inside of his hat. He'd ignored Shiloh when she'd spoken his name, preferring to use the time to mull over what was happening. The ridiculousness of it all was almost laughable. He'd survived every major battle of the Texas Revolution seven years before, and after that had cheated death in countless Indian raids and the Mexican army's forages into the Rio Grande valley. More recently, he had avoided being killed on the Mier expedition. His superiors in Washington considered him one of the most discreet, elusive agents in Texas.

Yet a mere slip of a girl had managed to seize him. He wondered if the little spitfire was aware of the fiasco she'd caused. He'd been trying to make contact with

Raoul Delgado, a Mexican operative who had vital information about the Accord. It was no accident that Harmon West had sent Shiloh to Washington-on-the-Brazos in time to foil the contact, but did she know that?

Probably not, Justin decided. As far as Shiloh knew, she was merely bringing him to Jessamine. Jessamine. A sharp image of plump white breasts and a rosebud mouth came into focus in Justin's mind. Among Stripling's personal effects he'd found a scribbled note suggesting that Jessamine might be induced to shed some light on her father's scurrilous activities. So Justin had approached her, and found her more than willing to strike up an acquaintance. The sweet southern belle facade had rapidly fallen away to reveal the girl's healthy interest in fleshly delights. In addition to a few tidbits about Harmon West, Justin had been treated to a large dose of Jessamine's charms. She'd been a mildly pleasant diversion.

The one thing Justin had underestimated was her possessiveness. She'd quickly made it clear that he was the man she wanted to wed. Justin had thought he'd succeeded in persuading her otherwise, but apparently he had not.

He groaned audibly as everything fell into place. Harmon had hit on a perfect solution for halting the United States' investigation. The judge intended to make the government's chief agent his son-in-law. That would neatly destroy Justin's credibility as an impartial operative, for Harmon was known for buying people. Too, it would placate Jessamine's spoiled nagging.

If marrying the girl was personally unappealing to Justin, it was out of the question on a professional level. He hadn't left his native plantation in Virginia eight years earlier to pursue a life of obscurity in Texas. He meant to do something that counted, and Jessamine couldn't be included in his plans.

His father's angry words, spoken years ago at Justin's final parting from his Virginia plantation, came back, hauntingly clear in the quiet of Justin's mind.

"You'll regret going to that godforsaken frontier," Angus McCord had warned. "Texas will milk you dry, and if you aren't killed by a Mexican saber, you'll wind up beaten by the land itself. The day you were born I promised the Grangers you'd marry their daughter Ivy and our plantations would merge. I know how you feel about that, but believe me, you'll thank me for it one day."

Justin had rebelled against the arranged marriage, yet now a similar one seemed imminent. Harmon West would be well within his rights to force a wedding. Laws in Texas tended to be an individual code, and many would admire the judge for protecting his daughter's honor.

There had to be a way out. Justin knew that with a little maneuvering, he could easily break free from Shiloh Mulvane. But that would only buy him a little time. The moment he showed his face in Houston, West would pounce on him and carry out his manipulative plan. No, what Justin needed was a much more permanent solution. . . .

A sudden splash startled him out of his musing. He swept his hat from his face and sat up, looking toward the creek. The sight that greeted him drove all thoughts of Harmon West's treachery away.

Shiloh's moon-silvered shoulders glistened as she bathed herself in the creek. She was rinsing soap from her hair, the foam being swept downstream. Justin caught sight of her profile: a high, clear forehead, a small, slightly upturned nose, a proudly angled chin.

At first he'd thought the girl plain, almost homely, but in this unguarded moment he recognized a subtle,

27

yet undeniable beauty. The revelation was confirmed when Shiloh emerged slowly from the water.

Her nude body, its contours shining, was perfection. Lean, yet shapely, her legs carried her to the shore with unconscious grace. Her breasts were little more than rises of soft flesh, but the sight of her tight coral nipples sent a flood of liquid fire to Justin's loins. She had a tiny waist and flat belly, and barely rounded hips. Her thighs, beautifully muscled, were topped by the pale, enticing mounds of her buttocks.

As she stooped to pick up a rough blanket and began drying herself off, Justin drew in his breath with a hiss. He didn't remember ever wanting a woman as badly as he wanted Shiloh just now. As she donned a clean shirt, leaving it open for a cooling breeze to caress her, Justin steeled himself against the urge to tear his ankle from the leg iron and enfold the lovely body in his arms.

But he didn't. He relaxed onto his bedroll and let a slow smile spread across his face. Like the moon bursting from behind a bank of clouds, a plan began to take shape in his mind.

Feeling utterly refreshed after her bath, Shiloh drew a wooden comb through her matted curls. Suddenly, a chill touched the base of her neck. A wolf howled, intensifying the feeling Shiloh had of being watched.

Glancing over at McCord, she gasped and dropped the comb. He was lying on his side, propped up easily on one elbow.

"I take back what I said earlier," he drawled, "about there not being much of the woman in you."

Shiloh dove for her Colt's, holding her shirt closed with her other hand. Her grasp wavered as she leveled the gun at him.

"Damn you!" she hissed. "How long were you—have

you been—"

McCord grinned, his dimple making a dark impression on his face. "Long enough to know that you're every inch a woman, from the freckles on your nose to your incredibly shapely legs."

A burning blush crept over Shiloh as she gritted her teeth. She raised the gun.

"Damn you," she said again. "I could kill you for—"

McCord's laugh angered her further. "If I thought it would do any good, Miss Mulvane, I'd apologize. But I honestly didn't do anything wrong. *You* were the one who disturbed *me*, splashing around like a water nymph." His eyes traveled insolently down her legs.

She cocked her gun. "Turn around, Mr. McCord."

He laughed. "I doubt Judge West would be willing to pay for a corpse." But he turned obligingly, pulled his hat down again, and said no more.

Shiloh hurriedly donned her breeches and lay down, but sleep would not come. No amount of tossing and turning could dispel the image of McCord's flinty eyes, silvered by moonlight, watching her with a strange mixture of hunger and cold calculation.

He was aware of her as a woman now, and during the next day's drive she felt his eyes on her almost constantly, studying her profile or the curve of her breast, his hand actually brushing her thigh from time to time. The miles of red clay mounds and heat-shimmering yellow-green fields seemed to crawl by.

When they stopped at nightfall, some twenty miles west of Houston, Shiloh's nerves were stretched taut, dangerously close to the surface.

"I think you liked me better before I found you so damned attractive," McCord said.

Agitated, Shiloh fumbled with the leg irons. "It's not

29

my place to like or dislike you, Mr. McCord. My only concern is to deliver you to Houston."

He flexed his booted ankle slightly. "Oh yes, to my wedding."

Shiloh finished with the leg iron and looked up. "I believe that's what Judge West had in mind for you. It won't do you any good to try and get out of it."

He grinned charmingly. "Oh, I intend to be married, Miss Mulvane. Even sooner than you might think."

There was no warning. One moment McCord was lounging easily on the seat of the wagon, and the next he moved like a striking snake. He grasped Shiloh by the wrists and kicked off the leg iron, which hadn't latched properly. With one great angry tug, he broke the handcuffs away from the wagon, splintering the dry wood.

He let go of Shiloh so abruptly that she fell, surprised and sputtering, to the dust. With an air of studied casualness, McCord ambled over to a live oak, where Shiloh had stowed the guns and keys out of his reach. He freed himself from the handcuffs, shaking them off in an annoyed manner. Then he bent and holstered his own gun and emptied hers, tossing the bullets into the nearby stream.

Shiloh recovered quickly. While McCord's back was turned, she scrambled to her feet and edged around to the back of the wagon, where a loaded rifle was stashed beneath some hopsacking. Although McCord was facing away, he seemed to read her thoughts.

"I wouldn't go for the rifle, Mis Mulvane. You'd never be quick enough to use it." Slowly he turned, smiling, and approached Shiloh, holding her eyes with his.

She backed against the wagon, her heart thumping, her hands clutching at the rail. McCord walked toward her and didn't stop until they were inches from one another. Shiloh caught the scent of dust and cheroot. Absurdly, she found herself wondering how he'd gotten the small scar on his left cheekbone. It was very faint, shaped like a crescent.

"Let's get one thing straight, Miss Mulvane," he drawled, his breath warm on her face. "I'm not a man who takes to being chained up like a dog. It would behoove you to remember that in the future."

Shiloh's mouth felt dry as cotton. "What are you going to do?"

He smiled lazily. "I'm coming with you to Houston, if you don't mind my company. But I'm afraid we'll have to make a brief stop before seeing the judge."

He reached behind her. Shiloh tensed, thinking he was going to embrace her. But instead, he simply picked up the rifle, emptied it, and tossed the shot into the stream.

"Any coffee in there?" he inquired, jerking his head toward the hamper under the tree. He was as calm as if nothing had happened.

Shiloh nodded in a dazed manner. Confused, angry, and disappointed, she watched as McCord made a small, crackling fire and set the coffee brewing. She considered running off, but she knew she wouldn't get far. McCord's feigned nonchalance masked a tense vigilance.

"Relax, Miss Mulvane. I know I haven't given you any reason to trust me, but I'm not going to run out on you."

"That's the least of my worries," she retorted.

He shrugged and drew a small flask from his boot. Shiloh noticed with alarm that he had a Bowie knife sheathed there, and cursed her own stupidity in overlooking it. She'd been so smug about having captured him, but now she realized all the mistakes she'd made.

31

When he offered her the flask she took it and drank deeply. The fiery liquid nearly made her gag, but the second time she raised it to her lips it went down more smoothly. After a third drink she passed it to McCord. He didn't drink.

At last she found her voice. "I don't understand you, Mr. McCord."

He shrugged and sipped his coffee. "If Judge West had taken the trouble to check, he'd've spared you this trip. I bought the Stripling farm outside Houston just six weeks ago. Planned to make it into a horse ranch. In fact, I was going to look at some livestock when I made your charming acquaintance."

Shiloh looked at him sharply. "I didn't notice any horse traders in Washington-on-the-Brazos."

"I had other business as well." He didn't elaborate on that. "So you see, I'm quite willing to return to Houston. If Miss West is expecting a child, I'll make the necessary arrangements."

"But you won't marry her."

"Nope." He flicked the stub of his cheroot into the fire. "By the time we reach Houston, that will be quite impossible. Jessamine may find that I'm not the eligible bachelor she thought I was."

Shiloh reached for the flask again, wondering what heinous truth he would reveal about himself that would turn Jessamine away. "I don't have to tell you that won't sit well with the judge. Besides, won't you be needing a wife if you're starting up a ranch?"

"Could be." The flinty eyes looked at her squarely. "But if I do, it'll be on my own terms, and not because I've been prodded into it. One of the reasons I left Virginia and came to Texas in the first place was that I resented my father's trying to pair me off."

Shiloh looked at him. She couldn't imagine a man like McCord even having a father, much less one who believed he could keep a son like Justin in line. She traced her finger in the dust, wondering what sort of life he'd left behind in Virginia.

"You could do worse than Jessamine," she suggested. Personally, she found the young woman cloyingly sweet, with a subtle streak of feline nastiness. But Jessamine had the plump, yellow-haired looks that brought men to their knees, and she knew how to simper and giggle expertly.

McCord chuckled. "Ah, the delectable Miss West. She has all the conversational interest of a mocking-bird. No, I'm not prepared to spend my life gowning her in silks and escorting her to social functions."

In spite of everything, and because of the whiskey that warmed her veins, Shiloh laughed. For some reason it pleased her that McCord's impression of Jessamine matched her own. Some of the tension of the last two days seemed to leave her.

"I'd say you're in a heap of trouble, Mr. McCord. Whatever made you take up with Jessamine if you don't even like her?"

He shrugged. "I like women. And Jessamine made no mention of future commitments when she threw herself at me."

Shiloh scowled. "That's a pretty arrogant thing to say."

"You asked." He shifted, and was suddenly sitting closer to Shiloh. Again she caught his scent, and noticed the play of muscles in his thigh as he drew his knee up to his chest.

"I don't much fancy talking about myself, Shiloh. I'd rather hear about you."

It was the first time she'd heard him use her given name. He slid into using it easily, as easily as his arm moved behind her, barely touching her as he rested his hand on the ground. Shiloh drank some more of the

33

whiskey.

"I live in Houston with my father. He brought me back there when I didn't do so well at the girls' school in the East. I've been working with him for two years."

McCord nodded. "I could tell you were no amateur. You handle a gun pretty well. You'd've had me nailed if you hadn't been so softhearted with me."

She straightened up, frowning. "Softhearted? Me? Don't flatter yourself, Mr. McCord."

"If you'd really meant business, you would have trussed me up like a spring turkey and thrown me in the back of the wagon. I'd've been none the worse for the wear."

Shiloh fumed. He was right, of course, although she'd never admit it to him. Privately, she vowed to follow his advice the next time . . . if there ever was a next time. Justin McCord might well have ruined the career she so desperately wanted to pursue. She studied him long and hard, wondering how cooperative he could be. She had to try.

"Mc—Justin." She shifted, putting her shoulder against the tree to face him. A bird called, a yearning sound in the night. "I agreed to work for Judge West because my father and I need money—badly. But there's also another reason."

He gave her his full attention, looking at her intently.

"Father has never taken me seriously. When I wanted to work with him, he had me shuffling papers and pouring over account books, occasionally writing a report.

"Four weeks ago, he was stabbed in the leg and the wound festered. He's been bedridden and doesn't know I took this job. He'll be furious when he finds out. He'll never trust me again when he learns that you—that I botched everything. But if I succeed—"

"You'll have proven yourself," McCord finished for her.

Shiloh nodded, her eyes large and luminous in the moonlight.

"It means a lot to you, doesn't it?"

Again she nodded. "More than I can say."

"And all I have to do is let you haul me into town, as if you'd dragged me—fighting and hollering—every inch of the way."

Shiloh gave him a dubious look. "I know it's a lot to ask—"

He touched her and she gasped. His long-fingered hand traveled, ever so lightly, up the side of her arm. Gently, he lifted the curls away from her neck and caressed the leaping pulse at her throat.

For a moment, Shiloh was mesmerized by his touch, fascinated by the wave of intense sensations that washed over her. The hard-planed face drew down to hers, closer . . . Shiloh could almost taste his lips on hers.

His mouth poised just a whisper away, he said, "That's a mighty big favor you're asking of me, Shiloh. But I might consider it if you'd—"

A chill came over her, snuffing out the sudden hot longing that had seized her. She slapped his hand away.

"No deal, McCord."

He laughed, seemingly unabashed by her rejection. "A minute ago you wanted something badly enough to—"

"Not enough to warm your bedroll for a night, McCord. I've no doubt you know many women who would settle for that, but I'm not one of them." Shiloh jumped up and stalked over to the bubbling stream. She filled her cupped hands with cool water and bathed her flaming cheeks, trembling with outrage. She felt him come up behind her. He knelt and spoke intimately into her ear.

"No moonlit swim tonight, Miss Mulvane?"

She tossed her head in angry denial. "You've already shown that you can't be trusted."

"But you won't mind if I do," he said, a smile in his voice. "I'll want to look presentable for tomorrow."

"Do as you please," Shiloh snapped. She whirled around, intending to brush past him. Instead, she found herself staring point-blank at the incredibly broad expanse of his bare chest. Powerful bands of muscle stood out, tapering down to a flat belly. His skin glistened in the moonlight. There was a curious absence of hair, but that only served to heighten the image of unadorned masculinity. Shiloh had an urge to study him closely, from the deep, arrowhead-shaped scar on his right shoulder to the narrow waistline of his trouser tops, but she forced her disconcerted gaze away.

"Excuse me," she muttered, and hurried to her bedroll, where she buried her face in her arms and refused to look at him. His low, mocking laughter told her he'd fully understood his effect on her.

The wagon creaked over deep ruts in the clay road, jolting the two silent passengers. They passed by a small farm with a tiny log house and a few thrown-together outbuildings, all covered with a fine coating of reddish-brown dust. A thin, weary woman carrying a small child on her hip emerged from the cabin and blew on a long, hollowed-out horn, summoning her husband and sons in from the fields. It was a lonely, plaintive sound, devoid of any brightness. The woman shaded her eyes and stared, unsmiling, as the wagon drove past.

Shiloh felt sorry for the woman, whose life undoubtedly consisted of scratching out a living on the prairie, being faced with Indian raids and drought, and subjugated daily by her husband. Silently, Shiloh renewed her commitment to pursue her career, to live independently as she pleased. She only hoped that her blunder with McCord wouldn't prove to be fatal to her ambition.

From the top of a sharp rise in the road, Houston came into view. It was a sprawling, mud-spattered town clinging to the brown banks of Buffalo Bayou. One of the most populated places in the Republic, it boasted numerous grog-shops and inns, government buildings, and trading posts. Settlers arrived daily, from the East, from Europe, from Mexico, and from the port of Galveston. None of these hurrying strangers found anything remarkable about the tense-looking couple approaching from the west end of town.

Justin pulled the team to a halt and looked at Shiloh, a question in his eyes. She lifted her chin and glanced away, unwilling to speak to him. He shrugged and drew the wagon up to a small whitewashed church. A rainbow of untended wildflowers grew in profusion beside the steps leading to the double doors. Shiloh looked dubiously at Justin.

By now, Justin McCord had done the unexpected too many times for her to be surprised. She raised an eyebrow at him.

"Come to repent for your sins?" she inquired sarcastically.

He reached behind the seat and took out her serape. He placed it around her shoulders and softly answered her question.

"No, Miss Mulvane. I've come to commit one."

Shiloh froze as she felt the thrust of his six-gun against the small of her back. She tensed, ready to spring to the ground.

"I wouldn't," McCord threatened, his voice still soft, almost intimate. "You've backed me into a corner, Shiloh, and I don't much care for it. Let's go."

Heart pounding, Shiloh got down. She glanced quickly about, seeking help. But the narrow lane leading to the church was deserted. Besides, McCord's gun was concealed by her serape. To the unsuspecting eye, they would undoubtedly look like a couple in love, with Justin's hand guiding her solicitously up the steps.

Shiloh hesitated at the door. "What are you going to do? I think I have a right—"

He pushed her, none too gently, into the church. "You gave up any rights you might have had when you went to work for Judge West, Shiloh. Now, keep your mouth shut and you won't get hurt."

The church was empty. Golden shafts of afternoon light slanted in through the high, half-wheel windows. Benches were arranged in neat rows facing a raised pulpit. Justin pushed Shiloh up the aisle and through a door in the back. This led to a small, dim drawing room. A faint smell of roasting meat hung in the air.

"Hello!" Justin called out.

Shiloh heard the sound of a scraping chair, and then a small, rotund man appeared, wiping food from the corner of his mouth with a napkin.

"Howdy, folks," he said, eyeing Justin with a faint flicker of nervousness. "What can I do for you?"

"We want to be married," Justin stated. "Now."

Two

Shiloh staggered, her mouth working in shocked silence. Justin held her tightly against him, his gun a constant reminder of his cold ruthlessness.

The preacher seemed flustered. "Now look, mister, I can't just—"

Justin drew a small cloth bag from his pocket and tossed it carelessly on a low table. Yellow-gold coins spilled out. Shiloh guessed there was better than a hundred dollars in double eagles there.

The preacher's moon-shaped face grew suddenly very friendly. He picked up the coins and stashed them carefully in his vest pocket.

"I suppose," he said agreeably, "that we could get things going pretty quickly. Now, my wife knows a good hymn or two, and she's just in from cutting flowers in the garden. For a bit more, you could—"

"That won't be necessary," Justin interupted. "Just do what you have to do to make it legal." He glanced down at Shiloh, whose face had drained of color. As she studied the lattice design on the mauve carpet which covered the floor, Justin felt a small, unfamiliar stab of regret. She looked so vulnerable, so damned childlike.

He'd seen more cheerful faces on men doomed to be executed.

Justin let out his breath with a soft hiss. He reached into his pocket and tossed out another coin. "I guess a flower or two wouldn't hurt."

"Of course," the preacher said hastily. "I won't be a moment."

Suddenly Shiloh seemed to snap out of her stunned silence. "Wait!" she cried.

The preacher turned, eyeing her curiously.

"Sir, you can't do this," she said hurriedly. "This man is a stranger to me. He's forcing me against my will—" She gasped as she felt the gun press painfully into her back.

"There now, sweetheart," Justin drawled, sending the preacher a knowing look. "Don't make a fool of yourself in front of the gentleman." He appeared to give her a reassuring squeeze, but actually he thrust the gun even more firmly into her.

Then he faced the preacher. "I guess she can't believe she finally got me to the altar." He grinned. "Trailed me all the way to Washington-on-the-Brazos just to get me hitched, didn't you, sweetheart?"

Shiloh shook with outrage. "I—I—*damn* you . . ."

Justin gave the preacher another coin. "A little case of cold feet, that's all," he exclaimed easily. "She'll be fine."

The man scurried away to fetch his wife.

When they were alone, Shiloh turned to Justin. Hatred shimmered from her moss-green eyes and her voice dripped venom.

"You'll be sorry you did this, Justin McCord," she vowed, trembling with rage.

His flinty eyes met hers, hard as granite. "I've no doubt you'll do your best to make me regret it, Shiloh. But you left me no alternative—"

40

He broke off abruptly as Shiloh began a desperate struggle. She twisted in his steely grip and kicked out viciously. Justin nearly lost his hold on her, but he finally subdued her by squeezing her so tightly that she nearly lost consciousness.

"I'm calling your bluff, McCord," she gasped, green eyes shooting daggers of loathing at him. "Go ahead and shoot me. I'd rather die than become your wife."

"You don't mean that," he told her sternly. "What would your father think if you got yourself killed on your first job? And didn't you say he was ailing? He may not be able to get along too well without you."

The mention of her father seemed to subdue her. The anger in her eyes melted into quiet defeat. She deflated a little in his arms. Still, the spark of defiance hadn't quite gone out.

"You won't get away with this, McCord," she muttered, raising her chin a little.

The preacher bustled in again, followed by his wife, whose plumpness and round face matched his. She held out a bunch of wildflowers: lavender foxglove, yellow agarita, tender little wild roses. Shiloh took them, trying to keep her hands steady. His face unreadable, Justin plucked a single rose from the bunch. It was perfect: dewy, on the verge of opening fully, the color of fresh-churned butter. He gently tucked the blossom into Shiloh's hair.

With a grunt of satisfaction he turned back to the preacher. "Let's get on with it," he muttered.

The preacher cleared his throat and opened a small black book to a page that was marked by a red ribbon.

"Dearly beloved," he began, "we are gath—"

Justin shifted impatiently. "Can you make this as short as possible?"

The preacher looked up, one eyebrow raised high. He glanced over his shoulder toward the door, obviously thinking of his unfinished supper. Shrugging, he flipped forward a few pages. "I don't suppose you have a ring."

Justin started to shake his head, and then hesitated. Working with his thumb, he slipped the curious gold ring from his fourth finger and handed it to Shiloh. Dazed, she placed it on her left hand. It felt warm, comfortably heavy, and the small design of a willow tree glinted in the dim light.

The preacher was already speaking again. ". . . and by the power vested in me by the Republic of Texas, I hereby declare the two of you man and wife."

Silence reigned. The preacher and his wife were looking at them expectantly.

"It's customary to kiss the bride," the preacher prompted.

Shiloh opened her mouth to protest, but Justin's eyes cautioned her. He leaned down, taking his time for once, and captured her lips. His mouth held hers, for perhaps a beat, but in that moment his action conveyed volumes. She belonged to him now, that was obvious from the possessive way he kissed her. Shiloh felt weak with relief when it was over.

They signed the preacher's register and a document printed on cheap paper, which the preacher sealed with a stamp.

Numb with disbelief, Shiloh lost her footing as she climbed up onto the wagon. Justin's strong arms were there to catch her. As he held her firmly, amazed at the softness of her body, she felt small and oddly vulnerable to him.

Yet her reaction was terse. "I can manage by myself," she snapped, and brushed him away. Justin shrugged. He didn't blame her. He knew he wouldn't be feeling too kindly toward someone who'd just forced him into marriage without his consent.

As he drove away from the church, Justin studied Shiloh's profile. She held her chin high and looked straight ahead. She had a small, well-shaped nose that was sprayed with tiny freckles, and pretty coral-colored lips. In the past few days, Justin had grown to appreciate Shiloh's looks. She could never be termed a great beauty, not with such an intense face and lean, almost spare body. But there was something about her that he found incredibly appealing. It was more than the pale, perfect vision he'd glimpsed when he'd watched her bathe; it was her spirit, her quick mind, even her sharp tongue that intrigued him. And although Shiloh was fiercely independent, he knew that her bravado masked a wealth of softer feelings. This mixture of gritty self-reliance and childlike vulnerability made Shiloh different from any woman he'd ever known. He wanted nothing more to do with lush, lying beauties like Isabella Hernandez or the grasping Jessamine West.

It was a pity he'd had to treat Shiloh this way, to involve her in the twisted, murky web of affairs Thaddeus Stripling had charged him with. Justin decided that Shiloh deserved some explanation.

"I'm sorry about what happened back there."

She turned quickly, green eyes smoldering. "You don't need to bother apologizing. It's not going to change the fact that you just forced me to marry you."

Justin shrugged. "The idea of a shotgun wedding didn't seem to bother you much when *I* was the one being forced. As I remember, you were dead set on presenting me to Jessamine West."

"That was different. I was doing a job, performing a service."

He leveled his gaze at her. "I, too, have a job that must be done. It would have been disastrous if I'd had to marry Jessamine."

Shiloh sniffed. "You should have thought of that

43

when you seduced her."

Justin scowled. It was true, but he'd had something entirely different in mind as he'd wooed Jessamine. How was he to know that what he thought was a casual affair would mean so much to the judge's daughter?

He guided the wagon down Texas Avenue, wishing that Shiloh weren't so damned silent. Why didn't she rail at him, call him all manner of names, ask a passerby for help?

"Where do you live?" he inquired. "I think the first thing we should do is see your father."

She swung around abruptly, her eyes troubled. "No! I don't want to see him."

"Why not? You've been gone at least a week. Won't he be worried?"

"I told him I was going to visit my Aunt Sharon at her farm north of town."

Justin frowned. "You mean you came after me without his knowledge?"

"Of course. I told you, he'd never have allowed it."

Justin let out a low whistle. "Damn. I expect he won't be too happy when he hears we've married."

Shiloh smiled grimly. "On the contrary, he'll be delighted that someone's agreed to take me off his hands. He's been badgering me to 'settle down' since I was sixteen."

"Then why don't you want to see him?"

Shiloh didn't answer right away. As Justin watched intently, she looked down at her small, work-roughened hands. Deep auburn lashes veiled her eyes. She blinked, and swallowed as if fighting back tears. Justin's jaw tightened as he suddenly realized the pain she was in. The pain of having an uncaring father and the pain he'd inflicted on her. Cursing himself, he drew the wagon to the side fo the road and halted it beneath a broad live oak.

Gently, he touched her arm. "What is it, Shiloh?"

She pulled away as if stung and regarded him fiercely. "I don't know why you bother to ask, but if you must know, you've ruined all I've ever dreamed of."

Justin cringed inwardly. "Was there another man, Shiloh? Were you courting—"

"No! I never have. That sort of thing means nothing to me." Her eyes sparkled with the sheen of unshed tears. "All I've ever wanted was to be a detective, like my father. Don't look so dubious, Justin. A few women have done it quite successfully. Doña Estebana of Goliad, for example. But my father was like you. He didn't think a woman could make it. Even when I learned to ride and shoot like a man, he thought it was only a matter of time before I closed my world until it was nothing more than a hearth and home, a husband and children."

"But you had other ideas."

Shiloh nodded, her eyes still moist, but oddly cold. She spoke not to him, but almost to herself, staring at some distant point beyond the bayou.

"For as long as I can remember, all I wanted to do was be a detective. I knew I was good, from the time I found a Mexican arsenal stored beneath the hall of justice in San Antonio when I was fifteen years old. There was enough ordnance there to bring down half the city, but I saw that it was given over to the proper authorities. After that, my father let me play at spying, posing as a belle at a Spanish baile, or delivering correspondence here and there. Father would never admit it, but I was getting good. Detective life was ruining him, driving him more and more to his bottle, but I was thriving."

She shot Justin a contemptuous look. "I know you proved my ineptness, but this is the first time I made such a large error in judgment."

He could see that she was trembling. She looked small and fierce, like a cornered bobcat. Again he touched her arm.

"This job that Judge West sent you on—it was important to you, wasn't it?"

She nodded. "The judge paid well, and my father had some pressing debts. I had hoped to prove myself to him, so he'd take me seriously at last."

Justin felt an unaccustomed tightening in his gut. Wrapped up in his own affairs, he'd never paused to consider Shiloh. He'd merely used her as a vehicle to avoid being placed under Harmon West's control. Now, too late, he was discovering that she was more than a money-grabbing bounty hunter. She was a many-faceted individual, with hopes and dreams of her own.

Justin frowned as a wave of guilt washed over him. He spoke gently, wanting to soften the hard line of Shiloh's pressed-together lips and the creases in her brow.

"I still think we should see your father. You can't put it off indefinitely."

Shiloh expelled her breath slowly. Without looking at him, she said, "Main Street, the east end."

Eb, the aging freedman who worked for Nate Mulvane, came around to the front of the dusty white frame house to see to the wagon and team. His bright, expert eye quickly evaluated Justin's fine mount, a deep bay.

"Evenin', miss," Eb said. He nodded his grizzled head at Justin, taking the man in with a sweep of his eyes, and led the team away with an obvious lack of curiosity.

Looking after him, Shiloh suppressed a wistful sigh. Only Eb understood her ambition, and in his quiet way encouraged it. How proud he would have been of her if she'd only pulled this off. . . . Feeling Justin's eyes on her, she tossed her head.

"This way. I expect my father will be having his supper." She led the way into the house. There was a large room with a heavy table and benches and a good-sized kitchen hearth. Eb kept the place tidy and swept, and a pot of his good beef stew filled the air with a delicious aroma. An iron safe stood in the corner, its top stacked with numerous papers and account books.

"Eb? Eb!" A gruff voice called from beyond a curtained doorway.

"It's me, Father," Shiloh answered. "I'm with my—with a visitor." She cringed inwardly at the slip. Although she'd gone through with the sham of a ceremony and put her name to a piece of paper, the word "husband" stuck in her throat.

"Well, come on in, girl," Mulvane blustered.

They stepped inside the tiny bedroom. The air was thick with blue-gray smoke. Nate Mulvane sat propped on his bed, his lap strewn with papers and ashes. A plate of stew was on the table beside him, untouched. A bottle of whiskey and a small glass stood beside it, the bottle half empty. Mulvane looked up, his florid face seeming even more ruddy because of his great profusion of red hair. Eyebrows as thick as cattails descended as he viewed his daughter and her guest. He rubbed a hand across his unshaven face.

"How's Sharon?" he inquired.

"She—Father, I didn't go to see Aunt Sharon."

His green eyes, aging mirrors of her own, narrowed slightly. "Oh?" Then where the hell have you been?"

Shiloh glanced briefly at Justin. He leaned easily against the door frame, his face impassive, but she wondered if he was shocked by the crudeness of her father. Drawing a deep breath, she framed an explana-

47

tion.

"Judge West paid me to go to Washington-on-the-Brazos after this man—Justin McCord."

Mulvane's fist came down, scattering the papers in his lap. "Damn it, girl, why didn't you tell me?"

"Because you wouldn't have let me go."

"You're damned right I—" Mulvane looked fiercely at Justin. His thick red brows drew together. "What does Harmon want with you?"

Justin sidled into the room, clearly unabashed by Mulvane's blustering.

"I suspect he had a number of things in mind, but he had some idea that I should be compelled to marry his daughter."

"Hmph." Mulvane puffed on his cigar, bringing the dwindling ember to life. "I'd heard Jessamine's finally set her sights on one man." His eyes flicked over Justin's uncombed hair and dusty clothes. "Didn't figure it'd be someone like you."

"Don't worry, Mulvane. It won't be."

The bushy eyebrows shot up. "What the devil's wrong with you, boy? Jessamine's damned pretty, and rich to boot."

Justin shrugged. "It doesn't matter. I couldn't marry her. Being Harmon West's son-in-law would be directly at odds with my work."

"Are you a Ranger, boy?"

"No. Why do you ask?"

"You've got that look about you. Cold eyes, fast hands, a go-to-hell attitude—"

"I've ridden with Jack Hays and Big Foot Wallace."

Mulvane nodded. "It figures. Well, son, since you're not going to say anymore about what you do, why not tell me how it is that you let a hundred-pound girl drag you back to Houston?"

Shiloh gritted her teeth, but Justin grinned broadly.

"She did a damned good job. Nailed me when I had my back turned outside a saloon."

Mulvane scowled at his daughter. "I spent most of my life savings sending you to that fancy girls' school in the East. Didn't they teach you not to go near saloons?"

Justin gave a short laugh to dispel the momentary tension. "Her sombrero and serape completely concealed her identity."

Mulvane relaxed against his bolster. "Well now, maybe this deal wasn't as foolhardy as I'd thought. How much did Harmon pay you, Shiloh?"

She merely stared, her gut twisting in anticipation of her father's reaction when he learned the truth.

"Well?" he prompted.

"Justin didn't tell you everything," she said, her voice soft and toneless. "He overpowered me, and—"

Mulvane sat forward, his hand going for the barrel of his six-gun, which lay on the floor where he'd been cleaning it.

"And what? Speak up, girl."

"—and we were married." The admission was little more than a whisper in the smoky haze of the room.

Mulvane froze in midaction. His green eyes narrowed and his lips thinned. Then, suddenly, he threw back his head and burst into laughter. It was the worst possible reaction in Shiloh's eyes. She could have withstood his anger much more easily.

"Married!" Nate roared. "Sweet tarnation, my daughter's married! Eb! Bring a glass for Mr. McCord. We've got some celebrating to do. Now, get over here, son, and shake my hand. I'd stand and salute you if it weren't for this dad-blamed leg. You're a rare man indeed to stand up to Shiloh's nonsense. I can't tell you how many perfectly decent men she's chased off." Mulvane's broad grin disappeared for a moment. "That isn't to say, Justin, that she won't make you a

49

good wife. In spite of all her malarkey about careers and such, my daughter's a fine woman."

Justin looked from Nate to Shiloh, his face oddly tender. "I know," he said quietly, and took the proffered glass from Eb.

Mulvane looked at her too, and spoke brusquely. "Go on, now, Shiloh. We've got some serious drinking to do. Go get yourself cleaned up, and for God's sake, put on a dress. It's your wedding day!"

Slowly, Shiloh backed out of the room. She couldn't decide who she hated more, McCord, her father—or herself.

As she lay on her rope-frame loft bed, watching gilded dust motes spin through the air, Shiloh bit hard into her lower lip. What was happening was so awful that there was a sense of unreality about the whole situation. She felt as if her life had ended, when it should have been just beginning. A dull ache throbbed behind her eyes. She had no idea what would become of her. She didn't know how to be a wife. All she knew was the uncertainty of a detective's life: endless days in the saddle, stealthy observations, the tingle of imminent danger, the sense of supreme satisfaction when a job was done . . . there would never be any more of that for her.

Shiloh squeezed her eyes shut. Conversation, punctuated by her father's deep laughter, drifted up to her ears. Unable to resist, she listened to learn more about the man who had forced her to marry him.

Nat Mulvane chuckled. "Most of these things should be settled before the marriage, but you didn't come to me on bended knee, begging for her hand."

"I had to act quickly, Nate."

"Don't worry. I'm not complaining. But I would like

50

to know where you come from."

"I was born in Virginia. My parents come from old families and it was always assumed that I'd carry on the family tobacco plantation. But my father and I didn't see eye to eye on a lot of things. Finally we had a major falling-out and I joined a group that was coming West. That was in 1835, eight years ago. The Texans had already begun their campaign against Santa Anna. Soldiering didn't appeal to me, but I've got a good eye for horseflesh and can sit a mount decently. Hank Karne, the Ranger, made me a scout. I did a lot of work for him, even after San Jacinto." There was a clink of glass as he refilled his drink. "Recently, I got mixed up in the Mier Expedition, but I managed to escape."

Nate gave a low whistle. "I heard that all the survivors were marched to Mexico City and never heard of again. How'd you get away from those Red Cap devils?"

"I made a friend. A good friend."

Shiloh grimaced. She couldn't imagine anyone as unscrupulous as Justin having a friend. More likely, he'd slit the throat of his guard and stolen off, or perhaps bribed his way back to Texas.

"I'm surprised I didn't hear about your escape," Nate said. Shiloh recognized the keen probing beneath the casual comment.

"There's a reason for that, Nate. I'd rather not go into it now, but we can talk later."

"You'd be a hero, son—"

"Not interested. There are a lot of things more important than personal recognition."

"Such as . . .?"

"Annexation. I want to see Texas become part of the United States."

"That's a big dream, McCord. A lot of folks are in

favor of it, but not the right folks."

"It's something I've been working for since San Jacinto."

"Working for statehood won't feed my little girl, Justin."

"I have a good piece of land and a house up north of town. It used to belong to Thaddeus Stripling. I'm planning on turning it into a horse ranch. Samuel Colt's Texas-model pistol has made the Rangers a lot more effective, but they could use some better horses. I've seen a lot of good men having to use farm plugs against Comanches."

"Shiloh might like that," Nate mused. "She's always been good with horses."

With a snort of digust, she sprang from the bed. Justin and her father were cronies by now, drinking and talking without a care in the world. She heard Nate suggest a bath and change of clothes for Justin and decided that she, too, needed to clean up after the dusty, draining trip. She went to the washstand, bending low beneath the roof beams, and poured water into the basin. Sighing gratefully, she peeled off her travel-stained clothes and splashed the sweat and dust from her skin. She used honeysuckle soap liberally, almost defiantly. Both Justin and her father had accused her of being less than feminine, and she meant to prove them both wrong.

She had a few dresses hanging from wall hooks in the corner. None of them were particularly pretty, but the green sprigged cotton frock complimented her coloring and the full skirt and shirred bodice gave the illusion of fullness to her figure. She brushed savagely at her profusion of carrot-colored curls, not relenting until her hair shone. She swept it back from her face with a pair of tortoise shell combs, leaving it long in the back. A tiny oval looking glass, cracked years ago when her father was in his cups, showed an image that was barely satisfactory. Days in the sun had darkened her skin and the spray of freckles across her nose. Hastily, Shiloh took up a shawl and used it to cover her amber-tinged arms. Taking a deep breath, she descended the ladder.

She hesitated on the bottom rung, looking down with mounting anger at Justin McCord. He was seated at the thick oak trestle table, looking over a sheaf of papers. He was wearing clean clothes: a loose white shirt and thigh-hugging buckskins. His newly washed hair gleamed yellow-gold in the lamplight. His face, clean-shaven now, was drawn into an expression of intense concentration. There was no denying the phsyical appeal of Justin McCord. Lean and bronzed, with his sculpted features, he was a man of uncompromising masculinity.

Shiloh made a small movement on the ladder. McCord looked up quickly, his eyes wary, and hastily gathered up his papers, stuffing them back into his saddlebag.

"What are you doing?" Shiloh demanded.

He grinned slowly, taking in the snug bodice of her dress and the turn of her bare ankle with obvious appreciation. "Your father celebrated himself into a long nap. I was just going over a few things." He indicated a large pot on the cookstove. "Coffee?"

Shiloh shook her head. "Where's Eb?"

"He said something about getting one of the horses shod. One of your team threw a shoe."

Shiloh gritted her teeth. Why hadn't she seen that? She'd always been attentive to the animals' needs . . . but she'd been so preoccupied with McCord that she hadn't noticed. She was sure Justin would remember this further example of her incompetence. Without

53

another glance at his handsome, smiling face, she went out to the porch and stood leaning against the railing.

Twilight had given way to another crystalline night. Stars were sprayed across the sky, and the tall, still pines were silhouetted against the light of a waxing moon. The animals in the shed behind the house stamped and snuffed, bedding down for the night.

Familiar sounds, comforting sounds . . . but Shiloh's agitation did not abate. She stiffened when she felt McCord's presence behind her. He was so close that she sensed his warmth, smelled his faint scent of soap and leather.

"For what it's worth, I'm sorry about the way things turned out for you."

She whirled on him, gasping a little as her bosom brushed against his shirtfront.

"Spare me your pity, McCord. It has a hollow ring to it."

"Come on, Shiloh. I think you're making too much of this. I promised your father I'd treat you decently, give you a good life—"

Her green eyes blazed in the moonlight. "Have you ever wanted anything, Justin, wanted it so badly you could taste it in the air you breathe, and hear it on the wind every night? Wanted it so much you went to sleep thinking about it, and woke up with it still fresh in your mind?"

He stared, the lines of his face softening the slightest bit. His eyes took on a veiled, distant look. "Maybe I have, Shiloh."

"Then why can't you understand what this means to me—"

"Because it's wrong, damn it, and you're a fool for dreaming about it. You're a woman, Shiloh, although I didn't really appreciate that at first. You can't go around masquerading as a man, doing a man's work.

Give marriage a chance, girl. You're ripe for it."

Insolently, he flicked her shawl away and touched the flesh of her shoulder. Trapped between McCord and the porch railing, Shiloh decided to stand firm, and show him that she was not one to succumb to his evocative touch, even though his nearness caused a tingling to begin deep inside her.

"I'm not interested, McCord. That piece of paper we signed today doesn't change that," she hissed. Still a curious lassitude was creeping over her, induced by the small, sensual motions of his hand on her bare shoulder.

"So you say," he whispered. "But you're lying." Slowly, he bent and tasted her flesh. His teeth grazed the side of her neck, and his hand slid lower to rest against the curve of her breast.

"Don't —" she pleaded, but her voice sounded small and distant, so weak a protest that it almost resembled an invitation.

Justin sought her lips, savoring them, devouring their fullness. His arms encircled her, gathering her against him so that she felt the heat of his passion. The lassitude deepened, warming her in places she'd never felt before. His hand played along the narrow length of her back, defying her to make him stop. With a tiny moan of denial, her lips parted, inviting the velvety caresses of his tongue. Unable to resist his closeness now, her arms crept around him, hands roving over the sinews beneath his shirt. Encouraged, Justin pressed forward until Shiloh arched back over the railing, his strong arm keeping her from falling.

Her heart leapt wildly as his fingers loosened the buttons of her dress, freeing her breasts. Still kissing her deeply, he fondled her, circling her nipples with his thumbs. Then he dipped his head and assailed her bosom with his swirling tongue. Shiloh was rocked by new sensations, her ears ringing and the world closing down around her, until all that existed was Justin, his bold hands and hungry lips.

Desire knifed through her as she arched against him, beyond thought, beyond reason. Only a moment ago she was hating him for taking away her freedom, yet now she wanted nothing more than to clasp him to her, to beg him to quench the flames of her desire. Wave after wave of aching engulfed her, sapped her legs of their strength to stand.

Justin lifted her passion-weak body, staring hotly down at her. His flint-dark eyes bored into hers.

"Say you were lying about not wanting me." His hand flicked tantalizingly across her naked breast.

"I—"

"Say it, Shiloh."

The night breeze cooled her bosom and left her longing for him to continue his caresses. Her faint whisper was nearly drowned out by the buzzing of cicadas.

"I lied, Justin. Damn you." She closed her eyes in anticipation of his next searing kiss. When he made no move, she opened them again.

The barest hint of a smile curved his lips. Gently, he set her on her feet and pulled the bodice of her dress back in place. While Shiloh stared in confusion, he reached around and did up the buttons. Finally, he drew her shawl back around her, brushed his lips across her brow. His arms dropped to his sides.

"I'll be bedding down out back, with Eb," he said. "Holler if you need me." He ambled slowly down the steps and around back, whistling.

Hate flooded into Shiloh's every nerve as she gaped, speechless, after him. As he had so many times before, Justin McCord had made a fool of her. Brought her, with his masterful hands and sensual lips, to the brink of surrender, only to leave her stone-cold and seething, despising her own weakness as much as she loathed the man who brought it out in her.

Nothing short of revenge would satisfy her. Looking up at the winking stars, Shiloh vowed to get even with Justin McCord.

Justin scowled up at the dawn-gray cracks in the top of the shed. Nearby, Eb snored softly, and the horses were just beginning to stir. Justin had passed a nearly sleepless night, haunted by a vision of wide, moss-green eyes, pale, silken skin, Shiloh's artlessly passionate lips. He couldn't explain what had induced him to begin to make love to her the night before. It was bad enough that he'd made her marry him; he hadn't meant to complicate things further.

But something about Shiloh's contemptuous attitude had challenged him, made him want to prove to her that she was a woman ready for love. Perhaps he'd wanted to show her that, contrary to what she believed, marriage to him wasn't the end of the world.

It had taken every ounce of his restraint to leave her, just when she would have given herself to him. But he knew she wasn't ready, although her body had responded to his touch. She would have come to her senses soon enough and despised him all the more for taking advantage of her.

Justin sighed wearily. He was as unready for marriage as Shiloh. There was too much to do, too much uncertainty in the future. He decided that, come morning, he'd explain as much to Shiloh. He'd hold her to their marriage only until the threat of Jessamine West was past, and then he'd give her back her freedom. Surely even Shiloh would agree that that was reasonable.

Although a small voice in the back of his mind protested letting a woman like her go, Justin thought it a satisfactory solution. Flinging his arm across his eyes, he decided to try and get a little sleep.

Just as he was drifting off, he felt a circle of cold metal against his neck and froze. Shifting on the bed of straw, he found himself looking into a vengeful pair of moss-green eyes.

Three

A morning rain had dampened the lush green lawn of the Villa, Judge Harmon West's new house beside Buffalo Bayou. Small, yet cunningly styled after the graceful plantations of Georgia and the Carolinas, the Villa had glass windows and a white-railed verandah wrapping around the flower-decked front porch.

The sparkling lawn bloomed with drooping lavender wisteria and clipped bushes of white-flowering hawthorne. Spanish moss dripped from ancient live oaks. Yellow blossoms of jessamine, for which the judge's only daughter was named, draped a wrought-iron fence. It was a picture of formidable wealth, which Harmon West had come by, some whispered, without total regard for the laws he now upheld.

Justin McCord shifted uncomfortably on the hard cart-bed and was jolted when it came to an abrupt halt on the drive in front of the house. He stared angrily at the stiff, narrow back of his utterly defiant wife and tried to rub his painfully shackled wrists. Glowering, he chastised himself roundly for having goaded Shiloh into her vengeful act. He'd been too damned sure of himself, too hasty in dismissing her, thinking she'd given up her crazy notion of delivering him to Judge West.

It was not like him to be so incautious; in his line of work one couldn't afford to make stupid mistakes. But he'd done just that, convinced by Nate Mulvane that the girl had been tamed, letting himself be provoked by Shiloh into taking her into his arms last night.

"You're making a mistake, Shiloh," he muttered darkly.

She swung around, her eyes hard as emeralds. "No, Justin, the mistake was yours. You and my father are both dead wrong about me. It's going to take more than that worthless piece of paper—and a few kisses—to turn me into a meek little homebody."

He saw the hot blush that stained her cheeks, and he started to apologize. Then he clamped his mouth shut. What the hell did he have to be sorry about? He was the one being dragged before a man who could quite possibly murder him when he found out he'd been duped. Shiloh's treachery shouldn't surprise him. It wouldn't be the first time a woman had betrayed him.

Justin let a sneer curl his lip. "I'd never accuse you of being meek, my dear, but last night I got the idea that you might be just the slightest bit interested in being a wife to me."

Her face drained of color. He could see that her hands shook as she held the reins.

"You had no right to do that to me, Justin McCord."

"On the contrary, Shiloh, as your husband, I have a right to far more than I took last night. I hadn't planned on taking advantage of it, but this latest stunt of yours may cause me to change my mind."

"You wouldn't dare—"

A servant came out of the great double doors and two mulatto grooms appeared to see to the cart and team.

Shiloh nodded at them and turned to the servant. "Tell Judge West it's Shiloh—Mc—Mulvane." She glanced back at Justin, her eyes full of venom. "Making the delivery he requested."

Justin refused to rise to her bait. He grinned lazily, inclined his head. "Congratulations, Shiloh. You brought this to a successful conclusion, after all." He stretched out his iron-bound ankles.

Shiloh lifted her face to the morning sun. Justin noticed again the curiously endearing dusting of freckles across her small, upturned nose. It was incredible that one who looked so sweet, almost childlike, could act like this. He reached up with both shackled hands and ran them suggestively along the silken flesh of her bare arm, flesh that was warm and honey-colored from the sun.

Shiloh drew quickly away. "You'd better save your caresses for Jessamine."

"You're a cold woman, Shiloh."

Her green eyes, which on occasion looked as soft as dew-laden moss, grew hard. "You're nothing to me, Justin. Nothing but a hundred dollars in my pocket as soon as Judge West gets out here."

Justin shook his head. That kind of hardness seemed unnatural in one so young.

"I'm curious, Shiloh. How do you propose to get around the fact that we're married?"

She scowled darkly at him. "The judge himself will take care of that. No court in Texas would uphold a marriage made by force. Or one that hasn't been consummated," she added pointedly. Spots of ripe-peach color appeared on her cheeks.

Justin shook his head. "It's your word against mine. Your father was mighty pleased with the way things turned out. He's not about to let anything jeopardize our marriage."

Shiloh pursed her lips. "We'll just see about that, Justin." She turned her back and refused to look at him again.

Presently Harmon West arrived, flanked by two burly black men, walking slowly to the cart. He was a man on whom middle age looked well: tall, silver-haired, still trim around the middle. He was impeccably clad in a tailored black frock coat and trousers. His polished hardwood cane was probably an affectation, as West had the gait of a much younger man.

He barely nodded at Shiloh, but took the keys she offered and freed McCord's hands and ankles. The two guards stood close by, watching for trouble. Justin flexed his wrists and jumped down.

"I appreciate the reception, Harmon," he said easily.

"Let's go inside, McCord. We have some business to —"

"Justin!" A feminine voice rang out. Jessamine West ran across the lawn, her ribbon-trimmed yellow dress drawn back over a lacy petticoat. Her plump pink cheeks were flushed with exertion, her blue eyes wide and shining. Yellow ringlets bobbed about her face.

Justin groaned inwardly. For perhaps the hundredth time he rued his indiscretion with the girl. The liaison hadn't been anywhere near as fruitful as he'd hoped. Jessamine had been willing enough to talk, but her knowledge of her father's involvement with the British and Mexicans had been scant.

He removed his hat and nodded a greeting. Jessamine thrust her small, moist hand at him. As he bent and raised it to his lips, he heard Shiloh's soft snort of disgust.

"I'm ever so glad you're back," Jessamine breathed. "I was afraid you'd gone for good."

Justin extracted his hand from hers. "You'll have to excuse us, Jessamine. Your father and I were just

62

going in to talk over some business." He turned to follow Harmon into the house.

"Judge West." Shiloh called him back.

The gentleman turned, his jaw twitching in irritation. "Yes? What is it?"

"There's a small matter I must discuss with you." Shiloh's back was held stiff in a businesslike demeanor.

The judge coughed. "Oh yes, of course. I'll send Mr. North out to pay you."

"Judge, it's not—"

"Now look, miss, we agreed on what the payment would be."

"But I—"

Jessamine turned, as if noticing Shiloh for the first time. She frowned, and her small rosebud mouth drew into a pout.

"Payment? What payment?"

Feigning innocence, Shiloh raised her eyebrows. "Oh dear, Jessamine, I thought you knew. Your father thought Mr. McCord might need to be persuaded to return to you, since it didn't seem likely he'd come back on his own."

Jessamine's cheeks flamed and her curls bounced wildly, the longer ones striking her ample, heaving bosom.

"You're a liar, Shiloh Mulvane! You're just jealous because you'll wind up a skinny old maid, parading around in boys' clothes."

Shiloh appeared unruffled by the attack. She tossed her head. "I intend to, Jessamine. Just as soon as my business with your father is concluded."

Justin suppressed a grin. Jessamine was no match for Shiloh. He caught her eye and winked. She looked disdainfully away and turned to face the judge.

Before she could speak, he waved his hand. "Mr. North will be out presently." With a nod of dismissal, he turned and went into the house.

Justin looked back at Shiloh, who for once was at a loss. But the stare she gave him promised that she hadn't given up. Not at all.

Harmon West's office was predictably tidy and handsomely appointed. Books lined the shelves from polished floor to wainscoted ceiling, and the furniture was of finest fruitwood, polished and fragrant with verbena. West was one of the first to bring eastern style to Houston, which was fast growing from a boggy outpost into a city.

Justin waved away a servant who offered him whiskey, and seated himself on a leather wingback chair.

"What can I do for you, Harmon?" he asked mildly.

The judge selected a fat cigar from the humidor on his desk and clipped the end with a vicious stroke. "I don't much like the way you treated my daughter, McCord."

Justin's lips thinned. "And I don't much like your sending Shiloh after me."

Harmon chuckled. "A blow to your ego, McCord?"

"No, damn it!" Justin's fist pounded the arm of his chair. "What the hell were you thinking of, sending that girl off alone? You know what it's like on the trails—"

"The young lady assured me she had no fear of outlaws, redskins, or Mexican bandits."

"I don't doubt that that's true, Harmon. Shiloh fears nothing. But you sent her off knowing of the dangers involved. What the hell kind of man are you?"

Unruffled, the judge steepled his hands. "The question is, McCord, what sort of man are *you*? Your concern for the Mulvane girl is touching, but we are here to discuss a more important matter: you and my daughter."

64

"I have no interest in Jessamine. You wasted Shiloh's time and your money bringing me here."

Harmon West had small eyes of no particular color. They narrowed in a cold, calculating way. "Jessamine needs a husband. Since it was you who stole her innocence, then it will be you who will wed her. You should consider yourself lucky. Men in these parts have been killed for less."

Justin declined to mention that Jessamine's innocence had been long gone by the time he'd taken up with her, knowing that it wouldn't matter to the judge.

West drew a document out of a drawer. "Here is the contract. I've been generous with Jessamine's dowry—"

"Sorry, Harmon. I can't marry your daughter."

"You don't have a choice, McCord. You sealed your own fate six weeks ago, when you seduced Jessamine."

Justin's jaw tightened. "Is she pregnant?"

"No. But that doesn't change a thing. You're still responsible."

"I won't sign that contract."

With the quickness of a much younger man, Harmon drew his heavy revolving pistol from the drawer and pointed it with a cold metallic click at Justin's chest.

"No one would raise a finger of protest if I killed you now."

Smiling slightly, Justin leaned back in his chair. "I can understand your wanting to marry Jessamine off, Harmon. God knows, the girl spends enough of your money. But my marrying her would make me a bigamist, and that could taint your image pretty badly."

"What the devil are you talking about, McCord?"

Justin spread his hands in guileless fashion. "I'm already married." He leaned forward and helped himself to a cigar from Harmon's humidor.

The older man lost his composure for a moment,

letting his jaw drop. Recovering, he said, "That's a damned lie. You said you were a bachelor the first night you met Jessamine."

"I was. But then I met Shiloh Mulvane." Justin was a little surprised at the pride he heard in his own voice. He'd never wanted a wife, preferring the nomadic life as an agent of the government. But now that he was compelled to settle down, who better to do it with than the volatile, intriguing Shiloh?

Judge West shook his head in confusion. He lowered the gun, but kept his hand close to the handle.

"Perhaps you'd better tell me about this."

Justin grinned. "Shiloh and I were married yesterday. It's all perfectly legal—"

"Either you're lying, McCord, or Shiloh is as crazy as people say. If she's your wife, then why in tarnation did she deposit you here?"

Justin's grin faded a little. "Shiloh and I haven't smoothed out all of our differences. After all, we didn't meet under the most ideal circumstances. And you know how it is with young folks just starting out. Shiloh has some fool idea about taking up with her father. She accepted your job to prove to Nate that she could do it on her own."

Harmon's hand came down hard on the desktop, causing the lamp and inkwell to jump. "I paid that woman good money to bring you here."

"And she did, Harmon. I don't believe she was charged with insuring my bachelor status. If the money means that much to you, I'll see that you get it back." Justin's eyes grew suddenly hard. He made no effort to conceal his dislike of Harmon West.

"But it isn't the money at all, is it, Harmon? And it's not Jessamine's happiness you're worried about. The only reason you wanted me to marry her was to get me under your thumb. So I wouldn't stand in the way of your plans to prevent statehood for Texas."

Judge West smiled grimly. "So the cards are all out on the table now, aren't they, McCord? It doesn't matter, though. I admit, things would've been a lot easier if you were one of the family. But I'll manage." His hand moved caressingly, meaningfully, over the butt of his Colt's. "And you'll be one sorry son of a bitch before I'm through with you."

Justin smiled. He didn't underestimate Harmon's power, but neither was he afraid of the unscrupulous judge. He stood and slowly ambled from the room, his mind already on other business.

He rode hard over the rolling acres of meadowland, rounding a deep, murky pond and climbing the rise that led to the ranch he'd named Post Oaks. Thaddeus had left some livestock, and a few Mexican workers had stayed on to work for Justin. The amount of work that had to be done on the house was staggering, and Justin hadn't been around enough to see that it got done. Now, though, he'd have plenty of time to make improvements.

Justin let himself in through the heavy front door. The house smelled musty, of disuse. Most of the furnishings were still draped with sheeting. The small study was the one room Justin had opened. The hand-hewn furniture was unattractive but sturdy, and the desk was well equipped with paper, ink, and wax for his correspondence. With muttered curses, he rifled through his papers. He drew out the documents he'd gone to pass on to Delgado in Washington-on-the-Brazos and frowned. Shiloh had seized him before he'd been able to meet with his colleague. And now Delgado would miss the opportunity to present damning evidence against the Accord at a hearing in San

Antonio.

Harmon West had known that. He'd succeeded in outsmarting Justin on that count. But there was one thing he'd overlooked. Justin's lips thinned into a cold smile. Shrewd as Harmon West was, he had erred badly in sending Shiloh after Justin. She'd provided the perfect dodge.

Perfect? Justin frowned again. He paused to consider the type of woman he'd married. Hoydenish, temperamental, and proud, she was enough to give any man pause. When she was angry, nothing was safe from her wrath. Yet when she smiled — rarely enough — the whole world seemed to light up. And there was an aura of sensuality about her that she didn't even know she possessed. Justin had first glimpsed it when she'd bathed in the river. And last night, when she'd responded to his kisses with surprising intensity. She was naive and untried, but Justin recognized the promise of passion.

It was a promise he was tempted to see fulfilled. Something about Shiloh challenged and defied him. He wasn't about to let her insult of this morning pass. Last night he'd considered releasing her from the marriage as soon as it was prudent, but that was before she'd acted so vindictively. Justin smiled. The little wildcat. She was begging for a fight.

He returned his papers to the safe and went to find Ina. The maid was in the kitchen, her inky hair braided and her apron smeared with grease.

"There will be two for supper tonight. And put fresh linens on the bed. My wife will be joining me."

Shiloh jumped down from her lathered mount and led it around to the yard behind the house. She'd spent the morning riding hard, ranging through the wild

68

bayou country as if pursued by demons. Finally she'd turned her big piebald stallion to the north, where her Aunt Sharon lived. Two ferns on pedestals stood inside the door, quivering as Shiloh burst inside.

"Aunt Sharon! It's me, Shiloh."

A small woman came around from the kitchen, wiping her flour-dusted hands on her apron. Nate Mulvane's sister looked enough like Shiloh to be mistaken for her mother, with the same tightly curling red hair, green eyes, and a perpetually intense expression. But time and care had mellowed Sharon, made her cautious and prudent, where Shiloh was not.

"Land alive, child, look at you. Your dress is covered with dust and your bonnet's hanging down your back—" Sharon grew suddenly alarmed. "Is it Nathaniel? Has he taken a turn for the worse?"

"No," Shiloh answered quickly. "My father is still abed, but he seems to be mending."

Sharon wiped a hand across her brow. "Then what is it? It's been a long time since you've come bursting in one me." Smiling affectionately, she led Shiloh by the hand into her tiny calico-curtained parlor, and they sat down together on a fading brocade settee.

Shiloh swallowed hard. "Aunt Sharon, could I talk to you about something?"

The older woman's eyes softened. A childless widow, she had always lavished her love on Shiloh. "Of course, child. You know you can tell me anything."

Taking a deep breath, Shiloh began at the beginning, when Judge West had sought her out. The words poured out in a torrent, describing her triumph at capturing Justin McCord, and her mortification when he'd turned on her and forced her to marry him.

Sharon listened quietly, displaying neither surprise nor shock at Shiloh's tale. When it ended, she said, "My dear, you should have considered the consequences of going off like that, without your father's knowledge."

"I thought I was prepared for any possibility, Aunt Sharon. But how could I have known that he would make me wed him?"

"I suppose you couldn't have foreseen that. What sort of man is this Justin McCord?"

"He's . . . he's—" Shiloh frowned and thought for a moment. "Some women might call him handsome: tall and broad, with a great shock of blond hair and white teeth and a dimple. He's from a wealthy Virginia family. I heard him tell my father that he came West after a falling-out with his father, and then he served as a scout in the revolution. Now he's planning on starting up a horse ranch. Father seemed to like him, but I know better. Justin's impossibly arrogant, scheming, and unscrupulous."

"Oh dear, did he hurt you, Shiloh?"

"No, no, nothing like that. He was quite gentle with me, in fact. I don't know why, but at the wedding he put a flower in my hair and gave me this ring." Shiloh held it out for her aunt to see.

"You could do worse than a man like that."

"But I don't want to be his wife, or anybody's. Don't you see, Aunt Sharon, I'll suffocate as his wife. He won't ever let me work with Father as I'd planned."

"Are you sure of that, Shiloh? Have you asked him?"

She shook her head. "I'm sure he expects me to be a proper farm wife, seeing he's fed and his clothes are laundered." She lowered her voice almost to a whisper. "I just can't live like that." She twisted the ring around her finger.

The older woman stood and moved about the room in her brisk way. "Well, it's done. Now you must decide what you are going to do."

"I'll go to Judge West. He wouldn't listen to me this

morning, but now Justin's probably told him everything. Surely he knows a way to invalidate the marriage."

Sharon frowned. "I don't like Harmon West. Never have. When your uncle was with the Rangers he suspected that the judge was supplying the Mexicans with ordnance. Six weeks later Elihu was dead. Killed in a Comanche raid, or so they said. But I've never been able to get it out of my mind that Harmon had something to do with it."

Suppressing a shiver, Shiloh went and took her aunt's hands. "You never told me that. Why didn't you do something about it?"

"There was no proof. And nine years have passed. Yet I still believe Harmon is not to be trusted."

Shiloh nodded. She didn't like the judge either, but his money had made her overlook that. Still, she clung to the idea that perhaps he could do something about her predicament.

"He's a judge, Aunt Sharon. And it's to his advantage to help me."

"You don't understand, child. If Justin refuses an annulment and your father backs him up, there's no way anything can be done. I'm afraid we women have very little to say about such things."

Shiloh sighed, painfully aware of the truth in that. "I won't go to the judge, then. But neither do I want to be Justin's wife. Aunt Sharon, can I stay here with you?"

Sharon looked deep into her niece's eyes. "I was afraid you'd ask that." She gently smoothed a wisp of hair from Shiloh's cheek. "Child, I can't let you do that. You know I love you like a daughter, but if you stayed here, you'd be running away. You've never been one to do that. You're going to have to face up to this, and the sooner the better. Besides, your Justin McCord doesn't sound like a man who'd stand for that."

Shiloh looked out the window, across a sea of waving grass. Her aunt's words echoed in her mind. Shiloh never hid away from trouble, even when things were at their worst. She was at a low point now, married to a virtual stranger, but she knew she would only triumph if she found the strength to deal with Justin face to face. She pursed her lips in sudden decision.

"You're right, Aunt Sharon."

The older woman took her hands, her eyes moist. "Go to him, Shiloh. Talk to him. Maybe things aren't as bad as they seem."

The sun was lingering low as Shiloh climbed the steps to her father's house. She'd ridden long and hard to Aunt Sharon's and back, but in a way the ride had purged her, and at least her talk with her aunt had made her feel better. Nothing had changed, but she'd resolved to work something out with Justin. Perhaps he would be reasonable after all. Despite everything, she couldn't deny that there seemed to be a thread of decency in Justin. She remembered the yellow rose and the ring on her finger, and told herself that maybe he'd understand—

Shiloh gasped as a pair of strong, unyielding hands grasped her from behind, one of them clamping over her mouth to stifle a protest. She recognized Justin instantly from his scent and the low chuckle that rumbled in his throat.

"Evening, Shiloh," he drawled. She struggled ineffectually against his tall, hard frame. "You know," he said, "I don't take kindly to being tricked. You bested me this morning, but it won't happen again. The game is over. Let's go home." He dropped his hand from her mouth when her struggling ceased.

"This is my home," she said through gritted teeth.

"Not anymore. And I'm sure your father agrees with me."

As if summoned on cue, Nate Mulvane appeared on the porch, leaning heavily on a gnarled cane. Shiloh gave him a pleading look. If ever she'd wanted something from her father, it was this.

Don't make me go, she said in a silent message with her eyes. Don't make me go.

A shadow crossed her father's face and he looked away, concealing an odd glint in his eyes. He spoke to Justin.

"Take care of my girl, McCord."

Shiloh couldn't believe her ears. *"Father—"*

Nate shook his head. "It's for the best. Justin will give you better than I ever could."

Justin nodded curtly to his father-in-law. Without warning, he scooped Shiloh up and placed her on his horse, mounting easily behind. The bay sidled and surged forward, clattering through the town and northward, to Post Oaks.

Stiff with anger, Shiloh preceded him into the house. At one time it had been quite comfortable—grand, even, by frontier standards—but now the mustiness of neglect hung in the air. By the light of a table lamp in the large main room, Shiloh noted the dusty wainscoting and the cloth-draped parlor furniture. Fading wallpaper peeled from the wall leading upstairs.

"What do you think?" Justin asked mildly, studying her for a reaction.

She whirled on him, eyes full of venom. "I think you are a boor."

Justin laughed. "I know that. I was talking about the house."

"It's a relic." Shiloh sniffed. "It should have been left

to die a natural death."

"Perhaps it just needs a woman's touch," he suggested.

"Look, Justin, I'm not going to spend my days cleaning up your house."

"Of course, you won't. We've a maid for that."

Shiloh stared in surprise. "A maid?"

Justin nodded. "Ina. You'll meet her later. But now it's time to get ready for supper. This way." He started up the stairs.

Shiloh opened her mouth to object, but she knew by now that Justin was oblivious to normal reasoning. She followed him up to a large room, the master bedroom. This room, at least, had been aired out and the furniture uncovered. There was a pair of matching armoires, the blond pine doors gleaming with polish. A heavy table and chairs were arranged in a corner and there was a pair of sturdy chairs at the hearth. But the focal point of the room was the huge tester bed. It was draped with colorful quilts and bolsters, and looked almost decadently soft.

Justin went to the hearth and stirred the fire to life. He opened a door to reveal a good-sized dressing room. There, a copper tub steamed.

"I thought you might like a bath," he said. Returning to the room, he indicated one of the armoires. "I also took the liberty of getting you some clothes. There wasn't much to be had ready-made, so I bought some bolts of cloth as well. Ina is clever with a needle; she'll help you."

Shiloh planted her feet obstinately. "I have my own clothes."

"Dungarees, men's shirts, moccasins, a faded dress or two." Justin laid his hands gently on her shoulders. "You're not a little girl anymore, Shiloh, playing at being a spy." Abruptly, he turned on his heel and left.

Shiloh glared at the closed door, seething. Never had she felt so trapped, so helpless. After talking with Aunt Sharon, she'd had a small hope that she could reach some sort of understanding with Justin. But he'd proved her wrong by unceremoniously snatching her from her father's house and dragging her here.

Sighing, she went to the dressing room. She stood for a moment looking at the tub. She'd never had a real bath, not even at school in the East. It did look inviting, the steam rising in gentle wisps, a fresh cake of soap and a pile of snowy linens nearby. Shiloh wondered if it would seem like she were giving in to Justin if she took advantage of the inviting facilities, but convinced herself it would not. She shed her clothes and stepped into the tub, submerging herself up to the neck.

The luxury of basking in the warm, soft spring water engulfed her. For a moment she forgot her troubles and gave herself over to the exquisite sensation of the water lapping up between her breasts, around the tense muscles of her shoulders. She lifted a languid hand and watched the droplets run down her arm. Taking up the cake of soap, she rolled it slowly between her hands.

Honeysuckle. The scent of the lather wafted up, taking her by surprise. Was it possible that Justin had—no, of course not. It was an accident that he'd found her favorite soap. Never would she credit him with such an act of thoughtfulness. With a shrug, she washed herself, taking her time to soap herself from head to toe.

It was then that she noticed a cut-glass decanter and glass on a small stand by the bath. Removing the stopper, she sniffed it. Sherry. Aunt Sharon usually kept a bottle for occasions that demanded something more than tea. Shiloh poured herself a glass and drank it quickly. It tasted so pleasant that she had another. By the time she'd downed her third glass, the warmth pervaded her and augmented the languor of the warm bath.

When she finally, reluctantly, emerged from the bath, Shiloh's mood had lightened. She'd never felt so fragrantly clean, or so totally relaxed. Her skin glowed as she patted it dry. Her hair fell in dozens of damp, gleaming ringlets down her back. She stepped into the bedroom, which was dimly lit by the fire. The bed, with its rounded billows of quilts, beckoned irresistibly.

Shiloh went over and sat down. The languor imparted by the bath and the sherry overwhelmed her. She sank back onto the pillows and slid beneath the sheets. She hadn't forgotten that Justin was waiting for her. Let him wait, she thought, with a slow, catlike smile. He'll just have to learn that I'll not be at his beck and call . . . stretching luxuriously, Shiloh dropped off to sleep.

The lamp on Justin's desk wavered. He looked up from his work, rubbed his eyes, and folded up the map he'd been studying. Glancing at the clock on the mantel, he saw that more than an hour had passed since he'd left Shiloh. She'd had more than enough time to bathe and dress. He knew that many women regularly spent hours preparing themselves, but not Shiloh. Frowning, he climbed the stairs to see what was keeping her.

He knocked. No response. Swearing, Justin swung the door open. He'd half expected her to flee, but not this soon. Not without being noticed by him or any of the ranch hands, who had been alerted. The room was quiet, except for the soughing of the night breeze through the window.

Justin's tenseness left him when he saw Shiloh asleep

on the bed. He approached quietly so as not to awaken her. He sucked in his breath at what he saw. This was Shiloh as he'd never seen her before. Her hair was splayed out in a gleaming riot across the pillow. One hand lay beside her face, the fingers curled slightly inward. The lines of her small, intriguing face were soft, the lips moistly parted. The quilt had fallen away to reveal a pale shoulder and the rounded swell of a breast.

Fire leapt to Justin's loins. He hadn't had a woman since — Jessamine. Her blond plumpness couldn't compare with the lithe, quiet beauty of Shiloh. She stirred a little in her sleep, exposing her foot and slim ankle.

Supper could wait; the heat in Justin's blood couldn't. He bent and nuzzled her cheek. She smelled of sweet honeysuckle and — Justin laughed softly — sherry. Her hand reached toward him, touched the fabric of his shirt. Encouraged, Justin reclined beside her and tasted her lips, gently at first so she wouldn't be startled when she awoke. As his tongue traced the soft flesh of her mouth he felt the beginnings of a response. Shiloh arched toward him and wound her fingers through his hair. His hand strayed over her shoulder and down to her breasts, his fingers teasing the nipples to hardness. With a sigh, Shiloh pressed closer, and Justin's hand played across the lean expanse of her middle and then lower, to stroke the untried softness of her inner thighs.

Shiloh gasped and her eyes fluttered open. "Justin! What — what are you doing?"

He smiled and nipped at her ear. "I just came to see if you've made yourself at home." His hand moved up her thigh. "You seem to be quite comfortable."

"Yes . . . yes, I have." She sounded groggy from sherry and from sleep. She brought her bare leg up and draped it over Justin's, eager for his caresses.

He looked down at her tousled hair, her heavy-lidded bleary eyes. As suddenly as passion had come upon him, it cooled. He wanted Shiloh, probably more than he'd ever wanted any woman, but not like this. Not with her mind and sensitivities muddled with sleep and drink. He knew that if he took her now, she'd regret it in the morning. It would be just like her to accuse him of taking advantage of her. With a muttered oath, he disentangled himself and stood up.

Shiloh brushed a curl from her cheek. "What's wrong?"

"Supper's waiting," he told her curtly. He crossed the room to the armoire and began flinging things onto the bed. A chemise, a wispy pair of pantaloons. "The lady in the drygoods store told me these were necessary," Justin explained. Last, he took out a yellow cotton dress.

Shiloh sat up in bed, sputtering with anger. "I don't understand you, Justin McCord. One minute you're — you're making love to me, and the next you're ordering me about." She was so angry that she didn't protest when he held out the chemise and slipped her arms through the sleeves.

"I married an unwilling woman," he said. "I figure the least I can do is wait until you're completely willing to be bedded."

"But I —"

Justin shook his head, trying to ignore her softly glowing skin. "I apologize for what just happened. You were asleep, and a little fuzzy from the sherry. Now, let's get the rest of these clothes on." He held out the pantaloons, which she snatched away with an oath that would have done a Ranger proud. Keeping the quilts over her, she donned the undergarment. Patiently, Justin held out the dress.

Rising from the bed, Shiloh stepped into it. As

Justin fastened the buttons in back, she asked caustically, "Are you to be my nursemaid as well?"

Justin rested his hands at her waist, marveling at her slimness. He leaned forward and inhaled the scent of her hair. "I could be a lot more to you, if you'd let me."

She spun away, curls flying and eyes flashing. "I want nothing from you, Justin."

Anger pricked at him. He'd gone to no little trouble to get her some decent clothes and prepare the room for her, yet she threw everything contemptuously back at him. He couldn't figure the woman.

As she sullenly picked at the large, flavorful meal Ina and Prairie Flower, the aging Comanche cook, had prepared, Justin began to wonder about the advice Nate Mulvane had given him. *Romance the girl a little, no need to be heavy-handed. She'll come around.* Justin doubted it seriously. Nate had underestimated his daughter's stubbornness.

He watched her eyes flick around the dining room. It had been pleasant in its day, with a beamed ceiling and double doors facing out onto the rolling, oak-studded grasslands. But now the wallpaper and curtains were faded and dusty, and the furniture was dull from neglect.

"You haven't said what you think of the place," Justin said.

"Does it matter?"

"I want you to feel at home here."

Shiloh looked at him suspiciously, as if she didn't quite believe him. "How long have you owned Post Oaks?"

"A few weeks. But I haven't been around much. The house has been neglected, as you can see."

She glowered at him. "I know nothing of making a home. Back East they taught me how to serve tea and go calling. But I've forgotten that as well."

Justin couldn't suppress a smile. What a little hellcat she was, defiant, spitting her anger at him. "Tell me, Mrs. McCord," he drawled. "What *can* you do?"

She tossed her head proudly. "I can sit a horse for twenty hours without stopping. Hit a mark at fifty yards. Read sign on almost any terrain. Track a man with the stealth of a Comanche. Oh yes, I can also read and write and cipher. But I don't suppose those are traits you value in a woman."

Justin was taken aback by her vehemence. He'd known from the start that she was an able spy, needing only more experience to make her truly accomplished, but he'd underestimated her ambition. He rose and rounded the table to stand behind her. Gently, he lifted the curls from her shoulders.

"You won't be a caged bird here, Shiloh. I don't expect you to be a housekeeper. You're free to come and go as you please. But I can't let you do anything dangerous."

She turned and tilted her head back to meet his eyes. "Your concern for me is touching, Justin."

He clenched his jaw against an angry retort. There was simply no pleasing the woman. Shrugging, he said, "It's time we got to bed. Don't worry, Shiloh. You can have the bedroom all to yourself. If you need me, I'll be in the bunkhouse with the ranch hands."

He turned sharply and strode from the dining room.

Shiloh blinked slowly at the ray of sunlight that had slid across her face to awaken her. She sat up in sudden realization of where she was. She ran to the window and looked out. The sun was high over the fields. A pair of hands were driving posts around a corral, their shirts damp with sweat. It was practically the middle of the day. Frowning, Shiloh wondered why no one had awakened her.

Then she remembered. There was no reason for her to be up and about. Justin didn't need her, and she'd refused to run the household. She was nothing but a useless ornament. . . .

She caught sight of herself in a tall oval looking glass. Ornament? That was a ridiculous description of the creature who stared back out of the glass. A blur of rumpled red hair, eyes slightly bleary from the sherry last night, the wrinkled chemise she'd slept in. She looked dreadful. And worse, the fact that her appearance concerned her was alarming. She'd never cared about how she'd looked before.

Sighing, she went to the dressing room and poured water into the basin. She bathed away the puffiness from around her eyes and pulled a brush through her hair, bringing it away from her face with a pair of combs. In the armoire she found another ready-made dress, this one a simple morning gown printed with small lavender flowers. Like the other, it fit her well, hugging her bosom and waist and just brushing the tops of the new black slippers she'd found.

For all his other faults, Justin had done a remarkable job of finding clothes for her. In addition to the two ready-made dresses, there were underthings, stockings, and bed gowns, as well as several bolts of cloth and numerous trimmings. With a twinge of resentment, Shiloh decided that Justin's gesture wasn't made out of thoughtfulness, but out of his compulsion to make a proper wife of her.

Studying her much-improved image in the looking glass, Shiloh said, "It will take a lot more than pretty clothes to change what I am."

"Who said anything about changing you?" asked a lazy, deep voice.

Shiloh spun about to face him. "It's obvious that you

81

don't care for me the way I am."

He shook his head, giving her a dazzling grin. "I'm not going to get into it with you now, Shiloh. I just came to tell you I'm going into town. I'd be obliged if you'd accompany me."

Shiloh started to refuse immediately, but the afternoon stretched long and tedious before her. Snatching a bonnet from the armoire, she followed him down to the stableyard. A Mexican boy waited beside a handsome cart, drawn by a gleaming pair of matched grays. The boy eyed her curiously, but said nothing.

Amused by his round-eyed interest, Shiloh smiled brightly and took both his hands.

"I'm Shiloh," she said. "What's your name?"

"I am Tomas." He smiled proudly. "I work for Señor McCord."

"I'm sure you do a wonderful job." Her bright smile faded quickly when she felt Justin's hand at her elbow. She pulled away and climbed into the cart on her own. She saw his jaw clench with annoyance and smiled to herself. She'd decided it was wise to court his dislike; with luck, he might lose patience with her and agree to end this farce.

But as they drove toward town, Justin was smiling again. "Tomas was pretty taken with you. You're probably good with children."

She gave him a sideways glance. "With other peoples' children, maybe. I don't know the first thing about raising them."

"I'm told it just comes naturally."

"I'm in no hurry to find out," Shiloh retorted. It was ridiculous to even consider having a family with Justin. Fortunately, Shiloh felt safe from that possibility for the moment. He was being unusually reasonable about the intimate aspects of marriage. Twice he could have had her—she admitted that his kisses had some strange, drugging power over her — but he'd backed off.

An unwelcome thought niggled at her as the cart jolted along. She'd assumed that Justin was showing admirable restraint, even after his will-crumbling caresses had destroyed hers. But what if something else had held him back? What if he simply didn't find her attractive? Justin was obviously a man of the world, accustomed, no doubt, to sophisticated women. The idea bothered her more than she cared to admit.

·Houston was in full swing. The heat-shimmering streets were crowded with people of all shapes, sizes, and color. Laughter and music issued from the numerous grog shops and saloons, and traders worked from hastily constructed storefronts. A sidewheeler that had steamed up from the port of Galveston was swarming with newcomers eager to settle in Texas, where the wild land was practically free for the taking.

Justin rolled the cart to a stop in front of a small log building.

"I'll just be a minute," he said, jumping down. "There's a lunch in that basket if you get hungry."

Shiloh watched him amble away, his bootheels clicking on the wooden planks that led to the office. She squinted at a small brass plaque beside the door. Lamar B. Coulter, Solicitor.

Taking a biscuit from the basket, she took a bite and chewed thoughtfully. She knew little about Mr. Coulter, who'd had business with her father some months ago. Her father had declined to discuss the nature of the business, but in reckoning the account books, Shiloh had discovered that the man had paid handsomely for Nate's services.

Frowning, Shiloh remembered something else about Coulter. He'd come to Nate's house one day, and Nate had been with Captain Charles Elliot, the British chargé d'affaires in Texas. Before Shiloh could show him in, Coulter had mumbled some excuse and fled, as if fearful of meeting the Englishman.

She wondered what business Justin had with the man. Shifting impatiently, she decided to find out for herself. She climbed down and stepped into a hot, airless room.

Justin and the solicitor, a tall, rangey man of middle years, were in a small office in the rear, visible through the doorway. They hadn't noticed Shiloh and were conferring in urgent tones. She strained to hear.

. . . pretty sure the rumored British offer will turn up in San Antonio," Coulter was saying.

"Christ, no wonder Harmon sent Shiloh after me," Justin said, shaking his head.

"Who the hell is Shiloh?"

Justin laughed harshly. "My wife."

"Your *wife*?"

"It's a long story, Lamar. She fancied herself a detective, like her father, Nate Mulvane, and was hired by Harmon West to intercept me in Washington-on-the-Brazos. It was no accident that she showed up just before I made contact with Delgado. Harmon didn't just want to marry off his daughter, he must have known about the meeting."

"Damn! Then there's nothing we can do."

"I'll go to San Antonio and find Delgado myself."

Lamar shook his head. "It's too late, Justin. Raoul Delgado was murdered yesterday. I had word from a rider this morning."

Justin let his breath out in a thin hiss. "Any word on the letters?"

"Gone. Along with everything else we'd planned to present to the President. I've got these other reports if you want to take a look—" Lamar Coulter stopped

84

short when he reached for a parcel and spied Shiloh.

She crossed the room quickly, as if she'd just come through the door. Smiling guilelessly, she extended her hand to Lamar.

"I'm Shiloh Mul — McCord," she said. "I'm afraid you've kept my husband a little too long."

Coulter cleared his throat. "Yes, yes, of course. I apologize, ma'am. Well, I think our business is concluded, don't you, Justin?"

Justin's steel-gray eyes were narrowed dangerously. He strode to the door, taking Shiloh by the arm none too gently. "I'll be in touch, Lamar."

As they walked toward the cart, his grip bit into her. "Don't ever do that again, Shiloh," he said, his voice full of quiet rage.

She pulled away, surprised by the intensity of his reaction. The matter he'd been discussing with Lamar Coulter must be very confidential indeed. Perhaps, Shiloh decided with a sly smile, she'd found a vulnerable spot in Justin McCord.

"You look pretty damned pleased with yourself," he growled as they started up Main Street.

"Well, I'm not," she retorted. "I didn't appreciate being left to bake in the hot sun while you passed the time of day with Mr. Coulter."

"I thought you were Texas born and bred. The heat shouldn't bother you." They drove along in tense silence for a while. Then Justin turned to her.

"How much did you hear, Shiloh?"

She gave him a wide-eyed look of innocence. "What do you mean?"

"That was private business between Lamar Coulter and me. You shouldn't have walked in on us."

"I didn't realize husbands kept secrets from their wives."

He turned his hard-eyed stare on her. "You're my

wife in name only, Shiloh. Until you're ready to share yourself fully with me, I won't be able to trust you with my confidences."

"I see," she said tightly. "Well, you needn't worry. I don't know what you and Mr. Coulter were talking about. But I think that if you're in some kind of trouble I have a right to know about it."

"I often have business that must be conducted secretly. I have to travel a lot, too. I'm leaving tomorrow, as a matter of fact, for a couple of weeks. I hope you don't get it into that head of yours to go nosing around, Shiloh."

She narrowed her eyes at him. "Don't worry, Justin. I wouldn't dream of tampering with anything that takes you away from me."

He laughed then, mockingly, and appeared to relax. They made several more stops, laying in supplies for the ranch and ordering some building materials. Shiloh knew that these errands were only a front for Justin's meeting with Coulter. And, despite what she had told him, she vowed to find out everything she could about his "business."

They were met at the southern gate of Post Oaks by an agitated Tomas. The boy came running up the dusty track, waving his arms.

"Señor McCord, come quickly! It's the big mare. She's foaling right now—this minute!"

Justin extended a hand to the boy and hoisted him up into the wagon. A flick of the reins had the team bolting forward.

Justin seemed to have forgotten Shiloh. When they reached the stableyard he jumped from the wagon and hurried toward a small outbuilding in the western field. Shiloh followed, her curiosity piqued by Justin's concern.

Sunset was gathering on the grassy knoll where the shed stood. A man about Justin's age motioned them inside.

"What's up, Wylie?" Justin demanded.

The man grinned, revealing a rather poor set of teeth. "The mare's been laboring since this morning. Should be any time now. Now that you're here, I think I'll go get some supper."

"Thanks, Wylie, for staying with her."

Wylie lifted his hat. "Sure. And I hope you get that filly you've been wanting."

Inside, the smell of dust and sweat hung in the air. A beautiful roan, her sides swollen wide, stood in a hay-covered stall. The mare's eyes, a deep, velvety brown, blinked slowly and rolled back as she grunted with pain.

Justin approached her slowly, hand outstretched. He spoke softly, in a comforting way.

"There now, girl. Easy . . . what's ailing you, Sugar?"

Sugar tossed her head and sidled away, but then seemed to nod, inviting Justin's approach. He dodged the softly swishing tail and rolled up his sleeves to examine her.

She sidled again, swinging her head around to regard him in silent reproach. Moved by the mare's obvious pain, Shiloh came forward and gently took hold of her bridle. Stroking her neck, she began to murmur soothingly. The mare steadied and held still while Justin continued working.

"Is she all right?" Shiloh asked.

He looked up, as if noticing her for the first time. He gave her a smile so dazzling that it took her breath away. "She's fine, Shiloh. She's about to become a mama."

But the mare was in no hurry. Time seemed to crawl by, the moments punctuated by the animal's grunts and snorts of pain. The sun slid below the horizon and Justin lit a pair of lanterns and hung them in the stall. An owl screamed somewhere in the distance and a wolf set up a baleful cry to the rising moon. The mare suffered, weakened by each successive pain.

"Isn't there anything we can do?" Shiloh asked.

Smiling strangely, Justin came around and daubed at her flushed face with a handkerchief. "You know, Shiloh, you're really —"

The mare let out a high-pitched squeal, and he returned to her. "The hooves!" he said. "It's coming — damn!" His hands had slipped.

"Let me try," Shiloh insisted, brushing past him. "You'll hurt her with those big hands of yours." Gritting her teeth, she reached in and grasped the foal. Her eyes lit with triumph as she felt it surge forward. Just as suddenly, it slipped back and tears of frustration sprang to her eyes. "I can't —"

"Hold on, Shiloh. You can do it, sweetheart."

Too intent on what she was doing to notice the affectionate term, she grasped hard. Another contraction, and she pulled with all her might. Justin put his arms around her waist and pulled too, nearly squeezing the breath from her.

The foal descended. At long last, a pair of tiny, perfectly formed hooves emerged. Shiloh fell back, awed by the sight. The next happened so fast that she wasn't sure she'd seen it.

With an unearthly squeal, the mare pushed the foal out onto the bed of straw.

Shiloh dropped to her knees beside the limp, still creature. It was tiny, glistening dark and motionless, as quiet as the night air.

"It's stillborn," she said, her voice hollow and her

whole being empty of all feeling. "The foal is—"

But Justin ignored her. He brought the mare around, patting its damp neck. "Here it is, mother. Looks like a fine filly."

Shiloh stared at him as if he'd lost all reason. "Justin, don't you realize—"

"Hush," he said quietly. "Watch."

The mare nuzzled the still form in the straw, nibbling the slick sac that surrounded it. Suddenly the tiny filly twitched and gasped, breathing in life for the first time on its own. It let out a thin wail.

Moved to her very soul, for she'd never witnessed the miracle of birth before, Shiloh collapsed against Justin. "Thank God," she whispered. "Thank God."

"I think you and your clever little hands had a little to do with it, Shiloh," he murmured.

She watched the mare as it meticulously cleaned the foal. Unconsciously, she reached for Justin's hand. "Look, it's got a blaze on its face. Oh Justin, have you ever seen anything so beautiful?"

He turned her in his arms so that they were facing each other. "You," he said huskily. "You're beautiful."

Shiloh froze. She searched his face for a hint of the now-familiar mockery. She'd never been more unattractive in her life. Drenched with sweat and soiled by the mare's blood and fluids, she knew she must look and smell abominable. Frowning, she pulled away.

"Justin, this is no time to make fun of me. I'm tired, and—"

"Damn it, Shiloh, I wasn't—never mind. If I told you today was Tuesday you'd say it's Wednesday." Abruptly he left her side and held the door of the shed open. "Let's go back to the house."

For some reason, Shiloh felt apologetic, although she said nothing. She still couldn't be sure Justin had been sincere when he'd said she was beautiful. Shaking her head in confusion, she followed him out of the shed. She was amazed to see the first light of dawn rolling down over the fields. They'd been with the mare all night. She stopped in the doorway and breathed in the sweet, moist morning air. She smiled and looked back again at the new little filly. It was already raising its head, feebly, but with gathering strength.

"What are you going to name her?" Justin asked.

She frowned up at him. "Name her?"

"The filly. She's yours, you know. She wouldn't be here if it weren't for you."

Shiloh reached out and impulsively squeezed his hand. "Thank you." A sheen of unbidden tears spread over her eyes as she looked out at the dew-colored fields.

"Dawn," she said finally. "I'll name her Dawn, after the most beautiful hour of the day." She looked to Justin to see if he approved, but he was already bolting the door against wolves and coyotes. Then he strode toward the house.

Shiloh had an inexplicable urge to run to him and fling her arms around him, but she resisted it. Justin wasn't an easy man to approach, not even to express simple gratitude.

Weary and filled with a muddle of unfamiliar emotions, Shiloh followed him to the house.

Four

Lightning tore through the night sky, bringing Shiloh to her feet. She had been sleeping soundly after spending the day with Sugar, the mare, and the new filly. She'd marveled at the mare's attentiveness to her foal, so meticulous in her cleaning and care, so encouraging as the little creature struggled to its feet to nurse.

Now Shiloh wrapped herself hastily in a robe and ran to the window. The storm had burst upon the fields with ungodly wrath. Leaves were ripped from the trees as rain slashed in through the open window. Lightning struck relentlessly like livid, vertical needles. During one deafening crash, the fields were momentarily lit for Shiloh's eyes. It struck so close to the shed where the new filly lay that she was sure it had been hit. Without stopping to put on shoes, Shiloh rushed downstairs and out to the fields.

She was immediately drenched by a thick curtain of rain, the hem of her bed gown and robe soiled by splattering mud. Driven by a sense of urgency, she ran all the way to the shed.

Her lungs felt close to bursting by the time she reached it. Wet hands fumbling, she unlatched the door and let herself in. It was dry inside, and the horses were fine. By the bluish glow of another flash, she could see that the mare was standing nervously against the side of the stall. The filly was bedded down in the hay, unperturbed by the storm.

Shiloh stroked Sugar's neck and caught her breath. After spending a few minutes satisfying herself that everything was all right, she went back out into the tempest and secured the door.

"Shiloh!" She heard Justin calling her name, his voice nearly drowned out by the rain and thunder. The sky lit up for a split second and she saw him running toward her, rounding a small oak grove. Waving, she started toward him.

Her foot caught on an unseen root and she slipped, cursing, to the ground. At the same moment, lightning struck. It split a tall, ancient oak tree down the middle. Half of it fell with an ear-splitting crack.

Shiloh froze, watching in horror as the huge branches descended on her. She tried to scramble away, but her gown and the mud-slick grass impeded her. She closed her eyes and waited to be crushed. But the oak didn't quite reach her, and she was only brushed by small top branches.

Suddenly, a pair of hands gripped her and yanked her to her feet. Weak with relief, Shiloh collapsed against Justin's chest, laying her cheek on him to feel the moist warmth of his sodden shirt.

As he stroked her rain-wet curls, she almost imagined that his hands were shaking. When he smoothed the hair away from her face, she knew she wasn't imagining it. She looked up, eyes wide with amazement at her concern.

With one sweeping movement, he gathered her up into his arms, lifting her from the ground. With a little cry, Shiloh placed her arms around his neck, clinging to his strength.

Without warning, his mouth crushed down on hers, his lips firm and insistent. And the fury of the storm seemed suddenly insignificant compared to the feelings that engulfed Shiloh. She let her lips part to invite the caresses of his tongue. A roar of thunder only heightened the urgency of Shiloh's desire. She answered the questing tongue eagerly, stroking it with her own, amazed at her own wanton boldness. While the wind and rain whipped around them, they brought each other to a fever of passion.

When Justin dragged his mouth away and carried her down to the house, Shiloh was sure their time had come. He thrust the door open with his knee and strode up the stairs, taking them two at a time as easily as if he carried no burden at all. The intensity of the look on his face as he set her down in the bedroom took her breath away.

"Are you all right?" he demanded.

Shiloh wished she had the words to tell him of the longing he'd sparked within her, but she found it so hard to speak that she could only nod.

He gripped her upper arms and bent low. "Christ, you gave me a scare. I thought that tree had fallen on you. What the hell were you doing up there?"

"I—I was worried about the horses."

He stepped back, his eyes suddenly cold. "Well, it was a damned fool thing to do, going out on a night like this."

"But I—"

"You were almost killed."

Shiloh began to laugh softly, touched by the brusqueness that masked his concern.

"What's so funny?"

"You," she said, fingering a damp lock of blond hair. "You really do care what happens to me, don't you?"

He took her hand and removed it from his hair, the sculpted angles of his face gone hard. "Obviously, I must," he replied curtly. "I'm sure Jessamine would gladly accept a widower. Besides, I promised your father I'd take care of you."

Shiloh swallowed and looked down to hide a hot blush of humiliation. She was appalled that she'd read him so wrong. He might have been moved to kiss her out in the storm, but apparently that didn't mean he felt anything for her.

"I see," she said quietly, fighting a terrible rage. "How thoughtless of me to jeopardize you like that."

"Shiloh, I didn't mean—"

Now her eyes were as cold as his. "I know exactly what you mean. Now, hadn't you better get some sleep before you leave in the morning?"

Justin tightened the straps of his saddlebag and glanced back at the house. The storm had passed by dawn, leaving brilliant green freshness in its wake. He knew better than to expect Shiloh to see him off, especially after last night. He knew he'd hurt her, but he also knew it would have been wrong to give in to the passion she aroused in him. Things were complicated enough without bringing in any emotional entanglements.

He turned and hooked his hand over the saddlehorn, forcing his mind to the journey ahead.

"I don't suppose you'd care to tell me where you're going."

Justin looked back. He hadn't heard Shiloh come out of the house, but there she was, standing stiffly on the porch with one hand on the railing. She was wearing the yellow dress he'd bought, and had pulled her hair severely away from her face. Freckles stood out on the pallor of her face. Her eyes were darkly smudged, as if she hadn't slept well. Justin felt a twinge of guilt.

"Galveston," he said, mounting the steps. "I'll be back in a week or two. If you need anything, tell Ina or one of the hands." Bending slightly, he brushed his lips across her forehead.

"Take care, Shiloh." Hurrying away from the sweet scent of honeysuckle that clung to her, he mounted and spurred his horse. When he turned to lift his hat to her, he saw that she was watching him, unsmiling, her hand raised in farewell.

Justin spent the ten-hour trip on the sidewheeler *Progress*, planning his agenda and avoiding thoughts of Shiloh. By the time he reached the bustling port city, he'd managed to temporarily forget the small, vulnerable girl on the porch.

He went directly to the Tremont Hotel and sent for William Murphy, the U.S. chargé d'affaires in Galveston. While he waited in the big main room, his sharp eyes took in the people as they came and went.

There were more of them each week, from all ports of the world, and each of them was driven by the conviction that Texas would be their paradise.

And well it could be, Justin thought as he lit up a cheroot and drew in the pungent, sweetish smoke. Texas had much to offer, but not in its present state. The government was splintered into warring factions and was hopelessly bankrupt. The Mexican army threatened from the south and the Indians from the north and west, and President Houston had been forced to reduce the Texas army by half. When the republic crumbled, and Justin had no doubt that it would, it would be fair game for any nation.

Only statehood would protect it from English,

95

French, and Mexican interests. Justin hoped that the news from Washington would be favorable.

William Murphy appeared, a bewhiskered, meticulously groomed little man. Justin rose and shook his hand and they seated themselves on velvet-covered chairs behind a tall potted plant.

"Good to see you, Justin," Murphy said. "We were sure we'd lost you back in March when you were down in the Rio Grande valley."

"Damned near got myself killed," Justin said ruefully. "If it weren't for Thad Stripling I would have been. Why didn't I know he worked for you?"

"There was no need."

Justin clenched his jaw. He disliked Murphy's unwillingness to disclose everything. Still, he'd been treated well enough by his superiors and so had few complaints.

"I don't need to tell you there was nothing to be found at the border," he said. "No armaments, no ordnance, nothing to link the Accord with the Mexicans. But they were on to me," he added darkly. "I was shot, and then the woman who was caring for me turned me in to Huerto."

Murphy shrugged. "These things happen. Under the circumstances you handled yourself well."

"You might not think so when I tell you what's happened. Harmon West knows who I am, what I'm doing. Stripling's house had been ransacked by the time I got to it, and I suspect Harmon got it into his head that I should marry his daughter. A bit of nepotism to make it look like I'd been bought."

"Jesus, why didn't you—"

"Don't worry, Will. I arranged it so it would be impossible for me to marry Jessamine."

"How did you accomplish that?"

"I married someone else. Another long story."

96

"Well — er, are congratulations in order?"

Justin grinned. "I haven't made up my mind about that yet."

Murphy looked at him quizzically for a moment and then went on to other things. "I understand the meeting in San Antonio de Bexar didn't go through."

Justin nodded ruefully. "I was waylaid in Washington-on-the-Brazos and Delgado was murdered. Much of the evidence we'd gathered against the Accord has disappeared. It's a serious setback. Especially since things in Washington aren't progressing."

"What do you mean by that?"

"There are a lot of people who oppose annexation. Mostly Northerners. They're saying they don't want another slave state."

Murphy nodded thoughtfully.

"I'm with the abolitionists, when it comes down to it," Justin said. "But the alternatives are worse. Texas could easily become another English territory within the next few years."

"There's another thing. The minute Texas signs a treaty with the United States, we'd be at war with Mexico."

Justin nodded darkly. "I'm aware of that. Mexico is always lurking like a shadow in the south." No sooner were the words out of his mouth than a flash of brilliant red caught his eye. Through the fronds of the potted plant, he saw a lush form, draped in satin and black lace. Like a dream, a hauntingly beautiful profile was silhouetted against a window across the room.

Forgetting Murphy, Justin rose and covered the distance in a few long strides. Large brown eyes turned to him and widened in unconcealed terror.

"Justin —"

He stepped closer and gripped her elbow, watching the once-familiar swell of her bosom.

"Hello, Isabella."

Shiloh moved restlessly about the bedroom, setting down the book she'd been reading. In the two days since Justin had gone, the hours had crawled by. There was nothing to do. Her meals were prepared by Prairie Flower and served by Ina. The ranch hands took care of the livestock and fields. She had never felt so idle in her life, and she deeply resented Justin for putting her in this position.

There was a knock at the door. "It's Ina, Mrs. McCord."

Shiloh let the maid in. "Please, Ina, you must call me Shiloh. I insist."

"Yes ma'am—Shiloh. I was wondering if you'd like to get started on your dresses."

Shiloh smiled apologetically. "I'm afraid I'm not very good with a needle, and I haven't the slightest idea about designing a gown."

Ina looked at her, her olive-tinted face a little shy. "I'm told I can put together a dress quite cunningly. I was taught about it at the mission school in Goliad. All you would have to do is stand for fittings and tell me your preferences."

"Ina, you don't have to—"

"Really, I enjoy it. And with Mr. McCord gone, there isn't much to do around the place."

"Very well. If you really don't mind. . . ."

Ina hurried to the armoire and opened it wide. She deposited a number of bolts on the bed and took out a drawerful of trimmings. She smiled up at Shiloh. Her middle-aged face was softly handsome, wide, but modest. "He has a good eye, your husband. He chose beautiful things for you. Few men are so well aware of their wives' needs."

98

Shiloh sniffed. "He presumes too much."

"Do you not find his choices pleasing?"

Shiloh moved her eyes over the pile of fabric, taking in a rich length of gold cotton, an emerald satin, several bright calicos and some soft pastels. There was no denying that the fabrics were lovely, but she disliked them because of what they represented: Justin's virtual ownership of her, her total lack of freedom to make her own choices. But Ina looked so eager that she smiled.

"I've no doubt that you can turn these into wonderful gowns."

Ina nodded vigorously. She drew several folded pages from her apron pocket and spread them out for Shiloh to see.

"These are from London and Paris," she said excitedly. "Mr. McCord gave them to me. He knew I was interested in fashion. The drawings are several years old, but are beautiful still." She indicated a sketch of a traveling suit. "The cut of this jacket and skirt will look well on you. And this ballgown—think how graceful it will be in the emerald satin. Very simple, but with your coloring it will be stunning."

Shiloh looked at Ina in surprise. The woman must have a vivid imagination to believe she could ever be called stunning.

"These are lovely, but why would I ever need such things?"

"Your husband is an important man. He attends many functions. He has been received many times by President Houston and the Allens. You must look your best when you accompany him." Ina's manner became brisk. "Come, let us measure you for your new dresses."

Shiloh submitted patiently to Ina's marked-off ribbon and pins, lifting her arms and turning when instructed.

"You are very small," the woman murmured, noting

the size of her waist and bosom.

"I'm told my mother was tiny, but I don't remember."

Ina lowered her lashes. "I, too, lost my mother. My father, too, in the Revolution of 1810. And the *niños*—my brothers and sisters—were sent back to distant relations down in Mexico. I alone was allowed to continue my schooling at the mission. It was said I had a good mind and a great faith in God."

"I think you're remarkable," Shiloh said sincerely. "I envy you for the way you take care of yourself."

Ina stared at her. "I take care of myself, that is true. But there is nothing enviable in it. I would like nothing better than to leave it all to someone else. You are lucky to have a man to look after you."

Shiloh snorted. "It was not my choice to marry Justin. I feel he stole my freedom from me. This house, the clothes, everything—I'd give it all up if only I could be on my own again."

Ina laughed. "What a pair we are, each wanting what the other has." She sighed. "Ah well, perhaps some day . . ." She let her voice trail off and turned her attention to her work.

The next day, Shiloh tried her hand at helping Ina, more for the woman's company than from any desire to learn to sew. But she was so hopelessly inept with scissors and needle that she gave up, with Ina's relieved blessing.

"I'm going riding," she announced after she had cut all the knots out of the seam she'd been sewing.

Ina raised an eyebrow. "Alone?"

"Of course."

"But you cannot! Mr. McCord said—"

Shiloh looked at her sharply. "Said what?"

"Nothing," Ina mumbled, blushing down at her work.

"I insist that you tell me. Did Justin say that I wasn't to leave?"

Ina nodded without looking up. "Don't be angry, Shiloh. He is only concerned for your safety."

"The hell he is!" Shiloh said loudly, disregarding the older woman's cringe at her language. "Justin has no right to keep me here. I won't stand for it!" She flew from the room and went up to don her trousers, shirt, and scuffed boots. Glimpsing herself in the mirror, she smiled grimly. This was the old Shiloh, plain and unadorned, with a devil-may-care, defiant gleam in her eyes.

Her ride took her down along the murky bayou, around thick cane brakes and kudzu-draped forests. She galloped wildly until she felt her anger abate to a dull ache. Slowing her mount to a canter, she headed toward town. It was time to prove to Justin that she'd not allow him to control her. She *would* work, pursuing the career she'd chosen for herself. With renewed determination, she burst into her father's house.

Nate Mulvane showed mild surprise at his daughter's sudden appearance. He was sitting in a chair, his leg propped up on a stool.

"Hello," Shiloh said. "Looks like you're mending."

"Doing better. Could be Eb's infernal liniment is doing some good, after all. What are you doing here, Shiloh?"

She paced up and down the room, trying hard to hide her anger. "I thought you'd realize that you can't just transfer me to another man like so much horseflesh."

"Shiloh, I didn't —"

"Yes, you did. You knew. I had no desire to be Justin's wife."

101

"He's a good man, Shiloh. He'll take care of you."

With an effort, she refrained from stamping her foot in frustration. "I don't want to be taken care of. I want to live my own life!" She swallowed hard. "Let me work for you. I know money's getting scarce, and you're still in no shape to work. And with new people arriving in Houston each week, you must be inundated with jobs, finding relatives, and—"

Nate shook his head. "Sorry, Shiloh. Things are getting too rough."

"But I—"

"No."

They stared at each other with eyes so alike, yet so at odds. Shiloh searched for the slightest softening in his, but found none. Without another word, she turned on her heel and left.

Feeling defeated, she returned to Post Oaks. The house on the hill was tinted amber by the lowering sun, and a few horses in the west meadow were silhouetted against a wide, pink sweep of clouds. Shiloh sighed. There was nothing about this place that beckoned her, no welcome in the white-railed porch or the upper dormer windows. To her it was more a prison than a home, in spite of its beautiful setting.

Then she noticed the buckboard in the drive. A driver stood nearby, holding a lantern. A black girl, her face shaded by a wide-brimmed hat, waited on the seat. Shiloh rode up to the house and gave her horse to Tomas, wondering who had come to call. She stepped through the door and glimpsed the lace-encrusted hem of a dress. She stopped at the entrance to the parlor, her eyes narrowed to meet the challenge.

Planting her feet and placing her hands at her hips, she faced the visitor.

"What are you doing here, Jessamine?"

The girl set down her teacup and wiped a crumb of

biscuit from her ripe mouth.

"Why Shiloh, I'd almost given up on you."

Shiloh crossed the room, which was pervaded by the scent of gardenia emanating from Jessamine.

"What can I do for you?"

"I've just come to call on you. Isn't it customary for a new bride to receive visitors?"

"I wouldn't know."

Jessamine sighed prettily. "No, I don't suppose you would. You never were one to practice the social graces." She gave Shiloh's dusty clothes a meaningful look.

"Since I'm such an oaf, Jessamine, why don't you leave?"

Yellow ringlets bobbed as Jessamine laughed. "I'm just curious about you, Shiloh. I was wondering what you did to make Justin marry you so suddenly."

Shiloh returned the girl's laugh. "Oh, that was easy. All I did was tell him he was going to be forced to marry you. The next thing I knew, he was placing his ring on my finger."

Jessamine's smiling facade fell away. "You're lying! Justin loves me, not you."

"You're right in thinking there's no love between Justin and me."

"Then why did you trap him into this?"

"I did no such thing. But I'm not going to stand here and argue about it with you."

Jessamine rose and flounced about the room, wrinkling her nose in distaste. She spoke almost to herself. "Look at this place. It's a disgrace. The paint is flaking, the wallpaper and curtains are faded . . . no self-respecting woman would allow her house to look like this."

Shiloh bristled. She didn't care what Jessamine or anyone else thought, but it went against her grain to

103

listen to insults.

"Get out," she said tightly.

Jessamine went to the door, her china-blue eyes gone hard as ice. "It won't take long for Justin to realize the mistake he's made. He'll soon see you for what you are—a scruffy, no-account little opportunist!"

"Sorry, Isabella, but I'm not buying it." Justin flicked his cheroot over the saloon balcony and looked coldly at the Mexican beauty. "No one forced you to turn me over to Huerto." Isabella had managed to elude him, after that first meeting at the Tremont ten days earlier, but now, on the eve of his departure for Houston, he'd cornered her.

"Justin, please, listen! I had no choice! The *alcaldé*'s son, who was once my *novio*, found out that I was hiding you. I would have been punished severely if they'd discovered you." She swayed seductively toward him, moistening her lips. "No one would have been able to understand what we had, would they, *caro*? We were special. . . ." She let her voice trail off and leaned toward him, pressing the fullness of her bosom to his chest.

At one time, her buxom nearness might have aroused him, but now he felt only distaste for her soft body, her heavy scent, her full, lying lips. Gently, but resolutely, he set her away from him.

"That won't work anymore, Isabella." He leaned easily on the railing, studying her. "Now, suppose you tell me what you're doing in Galveston."

A guarded look came over her. "I am here with my uncle. He owns interest in a small merchantman out of Vera Cruz and has come to do some trading."

Justin shook his head. "You'll have to do better than that, Isabella. I saw you with Captain Elliot last night, and I could tell the two of you were no strangers. What does the Englishman want?"

"How should I know? Perhaps he is lonesome and in need of company."

"Your lies aren't working, Isabella. Elliot is mighty friendly with the Mexicans and I want to know what he's up to. Now, either you can tell me, or—"

He stopped short, sensing movement behind him. Two thick-set men, dark-skinned and mustachioed, stepped through the curtain onto the balcony. They were as alike as the tooled knife handles they held in their hands.

Isabella smiled maliciously. "You were saying, Justin . . . ?"

He returned her smile as the thugs advanced on him. Then, lazily tipping his hat, he vaulted over the railing and leaped to the street below. He landed on his feet and ambled away slowly, whistling a tune.

At first Justin thought it was relief after a long, fruitless trip that made the house at Post Oaks look brighter, more vivid, than he remembered. As he galloped up the drive, he realized the house had been transformed. Stopping in front, he stared in amazement.

A fresh coat of brilliant white paint adorned it, the trim a handsome grayish blue. The wild tangle of brush had been cleared away from the base of the porch to reveal neatly trimmed hawthorne and azealea bushes. The porch had been swept and a pair of chairs brought out, flanked by potted ivy on wooden stands.

"Señor McCord!" Tomas's boyish voice rang out as he ran forward to take charge of the horse.

Justin dismounted and tossed him the reins. "What's going on here?"

"Your wife, señor, she has had everybody working for over a week."

Shiloh was full of surprises, Justin thought as he went inside. This, too, was greatly improved. The floors and furniture had been cleaned and polished. The faded wallpaper was gone, the walls painted a pale shade of blue. New curtains graced the windows and sparkling jars full of wildflowers stood on the parlor mantel and table.

Justin leaned against the door frame, breathing in the scent of lye soap and flowers. He reflected briefly on the home of his boyhood, a plantation called the Willows. The place had dripped with elegance, decorated by his mother to fussy perfection and changed every few years or so. Looking around at his present dwelling, he realized how much he preferred it, with the homey touches of a faded quilt on a stand, a collection of Prairie Flower's baskets at the hearth. After years of living in rough boardinghouses and under the open sky, he found having a home again a welcome change.

He went to find Shiloh, to see if she, like the house, had somehow been transformed. He found her in the kitchen, down on her hands and knees, scrubbing the brick of the great cooking hearth. She looked small, yet oddly strong and determined, as she scrubbed away. Her hair was knotted low on her neck, stray wisps curling about her face. She was humming as she worked, her voice sweet, almost childlike. Unaware of his presence, she made an endearing picture.

Justin cleared his throat. "My compliments," he said. "I hardly recognize the place."

Shiloh dropped her brush, startled. As she rose, a ripe-peach blush stained her cheeks. She brushed a stray curl from her brow, smearing it with a thumb-print of gray ashes.

106

"Hello, Justin. Welcome back."

He smiled wryly at her words. There was not a hint of welcome in her defiant green eyes.

"I see you've been busy," he said mildly.

She tossed her head. "I had to do something. If I'm to be forced to live here, I might as well make my surroundings pleasant."

"Shiloh, no one's forcing you."

"What choice do I have? My father will have nothing to do with me, my aunt has some fool idea that I belong here, and I have no money to live on my own."

"I want you to be happy here."

"Then you're asking the impossible. But I'd rather be scrubbing floors than mooning idly about."

Justin ambled over to the sideboard and sampled a crust of Prairie Flower's dark bread. Chewing slowly, he regarded her. "I don't suppose you'd accept my thanks for all you've done."

"It wasn't for you," she said obstinately. "And you won't be so grateful when you find out what I spent on your credit in town."

His eyes twinkled with amusement. Money was one thing he didn't have to worry about. He had a trust from his grandfather that would allow him to live comfortably for years.

"I don't mind, Shiloh. I told your father you'd want for nothing."

She sniffed and wiped her hands on her apron. "It'll be time for supper soon. I'm going to get cleaned up." She smiled at Prairie Flower, who came in from the kitchen garden with a basket of greens and onions. Giving a last glowering look at Justin, she went to empty her cleaning bucket.

Prairie Flower watched her with satisfaction, the lines of her nut-brown skin creased around her small bright eyes.

"Good woman," she said to Justin. "Hard worker."

"That she is," Justin agreed.

"She is not happy, McCord."

He nodded his head. "She makes no secret of that."

"She has a fire in her, a spirit. A great desire to prove herself. But she will not do that by simply being your wife." The wizened face challenged him.

Justin patted the elderly Comanche woman, who had come into Thad Stripling's employ under obscure circumstances, on the shoulder.

"I'll keep that in mind."

Ina caught Shiloh's eye as she served a generous supper of venison, greens, and field peas. Shiloh knew that Ina was wondering how she liked her new gown, a simple dress of gold cotton. She smiled, and then looked at Justin. He hadn't noticed the dress, or at least he hadn't commented on it. He was eating in a distracted way.

Finally, as the candle on the table burned down to a stub, he spoke.

"I have some things to tell you about myself. I'm sure you've realized that I have other responsibilities besides this ranch."

She gave him her coolest stare, resting her chin in her hand. "You're an agent of the United States government, directly responsible to a Mr. Pinckney Henderson in Washington. Your work is supposed to lay ground for an annexation treaty."

He raised an eyebrow at her. "How did you—"

She laughed, enjoying her small triumph. "You made it far too easy on me. That outmoded safe in your study isn't much good for keeping secrets."

He set his glass down, tensing in anger. "Damn it, Shiloh, can't you keep your nose out of my things?"

She gave him her sweetest smile. "I'm afraid not, Justin. I guess it's in my blood. I'm my father's daughter."

He lit a cheroot and leaned back. "You've pieced it together nicely. But things are not that simple. It's not just a question of negotiating a treaty. There are plenty of influential people around who will go to great lengths to prevent annexation."

"And Judge West is one of them."

"That's right."

Shiloh swallowed as a cold feeling gripped her. In going through Justin's letters, she'd learned a lot, and now she had it by his own admission. She knew now how completely Justin had used her to shield himself from Harmon West. The cold feeling turned to bitterness. The marriage had been a wise move for Justin, but what did that make her? Three weeks ago she had been an independent woman, pleased with her lot in life. Then Justin had reduced her to his wife, an object of convenience.

She wanted to run from the room and hide from Justin's piercing, steel-eyed stare. But she remained seated, knowing that she must do something to gain back her self-respect.

"I want to work with you on this, Justin," she said with quiet determination.

Unhesitating, he shook his head and flicked his cheroot into the grate. "Sorry, Shiloh. I can't let you do that."

"Justin, I'm good at this sort of thing. You said so yourself."

"Your father taught you well, but I won't have you getting involved in this. It's too dangerous. Besides, I don't have the authority to bring you in. It's up to my superiors in Washington."

"That's a lie!" Shiloh snapped. "You have a letter

from Mr. Henderson giving you license to do whatever you see fit to achieve your goal. I'm sure that includes getting help from—"

He smiled, shaking his head as one does at an overindulged child. "You really dug deep, didn't you, Shiloh?"

"I wanted to know what you were hiding from me. Justin, I'm offering you my help."

He leaned back, folding his arms across his chest. "There is something you can do."

A spark of hope flared within her. She felt the hardness leave her eyes. "Tell me," she prompted.

"There's a ball in San Antonio next month, a big deal put on for the foreign legates in Texas. A lot of important people will be there. I managed to get myself invited. I'd be much less conspicuous if I arrived with my wife."

Shiloh masked her disappointment, but not her anger. "In other words," she said coldly, "I'd come along as part of your disguise."

Equally cold, Justin stood up to leave. "Just be sure you have something decent to wear."

Shiloh stared after him, making a silent vow to defy his obviously low opinion of her. She'd go to San Antonio de Bexar, but her presence wouldn't make Justin inconspicuous. Far from it. A satisfied smile tugged at her mouth as she picked up the candle and went upstairs.

Five

Shiloh lifted a leather flap and looked out the window of the hired coach as it creaked its way along the old San Antonio road. She'd stopped counting the hours of travel long ago, her mind numb with the monotony of the trip.

Ina rode behind in a similar, hooded wagon with — of all people — Nate Mulvane. For some reason, he'd decided to go along and had volunteered readily to drive Ina and Shiloh's ridiculously large load of baggage.

Across from her, on a fading upholstered seat, Justin sat, as absorbed in his thoughts as Shiloh was in hers. She glanced at him briefly and looked away, out the window at the endless summer sky and green rolls of grassland. Shifting uncomfortably, she reflected on the past month.

The first four weeks of her marriage had been fraught with tension. Justin refused to discuss his business with her and actually seemed to avoid her. While she continued with her massive clean-up of the house, he threw himself into developing the ranch. He and the hands repaired the main barn and well-house and built a sturdy corral. A dozen horses were added to the stock. And already there had been plenty of buyers with ready cash.

On the surface, it looked as if the newlyweds were prospering early in their life together. But beneath that thin surface, there existed nothing but discontent and occasionally dangerous moments of passion.

Shiloh shivered in spite of the heat, remembering. Most of the time, Justin maintained a maddening aloofness. But every once in a while, when she made a cutting remark or defied him some small way, she would find herself caught in his steel-banded embrace, her mouth plundered by his hot kisses until all resistance was driven from her. She hated the weakness of her own flesh, even more than she hated the hollow, empty feeling when Justin left her raw with desire, as he invariably did. He claimed she wasn't ready for his touch, even when her body cried out for his caresses. And she was too proud to disagree with him.

As she tried to push aside the turmoil of her thoughts, Shiloh sensed a subtle change in the land outside. The long stretches of nothingness became tamer, the small farms more frequent.

"La Villita," Justin said, indicating a row of diminutive houses.

"Are we nearing San Antonio?"

He smiled brilliantly. "We've arrived, Shiloh. Look up to the north."

She moved to the opposite side of the coach. In the distance the sand-colored facade of the Alamo rose against the late afternoon sky. Shiloh drew in her breath at the sight of the infamous mission. She'd grown up hearing tales of the brave, doomed Texans who had fought and died there. Now the building looked ordinary, unremarkable, vendors plodding past with their flatbed carts and cats sitting upon its walls.

Shiloh couldn't imagine those same walls breached by the bloodthirsty host that had slaughtered every last man within. Yet she knew it had happened, and an almost reverent feeling welled in her heart as they passed the mission.

"Did you know any of them?" she asked Justin.

He nodded his head, and his voice was gravelly with emotion. "Nearly all. I was on a scouting mission down San Pedro Creek. By the time I got back it was too late. I never felt so damned helpless. . . ."

She felt her throat constrict at the look of pain etched on his face. The Alamo had been a horror indeed, to affect a man of Justin's hardness. She had a sudden urge to reach for his hand, to squeeze it reassuringly. But she didn't dare. That might make him angry, or worse, he might pull her into his arms for another of his punishing embraces.

The coach rolled to a stop beside the clear, quiet river that meandered just east of the city. Justin got out and Shiloh followed, eager to stretch after the long journey. He caught her by the waist and swung her down, his eyes laughing at her surprise.

"We're in San Antonio now, remember? You've got a role to play."

She forced a honeyed smile. "Don't worry, Justin. I'll see to it that no one guesses I'm anything but your docile wife."

His look told her he didn't believe her for a minute, but he offered her his arm and they entered San Antonio by way of a footbridge. It was an attractive old town, with tall trees, the brick and adobe houses graced with bright summer flowers. They walked through the plaza, which was dominated by a clock tower and a giant cypress in one corner. Justin took her to a small but well-built hotel where they were greeted by a congenial Mexican gentleman who appeared to

113

know Justin.

"For you, Señor McCord, I have a terrace room overlooking the plaza. You will find it most pleasant."

"We're traveling with my wife's maid and her father."

The gentleman knitted his brow. "Every place in town is full, I'm afraid. But I will find something."

A young girl led them up to their room. It wasn't elegant, but it was clean and comfortable and rather spacious. The iron-railed terrace was decked with potted plants, the tall French doors draped by sheer white curtains that billowed in the summer breeze. A dressing area was marked by a folding room divider and furnished with a washbasin. Shiloh didn't bother hiding her delight when she spied a copper tub. She was looking forward to washing away the days of travel.

The girl left, closing the door behind her. Justin looked at Shiloh.

"What do you think?"

She refused to admit to him that she'd never seen the inside of a hotel room before, and so had nothing to compare it to.

"There's only one bed," she said dubiously.

He laughed. "What did you expect?"

Blushing, she stared out the window. She tried to avoid thinking about the intimate aspects of their marriage. Only the people at Post Oaks, who would never dare question Justin, knew that they didn't live as husband and wife.

"I could try to find another room," Justin suggested, "but I'm afraid that wouldn't be very convincing."

"There's no need," Shiloh answered. "We're both adults. We can be reasonable about this."

She thought she saw a hint of derision in his eyes. "Of course, we can." He went to the door. "I'm going to check on Ina and your father."

Soon after he left, Shiloh's baggage arrived. With

great relief, she shed her traveling gown and washed at the basin. Then she donned her lavender cotton frock and went out. She knew that Justin had intended for her to stay where she was, but she didn't think twice about displeasing him. Nothing she did seemed to meet with his approval, not the improvements she'd made around the house, nor even the fact that Ina's dresses enhanced her plainness until she was almost pretty.

Holding her head up, she walked across the plaza, noting the stone and adobe shops and houses with their shady patios. She walked toward the setting sun, and before long came to the military plaza where she had discovered the cache of munitions one night five years earlier. Although she barely remembered the cathedral or the elegant dormered mansion of Jose Cassiano, she recalled with searing clarity the thrill of triumph she'd experienced at her own success.

Sitting on a stone bench, Shiloh felt a wave of desolation wash over her. She'd been so busy with the house that there hadn't been time to regret the abandonment of her career. At times she'd even forgotten her ambition. But now it all came back, the impossibility of it taunting her. She sat for a long time, watching the people pass, yet not really seeing them.

And then a shadow blocked her view and the sweet scent of magnolia assailed her senses. She looked up in surprise to see a black-clad gentleman smiling down at her. The first stars of twilight winked above his head.

"What a pretty sight you make," the man said, holding a cream-colored blossom out to her.

Surprised, Shiloh took it and murmured her thanks. She didn't much care for the man's manner, and quickly realized that she would be wise to return to the hotel before dark.

"I have been watching you," the man said, his

English enriched by the hint of a Spanish accent. "A more lonely lady I have never seen."

"Sir, I am not looking for company," Shiloh said, getting rapidly to her feet. "If you'll excuse me, I must be on my way." She started off and nearly collided with another man, more oily-looking than the first.

"Look, Franco, what I have found," the man was saying. *"La roja* . . ." He stepped much closer to Shiloh and she gasped. Behind him stood a third man, compact and handsome in the Latin way, whose face was leering avidly at her.

"A good find, Tonio," that one said. "I was hoping for luck in locating her."

Shiloh realized then that it was not chance that brought these men to accost her. But who were they, what did they want?

Tonio grinned. "Do not be frightened, señora. We would never harm you. Come, there is someone we want you to meet, there, in Madame Bustamente's fandango hall just across the way."

"I'm afraid I don't wish to go, gentlemen," Shiloh said. She was doing her best to remain calm, but the three of them had closed in on her and there was no way to elude them.

Tonio stroked the flesh of her bare arm, his laughter murmuring, suggestive. "Come now, you will enjoy our company."

Shiloh jerked away, only to find herself grasped from behind by Franco's arms. He circled her waist and dragged her against him.

"Look, Felix," he said to his companion. "I think she likes me."

Panic took over as Shiloh tried to wrench away. She struggled with every ounce of her strength, kicking viciously at booted shins, scratching at grasping hands and darkly laughing faces. She cried out, praying that someone would happen by.

"*Dios!*" Franco cried, releasing her to clutch at his leg. "*La diabla*—"

Shiloh seized the moment to run, but she didn't get far. Like great cats toying with their prey, Felix and Tonio caught her and tormented her with rough caresses. They passed her back and forth between them, laughing at her panic.

Shiloh knew she was at their mercy, that when they tired of their cruel game they would force her to go with them. Still, she couldn't stop fighting, couldn't cease her furious kicks and scratches. To do so would be to give in, and that was something she would never let happen.

But she felt herself growing fatigued. When a muscled arm wrapped around her neck from behind, she was robbed of air and felt herself sinking slowly, almost gratefully, into a deep velvet void of unconsciousness.

Seconds before she slipped over the brink, Shiloh heard a new voice above the jeering laughter of her assailants. An animal snarl, a growled oath . . . Shiloh forced her eyes open just in time to see a dark form spring forward out of the dark blue twilight. A flash of golden hair, a glint of steel in angry eyes—

"Justin!" she said, her voice a harsh whisper because of the pressure on her neck.

She heard a great crunch of bone against bone and a grunt as Franco released her and slithered to the ground. His jaw hung at a crazy angle, shattered by Justin's fist.

Justin lunged toward the other two, quick and lean as a cat. One blow split Tonio's lip wide and another glanced off Felix's cheekbone. Both men roared in pain. Felix cursed, and Tonio spat blood-drenched teeth to the ground.

Giving no quarter, Justin advanced again. But Felix

was ready now, and kicked him with swift force in the midsection. Shiloh heard his air passages empty out as he sprawled to the dust.

In the second it took him to scramble to his feet, both Felix and Tonio prepared themselves. Shiloh gasped as she saw flashes of steel. Each man had produced a knife, evilly pointed, honed to deadly sharpness.

Crouching low, they stepped toward Justin, stabbing out and slicing the air. He twisted away with the grace of a dancer, but still they pressed closer.

Felix jabbed and Justin caught his wrist, squeezing to force the knife from the man's hand. Felix yelped with pain but held fast, pushing the shining blade ever closer to Justin's enraged face.

While those two struggled, Shiloh saw Tonio move toward them. There was no time to think. Her feet left the ground as she leaped at him, falling on his back with all the fury of a hissing, spitting cat. Tonio sprawled face-first to the dusty stones and his knife dropped several feet away. Shiloh scrambled up, battling the fullness of her skirts, and seized it.

Her experience with knives was scant and she looked to Justin for help. But he was locked in combat with Felix, that blade being forced to and fro by high-veined, shaking hands. Tonio reached for her and instinctively she brought the knife up, tearing through his sleeve and cutting his arm.

"Puta!" Tonio spat, but the gash wasn't deep. He lunged for her again and she spun away, eluding him. Then, just as she poised the knife for her defense, a hand came from behind and grabbed it away. Shiloh froze, her heart sinking with the realization that Felix had bested Justin. Now he and Tonio would have their revenge on her —

But it was Justin's voice she heard behind her. His

118

words rumbled low with rage as he addressed Tonio.

"You lay a finger on my wife and you're a dead man."

Tonio's sharp eyes flicked from one fallen, groaning companion to the other. For a moment Shiloh thought he would continue to fight, but he turned and fled, his boots echoing through a darkened alley. The others limped and scrambled after, cursing the *diablo tejano*.

In the quiet aftermath, music drifted faintly from a dance hall. Shiloh took a deep breath, fighting a fearful trembling. Only now, when it was all over, did the terror of the incident strike her. She looked at Justin, eyes large and luminous in the pallor of her face. She took a step toward him, drawn to his strength. The intense look in his eyes made her hesitate. She swallowed, knowing better than to expect sympathy from him. She started to turn away.

"Shiloh." His voice brought her back around. Unsmiling, yet with an unmistakable softening of his eyes, he held out his arms to her.

With a cry of gratitude, she fell into his embrace. His arms curved around her protectively, crushing her to the warmth of his broad chest. As her trembling abated, he stroked her hair and her cheeks, murmuring softly into her ear. After a tender, breathless moment, he placed his arm across her shoulders and led her back to the hotel.

Justin sat in dimness and watched Shiloh undress. She was unaware that the lamp behind the folding screen silhouetted her slim, compact body in great detail. The shadow on the outside presented a feast for his eyes; the fine lines of her profile as she pulled the combs from her hair, the enticing curve of her breast, a shapely leg as she brought it up to roll down her stocking.

119

Suppressing a groan, Justin forced his gaze away. He didn't know how long he could go on like this, denying himself a thing he had every legal right to take. He didn't know what made his desire so strong. Perhaps it was the fact that Shiloh held herself aloof, wanted nothing to do with him. Or maybe it was the passion he sensed in her, her artlessly seductive response when he kissed her. An already complex situation would become even more complicated. Still, his desire grew with each passing day. He was finding it harder and harder to resist Shiloh.

She stepped from behind the screen, looking impossibly sweet and girlish in a floor-length white bed gown, which was pleated at the high bodice and gathered demurely at the wrists. Justin frowned at her. He knew his anger was a result of all he'd felt this evening, from the time he'd found her gone from the room until he'd discovered her in the midst of her struggle in the military plaza. It was too hard to face the fact that his dread of losing her might stem from his own feelings rather than his sense of responsibility for her. And so he frowned, wanting to hurt her for causing such gut-wrenching worry.

"Are you all right?" he asked curtly.

Shiloh nodded. She was still wide-eyed and pale, but she appeared quite calm.

"Then would you mind telling me what the hell you were doing out alone?"

"I wanted to walk around, stretch my legs, see some of the city. When I was here five years ago I didn't get a chance to see it."

"Damn it, Shiloh! Didn't it occur to you that it would be dangerous?"

She shrugged, managing to look both defiant and forlorn. "Not really."

He gave a snort of disgust. Shiloh drew herself up.

"Justin, there's something I have to tell you. Those men seemed to know who I was. They said something about taking me somewhere, to see someone—"

"*What?*"

"It's just as I said. Who could they have been?"

He blew his breath out in a great sigh. "The Accord. Probably the same thugs that murdered Delgado. . . ." He was speaking quietly, almost to himself.

"I don't understand, Justin."

"It's simple. Obviously someone doesn't want me at that ball tomorrow night, and they were trying to send me on a wild goose chase after you." He drove his fist into his hand. "Damn! I knew I shouldn't have brought you along. I've got enough troubles—"

Shiloh tossed her head. "You needn't bother chastising me about this, Justin. I admit I was wrong to go wandering alone in a strange city. Once again, I've proven my own ineptitude. I'm only sorry you had to get involved. But at least you know someone is working against you. Now, if I've spared you your tirade, I'd like to go to bed."

She slipped beneath the covers and pulled the quilt up around her, turning her face as if to hide from him.

Justin didn't much care for her attitude. The sight of her lying stiffly on the bed in that dismissive pose struck an infuriating chord in him. A growl, born of anger and frustrated desire, ripped from him as he crossed to the bed and flung aside the quilts. Shiloh turned quickly and drew her knees up in a gesture of self-protection. Yet she showed no fear of him.

"What's the matter, Justin?" she asked, her voice taunting. "Did I rob you of the opportunity to belittle me?"

He grabbed her by the shoulders and pulled her into a rough embrace. "That's not quite what I had in mind, Mrs. McCord."

121

His mouth forced its way down onto hers, exacting a harsh punishment for her behavior, while at the same time reminding her of her undeniable attraction to him. Shiloh moved helplessly in his arms, but her struggle only made him kiss her more determinedly. His tongue forced her lips apart as his hands plucked at the laces of her bed gown, pulling it down to bare her shoulders to the night breeze.

Shiloh felt her will crumble as Justin's hands moved over her, making a mockery of her resistance. His anger had taken a new and dangerous turn. His caresses were relentless, evocative, his hands seeming to know just how to stir her. His fingers roved over her bosom, teasing the rosy crests to urgent hardness.

With a strangled cry of protest Shiloh tried to tear herself away, but Justin only pressed her down on the bed, pinning her beneath him.

"You bastard," Shiloh hissed. "Don't touch me."

He laughed softly, wickedly. "You're begging for it, Shiloh. Stop kidding yourself." And he punctuated his comment by moving a hand up her thigh, to the honeyed warmth of her womanhood.

Shiloh's next curse caught in her throat as the white heat of passion consumed her. Despite her rage, she found that she was no longer struggling away from him, but toward him, toward the searing brand of his touch. Heated longing chased away all resistance, and suddenly Shiloh's desire became as fierce as her husband's. She reached for him boldly, in feverish want, her hands moving instinctively over his taut body.

It was her turn to smile as an involuntary groan issued from Justin. She knew then that she had a certain sensual power over him, and she meant to exploit it to the fullest. Guided by desire, she stroked and massaged his hard-muscled body and allowed her tongue a wanton exploration of the inside of his mouth.

After recovering from his initial surprise at her

122

boldness, Justin retaliated. All at once, his hands and mouth seemed to be everywhere, whispering suggestively into her ear while his tongue traced its outline, teasing her sensitive flesh with knowing caresses, evoking a sweet throbbing within her that begged for release.

His anger made him prolong the sensual torture until Shiloh hissed a curse into his ear.

He raised an eyebrow at her, smiling sardonically. "And all along," he drawled, placing himself between her legs and loosening his trousers, "I thought you were so innocent. . . ."

Shiloh didn't think she could cope with the rush of confusing emotions that washed over her. She dreaded what was to come next, yet she thought she would die if she was denied it. She swore again and wrapped her arms about Justin's strong neck.

There was a scratching at the door. Justin muttered something vile and tried to ignore it, but the caller persisted. He stood and straightened his clothing.

"I'm not through with you, Mrs. McCord," he promised, going to the door.

But the moment he left her, Shiloh vowed otherwise. The interruption was just what she needed to marshall her defenses, to free herself from his compelling control over her. Although her body still cried out for Justin's touch, she knew how wrong it would be to give in to him. This was that only thing he hadn't taken from her, and she meant to hold on to it. For she knew if she let him take her, like this, in anger, as a punishment, she would lose herself to him completely.

She drew her bed gown back around her and pulled the quilt up, watching Justin with wary eyes. The unseen person at the door had given him a letter, which his eyes devoured in the lamplight. She could tell by the attention he was giving the small, handwritten bit of paper that it was important, and that he'd all but forgotten her. She shot him a last malevolent look, silently thanked the person who had interrupted them, and turned over to go to sleep.

After scanning the note, Justin removed the lamp's blackened chimney and held the paper to the flame. He glanced over at Shiloh, who was doing a good imitation of sound sleep. Part of him wanted to return to her side and rekindle the wildfire that had started earlier, but the interruption had cooled his passion. Justin didn't want to have to cope with Shiloh's resentment along with everything else. He poured himself a glass of whiskey and sat down to think about the letter.

It was from a local Latino agent, confirming the worst of his suspicions. The government of the nearly bankrupt Republic of Texas was about to be bought. Lord Aberdeen, the British secretary of foreign affairs, had concocted a scheme in which England would pay interest on a loan to Texas. All that was expected in return was a promise to avoid annexation.

On the surface, it didn't sound as dangerous as it was. But Justin knew the price was dear. Not only would England insist on Texas's independence; it would expect many favorable trade agreements as well. While not exactly becoming part of the British Empire, Texas would become her puppet, bound by the strings of obligation.

Justin knew that if the public learned of such underhanded dealings, the cries of outrage would be loud enough to stop it. Although his information was sketchy, he knew that Captain Charles Elliot, the British chargé d'affaires, possessed a letter penned by Aberdeen himself, detailing the offer. Elliot would submit it secretly to a Texas official, whose name Justin hadn't been able to discover.

He had to intercept the letter; it was his sole reason

for making the trip to San Antonio de Bexar. His best chance would be at tomorrow night's grand ball at Las Alamedas. Elliot would attend, of course, and he'd have the letter with him. It was quite possible that the Englishman would actually try to pass it on at the party.

Justin vowed that Elliot would never have the chance. Before twenty-four hours were up, the Texas authorities would know about Britain's manipulative scheme.

With great confidence, Justin stripped off his boots and shirt and washed himself at the basin. Then he lay down beside Shiloh, on top of the covers to minimize the effect of her nearness.

But she wasn't about to let him forget about her. Although fast asleep, she seemed to sense his presence. She sighed and shifted slightly, nuzzling his shoulder in her sleep. Her hand crept across his chest. Justin stiffened at her touch, which seared his flesh and filled him with longing. Groaning, he wrapped his arms around her, marveling at her softness, and wished to God that morning would come before his control crumbled, as it nearly had just a short while ago.

A night shower had freshened the town, cleansed the stone and adobe buildings of dust. Shiloh stepped out onto the terrace and looked down at the plaza. In the brilliant morning sunlight, it was a colorful rustic scene. But now Shiloh knew that nightfall could transform the plazas and narrow alleyways into a haven for thieves and carousing gangs like the one she'd met last night. Her fear was gone, but the lesson would never be forgotten. She grimaced slightly. Justin wouldn't forget either. He hadn't said anything before he'd left on some obscure errand, but she'd seen him watching her critically, probably wondering if she'd repeat her blunder.

Waking up to Justin had been a shock. She'd opened her eyes after a sound sleep and found herself staring across the tanned, muscular expanse of his chest. His arms were around her. What stunned her more than anything was that their bodies seemed to fit together perfectly, as if they'd been designed for each other's comfort. Justin had awakened when she'd tried to extract herself from his embrace. He'd laughed at her, remarking on how much more agreeable she was asleep than awake.

Shaking her head, Shiloh went back to the room and tied on a bonnet. Her father had invited her and Ina to a picnic down at the riverside. She decided to wait for them on the patio, where she could sit and ponder her father's strange behavior. She'd never known him to go on a picnic in his life.

Shiloh wore one of Ina's many creations, a pale green dimity frock. She liked it because it was short-sleeved and cool, although she had to admit it did little to enhance her figure. The straight, simple lines of the bodice accentuated her slimness. Her hips lent no fullness at all to the skirts. But Shiloh didn't care. While other ladies were nearly smothered by tight corsets and voluminous petticoats, she was comfortable.

She locked the room and went downstairs to wait. The patio of the hotel was a shady, flower-decked refuge from the summer heat. She sat on a stone bench, watching the bees drift in and out of a row of ligostrum bushes and the mockingbirds that flitted through the branches of a fig tree. Just as she was actually beginning to feel like she was on holiday, her enjoyment was shattered by a shrill, falsely cheerful greeting.

126

"Why Shiloh! I'd heard you were here!" Like a great, billowing confection, Jessamine West swooped down upon her. She left her maid standing in the plaza and floated into the patio.

Shiloh fixed a smile on her face. "Hello, Jessamine."

"This *is* a surprise." The young woman's china-blue eyes took in Shiloh's appearance with one sweep. "I must say, you're looking rather well. That dress is rather charming. I mean, it's a bit plain, but a hundred times better than those shirts and dungarees you used to wear." Jessamine primped, adjusting the lace that frothed at her bosom.

"What brings you to San Antonio?" Shiloh inquired, refusing to rise to Jessamine's backhanded remark.

Pursing her lips, Jessamine said, "The grand ball at Las Alamedas, of course. But I don't suppose you would know about that. All the best people will be there, as well as many important European dignitaries. We mean to show our British and French friends that Texas has become a genteel nation, at least in the upper classes. So tell me, Shiloh what are *you* doing here?"

Shiloh gave her a cool stare. "Although I'm certain to disgrace all Texans, I'm going to Las Alamedas, too."

The blue eyes widened incredulously. "*You*? But of course, I'd nearly forgotten you're married to Justin. He's well accepted in our social circle. After all, his father *is* one of the richest planters in Virginia. But surely you know that."

Shiloh didn't, but she masked her surprise. She'd known that Justin's estranged family was well off, but she'd never thought much about it.

"Well," Jessamine continued blithely, "I assume Justin has told you how to act in such dignified company. But there's so much to remember! You must be consumed by nerves."

"Actually, Jessamine, I haven't given much thought to how I'll act. I'm sure that if I'm friendly and reasonably polite, I won't stain our reputation too badly."

Jessamine gave her a dubious look, completely missing Shiloh's sarcasm. Then, slowly, a honeyed smile appeared on her porcelain face. "I think we'll find your presence quite amusing tonight, Shiloh. I wish there were time for me to go over some of the finer points of etiquette with you, but I must go. I must start getting ready. It takes hours, you know."

She sailed proudly away, leaving Shiloh fuming on the patio. But suddenly her anger left her and she laughed aloud. Jessamine's jealousy was pitifully transparent. If she weren't such a bitch, Shiloh might feel sorry for her.

When Ina and her father appeared, she was in good spirits.

"How is your room?" she asked Ina. "I was afraid there wouldn't be accommodations for you."

Ina smiled her beautiful smile. "The innkeeper gave me a small room in the back. It is quite comfortable."

"That's more than I can say," Nate grumbled. "I spent the night with a bunch of drunken cowboys up over the livery." But his green eyes betrayed a twinkle. Shiloh guessed he'd found some agreeable cronies.

They walked down to the river, where willows swept down to dip their branches into the crystalline water. When Ina asked her if she'd passed a pleasant night, Shiloh nodded and looked away. There was no need to speak of the danger last night, for it wouldn't happen again. Besides, Shiloh couldn't bear the thought of her father's knowing.

She quickly turned the subject to other matters, asking her father what he knew of this widely anticipated evening at the villa called Las Alamedas.

Nate lay back on one elbow and idly threw a stone

into the water.

"Seems to me Justin would've told you all you need to know."

Shiloh let her hair fall forward to hide her blush. She wasn't sure how much her father knew of her and Justin's relationship—or the absence of it. She looked hard at a webworm as it crept along a blade of grass.

"Justin always seems to be busy. Besides, I didn't really give the party much thought until today. I ran into Jessamine West."

Nate nodded. "Harmon West is never far from big money and power. I'd heard he was bringing his daughter here."

"What is this really about? I mean, I know it's a social gathering to honor the European nations that have recognized Texas as a sovereign state, but I get the feeling something else is going on."

"You're right. You see, most folks in Texas are Americans, and to them statehood is a foregone conclusion. But I'm told that the powers that be see it differently. President Houston himself thinks it inadvisable. Mexico will declare war immediately if a treaty is signed. And the foreigners like things just the way they are. You'll see tonight, we're being romanced by the French and British alike. There'll be a lot of huckstering going on."

Shiloh mulled it over in her head, thinking back on the many thin-papered issues of the Houston *Morning Star* she'd been reading.

"Is it because of the slavery issue?" she asked.

Nate shook his head. "That's only part of it. The Yankees and British like to keep bringing it up. It makes them sound real high and mighty. But the British, especially, have other motives. They couldn't stand to see the United States get any bigger."

Shiloh and her father talked on, and for a time it was

129

like it had once been between them. They were equals again, having an intelligent discussion. It made Shiloh wistful for times past. Her father had never been affectionate with her. But his appreciation of her mind was something Shiloh valued even more. She didn't need fatherly indulgence so long as she had his respect.

During a lull in the conversation, she looked over at Ina, who had been watching both of them curiously, as if such talk between father and daughter were unusual.

"You must be tired of hearing about this," Shiloh said apologetically.

Ina shrugged. "Not really. I was just wondering what will happen when Webster leaves his post as secretary of state. There is no doubt he will, since he and President Tyler don't get on at all."

While both Nate and Shiloh looked at her with open-mouthed amazement, she matter-of-factly began unpacking the lunch they'd brought. Nate caught Shiloh's eyes and grinned.

"Still waters run deep, as the saying goes," he said.

They feasted on tortillas and spiced beans and strips of cabrito, idling the afternoon away. Shiloh gathered ripe plums and figs from the trees and they ate those when the other food was gone.

Then Shiloh lazed by the river, trailing her bare feet in the water. Behind her, Nate and Ina spoke in low voices, like comfortable friends. She couldn't remember her father's ever having a female companion. She looked back and saw Nate hand Ina a tiny figure he'd whittled from a bit of wood. Perhaps, Shiloh mused, smiling, perhaps Ina would be the one to soften her father's rough edges and turn him from his whiskey and carousing.

A sudden cry from Ina roused her from these pleasant thoughts.

"*Dios!* The clock in the plaza is chiming six!" She

began gathering up their things and led the way back to the hotel.

Shiloh couldn't believe the afternoon had passed so quickly. As she stepped into her room, she hoped that Justin hadn't gone to look for her as he had last night.

He hadn't. He was standing with his back to the door, facing the terrace. Shiloh stopped and caught her breath.

Never had she seen Justin this way. He was clad in a beautifully tailored suit of evening clothes, a black waisted coat with tails, and fine fawn trousers that were tucked into tall, highly polished boots. A gleaming top hat rested on the table beside him. His blond hair shone like locks of the sun's rays. He held himself stiffly, accentuating the perfection of his appearance.

Finally he spoke without looking at her. "I was wondering when you'd decide to come back."

"Justin, I'm sorry. I didn't notice the time—"

He swung around, and she stopped speaking as she gaped at the rest of his garb. His neck was encased by a high-starched collar and black cravat. A vest with brass buttons hugged his trim torso and pleated cuffs peeked out from his sleeves. He was so handsome that Shiloh nearly forgot to breathe.

Just as she was about to form some compliment, his eyes flashed with anger. A gaze of steel raked over her, from her tousled hair to her bare feet.

"Is this some sort of joke, Shiloh? Did you hope to make a fool of me by abandoning me tonight? Or is that what you're planning on wearing?"

"No, of course not. I just—"

"God knows, I ask little enough of you. All I wanted was to arrive at Las Alamedas with you on my arm. Damn, I should have figured you wouldn't give me even that small favor."

When Shiloh found her voice, she was equally angry. "I never asked to be married to you, Justin. And since you're managed to make me feel like nothing, it shouldn't surprise you that I'm at a loss when it comes to behaving like a wife."

He hissed out a sigh, too impatient to argue with her. "I'm afraid I won't be able to escort you tonight, Shiloh. I promised someone I'd meet him at six-thirty." He gave her another long, hard-eyed stare. "I've had a bath drawn for you. If you can make yourself presentable, you could come later with your father."

Snatching his hat from the table, he strode past her to the door. He hesitated there as if to say something else, but snapped his mouth shut and left, leaving the clean scent of bay rum behind him.

Shiloh fought an urge to weep. No, she told herself, this wasn't worth her tears. She ran to the window in time to see Justin gallop away on one of the horses from the livery. Her heart ached at the handsome picture he made as he clattered across the plaza.

Ina, beautifully groomed and gowned handsomely in black, bustled in, followed by a pair of chambermaids who carried in a green satin gown with almost reverent care.

"What are you doing just sitting there?" Ina demanded. "We must get you ready."

"I'm not going," Shiloh said dully, still looking down at the now empty plaza.

"What?"

"Justin left without me. He said I could come later, but I don't think I will."

"Do not be silly, Shiloh. Of course you will go. Here in San Antonio they keep later hours. No one is

132

expected to arrive until at least eight o' clock. It is the Spanish way."

Eyes bright with unshed tears, Shiloh whirled about. "You don't understand, Ina. I don't *want* to go. If you could have heard the things he said to me, the way he looked at me . . . Justin doesn't want me there, either. He obviously thinks I'll shame him as the plainest, most ill-bred woman there."

A canny gleam appeared in Ina's eyes. "There, you have proven it yourself. You must attend."

"But *why*?"

"To show Justin how wrong he is about you. When you appear in the gown I have created, he will—how do you Anglos say it?—eat his words."

Shiloh thought about this for a moment. Perhaps Ina was right. If she stayed here, cowed by Justin's insults, she'd only confirm his low opinion of her. But if she went to the gala, and was even a minor success, revenge would be hers. A smile spread slowly across her face.

"I'll have my bath now," she said.

Thirty minutes later, Ina was fussing over her like a mother hen. She toweled the flame-colored curls dry and brushed Shiloh's hair until it shone as never before. With artful twists and loops, she piled it atop the girl's head and secured it with pins, leaving the shorter tendrils to fall like tiny flames around her face and neck.

Then began the laborious process of clothing her. She slipped on a thin lawn shift and drawers, which Ina had painstakingly embroidered with white thread. Over that went yards of petticoats to give fullness to the skirt. The gown itself was a masterpiece. Even Shiloh, who had no eye whatsoever for fashion, knew that it represented all of Ina's considerable skill with the needle. It had a wide, low bodice and dozens of tiny pleats leading out to billowing gigot sleeves. Ina had designed a panel of shiny gold beads on the front of the bodice and at the wide hem of the gown. The emerald satin shimmered, catching the lamplight in its myriad folds.

Finally, Ina overrode Shiloh's protests and added faint smudges of rouge to her cheeks and lips and a hint of dark color about her eyes.

Shiloh stood before the mirror, feeling as though she were looking at a stranger.

"Oh Ina," she breathed. The creature that mouthed the words in the looking glass was truly beautiful. The upswept hairstyle added height to her small stature. The fullness of the emerald gown cut a shapely figure, sweeping gracefully to and fro. Shiloh's face, which she'd always considered plain, glowed softly, the freckles barely noticeable, the eyes enormous and slightly mysterious looking.

"You see, Shiloh," Ina said with a smile. "There has always been a great lady hiding within you. It had only to be brought out."

Shiloh laughed, enjoying the free-floating motion of her voluminous skirts as she swayed before the mirror. "I only hope that I remember to behave as well as I look."

"Do not worry; I will see that you do," Ina said with mock severity.

Shiloh was delighted. "You'll be there?"

Amazingly, a blush rose to the older woman's cheeks. "I will be escorted by your father."

Shiloh stared. *"My father?"*

"Yes. That is, if it doesn't bother you, Shiloh."

"Of course, it doesn't bother me. It's just that my father has never entertained a lady—a respectable one — before. I must say I admire you for putting up with all his gruffness and bad habits."

Ina smiled. "He is not so terrible, Shiloh. Beneath all his rough ways, he is a man of good heart. Perhaps he is a bit like you. Perhaps he just needs the right person to bring out his finer qualities."

Shiloh glanced at her sharply, wondering how she could be so wrong. Justin had the opposite effect on her. Being with him only made her overly sensitive and ill-tempered. In fact, she intended to avoid him tonight so that she could truly enjoy the evening.

Her father, looking uncharacteristically natty in his best black suit, proved to be an elegant escort. He conversed pleasantly during the short coach ride to Las Alamedas, an elegant Spanish-style villa north of town, which belonged to Don Henrico Valdez, whose family had settled in San Antonio a century before.

As they drove up between twin rows of graceful alameda trees, Shiloh felt butterfly wings of nervousness beating lightly within her. It was her first formal evening, and she was essentially untrained for such company. As a footman handed her down from the coach, she felt genuine nervousness.

As if he'd sensed her trepidation, Nate leaned down and whispered in her ear. "You'll do fine, girl. Just be yourself."

She smiled gratefully and followed him and Ina into the beautiful tiled foyer.

The double doors leading out to the flower-strewn patio were held wide open, revealing a glittering throng that danced in the glow of torches and hanging lanterns.

A pair of liveried men stood in the doorway, announcing the arrival of various guests.

Nate extended an arm to each woman. "Shall we, ladies?"

Shiloh held back, a glint of obstinacy in her eyes. "I think I'll go in alone. It will give the gossips something to twitter about."

Nate laughed knowingly. "And," he added, "point out your husband's bad manners."

Shiloh flushed and looked away, knowing her motives were obvious. Then, drawing a deep breath for courage, she followed her father and Ina to the doorway.

Six

A graceful quadrille ended and the dancers applauded politely, migrating toward the tables that flanked the patio to refresh themselves with *aguamiel* or chocolate. Justin stood leaning against a stone pillar, speaking in low tones with his associate, Duff Green.

"I'm glad you came early," said the compactly built, bewhiskered man. "I figured Elliot would have something up his sleeve tonight."

Justin scanned the throng on the huge patio and focused on a handsome man with silvering hair. "I'll watch him," he promised. "I just wish I knew who his contact is. I don't much fancy picking the Englishman's pocket."

"That may be the best way, Justin. The letter would be a damned good piece of evidence." A servant passed and handed them each a goblet of dark liquid.

Duff tasted his and grimaced. "What the hell is this stuff?"

Justin grinned. "Mustang grape. You have to develop a taste for it."

Duff set his goblet on the sideboard. "I heard you got married," he said, puffing on a thick cigar. "Thought you'd want to show her off tonight."

Justin looked dubious when he thought of how he'd left Shiloh in the hotel room. Barefoot, tousled-haired, head flung back in defiance. Narrowing his eyes, he inspected the surge of people on the patio, every one of them dressed in clothes fine enough for royalty. Glittering ladies smiled demurely behind fluttering fans, their polite laughter tinkling along with the clink of crystal and the bubbling of the fountain in the middle.

"Well?" Duff prompted, looking curiously at Justin.

"I doubt she'll come," he said ruminatively. "Shiloh isn't quite cut out for this sort of thing. She's . . . different. Plain, even simple, I guess some would call her, and not given to pretty dresses and socializing."

Duff beetled his thick brows. "That's a hell of a thing to say about your wife."

"Don't get me wrong, Duff. I don't mean to run her down, but Shiloh would be as awkward as a duck on a lake full of swans. But she's a good woman—"

He broke off as the steward announced a couple he recognized.

"Mr. Nathaniel Mulvane. Señora Ina María Ruiz y Garza."

They were an impressive couple, Nate with his fiery hair and beard and Ina darkly elegant beneath her black lace mantilla. But there was just the two of them.

"Mrs. Shiloh McCord," the steward called out.

Duff clamped a hand on Justin's arm. "Jesus," he hissed. "So this is your 'ugly duckling.' I can't say I blame you for wanting to hide her away, to keep her all for yourself."

Justin froze, his gaze riveted on the vision that stood in the arched entranceway. In the cool moss-green eyes and red-gold cloud of hair he recognized the Shiloh he knew. But she had been transformed. As she floated down into the patio on a shimmer of green satin, the

138

gold beads reflecting hundreds of points of light, Justin sucked in his breath. She smiled and extended her hand to Mayor Seguin, and then to his portly wife. Her face exuded a glow of beauty so intense that Justin felt a knot of something like pain in his gut, a flood of heat in his loins. Slowly, as if entranced by his wife's splendor, he began walking toward her.

Her entrance had not gone unnoticed by the other guests. Vaguely, Justin became aware of a sudden collective intake of breath, followed by low murmurs of pleasure and appreciation.

How had he missed it? Justin wondered, wending his way through the crowd. How could he have overlooked a beauty so fine, so brilliant that it was like an intense flame on the darkest of nights? As his eyes fastened on her coral-colored smiling lips and her shining eyes, he realized it had been there all along. He just hadn't been able to bring himself to acknowledge it fully, for fear of what it might do to him.

But now there was no denying who Shiloh was — what she was. And Justin knew he could no longer deny his response to her. He approached just as she finished speaking to Don Henrico.

She gave him a dazzling smile, taunting him. Justin's pulse thundered through his veins.

With a murmuring laugh, she turned to Don Henrico. "Here is my husband now. He was in such a hurry to get to Las Alamedas that he found it expedient to leave without me."

Don Henrico shook a finger at Justin. "Unforgivable, my friend. But then, a bird of paradise needs no escort, does she? Your wife, señor, is enchanting."

The sweet strains of a slow waltz filled the night air. "I couldn't agree with you more, Don Henrico." He slid his hand around Shiloh's waist, marveling at its uncorseted slimness, and led her to the dance floor.

Shiloh knew, as they whirled around the lighted fountain, that she and Justin had every eye in the house on them. Through a blur of flickering torchlight and swirling dancers, she saw the admiring glances, the smiles of approval.

She felt glorious. Even though Justin had abandoned her, she'd triumphed over his slight. And she could tell by the way he gazed down at her that he knew it. She had every right to flaunt her victory, but she said nothing. There was no need.

His expert lead during the waltz made the dancing effortless for Shiloh. She had been a bit doubtful about that part of it, having danced her last step some years ago at school. But it all came back as if she did this every day.

Finally Justin spoke. His hand rubbed intimately at the small of her back, causing a warm thrill to eddy through her veins.

"I forgot to say good evening," he murmured.

She looked up with a half smile and noticed the intriguing way the torchlight glinted off his golden hair.

"There's still time," she suggested softly.

He flashed a smile, showing his dimple and small fans of creases beside his eyes.

"Good evening, Mrs. McCord."

She inclined her head, hiding her reaction to his infectious grin.

"Do I need to tell you how beautiful you are?"

Shiloh swallowed. In spite of the overwhelming reception she'd been given, doubts still niggled in the back of her mind. Was she really like the plain caterpillar, emerging from the cocoon as a majestic butterfly? She had to know, had to hear it from Justin's lips.

She met his eyes, searching for a hint of the familiar mockery. Seeing none, she said, "Yes, Justin. You do need to tell me."

He pressed closer, squeezed her hand. "You're beautiful, Shiloh. You're so damned beautiful you make my head swim. When I saw you come through that door tonight, I thought I'd died and gone to heaven."

A warm glow spread through her, and with it, a tiny throb of longing for him. She flushed, and smiled to acknowledge his compliment.

As he spun her about, his lips descended and brushed the column of her neck, making her shiver with delight.

"Am I forgiven, then?" he asked, his breath warm beside her ear.

Shiloh moistened her lips. She'd come to the party nursing a grudge toward him, but she suddenly found herself in a forgiving mood.

"I suppose," she said, "that no respectable married lady has ever been so affronted. But then—" Here she grinned wickedly, "—most ladies have respectable husbands."

Justin bent low so that only she could hear. "Better stop smiling like that, girl. I might just show you how unrespectable I really can be." His hand began a slow, sensual exploration of the back of her gown, reaching up to her bare shoulder blades with roving fingers.

Just as Shiloh felt her knees begin to weaken, the waltz ended on a lingering note. Then, it was as if half the gentlemen on the patio converged upon her. Justin laughed at her confusion.

"Now that the formality of the first dance with your husband is over," he said, "it looks like you're fair game for anyone."

Her feet never rested as gentlemen of every age, shape, and size claimed her for quadrilles, gallopades, and contradances. She even danced the dangerously suggestive fandango with Mayor Seguin himself. Only when she was certain she'd trodden her green kid slippers through to the floor did she gravitate to the tables for a cooling drink.

"You're having a high old time for yourself," Nate Mulvane commented. With Ina at his side, he came to lead her to a chair.

Shiloh sank down, her face glowing with exertion and excitement. Her smile disappeared, though, when Jessamine West pushed her way to the table. She looked like a giant flower, Shiloh thought, in a pink bell-shaped dress that was cinched in so tightly at the waist that Jessamine's eyes appeared unnaturally wide, as if they might pop out of her head.

"You look quite well tonight, Shiloh," she said, allowing the slightest bit of amazement to tinge her remark.

Shiloh smiled. It was a totally new sensation for her to see envy in another woman's eyes. "Thank you," she said. "And you look lovely, Jessamine."

"Your dress is most unusual. A bit outmoded in the plain lines of it, but it seems to suit you. And—" she leaned forward conspiratorially, "—you must remember that people will talk if you continue to dance with each and every gentleman present." Jessamine glided off to attach herself to the Viscount Jules de Cramayel, the French chargé d'affaires.

Shiloh turned immediately to Ina. "Never mind her," she said. "Your dress is a triumph. I've been asked several times for the name of my seamstress."

Ina smiled softly. "It is not the dress, *mi amiga*, but the wearer who has caused such a stir."

Shiloh squeezed her hand and looked up to ask her father how he was enjoying himself. But he wasn't paying attention to her; he was staring intently across the patio.

"What is it?" she asked, following his gaze.

"That's Captain Charles Elliot," he said slowly. "I've been watching him all night." He glanced over at Shiloh. "So has your husband."

"Why?"

"I'm not sure. But I suspect it has something to do with that envelope he's carrying in his coat pocket. I'll bet Justin would love to get his hands on it—before someone else does."

Shiloh watched Elliot for a few moments. He smiled charmingly and spoke to a passing group, and accepted a drink from a tray. But she noticed the tenseness of his jaw, the watchful looks he cast about. In sudden inspiration, she stood.

"Excuse me," she murmured to Nate and Ina, and crossed the patio, politely declining several invitations as she went.

"Captain Elliot?"

He looked at her, distracted, and then with growing interest. His stare almost made Shiloh back away. He had the coldest pair of pale eyes she'd ever seen. His smile was suave, but did nothing to warm the icy chill of his gaze.

"I'm sorry, but you have me at a loss. Have we met, Miss—?"

She smiled at him. "Unfortunately, no. But I'd be delighted if you'd call me Shiloh." She covered her relief. She'd counted on his not knowing she was Justin's wife.

"An unusual name," he commented.. His British accent was so pronounced that it lent a haughtiness to his every word.

"My mother named me after the county where she was born," she explained. "She left her family back there and was always nostalgic about it."

143

"Enchanting," he said. He extended his arm. "I'm quite ignorant of your Texas dances," he admitted, "but for the sake of a beauty such as yourself I could try to blunder my way through."

"Oh please," Shiloh said, pressing close, "don't trouble yourself. To be honest, captain, I'd much rather take a stroll out into the water gardens. That is, if you aren't occupied with something else."

For the smallest fraction of a second, Elliot's icy eyes swept the room and then returned to Shiloh.

"I'd be delighted," he said, and led her back behind the orchestra, down a few stairs to the garden. As they walked slowly beneath the sweeping magnolia trees and down between a cement channel of running spring water, the sounds from the patio grew faint. What Shiloh spoke of she couldn't remember later, but she must have managed to allay any suspicions the Englishman might have had.

For when she affected a delicate shiver and asked for his coat to wrap about her shoulders, he readily obliged. Within seconds, she had found the small envelope and slipped it into the bodice of her gown, next to her rapidly beating heart.

When they returned to the patio, she knew she had to act quickly before Elliot realized what had happened. She returned his coat with smiling thanks and went back to the dance floor. As two different men approached to claim her for the zopilote, she put her hand to her brow.

She let her nervousness work for her, allowing her face to drain of color.

"Mrs. McCord, what is it?" someone asked.

She moaned slightly. "I—I feel dizzy. So lightheaded, and—" Letting her voice dissipate into the flower-scented air, she sank with dramatic slowness to the tiles. As she lay motionless, her eyes closed, she felt the press of the crowd about her.

"Stand back," someone ordered. "Give her air!"

"Smelling salts!" said another. "Bring smelling salts, and some water!"

Suddenly, Shiloh felt a pair of strong arms lifting her. She recognized Justin from his unique scent and the hard musculature of his frame.

She allowed her eyes to flutter open, weakly. "Jus— Justin, I'm ill," she breathed. "Oh please, take me back to the hotel—" She took a deep breath and feigned another swoon.

She was the only one who heard his vile whispered oath. Aloud, he spoke to her father.

"Nate. Could you—"

"Sorry, lad. I was just about to dance with this lady on my arm. Go ahead, take the coach. We'll get back another way, and I'll take your horse to the livery."

Shiloh felt Justin tense. Then he strode away so quickly that she could feel the wind in her hair. He paused twice on the way out. Once to promise a future meeting with someone called Duff, and again to decline Don Henrico's offer of a room in the villa.

Shiloh had planned on showing Justin her prize once they were in the coach, but as it bounced and clattered down the tree-lined lane, she thought better of it. If Captain Elliot overtook them, he was unlikely to commit the offense of searching her, but he wouldn't show that much restraint with Justin. The ruthlessness she remembered in his chilly eyes convinced her of that.

Besides, she reflected, smiling into the darkness, it was undeniably pleasant lying in Justin's lap with his arms about her, hearing his heartbeat and breathing in his clean smell.

Only when he had dashed with her up to the room and laid her gently on the bed did she allow her eyes to

145

open again.

By the light of a low-burning lamp she saw Justin's face and the golden gleam of his hair. All anger was gone from him as his brows knitted in concern.

"Shiloh . . . ?" He spoke her name gently and she smiled a little. "Shall I send for a doctor?" Before she could answer, he was going toward the door.

Bringing her charade to an abrupt end, she sat up on the bed. "That won't be necessary, Justin. I'm perfectly all right."

He whirled around to face her, his steel-gray eyes narrowing suspiciously. "Are you sure?"

She brushed a stray tendril from her neck. "Quite sure."

He returned to the bed and sat on the edge, holding her by her upper arms. "What happened back there at Las Alamedas? I thought something was seriously wrong."

She smiled in anticipation of revealing her triumph. "Nothing happened. I've never swooned in my life. But apparently I was pretty convincing."

His grip on her arms tightened. "But—*why?*"

Still composed, even in the face of his burgeoning wrath, Shiloh smiled again. "I thought it best to leave right away. I'll admit fainting was an amateurish ploy, but it was the best I could do under the circumstances. And it did work. Here we are."

Now the hands were biting into her soft flesh. "God damn." He gave her a rough shake. "God *damn!* Of all the foolish, idiotic—"

"Justin, please! You're hurting me!"

His face was very close to hers, darkly flushed with anger. "Not half as much as you deserve to be hurt," he raged. "Damn it, Shiloh, do you know what you just did? That party wasn't just a social engagement for me. I was there for a much more important reason. I had a job to do, and you stood in my way. I've spent weeks trying to pin down some evidence against the Accord, and now it's all lost. I'll never have a chance like this again. Damn! I was so close—" His tirade went on, punctuated by curses that even Shiloh found impressive.

She forced herself to listen calmly and resisted wincing in the steel trap of his hold on her. When he finally paused to glower at her, she slowly removed his fingers one by one, until her arms were free.

Looking with mild distaste at the reddened prints of his hands on her pale flesh, she asked, "Are you finished?"

"In more ways than one," he growled.

"Then perhaps you'll give me a chance to redeem myself," she suggested. Slipping a thumb and forefinger into the bodice of her gown, she extracted the envelope she'd stolen from Charles Elliot and held it out to Justin.

"Is this what you were so all-fired eager to get your hands on?"

The angry flush left his face as he snatched it away and broke the seal. His eyes scanned the tiny writing on the page. He looked up in amazement.

"My God. Shiloh, how the hell did you wind up with this?"

She permitted herself a touch of smugness. "I went for a stroll with Captain Elliot. He very kindly offered me his coat when the air got chilly."

"Why, Shiloh? Why did you do it?"

"I knew you were after it. I figured my way was a lot more discreet than your trying to pick his pocket. I don't know what that letter is about, but we would have been there all night if I hadn't acted."

An intriguing succession of emotions crossed Justin's face as he stared at her. Anger, suspicion, disbelief, and finally elation lit his eyes. Then, like the sun bursting from a thundercloud, he grinned his marvelous grin and let out a great whoop.

Shiloh's breath left her as she was swept into his embrace. His joy was infectious, and she brought her arms around him in response.

"Shiloh my girl," he said with a rich laugh, "my hat goes off to you. You've just outsmarted the wiliest fox that ever left England's shores."

She fell, laughing, against his chest, in the full flush of her victory. Then she looked up into his smiling eyes, still laughing.

Almost by accident, their lips met, bumping together as they smiled at one another.

Both froze, stunned by the chance meeting. Shiloh's smile faded as quickly as Justin's and they regarded each other from the distance of a single breath, a heartbeat, as a silken shadow crossed the light moment.

Now Justin's every movement became deliberate. With tantalizing slowness, he lowered his mouth to hers, drawing her soft gasp of surprise into his lungs. For a moment there was light pressure as his lips explored hers. Then he began a slow, sensual movement, deepening the pressure and wrapping his arms more securely around her.

He lifted his mouth to whisper, "Stop me now, Shiloh. Because if you let me go any further, I won't listen to you."

Stop? Her body wouldn't even allow her to consider it. She raised her mouth and kissed him.

A moist heat enveloped her, pervaded her most secret places. As with a will of their own, her lips parted, hungry for a taste of him. Justin's tongue traced the lines of her mouth and slid with unmistakable suggestion into hers. Slowly, he began a meticulous exploration of the silken inner recesses of her mouth, gliding his tongue over hers, running it along the sensitive tissues of her inner lip. Then the movement of his tongue became oddly rhythmic. At first, Shiloh didn't understand the meaning of it. His tongue thrust and receded, thrust and receded, lighting a wildfire in her that she couldn't control. Suddenly, as a moan escaped her, comprehension dawned. Justin's mouth and tongue were emulating the act that had always been a mystery to her. The knowledge of what he was doing drove her mad with desire.

Finally, when Shiloh lay weak and flushed in his arms, Justin lifted his mouth from hers. His eyes burned with an intensity she'd never seen before.

"Justin?" Her voice was breathless. "What — what is happening? You've never kissed me like that before."

He laughed softly, intimately. "That's because I never meant business before, Mrs. McCord."

She frowned, trying to still the quaking within her. "What's that supposed to mean?"

He traced his finger along the outline of her lips. "All these weeks I've watched you, Shiloh. But I swore I'd never force myself on you. I said I'd wait until you were willing. . . ." His fingers left her lips and trailed lazily down the column of her neck to the top of her bosom. "But now," he continued, "now, I can't wait any longer. You'd best tell me to go away now, Shiloh, or I won't be responsible for what happens."

She was mesmerized by the deep timbre of his voice, the fire in his eyes, the sensual circling of his hands. She didn't think before she spoke; the words seemed to form of their own accord.

"Don't go, Justin. Stay with me. Stay and show me —"

"What? Tell me, Shiloh." He urged the admission from her.

149

"Show me what you want from me. What—what I want from you."

Her words seemed to cause the fire in his eyes to blaze wildly. He gave her another searing kiss, his mouth pressing hers triumphantly. Then he dragged his lips away.

"Stand up, Shiloh."

"What?"

He stood and pulled her to her feet. His heated gaze swept over her and a smile of soul-searing intimacy crossed his face.

"That dress showed me how beautiful you are, Shiloh. But the creature beneath is something much, much more special." He punctuated his speech by drawing, one by one, the pins from her hair. Red-gold curls spilled over her shoulders and down the hollow of her back. Then his hands reached behind, unhurriedly freeing the gold buttons from their loops. He pulled at the fullness of her sleeves, bending to nuzzle her neck as the bodice of her gown fell to her waist.

With agonizing slowness, he pulled at the drawstring of her chemise, standing back to watch as it, too, fell away.

Shiloh heard the hiss of his indrawn breath as he feasted his eyes on her small coral-tipped breasts. The nipples were taut, tingling with anticipation. Both of Justin's hands came forward, cupping the pale mounds, thumbs circling the proud crests. He brought his mouth first to one, then the other, teasing the nipples with teeth and tongue until Shiloh gasped aloud.

He looked up, smiling. "Do you like that?"

"I—It's—"

"Do you, Shiloh?" It was as if he had to hear it from her lips.

"Yes," she sighed. "Oh, yes."

He kissed and caressed her breasts a while longer, until Shiloh was trembling, almost weeping with desire. Then Justin straightened and slid the gown over her narrow hips, pulling her toward him so she could step out of it. His hand untied the strings of her pantalettes and he slid them, along with her silk stockings, downward.

Shiloh's trembling increased as he knelt, revealing a triangle of red-gold hair and the curve of her buttocks. Sensation rocked her as he kissed every inch that was bared to him: the side of her hip, the whiteness of her thigh, the back of her knee. He removed her slippers and then her stockings, his tongue licking wickedly at her feet as he finished disrobing her.

Then he stood back and regarded her, like an artist admiring his own creation.

Shiloh blushed to the tips of her ears and brought her hands over her heaving bosom.

"Justin." Her whisper sounded distant, rough with both fear and longing.

He removed her hands ever so gently. "There is no shame in this, Shiloh. Be proud of your beauty." His hands coursed down her torso and around to stroke her buttocks.

"Undress me, love," he said.

She looked up at him, shocked.

"Come. I'll help you." He took her trembling hands and placed them at his lapels. She watched his jacket drop away. Then she cast aside his cravat and unbuttoned his vest and broadcloth shirt, her fingers clumsy and shaking.

His shoulders and bare chest gleamed with a sheen of moisture. The lamplight played over rippling muscles and tanned flesh that seemed to beg for her touch. Tentatively, then with growing confidence, she stroked his shoulders and strong arms and lay her cheek upon

151

his chest. She heard the thundering of his heart and marveled that it was she who caused his pulse to race.

Justin kicked off his boots and cast aside his belt. He brought her hand to the top of his trousers.

Shiloh pulled away. "Justin, I—I can't. I—"

He swept her into his arms, chuckling deeply. "There's no hurry, love. None at all. We can save that for later . . ." His words trailed off as he bent to kiss her, his mouth holding hers even as he laid her on the bed. The frame creaked slightly as he settled himself beside her. Propping himself up on one elbow, he lifted his lips to gaze down at her.

His other hand was everywhere, buffing her taut nipples, circling her flat belly, stroking her quaking thighs with long, sensuous caresses.

"You're a wonder, Shiloh," he said huskily. "A woman in every way, but still a child, too. Do you know anything about this—about making love?"

"I—" Shiloh reddened. "No."

He smiled. He was so achingly handsome. His words mingled with the feather-light kisses he showered over her face and neck and bosom. "I only hope, Shiloh, that I can do justice to your beauty—your innocence."

Then he began kissing her in earnest, relentlessly, while his hands played her as if her body were a tightly-strung instrument. He nipped and suckled at her breasts while one hand traveled downward, fingers twining into the red-gold nest of her womanhood.

Shiloh moaned and moistened her lips, powerless to resist his sensual assault. When he gently nudged her legs apart, they relaxed almost gratefully.

Suddenly his finger dipped and found the very core of her desire. Shiloh gasped at the shock his touch produced.

"Easy, love," Justin muttered, nuzzling the leaping

pulse at her throat. "Easy . . ."

She forgot to breathe as his fingers began a slow, tantalizing caress, drawing liquid fire from her loins. Then, while his thumb kept up a soul-shattering rhythm, his fingers went inside her.

Shiloh cried out, but again was quieted by Justin's soothing whisper. His questing finger was joined by another, and he kissed her deeply. Then, fingers and tongue began working in tandem, the rhythm that Shiloh now knew so well, wanted so burningly, quickening. His tongue thrust into her mouth and the motion was imitated below. And all the while, his thumb stroked relentlessly.

Shiloh felt her hips begin to rise, along with the rising flames of the wildfire within her. Her head pounded, almost unable to cope with the waves of sensation that flooded her. She felt herself on the brink of a precipice and waited, breathless, to drop over the edge.

Her eyes flew open as it happened. She was catapulted by passion into a dark world of sensation so intense that it caused her to cry out.

"Justin! What is—I don't know what I'm feeling—"

He laughed softly. "You don't have to know, love. Just feel it." He let her tighten around his fingers and kissed her until she finally relaxed. Then, as she lay bathed in the glow of passion, he slipped off his trousers.

Shiloh wanted to look away, but she couldn't. She was fascinated by the sight of his proud manhood, and shuddered as he lay down beside her.

"What shall I do, Justin?" she asked timidly.

He caressed her cheek. "Whatever your senses tell you to do. Whatever you want."

"But what about you?" She had to ask him. She realized that their lovemaking had been one-sided.

153

"You're everything I want," he said roughly. And then his hands went to work on her again, rekindling the fires that had never quite gone out. Before long, Shiloh was quaking in his arms, straining for completion.

But Justin was different now. Besides simply giving her the exquisite pleasure her body craved, he began to reveal, gently, demands of his own. His manhood grazed her belly, her thigh, searing her.

Shiloh touched him. She didn't know where she got the nerve to do it, but she bestowed on him a caress so evocative that he groaned aloud.

He knelt between her legs and moved both hands up to her thighs, his fingers flicking out at her softness. Then his hands dipped beneath her buttocks, raising her up to him. He looked at her, his face hard with restrained desire.

"I'll try not to hurt you, love," he whispered hoarsely.

Hurt her? Shiloh had no inkling of what he was talking about. She closed her eyes and gave herself up to him. His fingers parted her flesh and touched again the point of her desire, and then, moving so slowly that his body trembled, Justin came to her.

Shiloh inhaled as she felt herself being rent in two. She clawed at the rigid back, moving her head from side to side in protest.

Justin's lips whispered into her ear, crooning to her. "Just relax, sweetheart. It'll pass, you'll see. . . ."

He began to move. By now the rhythm was so familiar to Shiloh that she was able to forget the pain. Slowly, almost unnoticeably, the pain gave way to sheer pleasure. The rhythm Justin had taught her with his mouth and fingers took on a new form, one that was so exquisite that Shiloh felt tears spring to her eyes. She felt the moment build and again experienced ecstasy, this one even sweeter than the last.

Justin shuddered and thrust deeper than ever, and then relaxed, covering Shiloh's sated body with his.

They lay still, neither daring to move, to speak, in the moments following their coupling. Finally, when their heartbeats had slowed to normal, Justin kissed her sweetly and moved to one side.

"How do you feel, love?" he whispered.

"I'm—I never knew—never dreamed—" She stopped, unable to put what she was feeling into words.

He laughed softly and gathered her close, fitting her head into the crook of his arm.

"Regrets, Shiloh?"

She hesitated, wondering. He had stolen her freedom from her by marrying her, but she'd never felt like his possession. Yet now, bathed in all the new feelings he'd awakened in her, she knew that he had truly made her his own. She belonged to him as much as the stars belonged to the wide Texas sky. And he was asking her if she regretted that.

"No," she answered at last. "No, Justin, I don't regret what we've done."

He smoothed the hair from her face and drew a quilt up around them. Together, they held each other and drifted off to sleep.

Shiloh was awakened by an odd, tingling sensation. It was as if a feather was being drawn up and down the length of her side, from her ear to the back of her knee. It was so pleasant that she thought she might be dreaming, but when her eyes fluttered open, she knew she was not.

It was beyond the capacity of her imagination to conjure an image more exquisite than the one she saw. Justin reclined beside her, looking like a young god with his beautifully sculpted face and powerful build.

155

He had plucked a wildflower, a sprig of laceweed, from the jar on the bedside stand, and was trailing it lightly over her naked body.

"Did I startle you?" he asked.

Shiloh couldn't help smiling. "I've never been awakened quite like this before."

He grew bolder with the flower, dipping it down between her breasts and over her belly, to tease the responsive flesh of her thighs. Shiloh allowed the sweet torture to continue until she could stand it no more. Then she snatched the sprig away and cast it to the floor.

Laughing at her impatience, Justin gathered her to him and began working his magic over her once again. As she lay with him, Shiloh realized that a new part of her had been awakened. Nothing would ever be quite the same again.

Seven

A cloaked horseman plunged into the twilight shadows of a cane brake along Buffalo Bayou, looking this way and that, to assure himself he hadn't been seen. An owl screeched and an armadillo scuttled into the underbrush, but otherwise the murky locale was silent. The horseman slid to the marshy ground, tethered his horse, and went to a spreading live oak. There, another dark figure awaited him.

"Well?" asked Harmon West, peering at the approaching man.

"A disaster." Charles Elliot's clipped accent cut through the heavy night air. "The plan is ruined."

"Hmph. I thought so. What happened?"

"Lord Aberdeen's letter was stolen from me at Las Alamedas. By the charming wife of Justin McCord, I later learned."

"Damn! Don't tell me Washington has *her* working for them too. You should have been more careful, my friend."

"I? For God's sake, Harmon, you said you would take care of McCord. Weren't you going to marry your daughter to him?"

157

The judge nodded his silver head. "But McCord had other ideas. He married Shiloh Mulvane. She's always been regarded as an odd bird hereabouts. Fancied herself a detective, for private hire. Meddlesome woman!"

"This whole thing could have been avoided if you'd been there, Harmon."

"I was laid up with the damned gout. Couldn't move a muscle."

"What are we going to do about the letter?"

"No point in trying to get it back. Justin McCord wouldn't let it slip through his fingers. No doubt he's waiting for Sam Houston to return to town, so he can present it to him."

"I'm not worried about President Houston. Lord Aberdeen will, of course, deny any knowledge of the letter, and that will be that. But the real tragedy is that an ingenious plan can never come into being. The Americans would cry foul the minute they heard of it."

"You're right about that. But we don't need to get alarmed just yet. Houston isn't leaning too hard toward annexation, and the Texas legislature won't be meeting for a couple of months, at least. We've got plenty of time to think of a plan of action."

Elliot sighed wearily. "Whatever we do, let's try to keep McCord and his wife in the dark about it. I've a feeling those two don't miss much."

Harmon West snapped his fingers as a sudden inspiration came to him.

"That's it, Charles. The *two* of them. We were on the right track when we tried to have the woman abducted in San Antone. If we can somehow get them working against each other, instead of together, they'd be a lot less effective."

"That's ridiculous, Harmon. They're husband and wife."

"Sure they are. But we already know their marriage was no love match. It shouldn't be too hard to pit them against each other, maybe even get the girl to sympathize with us. We could use the slavery argument. Her father's a known abolitionist, and Shiloh probably agrees with him."

Elliot shrugged. "I suppose it's worth a try. It certainly would make our job easier. What do you propose we do?"

Harmon West chuckled darkly. "Get them fighting. Justin has a reputation as a real ladies' man and I doubt Shiloh would sit still for any of his fooling around. I'll get Isabella Hernandez to come in from Galveston. She managed to turn his head once, down at the border. And meanwhile, Charles, you can talk to Shiloh."

Elliot laughed sharply, his cold eyes narrowed. "Good God, Harmon, I'm twice her age."

"I'm not suggesting you sweep her off her feet. But you've got a way with words. Let her think your sole purpose is to prevent the United States from winning another slave state. She might like that."

"Very well," said Elliot. "Now, what are we going to do next?"

Harmon grinned into the thick darkness. "I think it's time we brought our Mexican friends into play. We've had them waiting down at the border for a long time. I think now would be a good time to demonstrate to people just what would happen if a treaty were made with the United States."

Just then, a dark shape slithered down the bank and dropped into the bayou with a small splash. Elliot recoiled.

"What was that?"

"A moccasin, probably. Poisonous as they come."

Muttering something about barbaric conditions, the

Englishman went back up to his horse.

"I don't believe you, Justin!" Shiloh snapped, whirling on him so quickly that her robe gaped open in the front.

He looked at her with unconcealed lust, eyes alighting on her soft, round breasts and the tiny red bite marks he'd bestowed on her the night before as they'd celebrated coming home to Post Oaks.

"It's business, love," he explained patiently. "You don't need to trouble your head about it." He stood and crossed the sun-flooded room, catching her against him, his arm slipping inside her robe.

Immediately, he felt her soften, become pliant in his arms. Desire flooded through him like a raging torrent and he bent his head to inhale the honeysuckle scent of her silken skin. No woman had ever affected him like this before. Her innocence and vulnerability were coupled with pride and strong will, and a passion that, when awakened, left him fighting for air like a drowning man. Justin refused to question his passion for his young wife. He didn't want to know why he was so drawn to her; he only wanted to feel and taste and smell her, and hear her unabashed cries of ecstasy ringing in his ears.

She lifted her lips for his kiss and he dropped his mouth to hers, tasting her sweetness. Already he wanted her; he couldn't get enough of her.

By the time the kiss ended, he was ready to fling her onto the bed. Her enormous green eyes regarded him steadily.

"Justin."

"Mmm?" His lips tasted her cheek, the edge of her jaw.

She placed her hands on his chest, pushing away

160

slightly so she could look at him.

"Tell me what was in the letter."

He groaned aloud. "Oh Christ, Shiloh. We've already been through this." He bent to kiss away her mounting anger, but she turned her head aside.

"I have a right to know," she insisted. "After all, it was I who got the envelope for you."

"I never asked you to do that."

"Nevertheless—"

"*No*, Shiloh. It's too dangerous for you to get involved in all this. I don't want anyone to have a reason to use you—"

Quick as lightning, she wrenched herself out of his embrace. "Very well," she said coldly, drawing her robe around her. "Then we have nothing more to discuss."

Justin's unrequited hunger fueled his anger. "Jesus, it didn't take you long to learn to use yourself as a weapon," he observed sarcastically.

"What's that supposed to mean?"

"You almost had me fooled, Shiloh. But you're no different from any other woman. The minute you don't get exactly what you want, you declare yourself off limits."

"That's not true!"

He raised an eyebrow sardonically. "Oh no? Think about it, Shiloh. If I'd shown you the letter, you'd be flat on your back, begging for me."

He watched a blush of outrage creep over her face. "How dare you talk to me like that!"

"It's the truth, girl. I think you know it."

She walked stiffly to the window, hiding her face from him. Suddenly, she turned again. "What about you, Justin? Now that I think about it, you showed your true colors in San Antonio. You wouldn't have been a husband to me if I hadn't shown up at Las Alamedas, dressed like a perfect lady. You didn't even

161

want me until it became obvious that other men found me desirable."

"Shiloh, I wanted you from the first time you paraded yourself naked before me the night we met. I only did you the courtesy of waiting until you were ready."

"And meanwhile you delighted in teasing me with an occasional kiss or two. No, Justin, I know all about you now. You were waiting to see if you could mold me into a proper wife. Well, you can't. I'm the same person you found so disagreeable at first. I still have the same dreams, the same goals. If you refuse to share your secrets with me, I swear I'll find out on my own."

"Shiloh," he said quietly. "Shiloh, listen. When I was in San Antonio I had a report about Raoul Delgado, my associate who was killed. It wasn't just a simple case of murder. The man had been tortured beyond belief. And then, after he told all he knew, they did him the favor of putting him to death. Don't go snooping around, Shiloh. It's too dangerous. You don't know who you're dealing with."

"Is it too dangerous for me?" she questioned, green eyes still blazing. "Or for your overblown ego? I think part of this is your humiliation at being outmaneuvered by me. You're jealous because I was able to get the letter."

Justin shook his head. "Of all the . . ." He stopped speaking. There was simply no reasoning with the woman. She just couldn't see that he didn't want her to have anything to do with the ruthless members of the Accord. Cursing under his breath, he pulled on his clothes and boots and took his hat from a peg by the door.

"I don't have time to argue with you, Shiloh," he said. "A couple of dozen wild horses are being driven in from Goliad, and there's going to be a lot of work to do around here in the next few weeks. But think about what I said. It's not a game, Shiloh."

"You did not touch your dinner," Ina observed, removing Shiloh's plate from the table.

"I don't have much of an appetite these days, Ina." Shiloh moved restlessly from the table. She was surprised to see the maid's handsome face smiling broadly at her.

"What's funny?" she demanded, getting to her feet.

"I was just counting. It has been seven weeks since we returned from San Antonio. Often that is soon enough to tell."

"Tell what?"

"Ah, Shiloh, I keep forgetting you did not grow up with a mother. There has been no one to tell you about the first signs of motherhood."

Shiloh stumbled back, stricken. She had never even considered the possibility of having a child—Justin's child. The thought filled her with cold dread. She wasn't ready for a baby; she never would be. Trembling, she looked over at Ina.

"Tell me more about these signs," she said.

"The symptoms are quite mild. I have never experienced them myself, but I am the oldest of eight children and I remember my mother well. A woman will feel nausea and headache. And, of course, the monthly bleeding stops—"

Shiloh brightened. "It does?"

Ina stared at her, first with disbelief and then with great sympathy. She put out a hand and smoothed a lock of red hair away from the girl's cheek.

"Poor little one," she crooned. "You are truly a child in many ways. Now. Do you think you are carrying a baby?"

"No," Shiloh breathed, weak with relief. "It's not possible. I had my courses after—after—" She swallowed, stifling a sob of misery.

Patting her hand, Ina said, "After Señor McCord moved back to the bunkhouse."

Shiloh nodded glumly. "I was so stupid. I thought everything was going to be all right, and then we had that terrible row. In the past month, Justin has either been away on business or busy with the ranch hands."

"There is a new herd to be broken, trained to the saddle. More space must be built for them . . . do not worry, Shiloh. He will realize soon that he has been neglecting you."

"But that's just it. I *want* him to leave me alone. I want nothing to do with him."

Ina regarded her sagely, with her large, liquid brown eyes. "Then why do you miss him so terribly?"

"I don't, Ina. I swear it! I've just been depressed lately because there is so little for me to do. If I were on my own I could be making a living the way I choose."

"You have been working very hard, Shiloh. You have been doing as much with the horses as any ranch hand."

"That's because there's nothing else to do. But I have half a mind to quit that, too. Justin doesn't seen to care one way or another."

"He cares, Shiloh. I have been watching him. You must understand a man like Señor McCord. He is proud, and has never failed at anything he has tried to do. He is afraid to find out whether or not he has won your love. And you are much the same, Shiloh. Stubborn. But if you want to put an end to this impasse, I think you will have to make the first move." Ina gathered the dishes from the table and left Shiloh to her thoughts.

She stood for a long time, looking out across the

wide, shimmering fields of autumn. The horses, sorrels and palominos, grazed within the confines of a newly built fence. The hands worked tirelessly, rapidly transforming Post Oaks into a prospering ranch.

Shiloh ran down to the stableyard, determined to have it out with Justin at last. She didn't know what she'd say to him, but Ina had made her realize that she could no longer tolerate this silent limbo. She squared her shoulders and stepped into the dimness of the stables. Tomas appeared, grinning broadly as he always did when he saw her.

"Where's Mr. McCord?" she asked.

"I am sorry, señora. He has just left for town. He said he had to meet with someone."

Shiloh pursed her lips. The afternoon stretched long and restless ahead of her, and she didn't relish the idea of waiting for Justin to come home.

"Saddle my horse," she said to Tomas. "I'll go get my boots on."

Justin sat at a battered table, clenching his jaw against an angry outburst. He, Lamar Coulter, and Duff Green had gone to hear Sam Houston's reaction to Elliot's letter.

"You have it right there in front of you, sir," he said quietly. "I don't know what more you need."

The president shrugged his massive shoulders and puffed on his cigar. He was the man who had chased Santa Anna back to Mexico, had tamed the Indians of the frontier. And he looked, Justin reflected, exactly like the hero that he was. But perhaps that was the problem, after all. How could a man as proud and powerful as Sam Houston allow the republic he'd built to disappear, joining the Union as a state?

Houston cleared his throat. "You've done the republic a great service in bringing this matter to my attention, Mr. McCord. Please extend my thanks to your associates." He shook his head in disgust. "Apparently the English see us as a bunch of money-hungry bumpkins, to think we'd fall for a deal like that."

Justin frowned. "Begging your pardon, sir, but your secretary of state didn't find the English proposal so outrageous."

Houston raised a bushy brow. "Anson Jones?"

"Yes, sir."

Houston shrugged. "The government's broke, that's no secret. There are a lot of people who would think this a reasonable solution."

"May I ask, Mr. President, what you intend to do about it?" Lamar asked.

Houston slapped his hands down on the table and rose to his full height, well over six feet.

"Nothing, gentlemen."

Duff Green moved agitatedly about the tiny office. "Just a minute, sir. I know we can't touch Elliot—he's a foreigner. But what about Harmon West?"

"He'll deny everything, as will the English."

"But he's got to be stopped! West is known to have a strong interest in Caribbean sugar and rum—"

"That's never been proven."

"He'll go to any length to prevent annexation. His next attempt might not be so discreet."

Houston went to the door and turned back, his roughly handsome features set in an apologetic expression.

"Sorry, gentlemen. Texans are always being accused of meting out justice rashly. We'll just have to let this one blow over." Taking down his hat, he left Coulter's office.

Duff Green let out a string of curses and followed him out, slamming the door behind him.

Justin hissed out a sigh. "I guess that's that. Come on, Lamar. Let's go get drunk."

Shiloh rode the length of Main Street, scanning the crowds for a glimpse of Justin. She caught sight of his deep-chested bay tethered at a hitching post outside a grog shop. It was the noisiest one in town, alive with piano music and loud yells and laughter, and the endless clink of glasses.

As she dismounted, she frowned pensively. Justin wasn't a drinking man, and didn't seem to have a penchant for card-playing. She wondered what he was doing in such a place.

She brushed the wrinkles from her skirts and took a deep breath. Ladies, of course, didn't ever show their faces in Houston's grog shops, but Shiloh reflected that her presence wouldn't shock many people. Her father had often brought her along on his drinking bouts, and occasionally she'd had to fetch him from such places after he'd imbibed too much.

She stepped inside and let her eyes adjust to the dimness. The air was thick with smoke, the taproom crowded with bodies. It was easy to spot Justin. Standing at the far end of the bar, he towered over all the others. He was grinning and speaking to someone.

As always, Shiloh's heart lurched painfully at the sight of him. Even in the murky environment of the saloon, his hat dusty and shirt damp with sweat, he looked unutterably handsome. Yet there was something unfamiliar in his eyes. They seemed to lack their usual sharp intensity. As he lifted a glass to his lips and tossed back the amber liquid, Shiloh realized what it was.

Justin was drunk. Not in a loud-mouthed, staggering way, but quietly in his cups. Shiloh couldn't help

167

the smile that crept across her lips. Justin wasn't the stoic she'd thought him. Perhaps he was more affected by the rift between them than she'd thought. A little shiver passed through her at the idea that she'd gotten to him.

She jostled her way down the bar, ignoring a few leering glances, a sly suggestion or two. Justin hadn't noticed her yet. He was still talking, laughing a little at some joke.

When she was only feet away, Shiloh froze. One of the men in front of her had moved aside to reveal Justin's companion.

She was a Mexican woman, her profile stunningly beautiful. Her hair gleamed ebony, her full lips a vivid red. A shining gown showed off lush curves, which she pressed intimately against Justin.

As Shiloh watched, cold with shock, the woman reached up to stroke Justin's cheek. He bent swiftly and wrapped his arm about her, his face suddenly intense, unsmiling. Shiloh knew the look of passionate hunger. She couldn't stifle a gasp of outrage when he bent low to the ripe ruby lips.

The woman stepped back abruptly. It was then that Justin spied Shiloh. Their eyes locked for a burning moment; she saw her name form on his lips. Her heart pounding wildly, she fled.

Justin burst from the saloon and called to her, but she ignored him and leaped into the saddle. She slapped her horse, urging it to a gallop, and rode as if the devil himself were at her heels. Her piebald wove in and out of carts and pedestrians as it bore her away from town.

She found herself wishing that a great wind would come up and carry her far away, never to return. Yet she knew there was no escaping the demons that pursued her. How many times had Justin gone to the arms of the Spanish beauty? It was no wonder he was content to spend his nights in the bunkhouse, if indeed that was where he slept.

Shiloh hated him. Hated him. He had robbed her of her freedom by marrying her, then awakened her passion only to discard her for a sophisticated beauty who undoubtedly had much to offer with her worldly ways. Shiloh had begun to believe that marriage was tolerable, but the loss of her dignity was more than she could stand. Probably half of Houston knew about Justin's wandering.

The landscape blurred before her, an expanse of painted flowers and grass as she thundered across a field to the north. She ducked low under the branches of a moss-hung tree and then gave the horse its head, not stopping until she reached the small, neat cottage that belonged to her aunt.

Minutes later she sat in the snug house, sipping lemonade and glowering angrily at the cold hearth.

"Can I get you something to eat?" Sharon asked gently.

"I'm not hungry."

"I won't pry, Shiloh, but let me know when you're ready to talk about it."

Shiloh held fast to her feeling of rage, knowing that she could dissolve into tears at any moment. Finally she began speaking in a flat monotone, telling her aunt about the trip to San Antonio, the terrible row they'd had their first day back at Post Oaks, and finally the scene she'd just witnessed in town.

Sharon tucked a wisp of gray-streaked red hair into her dustcap and looked hard at Shiloh, as if trying to see the true feelings that lay beneath the hurt and anger.

"What will you do?" she asked.

"I can't go back to Post Oaks. Whatever Justin and I

169

might have had is over now."

"Are you sure, Shiloh?"

"Of course I'm sure. Justin's made his choice. I know what I saw in that saloon today."

Sharon shook her head. "I don't know much about your husband, Shiloh, but I confess I did talk to Nathaniel about him. That business in the saloon doesn't sound like something Justin would do. Are you sure things were as they seemed? Perhaps the woman was an old friend. I think you need to give him a chance to explain."

Shiloh folded her arms obstinately across her chest. "Even if he bothers to explain, it'll all be lies."

They sat together in lengthening silence. A mockingbird trilled outside the parlor window, scolding one of Sharon's cats, which sat on the sill. Finally Sharon stood up.

"I just brought in a basket of field peas. I could use some help hulling them."

Shiloh ate little of her supper and hastened to clear up afterwards. Her stomach was a tight ball of nerves. She couldn't rid herself of the image that was branded on her mind: Justin, bending down to the inviting, dark-haired beauty. The vision tormented her, tore at her until her hands shook and her breath came in short gasps.

She could no longer deny what she felt. The thought of some other woman's touching Justin, possessing him as Shiloh had done once, filled her with such a raging jealousy that she couldn't see straight. Several times she started toward the door, but stopped herself. She was the one who had been wronged. Let him come to her, if he could manage to tear himself away from the Mexican woman.

As evening descended, a knock sounded at the door. Shiloh flew to answer it, noting only vaguely her aunt's knowing smile. She jerked the door open, aware that her face would reveal all that she felt, yet powerless to conceal it.

She found herself staring, confused, at the composed face and icy pale eyes of Charles Elliot.

"Captain Elliot!"

He smiled smoothly. "I'm pleased you remember me, Mrs. McCord." he used her name pointedly, reminding her that she hadn't revealed her identity to him in San Antonio. He looked past her inquiringly. "May I?"

Shiloh stepped aside, eyes wary. "Of course. Captain Elliot, this is my aunt, Sharon Bledsoe."

The two of them shook hands. "I apologize for the intrusion, Mrs. Bledsoe," said Elliot. "I have been wanting to speak to Mrs. McCord."

"How did you find out where I was?"

"I confess I spent the better part of the day looking for you. Someone at your ranch mentioned Mrs. Bledsoe's place."

Shiloh stepped away from him, watching distrustfully. "What do you want from me, Captain Elliot?"

He indicated the settee in the parlor. "Shall we sit down?"

Sharon looked uncertainly at Shiloh, who nodded. "I'll fetch something to drink," said the older woman, and hurried off to the kitchen.

"Imagine my surprise," Elliot began, seating himself comfortably, "when I discovered that a certain young woman had relieved me of a rather personal document."

Shiloh raised an eyebrow. "Was it so personal, captain?"

"I'm sure you know exactly what that letter said. My superiors in London were very specific."

"They were indeed," Shiloh bluffed.

"Young lady, do you know what you have done?" A tic of agitation began to jump beside his right eye. "In betraying official confidences, you have condemned the Republic of Texas to total bankrupcy."

Shiloh drew herself up. "Texas will not be manipulated by foreign powers."

Elliot watched her closely. "You're a proud woman, Mrs. McCord. And Texas is a proud nation. It surprises me that you wish your country to be swallowed up by the United States."

"No one will 'swallow us up,' captain. The people—myself included—want annexation."

"I don't understand you. Texas is a sovereign nation, independent of all others. If the United States takes over, you'll be subject to the whim of legislators thousands of miles away."

"If we don't sign a treaty, sir, we'll soon be so impoverished that the republic will simply dissolve."

The Englishman gave her a measuring glance. "Are you in favor of slavery, Mrs. McCord?"

"Certainly not." She accepted a glass of lemonade from her aunt.

"Then you should be sympathetic to the English plan. Slavery would be prohibited as a condition for the loan."

Shiloh quickly realized what the letter had been about. England was offering to help the Texas government out of bankruptcy—if certain prerequisites were met.

"I have a feeling, Captain Elliot, that abolition is not the only condition of the agreement. England is a great nation, but I doubt it can afford to be philanthropic. It's no coincidence that your interest happens to be in a fledgling republic that lies at the western edge of your greatest rival in trade."

"I've never met a woman quite so well versed in world affairs," Elliot admitted. "I am impressed."

"Thank you."

"I am also certain that you'll keep an open mind about things. You don't seem to be easily swayed. I hope your husband hasn't convinced you that his way is the only way."

"My husband has convinced me of nothing," Shiloh stated. "My views are my own. Your cause doesn't have my sympathy, captain, but I won't be too hasty to condemn it."

The Englishman stood, his mouth smiling charmingly but his eyes bitterly cold. "On that encouraging note, I must be going," he said. He thanked Sharon for her hospitality and rode off.

"What was that all about?" Sharon demanded.

Shiloh frowned. "I'm not sure. I think Captain Elliot might want to make friends with me. Perhaps he'd like me to ally myself with him against Justin."

"That was the feeling I got." Sharon shivered. "Dreadful man."

Shiloh's face hardened. "I won't need my persuasion to disagree with Justin. The way I feel about him now—"

She stopped, stiffening at the sound of distant hoofbeats. The horseman came to the top of a rise and drew up, shading his eyes to watch Captain Elliot as he disappeared in the opposite direction. Then he wheeled his horse and galloped toward the house.

"It's him," Shiloh said, her voice breaking.

"He's magnificent," Sharon commented. She looked at Shiloh levelly, daring her to disagree.

They stood on the small porch, watching as Justin dismounted and ambled on long legs toward them. An evening breeze lifted his golden hair as he removed his hat.

173

"Evening, Shiloh." He cracked a smile at Sharon. "Ma'am."

"I'm Sharon Bledsoe. Welcome, Mr. McCord."

"I'd be obliged if you'd call me Justin, ma'am."

"Of course, Justin." Sharon wiped her hands on her apron. "Please excuse me. I've got some washing up to do." She disappeared, closing the door firmly.

"You favor your aunt," Justin said, unsmiling.

Shiloh tossed her head, her curls glinting gold in the waning light. "So I've been told."

He took a step toward her. Shiloh was sure he could hear the wild hammering of her heart.

"What were you doing in town today, Shiloh?" he asked.

"I don't have to tell you that."

"Come on, Shiloh. You were looking for me, weren't you? Ina said so."

"So what if I was?"

"What did you want to say to me?"

Shiloh laughed bitterly. "I was going to ask if things would ever change with us; I was tired of going on like we were at Post Oaks. But I got my answer, didn't I? You found a very satisfactory way to cope."

"That wasn't what it seemed, in the saloon," he said, the lines about his eyes deepening with intensity.

"It's too late for lies, Justin. I saw you kiss that woman—"

"No, you didn't."

Shiloh tried to walk away, but she found herself suddenly in his iron grip.

"The woman's name is Isabella Hernandez. She's an old acquaintance. I was shot down at the border last March, and she helped me. But I didn't read her right back then. Come to find out, she's in with the Accord. She gave me over to the executioners of the Mier expedition."

"Charming," Shiloh said dryly. "No wonder you find her so fascinating."

"Just listen to me, will you? Isabella found me in the grog shop, and suddenly began acting very friendly. I humored her for a while, thinking maybe she'd let something useful slip."

"In other words, you kissed her in the line of duty."

"I didn't kiss her at all, Shiloh. I merely bent down to take something from her. From where you were standing, it probably looked like something else."

"The only thing I saw you take, Justin, was—"

Abruptly, he released her. Like a striking snake, he drew a tiny, evil-looking blade from his belt and pointed it at her. Shiloh gasped, thinking he'd lost his reason.

But he retracted the blade back into its elegant, almost feminine-looking handle of mother-of-pearl.

"A parting gift from Isabella," he said darkly.

Shiloh didn't want to believe his story, yet it made perfect sense. She looked hard at Justin, searching the flinty eyes for a trace of deception. She found none. Still, she felt she had been wronged.

"What were you doing getting drunk in a grog shop in the first place?" she asked suspiciously.

"I'd just come from a meeting with Sam Houston. I wasn't happy with what he'd had to say, so I had a few drinks to cheer me up. That was when Isabella found me."

"I understand," Shiloh said softly. She thought of her father. "I know all about men who turn to the bottle when things don't go their way."

His lips grew stiff with anger. "I couldn't think of a better alternative. Damn it, most men have a home to go to, a wife's soothing arms. I didn't see any point in coming to you. I've had nothing but cold stares and snide remarks for weeks."

"Forgive me if I'm not the woman of your dreams, Justin. I never pretended to be."

He let out a long, weary sigh. "I made a mistake, Shiloh. And I'm sorry. I know things haven't been easy for you, either. Let's say good-bye to your aunt and go home."

Shiloh planted her feet. "I'm staying right here."

Sharon stepped out onto the porch. "No, you're not, dear. Now, it's obvious you young people are unhappy, but running away from each other isn't going to fix that. You go on home and try to treat each other right."

"But Aunt Sharon—"

"Shiloh, you're married to the man. For better or worse."

"I—"

"Go home, Shiloh." Sharon smiled encouragingly. Then she grew severe and spoke to Justin. "I love my niece like a daughter, Justin. I'd like nothing better than to keep her at my side, if I thought that would be best for her. I'm trusting you, young man, to put the smile back into her eyes."

Justin placed his hat back on his head. "I'll do my best, ma'am."

Shiloh couldn't sleep. She'd bathed, hoping the warm water would relax her, but she only became more restless as she moved about the bedroom. Crossing to the window, she noticed that the night sky was as unsettled as she. Heavily bunched clouds scudded in from the Gulf across the moon, and heat lightning flickered in the distance. A hot, heavy wind blew the curtains inward, plastering Shiloh's robe against her body. The storm, when it rolled in off the Gulf, promised to be severe. Shiloh wrapped her arms across her chest and shivered.

"God, you're a sight," said a husky voice behind her.

She spun around, taken by surprise. Justin stepped close, his hands resting easily on her shoulders. He, too, had cleaned up. His hair glistened damply and his clean-shaven cheeks smelled faintly of bay rum.

"I couldn't forget you," he said, almost angry to have to admit it. "All those nights in the bunkhouse, all I could think of was your face, your body, your voice calling out to me. . . ." His lips descended, seeking hers.

It took all of Shiloh's willpower to turn her head aside. Despite the throbbing ache deep within her, she couldn't give in to her weakness. She had too many unresolved feelings to sort through.

Justin caught her chin with his thumb and forefinger and lifted her face to his.

"Don't do this, Shiloh. Let's forget all the arguments."

She shook her head, feeling the burn of tears in her eyes. She prayed he wouldn't notice.

"I can't, Justin. I can't forget that you wouldn't trust me enough to tell me about the letter. I had to find out from Captain Elliot —"

"Elliot?" His eyes grew hard. "I thought I recognized him as he rode away from your aunt's. What the hell did he want?"

She shrugged. "I'm not sure. I think he wanted me to know he's not the scheming villain you made him out to be."

"And were you convinced?"

She tossed her head back, curls flying. "Sometimes I feel I have less reason to trust you than him."

Tiny flames of restrained rage leaped to his eyes. "Oh really?" he snarled. "I didn't realize you were so frightened of me."

"I'm not frightened! I —"

Suddenly his hands were on her, igniting her flesh with knowing, masterful strokes. He laughed softly at her surprised gasp.

"Could it be, Mrs. McCord, that you're afraid of yourself? Afraid of all the things you feel when I touch you . . . like this . . . and this. . . ."

He brushed her robe aside and continued his relentless assault on her, finding all the places that were most sensitive. His hands cupped her breasts, branding her flesh with a heated caress. Then he circled her waist and pulled her roughly against him.

"Leave me alone," she hissed, battling the storm of passion that raged within her.

"You don't really want me to stop," he countered, stroking her intimately. His smile taunted her, let her know she couldn't hide her feelings from him.

His mouth descended on hers. At first Shiloh resisted, pressing her lips together and stiffening in his embrace. But as his hands blazed a path down her torso, she felt herself weaken. Even as she cursed her own failing, she felt her lips soften and part to admit his seeking tongue. Her captive body began to relax against his, leaning toward him, demanding completion.

Even so, she struggled for control, trying to retain something of herself. Yet Justin's determined assault continued. His hand traveled down to her thighs, toying insolently with the sensitive flesh until Shiloh's legs began to buckle.

In her head there were a hundred reasons why they shouldn't play this dangerous, erotic game. But the reasons seemed small in the face of the overwhelming power of their intimacy. Her hands, obeying her heart instead of her mind, sought the rigid lines of his body, moving slowly over his muscled flesh. With a surge of triumph, Shiloh felt his heart pounding wildly in his chest.

She raised her eyes, smiling. "Your heart is racing, Mr. McCord."

"Does that surprise you?"

Shiloh pressed closer. "I guess it does."

He shook his head, half annoyed, half amused. "Shiloh, why can't you just accept the fact that you're a beautiful, desirable woman? You make me crazy for you."

His mouth claimed hers again, tearing a moan of aching want from her. The final shreds of resistance fell away as Shiloh found herself engulfed by her husband—his hard, lean body, his male scent, the exquisite taste of him. His kisses, his searching hands, his intimate murmurs, filled her with hot longing.

Sensing her capitulation, Justin slid her bed gown from her, discarding it in a heap at her feet. His eyes drank in the sight of her nude body, devouring its slim lines until Shiloh began to blush. She moved toward the bed to conceal herself beneath the sheets.

Justin pulled her back to face him. "Don't hide yourself from me, sweetheart. Be proud of your beauty."

And the look he gave her, one of unabashed admiration, did make her proud. She held herself still as he disrobed. There was no resisting his magnificent body. Shiloh propelled herself toward him, and in one motion they fell to the bed, mouths locked and limbs tangled together.

They came together with a hunger that had been building for weeks, their senses exploding violently. Shiloh found that, once she'd started on the sensual odyssey, she couldn't get enough of him. One raging explosion led to another, and by the time they were finished, the storm rolled in with the dawn. As the tempest raged outside, so did the one in her heart. She knew she was becoming a slave to Justin's touch, but she was powerless to stop it. Drunk with his lovemaking, she finally fell into a deep, contented sleep in his arms.

He was gone when she awoke. The spot where he'd lain was a cold hollow, yet still his scent clung to the sheets and pillows. Shiloh felt a wave of fresh longing, an emptiness that only Justin could fill. Her cheeks flamed as she recalled the abandonment with which she'd behaved. He controlled her will with a single touch.

It was preposterous to allow him such power over her. Flinging the covers off, Shiloh leaped from the bed, full of renewed resolution. As she washed away the unsettling traces of their lovemaking, she vowed to be stronger, to protect herself from Justin. She couldn't let him turn her again into the weak, panting creature she'd been last night, or her whole identity would be lost.

Dressing hurriedly, she went down to see what the storm had wrought.

Eight

It was worse, even, than it had sounded. Rain lashed against the windows and thunder roared. The fields had been transformed into a network of streaming, wind-whipped rivers, the corrals deep with mud. Many branches were down. One of them had crashed through the top of the stables. Wiping the condensation away from a window, Shiloh saw the hands running here and there, frantically trying to bring the horses to the barn, which sat on higher ground, safe from flooding.

There were too many horses and not enough men. Even young Tomas wrestled with a balking mare. Shiloh ran from the house to help.

The downpour soaked her to the skin immediately, plastering her hair to her cheeks. Her feet sank into the reddish-brown mud as she ran across the stableyard to the corrals. She took the frightened mare from Tomas, slapping it on the haunches, and led it to the barn. It was a slow, slippery uphill climb, made more treacherous by holes that had been hollowed out by the streaming water. Shiloh took care that the horse didn't stumble.

She found Wylie Stokes in the barn, hurriedly clearing space for the livestock.

"Where's Justin?" she shouted over the din of the rain.

Wylie jerked his head. "Down by the bayou. He's rounding up the sorrel mare and her foal." He scratched his grizzled cheek. "Should've been back by now."

Shiloh's nerves twisted. She ran from the barn and headed down to the bayou. The sheets of rain were so dense that she was unable to see how swollen the bayou was until she nearly slipped into the water. Then she realized that whole trees were underwater, only their windblown tops showing.

She heard the terrified squeal of a horse and went toward it. The mare called Sugar stood on high ground, bucking and pawing the air, eyes rolling whitely in her skull.

Shiloh screamed when she saw the cause of the mare's distress. Deep in the eddying brown waters, Justin struggled to bring the filly to safety. The frightened young horse struggled wildly, hooves lashing out with violence.

Justin sank below the surface and then came up to gasp for air. He was holding fast to the horse's mane, trying to guide it to the edge. But the panicked animal twisted and bit out at him, impeding his efforts.

Shiloh paused only to discard her gown and petticoat, which would drag her under. Clad only in her soaking shift, she waded in.

She was a fairly good swimmer, but the current dragged at her legs. Reaching out, she could almost touch the flailing horse.

Justin was so intent on his battle that he didn't notice her until she called to him.

His face contorted with anger. "Shiloh! Damn it,

woman, you can't — "

"I'm here to help you," she shouted.

He shook his head, beads of water flying. But there was no time for arguing. The current was growing stronger by the minute and the filly's panic was rising. Shiloh planted her feet and took hold of the sodden mane.

The horse tossed its head back wildly, dragging her into the water. As she plunged beneath the surface, Shiloh's mouth and nose filled. She was frightened, yet her fear gave her strength. With a great kick, she came up and gulped for air. Setting her jaw, she hauled back on the mane. With Justin pushing from behind, the filly came forward, closer to the edge.

"Good girl!" Justin shouted. "One more time, sweetheart — pull!"

The filly advanced again, and its forelegs touched bottom. With the feel of solid ground under its feet, it surged toward its mother.

"She's out!" Shiloh yelled.

Justin's whoop of jubilation was cut off. The filly kicked out with the hind leg in a final effort to scramble ashore. The hoof caught Justin on the temple, opening a deep crescent in his flesh. As Shiloh watched in horror, he lost consciousness with a hiss and sank down. The current whirled around him and a cloud of bright red puffed out into the murky water around his head.

With a strangled cry of abject terror, Shiloh plunged in. The rushing water pulled him downstream, away from her. She had a sudden surge of strength, born of terror, and lunged after him. She dragged him to the shore. His inert, waterlogged body was abominably heavy, but Shiloh barely notice the weight. In seconds, she had him lying on the grass.

The sight of him filled her with dread so abominable

that it was like a physical pain. His face was colorless except for the gaping, curved gash at his temple. Blood pulsed from the wound. With a sob of fear, Shiloh staunched the flow with her wet gown. His flesh beneath her trembling hands felt cold.

Just as she began to wonder how she would get him back to the house, four of the ranch hands, led by Wylie Stokes, came running across the sodden grass. They assessed the situation quickly and gathered Justin up, forming a human litter by locking their hands and wrists together. As Tomas drove the mare and filly up to the barn, the others bore Justin to the house.

Shiloh ran alongside, holding the makeshift bandage in place, admonishing the men not to jostle him. She tried to avoid looking at Justin's prone form. For it was obvious there was not one sign that he had survived the accident.

The storm left the bayou as abruptly as it had descended. By evening, the rain had abated to a thin, steady mist, and the ranch hands were already at work removing the branches and debris from the stable area.

In the big bed upstairs, Justin lay motionless. Prairie Flower, assisted by Shiloh, had painstakingly closed the wound with a needle and a length of thread. It stood out like a black seam upon cool, grayish flesh.

Shiloh sat and looked upon her husband, hardly less terrified than when they had brought him in. He hadn't stirred, even when Prairie Flower had stabbed him with her needle. With a soft sob, Shiloh took his limp hand and brought it to her cheek, wetting it with frightened tears.

Prairie Flower came in with a tray of damp compresses and an array of herbs and special salves. She padded on bare feet to the bedside, her bright eyes assessing Justin and the trembling girl at his side.

"You love him well," said Prairie Flower.

Shiloh looked up, shocked to hear the words. She shook her head slowly, in mute denial. How could she love him, when she didn't even know what the feeling was? "I'm worried about him. And — and I feel responsible. I was trying to help him, but perhaps it would have been better if I hadn't interfered."

Prairie Flower gave a little grunt and bent over the tray, making a strong-smelling poultice.

Shiloh leaned forward to see. "What is that?"

"Beth root, wormwood, indigo . . . it will help in the healing." She placed a compress on the wound and expertly wrapped it to hold it in place. She looked up, patted Shiloh on the hand. "You rest. He will need your strength." She left quietly.

Shiloh sat on, until the candle guttered and she had to light another. She stared hard at Justin, watching his shallow breathing and stroking his hand, willing him to open his eyes. Prairie Flower's observation niggled at her brain, insinuating itself into her thoughts.

Love . . . could that be what she felt for Justin? Was that why the sight of him lying so still and pale tore a hole through her and left a great gulf of emptiness? She ran her hand through her tangled curls, wondering if she could make such an admission. Thinking back on her strange, lonely childhood, she knew she could not. She hadn't learned enough about love to recognize it when it touched her heart.

All she knew as she stared down at Justin was that she wanted him to be well, wanted it more than anything else. But he ignored her silent appeal and remained still throughout the night.

She was awakened from a nap in her chair by her

father.

"I came to see how you'd weathered the storm," Nate said gruffly. He gestured at Justin. "How's he doing?"

Shiloh blinked the sleep from her eyes and stretched her stiff legs.

"He hasn't moved," she said tonelessly.

Nate handed her a glass of water. "He'll buck up, girl. Just needs time to sleep it off."

"You don't know that," Shiloh said darkly.

"There now, you've never been one to give up hope." Nate gave her a canny look. "Or could it be that you've found a way out of being a wife—"

"How dare you?" Shiloh demanded heatedly. "How can you even think such a thing? I may not have wanted to be married to Justin, but that doesn't mean I wish him ill."

"There, there, of course you don't. It appears to me you care for the man. Leastways enough to sit up with him all night."

Shiloh looked down at her twisting hands. "I feel responsible for what happened."

"You should take credit for saving the man's life. Chin up, girl. Come on down and get something to eat."

"I'm not hungry. I'll stay here a while longer."

Nate reached out as if to touch her, but then hesitated and stuck his hand into the pocket of his breeches. "Let me know if there's anything I can do. I hope he gets better, Shiloh. For both of your sakes."

She squeezed her eyes shut and pressed her fists into them when she heard the door shut. She took Justin's hand and fell asleep again.

A light pressure on her hand awakened her. Her eyes flew open, blinking at the afternoon light that flooded in through the curtains.

At first Shiloh thought she was imagining what she felt. But Justin's long fingers closed around hers again, more firmly this time.

Her heart thumped wildly in her chest. "Justin?"

His eyes fluttered open, squinting against the sunlight. "Hello, Shiloh." His voice was gravelly with disuse.

"How do you feel?"

He groaned. "Like a herd of buffalo stampeded over my head. What happened?"

"You were kicked by the filly. She got out of the bayou, though."

Justin felt the bandage around his head. "It's worth it, then. Wasn't that your little foal?"

Shiloh nodded. "I should disown her after that. I'm sorry you got hurt, Justin. I feel like it was my fault."

He frowned. "Look, if you hadn't come along, both the horse and I would have drowned. That was some storm."

"It's over. The men have almost finished clearing up. Are you hungry? I could bring you some soup, or—"

He waved his hand in refusal. "I'd rather just keep you right here, Mrs. McCord. I kind of like having you nurse me. Do you realize we've just had an entire conversation without ending up at each other's throats?"

Shiloh stiffened. "So what?"

"So maybe, my dear, there's hope for us yet."

Shiloh turned her head aside, wondering if it could be true. She could not deny her relief at his recovery. But it was more than that. Perhaps Justin's brush with death would change the way they acted toward each other.

She took his outstretched hand in both of hers. "Time will tell, Justin," she said.

Justin's youth and strength served him well. Within a week, he was up and about and Prairie Flower had snipped the stitches from the gash. Shiloh cringed when he scaled up to the top of the stables to repair the broken beams, or when he worked with the wild horses, but she said nothing. She knew he wouldn't slow down, no matter what she said.

The only time he appeared to relax was at night. Although nothing was actually said, there was no question about his staying on in the master bedroom. For several nights they slept together, holding each other gently, making no demands. But inevitably the low-burning flames of desire flared up and there was no holding back.

By day, Shiloh blushed when she recalled their nightly passionate adventures, but all hesitation fell away when Justin gave her the hard look of desire and ignited her flesh with his masterful touch. She knew that his lovemaking left her weak and gasping, as pliant as clay in his hands, but she had no defense against him.

Some days, she caught herself smiling lazily as contentment crept over her. Still, there were other times when the old restlessness took over, after the work of the ranch was done or the endless jobs grew tedious.

On one such day, she went to her father's house.

When he recognized the glint of determination in her bright eyes, Nate Mulvane shook his head.

"Not again, Shiloh. I'm not about to put you to work."

"Come on, father. You need help. I heard about the cattle-stealing case. I could—"

"My answer is still no. This is a slippery one, dangerous to boot. A lot of Mexicans involved; they'll

188

knife you in the dark and ask questions later."

"I can handle that."

"I won't let you. Shiloh, you've got to stop trying to fill your life with my affairs. You have your own life now. Take care of your home, your husband, maybe have a couple of kids."

Her face reddened. "That's not what I want."

Nate shrugged. "Then talk it over with Justin. I imagine he has his hands full, what with all those new appointments in Washington."

She leaned forward. "What are you talking about?"

Nate pushed a newspaper across the table to her. "It's all there in the *Morning Star*. Apparently, Black Dan Webster had his final falling-out with President Tyler. There's a new secretary of state, name of Abel P. Upshur. He's a real pro-Texas man. Justin'll have to watch Harmon West like a hawk now. The old judge is sure to have something up his sleeve—"

Shiloh left before he had a chance to finish.

She was panting and sweaty when she burst into Justin's study, where he was puffing reflectively on a cheroot.

"Why didn't you tell me about Upshur?" she demanded.

He looked at her levelly. "I didn't think you'd be interested."

"Liar!" she hissed. "Just because we've been getting along decently for a change doesn't mean I've become a meek little housewife."

He studied the play of her fiery hair about her shoulders, the snapping green eyes, the incredible trimness of her figure in a crisp split riding skirt and jacket.

Unable to resist a smile of pure pleasure at her

appearance, Justin said, "I'd never make that mistake about you, Shiloh."

"Then why haven't you talked to me about this? It's as if half of you is a secret from me, while every night I give my whole self to you."

Justin's eyes narrowed, the lines around them deepening skeptically. "I didn't know there was a trade-off involved. Is that why you let me into your bed, Mrs. McCord? To swap your favors for my confidences?"

Her eyes widened in outrage. "How dare you—"

"I don't buy it, Shiloh. You're a man's dream at night, but I won't let you use your charms to milk me for information."

Shiloh stepped back, so angry that she almost spat her words at him. "If that's what you think, Justin, then I have nothing more to say to you." She stormed from the room, cracking the door shut with a mighty heave.

Justin rubbed his hand wearily through his hair. "No, Shiloh," he said quietly, "that's not what I think." He hated what he'd just said to her, but he had to do it. Had to sever the lines of communication for her own good. Shiloh was too damned smart to deceive; it wouldn't have taken her long to guess that he was about to investigate a dangerous matter. And she wouldn't sit still once she learned what was going on.

Justin sighed heavily. He should have known that the blissful time wouldn't last. But God, how he wished it could. The comfort of her arms around him after a long day was indescribable. Her company during meals and quiet times was more pleasant than he'd ever imagined it could be. If only Shiloh would forget her crazy notions and settle down . . . but of course, then she wouldn't be Shiloh. And Justin knew damned well that it was her fiery spirit that made her so appealing to him.

Forcing his thoughts away from Shiloh, he dialed the

combination on his safe and withdrew a letter. It had arrived only that morning from Francisco Reyes, a trusted contact in the border town of Matamoros.

As Justin had feared, the members of the Accord were wasting no time in reacting to Upshur's appointment. The new secretary of state was sure to press the issue of annexation, and Harmon West needed to act quickly to turn the tide of public sentiment against it.

The judge's plan was coldly simple. Reyes wrote that the Mexican forces in Matamoros were expecting a large shipment of arms from "an unnamed Houston gentlemen." Once equipped, a small but well-trained army would march up the Texas coast to Corpus Christi in a brash show of force. The impoverished Texas army would be powerless to stop them. And Texans everywhere would have a taste of what Mexico thought of annexation. Then, they wouldn't have much desire to join the United States.

Justin hoped to accomplish two things: to foil the planned march, and to catch Harmon West in the treasonous act of providing arms to the Mexicans. It would be both tricky and dangerous. But if he managed to stop West, it was worth the risk.

Drumming his fingers on the table, Justin searched his brain for answers. Like him, West probably had known about Upshur's appointment for some time. That would have given him time to get a shipment of British-made arms and ordnance from forts in the Caribbean. The question was, where would such a large shipment be hidden?

After a good deal of thought, he had an idea. Down the bayou from Houston, West had a derelict cotton warehouse with docks right out to the water. It sat on isolated marshland; no one would go near it.

Justin scanned the letter again. Reyes had done a thorough job. He'd found out that a Mexican boat

191

would go to collect the arms on October first. Tomorrow. Justin took up a stub of a pencil and scribbled the date and place on a piece of paper. He sealed it securely and went to give it to Leonicio, one of the ranch hands who couldn't read. Leonicio rode off to Houston, bearing the message to Lamar Coulter.

Justin stood on the porch, stretching and flexing his legs after hours of sitting. The night birds had arrived with the dark, mingling their voiced with the ceaseless buzzing of cicadas. In the distance, he heard Prairie Flower crooning to her chickens in her guttural native Comanche tongue as she closed their roosting house against marauding predators for the night. Faintly, he smelled her good venison stew in the air and realized he'd missed supper.

He wasn't hungry for food. In spite of the angry words, his body craved Shiloh's closeness. There was little hope of lovemaking tonight, but Justin was through with sleeping in the bunkhouse. He had every right to sleep in the master bedroom. Perhaps he'd even be able to coax Shiloh out of her anger.

He let himself into the dark room and shed his clothing. As he splashed water over himself at the washstand, he smiled ruefully. A few months ago, it never would have occurred to him to clean himself up for bed, not if bed was a dusty roll under the stars or a bug-infested boardinghouse mattress. Having a home and a wife had civilized him, without a doubt. And he didn't mind it half as much as he'd expected he would.

He slid beneath the covers, his arm wrapping around Shiloh's middle. She stirred in her sleep and settled against him with a sigh of contentment. Justin laughed softly into her honeysuckle-scented curls. At least her anger at him didn't affect her unconscious reaction to his closeness.

He willed away the surge of desire that filled him and

fell asleep.

Shiloh held herself still with a great effort. She knew she'd managed to convince Justin that she was asleep by remaining pliant in his arms, although she longed to push him away. She waited patiently, steeling herself against the warmth of his breath on her neck, until his breathing became deep and regular. Then, with painstaking slowness, she extracted herself from his loose embrace and slipped from the room.

In his study, her match flared and caught, and she lit the guttered stub of a candle. She went directly to the safe and whirled the tumblers around. It wasn't the first time she'd gone into the safe and she knew the combination by heart.

The door swung open. Shiloh moved aside an astoundingly large supply of bank notes and U.S. currency and took out a handful of papers. Setting the candle down, she thumbed through the pages.

A few finely printed documents, a number of letters signed by W.S. Murphy and Pinckney Henderson, all dated months ago. Their marriage certificate. Shiloh stared at Justin's firm signature, her own shaky one. She thought it strange that he considered the document important enough to lock away. But of course he would, she thought again. It was his safeguard against having to marry Jessamine.

Shaking her head, Shiloh continued her perusal until she found what she was looking for: a recently dated letter. It was written in poor English, signed by F. Reyes, Matamoros. As she read the letter, cold shock gripped her. If this Reyes was correct, and Justin obviously believed that he was, there would be a Mexican invasion. And it would undoubtedly be as ruthless and indiscriminate as other skirmishes in the past. She'd heard of outlandish atrocities, not just against the men, but against women and children as well. The Mexicans despised the Texans, whose ragtag army had driven them home years before. They meted out their revenge whenever they could.

It would all begin tomorrow, Shiloh noted. But how? Where? She leafed through the rest of the papers. Finding nothing, she replaced everything as she'd found it and closed the safe. Then she went to the desk and looked there. She saw only a stack of blank paper, a bit of graphite, an empty inkwell.

As she sat thinking, the candle flickered across the blank paper. A tiny impression, the shape of a letter, caught her eye. Justin had written something, and the top sheet bore the imprint of it. Holding the candle so that it cast a long shadow, Shiloh decoded the message. Justin had a firm hand, making the impression quite visible.

Tomorrow's date, and then a meeting place. The warehouse at LeBoyer's Crossing. Closing her eyes, she tried to think where she'd heard the name before. Nothing came to her. She decided to go back to bed and mull over the puzzle until she remembered.

The flame of the candle angled suddenly toward her. With a start, Shiloh saw Justin's tall form, framed by the doorway. Her heart leaped to her throat, but she managed to stifle her startled response.

"What are you doing?" he demanded, striding into the room. His robe, a belated wedding gift from Ina, flowed out behind him as he approached.

"I don't have to tell you that," Shiloh said haughtily. "I, too, am entitled to some privacy."

"Not in my study you aren't."

Suddenly the guarded look left Shiloh's face. It was ridiculous for her to pretend ignorance any longer.

"I couldn't help it, Justin. I knew something was up

by the way you talked to me this afternoon. I read Reyes's letter. And I know the Mexicans are going to LeBoyer's Crossing."

Justin cursed bitterly. "You have no business—"

She waved her hand to interrupt him. "The way I see it, Justin, we don't have time to argue about it. If the Mexicans get hold of that shipment, people will die!"

"Don't you think I know that?"

"Then what are you waiting for? All we have to do is get to the warehouse, make sure the arms are there, and dump everything into the bayou. Or, better yet, we could set fire to—"

" 'We' are not going to do anything, Shiloh. I'll handle it on my own."

"Justin, it's tomorrow. There isn't much time. Why bother waiting?"

He heaved a tired sigh. "You've got a lot to learn, girl. I can't just settle for getting rid of the shipment. I want to catch West in an act of treason. To do that, I'll need to wait until he is actually making the transaction."

Shiloh shook her head vigorously. "Too risky. Something could go wrong, and the deal could go through. I think it's more important to prevent the march on Corpus Christi."

He crossed the room and gripped her firmly by the shoulders. "What you think, Shiloh, doesn't matter. This is no game we're playing here. I've got a job to do, and I'll do it the best way I know how. Now, go back to bed."

She stared at him, trembling with anger. He neither wanted her help nor trusted her judgment. Her opinion meant nothing to him. It was the most wounding sort of rejection; one which confirmed how very little he thought of her.

Twisting out of his rough embrace, she went to the

door.

"Do what you will," she snapped. "But just remember, if anything goes wrong, you'll have the blood of Texans on your hands." Tossing her head, she jerked the door open and went upstairs.

Shiloh's hands clenched nervously around the porch railing. It was a glorious autumn day, alive with singing birds and colored by ripening fruits and vegetables in Prairie Flower's kitchen garden. Yet Shiloh remained pale with worry and lack of sleep. She was watching Justin as he prepared to leave. With growing alarm, she saw that he carried both of his revolving pistols and his bowie knife and had lashed a long rifle to his saddle. It seemed he packed away enough powder and shot for a small battle.

As she watched him mount up in the stableyard, she was struck by the idea that this could be the last she ever saw of him. If he was caught, he was a dead man. Harmon West would never allow him to carry tales of treason to the authorities.

She started toward him, not knowing what she would say. Then she hesitated. The words he'd said to her last night had laid open wounds that were still raw by light of day. She wasn't ready to forgive him, and it was obvious he wasn't of a mind to apologize. And so she stood quietly, hands clasped in front of her, watching him impassively.

He looked over at her and their gazes locked. Neither betrayed the slightest emotion. Autumn bees hummed through the flowers and there was a smell of ripe apricots in the air. After a tense moment, Justin raised his hat to her, wheeled his horse, and spurred it off down the road.

Shiloh watched until he was out of sight, and then

196

she ran back into the house to prepare for her own journey.

Four hours later she was traversing brambles so thick that her horse had slowed to a clumsy walk. The bayou, which she'd kept in sight, crept sluggishly toward the bay, obscured from time to time by dense brakes of cypress and cane, much of the growth cloaked in green kudzu vine. Strange birds, egrets and long-legged cranes, picked their way in and out of the marshes, poking their heads on thin necks into the silty ground. The mosquitoes were thick and merciless. Even with a coating of Prairie Flower's pennyroyal solution, Shiloh was plagued by the insects.

But not for one minute would she consider turning back. Her father had given her directions to LeBoyer's Crossing, and she meant to reach it as fast as was humanly possible. Maybe Justin wouldn't need her; maybe it was all a waste of time, but she had to be sure she was there in case something went wrong. If the Mexicans got hold of the arms . . . she tried not to think about it.

Voices drifted across the bayou, and she drew up her horse. Slipping to the ground, she went to investigate.

It was Judge West, standing upon a stout raft as if he were captain of a lofty vessel. He was dressed in his usual impeccable black and held a cigar in one hand while he gestured with the other. His burly slaves poled the raft down the bayou and listened indolently as the judge spoke.

Shiloh couldn't hear the words, but she could see that West was prepared for trouble. He himself was armed, as were the pair of buckskin-clad men with him. One of them was small and compact, with dark Latino features and a ruthless hard look about him.

197

The other was Anglo, tall and lanky, with eyes that lacked depth. Lackeys, Shiloh thought contemptuously as she returned to her horse. No doubt Judge West had selected them because they would follow his orders without question.

Although the raft was moving sluggishly, Shiloh felt a sense of urgency. She spurred her horse and whispered encouragement over the piebald's neck as it stepped through the tall reed marsh grasses.

She almost missed seeing the warehouse. Abandoned years earlier, when it had become known that the Allen brothers were taking their city farther north, it was overgrown by vines and grass and roof-high cattails. Had she not been looking for it, Shiloh might not have noticed the gray, weathered structure. But it caught her eye. She tethered her horse on dry ground and made her way toward it, carrying a heavy cloth sack over her shoulder.

She saw no one. The only sounds were made by birds and the quiet lapping of the water around the rotting dock. But Shiloh's stealth served her well. When she crept around to the front of the warehouse, she spied a man, a guard.

She recognized him from town. He was one of the scores of eager-eyed, hollow-cheeked newcomers, who'd probably spent his last cent getting to Texas and was now desperate for work. Shiloh doubted the man knew what he was doing. He'd shed his shirt and drawn his hat down over his face, evidently for a late afternoon nap. One hand rested on a rusting shotgun; the other loosely held a rope attached to a small rowboat.

Shiloh took a deep breath and pulled her hat down more securely, checking to see that no stray red curl escaped to betray her sex. She drew out her gun and stepped soundlessly toward the dozing man.

With one kick of her boot, she sent his rifle into the

198

bayou. At the sound of the splashing water, the man started.

"What the—"

Shiloh aimed her gun at his face. "Don't ask questions, mister," she said hoarsely, almost whispering. "Just get in that boat and start rowing downstream."

He tensed, but didn't move. His hungry eyes watched her, and his ribs poked through his gaunt frame. Knowing Judge West, the man wouldn't be paid until his job was done. Silently, she begged him to go. Aloud she said, "Don't make me use this, my friend."

She must have sounded convincing. The man scrambled down to the boat and began rowing with long, frantic strokes.

Replacing her gun, Shiloh stepped into the warehouse. She gasped, tasting dust and the tang of powder in her mouth. The building was packed to the walls with unmarked wooden crates. She guessed there were enough arms to outfit a small army. She climbed the crates until she reached the highest rafters, and then carefully put her head up through a jagged hole in the roof. She wanted to make sure the guard was well on his way before she proceeded.

He was on his way, all right. Although he'd headed downstream at first, he had circled back and was sculling swiftly toward Judge West's raft, perhaps a quarter-mile off. Shiloh had no doubt the man would alert the judge. And downstream was a sight that chilled her blood.

A shallow-draft shallop crept up from several hundred yards off. Although it was unmarked, even unremarkable, she knew it must be the Mexicans, come to collect their instruments of war.

Turning, Shiloh saw movement in the tall grasses a good distance behind the warehouse. The horsemen appeared for an instant, then receded again into the

199

foliage. In that moment, Shiloh recognized Justin's worn black hat and bay horse, and the slouching posture of Lamar Coulter.

They wouldn't know how close they were to danger. Not one, but two separate enemies were about to converge on them, the judge now warned by his confused guard. Shiloh knew she couldn't wait to see what happened. She had to act. Although she agreed with Justin that it would be best to catch Harmon West, it was more important to avert the coming disaster. And there was only one way to do that.

Once she'd made her decision, Shiloh's trembling ceased. She leaped agilely to the packed earth floor and drew a large jar of lamp oil from her sack. Working methodically, she sloshed it over the crates and the walls of the building. Outside, she emptied the jar in a circle around the entire structure.

Her hands began to shake again as she struck match after match, throwing the small flares around the building. None of them appeared to catch fire, or stay lit long enough to ignite the warehouse. Almost crying with frustration, Shiloh tore down a long brown-tipped cattail and loosened the pod until it resembled a ball of cotton wool. She doused this with the remaining drops of oil from the jar.

The makeshift torch caught fire, as did the grass and the outside wall of the warehouse when Shiloh touched it. She ran the entire perimeter until a steady blaze crackled and the flames licked toward the roof. Then, flinging down the cattail, Shiloh ran to her horse.

By the time she'd mounted and spurred, the fire roared. Shiloh looked back to see heat shimmering wildly above the bayou. Then, with an earthshaking explosion, the building detonated, sending plumes of fire high into the air and flinging debris in all directions. Several more explosions followed. Finally, the fire engulfed a black hole where the warehouse had once stood.

Shiloh smiled grimly. "So much for your invasion, Judge West," she murmured, and started on the long ride home.

Hours later, she was startled from a deep sleep by the bang of the bedroom door being flung open. Justin advanced on her, dark fires burning furiously in his eyes. His voice was a growl in his throat.

"You've gone too far this time, Shiloh."

Nine

Shiloh sat up and rubbed her eyes. Justin set a candle down on the bedside stand. His rage hung in the air between them like a thick fog.

"Don't try to deny it," he snapped, even before she had a chance to speak. He flung a heap of clothes onto the bed. Her trousers and the cotton shirt she'd worn on her journey down the bayou. They reeked of smoke and powder.

"I don't deny anything, Justin. I set that fire today."

His fist slammed against the wall. "Why, damn it?"

"Because I didn't want the Mexicans to get at the arms and munitions. I didn't want them to go anywhere near Corpus Christi."

Justin shook his head. "We were so damned close. Another few minutes and we would've had West, maybe even gotten a censure against Mexico."

"You're wrong," Shiloh said. "I saw what happened. Judge West was armed to the teeth. There was a guard at the warehouse. I sent him rowing downstream, but he doubled back to warn the judge."

"Well done," Justin sneered.

She ignored that. "The Mexicans coming up the river were probably armed, too. You and Mr. Coulter didn't stand a chance."

"I see. I suppose you think I should thank you for saving my life."

"I'm not asking for gratitude. But I wish you'd understand that there wasn't anything you could have done. Everything is fine now, Justin. No one was hurt. And no one will get hurt—"

"Until Harmon West tries something else. Thanks to you, he's free now."

Shiloh bit her lower lip. "I'm sorry he got away. But at least he has nothing to give the Mexicans now."

Justin hissed out a sigh and tossed his hat onto a hook. "I guess what's done is done." Shiloh saw his shoulders sag slightly with fatigue.

"Why are you so late?" she asked.

His steel-hard eyes bored into her. "Because, Mrs. McCord, I was looking for you. That explosion was big enough to take you with it."

"I'm not stupid, Justin," she said tightly. "I got well out of the way. Now, if you don't mind, I'd like to go back to sleep."

"Fine," he said, sitting on the edge of the bed and pulling off his boots.

"What are you doing?"

He ran his fingers wearily through his hair. "I'm going to get cleaned up and then come to bed."

"Oh . . ."

He gave her a sardonic smile. "Don't worry, Mrs. McCord. I won't bother you tonight. It's kind of hard to make love to a woman who makes a practice of lying and interfering in a man's work."

A week later, Shiloh was in the stables rubbing down one of the mares that had been brought from the wild to Post Oaks. The palomino flanks gleamed from the dedicated application of Shiloh's metal brush. The lean, rangy look of this mare and the others was gone since they'd been fattened on corn and good mash. Every one of them had been broken to the saddle. They were ready for the auction house.

Shiloh finished with the mare and moved on to a three-year-old, another palomino. She had taken to caring for the horses daily. It was something she enjoyed, and it was a way to avoid Justin.

He seemed to be satisfied with their lack of communication. Each morning he was gone by the time she awoke, working tirelessly on the ranch. At night he'd tumble, exhausted, into bed, after Shiloh was asleep. If they chanced to meet during the day, conversation was strained, and Justin seemed to study her with suspicious eyes as if wondering how she would betray him next.

"It's not as if I'd committed some great crime," Shiloh fumed, attacking the horse's flanks with her stiff-bristled brush. "I only did what I had to do." She went over and over it in her mind, trying to figure out if there could have been a way for Justin to seize Judge West and the shipment as well. But it was no use. If she'd stood aside and let him do it his way, he'd surely be dead by now and the Mexican army equipped. Yet Justin would never accept the truth of that. And now he was doubly angry, because Harmon West and his daughter had left town for a while, to lie low after the fiasco at LeBoyer's Crossing.

Sighing, Shiloh finished up in the stable. The mares they were taking to auction had never looked better. Their coats gleamed, manes and tails combed free of tangles and debris. Even their hooves shone with the polishing Shiloh had given them.

Looking down at her dusty trousers and sweat-stained shirt, Shiloh shook her head ruefully. She'd let her appearance go this week, not caring about the way she looked. The work clothes were functional, as was the thick tail of hair she tied at her neck. But she decided to make some changes for the trip to Houston. Buyers might take more notice if she looked decent.

Tomas brought water for her bath and Ina laid out her new riding habit. Once again, she had surpassed herself with the creation. The sky-blue skirt hugged Shiloh's hips and fell in a long, pleated line. The matching jacket covered a thin blouse trimmed with a bit of cream lace, tatted by Ina's own fingers. Ina piled her hair cunningly and pinned on a small hat. Then she handed Shiloh a small velvet purse.

"From your husband," she said.

Frowning, Shiloh loosened the laces and drew out a wide blue ribbon to which was attached an oval-shaped piece of porcelain, exquisitely painted. A brush no bigger than an eyelash had depicted a stalk of wild bluebonnet.

"It's beautiful," Shiloh whispered. "Ina, when did Justin—"

"Last night." Ina took the ribbon from her and fastened it around her neck. The shade of blue matched that of the riding habit perfectly.

Shiloh felt oddly nervous as she went downstairs. Her heart fluttered a little, reminding her that her feelings for Justin—such as they were—could not be denied. He was waiting for her at the foot of the steps, neatly dressed, his tall boots gleaming.

"Very nice," he murmured, unsmiling.

Shiloh nodded. "Ina is a genius with the needle." She reached up and fingered the brooch. "Thank you for this, Justin."

He shrugged and held the door open for her. "There's a German immigrant in town, name of Bruckner, who does that sort of thing."

As Shiloh passed in front of him, she caught his

scent and warmth flooded through her. She had to resist the urge to touch him. Her voice faltered a little when she said, "It—it's very thoughtful of you."

He tossed her the reins of her horse and took his own from Tomas.

"You earned it," he said matter-of-factly. "You've gotten these nags looking like champions for the auction. I expect they'll get us a hundred dollars apiece."

Shiloh sat stiffly in the saddle as they headed up the string of horses. She was angry at herself for having gone all soft over Justin's gift. She should have seen it for what it was: payment for services rendered.

"Maybe," Justin said, noticing that she'd fallen silent, "maybe it's a peace offering, too."

She glanced at him quickly, embarrassed that he'd read her thoughts. The corners of his mouth lifted slightly and a smile deepened the lines about his eyes.

"What are you saying, Justin?"

"That what's done is done. I'm willing to forget what happened last week if you are."

"I—I don't know, Justin."

"Look, Shiloh, it's ridiculous for us to act this way. We both want the ranch to succeed; we've worked our tails off for it. There's no reason for us not to be friends."

"Friends . . ." she repeated quietly. She'd never thought of being friends with Justin. He always seemed so unapproachable, but anything was better than what had been between them the past week.

She smiled over at him, feeling a little shy, and he raised his hat with mock cordiality. It was a tenuous truce at best, but immediately Shiloh felt some of the tension flow out of her. By the time they reached Houston and led the mares into the auction corral in Commerce Square, she was excited.

It was the first time they had appeared together at a

large gathering in Houston. Shiloh hadn't thought much about that, so she couldn't have anticipated the reception they received.

Mrs. Charlotte Allen, the wife of one of Houston's founding brothers, descended on her like a large, colorful butterfly. Her big, jowled face smiled, and her voice rang with deep, cultured tones.

"Shiloh Mulvane—or McCord, I should say. Who would have thought you'd end up like this." She embraced the girl, giving her a generous whiff of mimosa toilet water.

"It's nice to see you, Mrs. Allen," Shiloh said stiffly. The society matron had never said so much as "good day" to her before. Indeed, she'd been quite vocal about her disapproval of "that Mulvane girl," shaking her head as Shiloh passed through town at her unkempt father's heels.

But now, apparently, things had changed. As the ladies of the town gathered round to greet her, she longed to inform them that decent clothes and a socially acceptable husband hadn't changed the scruffy hoyden she had been.

"I always knew you'd come around, dear," said Vera Hanks, squeezing her hand. "It just took someone like Captain McCord to get you to settle down."

Shiloh looked quickly at Justin. "*Captain* McCord?"

"Of course," said Mrs. Hanks, clasping her hands. "And who would have thought you'd become such a beauty? Oh, the two of you make such a *handsome* couple. . . ." The woman gushed on as the others murmured agreement.

As politely as he could, Justin extracted Shiloh from the circle of women and led her to a seat overlooking the corral.

"Sorry about that," he said. "I should've realized you'd cause a stir."

"It's as if I'd been legitimized overnight," Shiloh remarked. She gave him a sideways glance. "I guess I have you to thank for that, *Captain* McCord."

He grinned. "Somehow, I don't think your goal in life is to join the ranks of 'proper' ladies."

She had to smile. "It's not. I doubt you'll find me joining quilting bees or church clubs. Justin, why didn't you tell you were a captain in the Texas army?"

"Would it have made you like me better if you'd known?"

"No."

He laughed deeply. "There you have it. I'd have wasted my time trying to score points with you."

They shared a smile, and Shiloh found herself relaxing even more. It was so much better this way, being friends. For the first time, she began to think that things might be all right between them.

Their horses were a great success, adding to her enjoyment of the day. They walked away from the auction that evening in high spirits, some eight hundred dollars richer.

Justin took her to Houston House, a hotel that had a reputation for good food and elegance.

His mood was understandably expansive. He ordered wine and a lavish meal of steak and potatoes, spiced squash and English peas. As they lingered over a dessert of Mexican flan and a delicious amber liqueur, Shiloh looked around the draped dining room, where the crowd had begun to thin.

"Shouldn't we be getting back to Post Oaks?" she asked.

"No need," Justin said, placing his napkin on the table. "We're staying here tonight, Mrs. McCord. I thought you'd like a change of pace, and there's a new string of wild mustangs in from Goliad. I'd like to buy a dozen or so in the morning."

"But I haven't brought anything to s[...]
protested.

He reached across the table and grasped [...]
His thumbs rubbed meaningfully into the soft[...]
her palms.

"The way I feel tonight, Mrs. McCord," he said
huskily, "you won't need anything."

Shiloh gasped at the look of naked desire on his face
and at the hot surge of sensation that flooded her. A
blush crept to her cheeks as she realized how badly she
wanted him again, like she had before.

Mesmerized by his intimate caress, his intent stare,
she rose from the table and followed him to the foyer.

The man at the desk handed Justin a key. "Everything has been arranged as you requested, sir," he said.

Discreetly, Justin pressed a coin into the man's hand.

Shiloh looked with wonder around the hotel's best
room. The canopied bed was enormous, billowing with
quilts and shrouded by a gossamer mosquito net.
There was a painted screen near the hearth that only
partially concealed an enormous zinc bathtub, bigger
than any Shiloh had ever seen. Steam curled from its
surface.

"Oh Justin," Shiloh breathed.

"A bit of luxury for the lady," he said with an
exaggerated bow. "Go ahead and have your bath. I
need to go down to the livery and check on the horses."

Shiloh turned and gave him a small smile. She knew
their horses were fine; Justin seemed to sense her
modesty. It wasn't the first time he'd shown unusual
sensitivity.

He dropped a kiss on her forehead and left. Shiloh
disrobed and sank down into the bath with a contented
smile. It was the first time she'd ever bathed twice in

_____, and she found she didn't object to it in the
_____. The water was the perfect temperature and felt as
soft as rain as it lapped up around her shoulders and
neck. She luxuriated for some minutes, closing her
eyes and giving herself up to pleasant sensations. She
heard the door open and close, the latch slide into
place.

"It's me," said Justin. "Can I get you anything?"

"I couldn't find any soap," Shiloh called.

He stepped around the screen, holding a glass of
brandy in one hand and a new, embossed cake of soap
in the other.

Shiloh instinctively hugged her arms across her chest
and drew up her knees.

He chuckled. "Modest, Mrs. McCord?"

She blushed deeply and her heart thumped at the
look on his face. "Just set it there, by the towels, thank
you."

But Justin only shook his head. He held the soap just
out of her reach. If she wanted it, she'd have to unfurl
her arms.

"Justin, don't tease," Shiloh begged.

His grin broadened, deepening the dimple on his
cheek. He leaned forward, but he still wasn't close
enough.

"You're impossible," Shiloh declared. Covering herself with one arm, she reached for the soap. Justin was
treated to a tantalizing glimpse of her pale shoulder
and the curve of her breast. Abruptly, he released the
soap and it dropped into the water.

"Sorry," he said as Shiloh began running her hands
along the bottom of the tub. "Here, I'll help."

"Justin, you don't need to—"

In seconds, he had shed his coat and shirt. Shiloh
gasped as he knelt and plunged his hands into the
water. Slowly, holding her eyes with his, he dragged the

bottom. Shiloh tried to shrink away from him, but his hands fluttered against her, stroking her silken flesh.

"Justin, please—" she begged, blushing now to the roots of her hair.

He stopped her protest with a deep, hungry kiss. His mouth mastered hers effortlessly, as easily as his hand, now holding the soap, began to lather her shoulders with slow, circular movements. The scent of honey-suckle wafted upward.

Shiloh knew she was lost as he lifted her partially out of the water and laved her breasts, stimulating them with the soft lather and his relentless hand. With a moan of agony, she lifted her arms and wound them about his neck, winding her fingers through his hair, drawing him nearer.

Justin rained kisses on her face, her neck, circling her ear with the tip of his tongue.

"I've missed you, my beauty," he whispered. His teeth nipped at her earlobe and then he kissed her again, giving her a taste of brandy from his own mouth. Sensing her complete submission, Justin slipped a hand beneath the surface of the water. He skimmed her belly and delved his fingers into the core of her desire, causing a wave of ecstasy that rocked Shiloh to her very soul.

"Justin," she moaned. "Oh, Justin . . ."

He laughed softly. Placing one hand beneath her buttocks and the other around her shoulders, he lifted her from the tub, heedless that she soaked him from neck to boots.

"I—I need a towel," Shiloh said helplessly.

But he only shook his head and carried her to the bed, parting the netting to lay her upon the quilts. Instinctively, Shiloh moved to gather the covers over her, but he held her hands still. A glow from the lamplight flickered across the sculpted lines of his face.

"Don't," he said compellingly. "I want to see you. All of you." He handed her a glass of brandy from the table. "Have a sip of this."

Thinking it would still her hammering heart, Shiloh took the glass and drank. But the brandy and the sight of Justin's lean body as he peeled away the remainder of his clothes only added fuel to the fire he had lit within her.

She closed her eyes and trembled as he sat down on the bed. His hands found hers and then trailed up her arms, to her torso, her breasts.

"Don't ever hide yourself from me, Shiloh," he said in his low, husky voice. "You're more beautiful than words can say." His hand tilted her chin up. "Here," he said, indicating her upturned face. His hand traveled to her small breasts. "And here . . ." Finally he parted her thighs with a swift movement. "And here . . ." he said, touching her.

Shiloh was so shaken by his sensual assault that she jumped. Brandy sloshed from the glass, spilling down over her breasts and pooling in her navel.

"Oh," she cried, and started to reach for the napkin that was wrapped around the bottle.

But Justin set the glass aside and pushed her back against the quilts.

"Allow me," he murmured. "It'll be my pleasure." And he proceeded to kiss and lick the droplets of brandy from her flesh, tongue swirling and teeth nipping wickedly at the dusky rose peaks of her breasts.

Just as Shiloh thought she could take no more of the exploding sensations, his mouth roved down to the tense muscles of her middle, his tongue lapping the liquid from her navel. She thought Justin had lost his reason when his lips went lower still, to the sensitive flesh of her liqueur-stained thighs.

"Justin," she gasped. "You can't—"

But he smiled and stilled her lips with two fingers. "You're so beautiful here," he said again. "Let me kiss you. . . ."

Shiloh thought she would die. She was powerless to stop the assault of his mouth and flicking tongue. She felt she was being torn to shreds by a passion so deep that bright light shimmered before her eyes.

A cry was dragged from her lips as she suddenly found the strength to draw Justin atop her.

"Please," she moaned. "I need you, Justin. I need—"

He slid effortlessly inside her, filling the void that cried out for him. His rhythmic movements finished what his mouth and tongue had begun. Shiloh's senses soared and exploded with earth-shattering release.

Soon after, she felt Justin stiffen and convulse, and then he collapsed upon her.

The moments throbbed by as, in silence, their bodies reveled in the relief they'd given each other. Finally, Justin moved aside and curled her against him.

"How do you feel, Mrs. McCord?"

She shivered slightly. "I don't know what to say, Justin. I feel so naive with you. I don't understand what happens to me when you . . . you . . ."

"Go on," he prompted, smiling at the blush of peach that stained her cheeks.

"When you do that to me," she finished weakly.

He stroked her gently, kissed her temple. "All you have to understand, sweetheart, is that you were made for love. There's no shame in anything we do together, so long as it pleases us both."

She nodded slowly, growing more comfortable with him as each moment passed.

Still, a question bothered her. "Justin," she began hesitantly. "Is it always like this—between a man and a woman?"

He gave her a thoroughly disarming smile.

"I didn't ask it to amuse you!"

"I'm not laughing at you, sweetheart," he said quickly, gathering her close. "It's just that sometimes I forget what an innocent you are. And to answer your question, no. Some women never allow themselves to feel pleasure. And a man can't always—that is, he's got to have some feelings for a woman in order to please her." He stumbled over the words, uncharacteristically awkward.

"You mean they have to be friends."

Justin laughed. "To say the least." He turned on his side and looked down at her, growing serious. "Shiloh, when I touch you, when we're close like this, I feel something deeper than friendship."

She waited, breathless, for him to continue. "Yes?"

"I feel . . ." he searched her face, as if looking for answers there. "You do something to me, Shiloh, that I—" Giving up, he leaned down and kissed her deeply, letting his mouth and hands say what he could not voice.

Shiloh was vaguely disappointed that he hadn't completely revealed his thoughts to her, but the feeling quickly vanished as lovemaking began anew.

In the morning he left her with a soft kiss before she had fully awakened. She gave him a sleepy smile and promised to be ready to leave when he returned. There was an almost sinful delight in lying naked between the sheets, hugging the pillow that still held Justin's scent.

Maybe, thought Shiloh, just maybe things would work out. If she could just find ways to soothe the restlessness in her, the unsettled longing for adventure. . . .

There was a knock at the door. Shiloh sat up,

214

clutching the sheets to her bosom.

"Yes?"

"A man to see you, missus," said a female voice. "Nigra by the name of Eb."

"Just a minute," Shiloh answered, springing from the bed. "Have him wait outside." She scrambled into her clothes and yanked a brush through her disarranged curls. Before she opened the door, she carefully pulled the netting around the bed, flushing when she thought of what had occurred there in the dark of night.

Then she let Eb in. The aging freedman moved slowly, with fatigue in his joints.

"Eb," she said, embracing his thin frame. "How did you know where to find me?"

"The name McCord is all over town. Your husband had a good day at the auction."

She saw the troubled shadows in his eyes. "What's wrong, Eb?"

"Your papa's in jail, Miss Shiloh. Drunken brawling. I couldn't find the cash to get him out."

Shiloh grabbed her reticule and spilled the contents into her hand. There were three double eagles and some silver.

"I've got enough," she said. "Let's go."

Nate Mulvane was sleeping soundly on the packed-earth floor of a small cell. Shiloh paid off the deputy, and together she and Eb managed to get her still-drunk father home.

Eb made coffee and Shiloh poured two cups down her father's throat, despite his angry protests and sputtering.

"You're out of money," she accused. "Flat broke. Why didn't you come to me?"

"I'm not going begging to my little girl," Nate

215

blustered. "Besides, it's only a temporary situation. I'm about to clean up on that cattle-rustling deal. Tonight, as a matter of fact."

Shiloh slowed down on the coffee when he said that. When Nate reached for his flask, she didn't object to his having a swig or two. She let him talk, and carefully remembered all that he said.

Mr. Clay Joseph, one of the biggest ranchers in the area, had lost hundreds of head of cattle to thieves. When the lawmen couldn't make any headway, Joseph had hired Nate to break up what appeared to be an extensive, well-organized ring of crime.

But one man couldn't be everywhere at once. Joseph's ranch encompassed thousands of acres, and the thieves struck at night.

"But I've got 'em now," Nate said, smiling and mellow from the whiskey. "Figured out why they never left any sign to speak of. They've been coming by raft. Take the herd right on down to Galveston and on to New Orleans."

"How do you know about tonight?"

Nate took another swallow. "Spotted their raft on the bayou. Biggest thing you ever saw. I figure I'll let them load up, and then bring the law down on 'em. They'll be like sitting ducks out on the bayou."

"It sounds too simple," Shiloh said dubiously.

"There could be a hitch or two. Joseph has a couple dozen *vaqueros*, and I suspect several are in on this."

Shiloh nodded slowly. Then, with false brightness, she said good-bye. She said nothing to Nate of her disappointment in him at landing himself in jail, or of her humiliation at having to bring him home. That had all been said before, and it had had no effect.

Eb insisted on seeing her back to the hotel. He spent a moment talking to Justin, and Shiloh caught him looking keenly at her. But she only smiled and started up the busy street.

Justin watched Shiloh carefully through supper that night. He couldn't seem to get enough of her; he would never tire of gazing at that small, intriguing face with the moss-green eyes that had such fathomless depths. Tonight, however, Justin had a purpose other than the sheer pleasure of feasting his eyes.

Eb had warned him that Shiloh might try to involve herself in her father's business. By now, Justin recognized the restlessness that drove her. She picked up one of Prairie Flower's specialties, a squash blossom stuffed with herbs, battered and fried. She sampled it distractedly and set it down on her plate.

"Not hungry?" Justin queried.

She smiled slightly and shook her head. "I was just thinking about my father. I suppose you know that's not the first time he's spent the night in jail." She turned her water glass around in her hands. "When I was young, Eb used to try to hide it from me, but I always knew. People talked . . . when we lived up in Nacogdoches ladies would sometimes come by with charity baskets from the church. They always made sure I knew exactly why they were there."

She spoke matter-of-factly, almost conversationally, but Justin saw in her eyes the lonely, frightened little girl she had been. In the determined set of her chin he could see the stiff bravado that had seen her through such times.

A wave of tenderness unlike anything he'd ever felt before washed over him and brought an unaccustomed hardness to his throat. He wanted to gather Shiloh to him, to shield her from hurtful things.

He reached across the table and took her hands. "Shiloh—"

Wylie Stokes burst into the dining room. "Justin!" He snatched his hat from his head. "Excuse me, ma'am. Justin, there's trouble with the new horses. They broke through one of the barriers and they're getting into it with the other horses."

Justin jumped up to follow him. He hesitated at the door and turned back to Shiloh.

"I'll see you later," he told her, and looked at her so that she could not mistake his meaning. She cast her eyes downward and nodded.

For the better part of an hour, Justin and the ranch hands labored to separate and contain the horses. Dodging flying hooves and viciously snapping jaws, the men managed to get in among the new horses and hood them with cloth sacks to render them helpless.

All the while, Justin cursed his bad luck. He'd meant to stay with Shiloh all evening, just in case she had any ideas about going out to the Joseph ranch to help her father. By now, she'd had ample time to slip away. Swearing under his breath, Justin hauled on the bridle of the last horse and brought it back into the corral.

Then, leaving the others to finish up, he raced back to the house. The dining room was empty and their meal had been cleared away. Justin burst into the kitchen to ask Ina and Prairie Flower if they knew where Shiloh was.

"Upstairs," Ina said. "She wanted to retire early."

Justin recognized the ruse. He ran across to the stables to confirm his suspicions. Shiloh's piebald was gone. His mouth set in a tight, grim line, he prepared to go after her, taking both revolving pistols and his bowie knife.

Fool woman, he thought darkly as he spurred his horse along the bayou path. Didn't she realize what could happen if she rode down among cattle rustlers? She didn't seem to understand that things had changed in Houston. With the tremendous influx of new-comers, what had once been a small bayou outpost had become a major trade center. And that meant that thieves were more professional, more ruthless than ever before.

"Fool woman!" he said aloud. Lying low over his horse's neck, he sped beneath moss-hung branches toward the Joseph ranch. He found the rounded-up cattle by the noise they made, lowing and grunting as they were jostled together between four shadowy, hard-riding forms.

Justin brought his horse to the edge of a clearing that was fringed by woods in a semicircle in front of the bayou landing. Shiloh was nowhere in sight, but that didn't mean anything. A hundred riders could have concealed themselves in the thick forest on this moon-less night.

"Aquí. Aquí, hombre." The clipped orders carried across the water. The men were trying to haul a log barge up to a muddy bank. Two riders came around to the rear, cutting across until they were practically on top of Justin. His hands poised themselves over his pistols.

"Are you sure somebody's over there, Jaime?" asked one of the riders. "Couldn't it have been a snake or a critter or something?"

"No way. I heard voices." The man called Jaime chuckled. "One of 'em's a female."

A low whistle. "Have you told Benito?"

"Nope. Don't intend to. He's mighty skittish; I don't want to worry him. We can take care of 'em on our own."

"Where are they?"

"Yonder, by that cottonwood. Wouldn't have heard a

219

thing, except a calf strayed over there."

"Think we can take 'em, Jaime?"

"No problem. We'll just swing around on foot. And use your knife, Cyrus. No point in making a lot of noise about it."

"But you said there was a woman!"

"Don't worry, we'll just rough her up a bit." Jaime snickered malevolently. "Maybe even have a little fun with her later. Let's go."

As they dismounted, Justin spurred his horse. Bunching the muscles of its haunches, the bay leaped from the shadows. His face contorted by a snarl, Justin raised one of his pistols and brought it down in an arc on the head of one of the men. As that one sank with a groan, the other let out a yelp of warning and started to run. Justin had always despised fighting, the feeling of inflicting pain on another. But he gritted his teeth, rode down the second man, and pistol-whipped him to the ground.

A shout rose from the bayou's edge. Justin heard the crack of a shotgun and the whiz of a ball behind him. As others opened fire on him and his flesh tensed in anticipation of being shot, all hell broke loose. The *vaqueros* left their posts and the panicked herd stampeded back toward the clearing. Justin's leg was crushed against the horse's flank as cattle rushed by. He ducked low to avoid the gunfire and urged his mount to fight its way out of the pack. By the time he plunged into a dense thicket, he was bruised and scratched, his horse lamed by a heavy bovine hoof.

But he was safe. The shouts of the *vaqueros* and boatmen receded as they gave up on the herd and escaped down the bayou. Justin began looking around for Shiloh, now more angry than concerned. No one but the two ranch hands he'd felled had known about her presence. The herd had veered around the cotton-

220

wood where she'd been hiding, so she would have had ample time to get away.

His horse faltered over a dip in the bank. With a soft oath, Justin dismounted to walk the distance to Post Oaks. He reached out and patted the bay, remembering to thank the valiant animal for getting him out of the scrape.

Fuming, he knew he'd have no such affection for his impetuous wife at the end of his two-hour walk.

Although it was nearly dawn when he arrived, Shiloh hadn't been to bed. She met him at the door, still clad in her snug trousers and boots.

For a fleeting instant, Justin saw relief wash over her when she spied him. But almost immediately, her green eyes snapped with anger.

"I hope you're pleased with yourself, Justin. Every one of those rustlers escaped tonight, because of you."

His own rage was fueled by hers. "I'd say that's a sight better than letting them get away with a small herd."

She stamped her foot. "Damn it, Justin, why did you have to interfere? We had it all set up so the law would catch them after they'd stolen the animals."

"Oh really?" he said sarcastically. "There was one thing you overlooked, my dear."

"And what is that?"

"It seems you couldn't keep your mouth shut and a couple of the ranch hands heard you. They were on their way to shut you up for good when I rode them down."

"I don't believe you. You know what I think, Justin? I think you can't stand to see me succeed at a man's job. I guess it does something to your overblown ego."

"My ego?" he raged. "Christ, woman, you're the one

who can't be satisfied with your own life. No matter how much I give you, you're always looking for something more."

"You're damned right I am," Shiloh snapped. "I never asked for anything from you, Justin, except to beg you to let me have a career of my own."

"Your so-called career, Mrs. McCord, would have been pretty short-lived if I hadn't stepped in tonight."

"So you say," she grumbled, shooting him a malevolent glance.

"It doesn't matter what I say, does it, Shiloh?" Justin felt his shoulders slump with fatigue. "Look, I don't know why we're wasting our time arguing. I just walked six miles with a lame horse. I'm going to turn in."

"Wait a minute, Justin."

He turned to see that her anger had abated somewhat. She was staring at him oddly, as if searching his eyes for something. He gave her the coldness of his flint-eyed glare.

She stepped toward him, fingers twisting together. "Justin, I hadn't planned on attacking you the minute you got home. But I was so damned mad about the rustlers and my father losing his payment that I forgot what I stayed up all night to tell you."

He was impressed by the way she suddenly gathered herself together, becoming coolly reasonable.

"Go on," he prompted.

"I've been doing a lot of thinking, Justin. About the two of us. I know we've had our moments when we got on well." She flushed a little. "But it's not enough. This marriage started out as something neither of us wanted, and nothing has been right since. We've done nothing but get under each other's feet, Justin. I'm afraid that if we don't do something soon, we'll tear each other apart."

"What are you getting at, Shiloh?"

"I think we should get out of each other's way, instead of being at each other's throats. I'll stay married to you for a while, I guess until Jessamine finds herself a husband. But we can't go on living like this. I'm going to stay with my aunt."

Justin thought he heard a note of wistfulness— sadness, even—in her voice. Part of him wanted to reach out to her, to ask her to try to work things out. Yet he couldn't argue with her cool logic. He stroked her flushed cheek.

"You're a fool woman," he said. "But I'll miss you."

She backed away. "It's better this way, Justin. You know it is. I'll be leaving in a few hours."

Ina loaded her trunk with tight-lipped disapproval. The anger in her quick, jerking motions as she flung clothing into the open box was not lost on Shiloh.

"Ina, please understand. It's the only way."

"Women do not simply leave their husbands just because things get a little hard. You must have patience with each other."

"It's no use. Justin and I will never get along. There's too much distrust between us."

Ina arched a dark brow. "Distrust? I think not. I think that, even though you will not admit it, you would trust Señor McCord with your very life. I am sorry, Shiloh, but it makes me angry that you would leave a good man when I, who for years have wanted to be a wife to someone, have nobody. I would settle for someone far less appealing than your husband."

Shiloh took her hands. "Oh, Ina . . ." Suddenly she understood. Lacking a husband of her own, Ina had pinned her hopes vicariously on another couple. The woman was taking this as a personal defeat. Then

Shiloh had a thought.

"Ina, my father needs help." She grimaced, thinking how close Nate had come to earning his pay from Clay Joseph. "Especially after last night. He'd never take money from me, but maybe there's something you could do."

An odd light flickered in the woman's velvet-brown eyes, although the handsome face remained carefully composed.

"Of course. If Na—er, your father is in need—"

"Maybe you could take him some things from the garden, a slab of bacon from the spring house. Perhaps even fix him a meal or two and mend his clothes. That is, if you've no objection."

"No, none at all," Ina said quickly.

Shiloh hid a smile behind a lock of hair. Her father, crude as he was, was hardly fit for the ladylike Ina, but one never knew. At least the idea had made Ina forget her anger.

Shiloh checked her dove-gray traveling suit in the mirror. Despite the lack of sleep last night, Ina had gotten her looking surprisingly well.

"I'm going to send Wylie up for the trunk," she said, leaving the room.

As she descended to the foyer, she saw an unfamiliar hat on the rack beside the door. Wrinkling her brow, she went to the door of Justin's study to knock. She hesitated at the sound of low, urgent voices.

No, she told herself, I'm through with meddling in Justin's affairs. But she couldn't help it. She stood and cocked her head to listen.

". . . could be in England by the end of November," said the stranger.

"I don't know, Will," Justin said. "That's a damned long time to be away. Now that I've got this ranch to look after—"

"I know it's a great inconvenience, Justin. Especially with you being newly married."

"That's one thing I'm not worried about at all," Justin replied. The coldness in his voice caused Shiloh's throat to tighten painfully.

"I guess there's no reason you can't bring the little woman along," said the stranger. "You'll have to pay for her passage, though."

"No, Will, you don't understand. I'm sure my wife would have no interest in going to England with me. In fact, I don't even want her to know where I'm going."

"Then I can count on you? We need you, Justin. You're unknown there, and won't sidestep the issues like Ashbel Smith has been doing. You'll go?"

Justin hesitated only a second. "Of course."

"Good. There's a merchantman called the *Falcon* in Galveston. It's going to call at port in the Caribbean and then proceed to England. It sails with the tide in two days."

"The *Falcon*?" Justin asked. "Has that smuggler gone legitimate all of a sudden?"

"It appears so, but don't count on it. Watch yourself, Justin."

Shiloh heard the clink of coins, the rustle of paper.

"Here's everything you need. Letters of introduction from Pinckney Henderson and myself, papers of identification . . . you may as well use your real name. And Justin, be careful. I can't stress that enough. The British are really hot on this issue. They'll go to great lengths to protect their interests."

The visitors stepped toward the door. Shiloh jumped back quickly and knocked.

Justin opened the door, his eyes narrowed in suspicion. But, seeing the wide-eyed look of innocence she affected, he seemed to relax.

"Shiloh," he said, unsmiling. "This is Mr. William

225

Murphy. Will, my wife."

A well-dressed man bent low over her extended hand. "Mrs. McCord, I'm enchanted," he said. He had the slightly nasal twang of an Easterner. "I must be going," he added. He paused to give Justin a nod and let himself out.

"Who is he?" Shiloh asked.

"An acquaintance. It's not important."

She wasn't surprised by his evasiveness and she knew better than to press for details.

"I'm ready," she said at last.

His eyes, hard as gunmetal, swept her up and down. "So I see." He went to the safe, whirled the knob, and took out a leather purse, dropping it almost disdainfully into her hand.

She weighed its heaviness. "Justin, I can't accept this."

"You can," he said coldly. "You will. You've earned it and then some."

"Earned it, have I?" Rage welled up hotly inside her. "Is that what I did—warmed your bed for a few coins?"

He shrugged wearily. "Let me know when it runs out. I'll send you more."

Shiloh drew her hand back, ready to fling it into his face. Then, reason took over. She'd need every cent if she was going to follow him secretly to England. Smiling tightly, she turned on her heel and walked away from him without saying good-bye.

Ten

"I'd like you to leave me in Houston," Shiloh said to Wylie Stokes, who was driving the cart.

"Ma'am?"

"I want to stop in town before going on to my aunt's. I've got some shopping to do."

"Whatever you say, ma'am. I don't mind waiting for you."

"I couldn't ask you to do that, Wylie. I'm sure to take all day. You can just leave me at Mr. Burdett's dry goods store. I'll hire someone to bring me out to Aunt Sharon's later."

"You sure, ma'am?"

"Quite sure, Wylie."

It was no accident that Burdett's establishment was in Commerce Street, directly across from the busy bayou wharves. Shiloh waited beside her huge trunk until the cart lumbered out of sight. Within half an hour, she'd gotten aboard a big sidewheeler and settled down amid a noisy crowd of traders, families, and slaves for the eight-hour trip to the port of Galveston.

She flipped through a collection of essays by Mr. Emerson. Normally his philosophy intrigued her and challenged her mind, but she couldn't concentrate. Her head was too full of what lay ahead.

She still was incredulous about her impetuous decision. She knew she had no business following Justin to England, but she had to go, had to find out what this was all about. Besides, everything fell so perfectly into place. She had her trunk containing all of her belongings, the money from Justin. Aunt Sharon wasn't expecting her, so she wouldn't be missed.

And adventure backoned tantalizingly. It was irresistible when Shiloh thought of the endless autumn and winter months ahead at her aunt's farm, the intolerable sameness of it all. She would have died of boredom. She smiled, pleased with the alternative she'd found.

The smile faded when the sidewheeler steamed past the burned-out shell of Judge West's warehouse at LeBoyer's Crossing. If Justin had been furious about her interference there, he'd be livid when he found her aboard the *Falcon*. Yet Mr. Murphy had suggested that he bring his wife along. Still, Shiloh shivered in the autumn air.

Eventually the fatigue of her sleepless night took over and she dozed. She didn't awaken until the steamer blew its piercing whistle, signaling the end of the voyage.

Galveston was a strange place to Shiloh; she knew the town only from brief visits when she'd gone off to school. The most populous city in Texas, it was a teeming port. The wharves were crowded with travelers, stacks of crates and puncheons, rolling hogsheads, and enormous, tightly bound bales of cotton. Carts and carriages were numerous on the waterfront road.

While a porter brought down Shiloh's trunk, she looked in confusion at a dozen high-masted ships. Finally she asked a passerby, a barefoot man with rolled-up trousers and a rolling gait, if he could point out the *Falcon*.

The swarthy, muscular man smiled appreciatively at Shiloh, but he babbled something in a language she didn't recognize and held out his hands.

Shiloh smiled vaguely and moved off to find someone else.

"You are looking for the *Falcon*?"

She turned, startled by the rich, creole accent of the speaker. She nodded quickly at a lovely, statuesque Negress.

"Yes, I am," she replied.

"Over there, in the farthest slip, missy. But are you sure it is what you are looking for?"

"Of course." But something about the dark-eyed woman's dubious glance unsettled her.

"It is not the place for you."

"I've already made up my mind," Shiloh said, almost to herself.

"There is danger on the winds that carry that ship," the woman said darkly.

Shiloh smiled. "It doesn't worry me."

The woman shrugged. She pointed to a ramshackle building at the end of a row of warehouses. "I am living there. If you need anything, ask for Sylvie."

Shiloh shook her head. "Thank you. But I'm sure I'll be fine."

Sylvie looked grim. "I, too, thought the same when I boarded the *Falcon*." She swung her head, long earrings jangling against her slim neck. Her disapproval as she studied the thrown-together buildings and dusty road, the sere sea grasses that waved in the autumn wind, was apparent.

"Take care, missy," she murmured, and glided off.

Shiloh gave the mysterious woman no further thought. She hired a porter to bring her trunk on a handcart to the *Falcon*. It was a tall, graceful vessel with sleek lines and clean, scrubbed-looking decks. There was nothing at all forbidding about it.

Mounting a plank to the upper deck, Shiloh hailed one of the sailors who was sitting with a lapful of rigging, mending it.

"Whom do I see to inquire about passage to England?" she asked.

The man jerked his head toward the raised stern. "See the captain, St. James," he said, his accent markedly British.

Shiloh stepped around crates and coils of rope as she made her way to the captain's quarters. The door was slightly ajar, and she took a moment to study the interior. It was more like a small, elegant drawing room than a ship's cabin. Evening light slanted in through windows on three sides, illuminating glowing walnut panels and bolted-down furniture, a rich Turkey carpet and a beautiful silver service on a sideboard.

A tall man stood looking over a spread of charts and strange-looking instruments on a broad-topped table. Shiloh stared with growing interest at the man. In a velvet jacket and fawn trousers, he hardly fit the image she'd had of what a sea captain should look like.

For one thing, he was young, perhaps of an age with Justin. His full head of curly black hair framed a profile that was so handsome that he looked more like an artist's sculpture than a human being. Hearing her tentative knock, he turned on her a face so beautiful that it was almost intimidating.

"Yes?" His voice didn't quite match his devastating looks. An odd mixture of British and Spanish, unexpectedly high in pitch.

Shiloh took a deep breath. "I'd like to sail to England, Captain St. James. I understand your ship sails tomorrow."

His eyes, dark brown with a vaguely Latin cast, a certain sleepiness, assessed her quickly. Apparently she pleased him, for he gave her a dazzling smile.

"Is that so, Miss . . . .?"

"Mulvane," she said quickly, using her maiden name. "Shiloh Mulvane."

He extended a slim, long-fingered hand. "Christopher St. James. Welcome aboard."

Shiloh looked at him incredulously. She hadn't expected it to be so easy. "You mean you'll take me . . . there's room?"

"There is always room on my ship for a lovely lady," he said gallantly. Then he gave her an arch look. "Provided, of course, she can pay."

Shiloh lifted her chin. "I'd like the best accommodations available, please." She placed a stack of double eagles on the captain's table.

"Happy to oblige," he said, his interest in her growing. "I'll show you there myself."

A ship's boy was polishing a brass bell on the stern. He ducked his head as the captain passed. The strong scent of musk cologne preceded Shiloh as St. James led the way down a steep ladder and along a cramped, narrow passageway. He opened the door to a tiny but immaculate cabin. There was a berth along one wall, a wooden stand with a brass lavatory on it, and a small secretary bolted to the opposite wall.

"Your home, Miss Mulvane, for the next several weeks," St. James said grandly. "If you'll send someone for your baggage, I'll have my steward set another place in my quarters for supper." He hesitated, lazy eyes holding hers challengingly. "You will join me, won't you?"

"Yes, thank you. Captain St. James, will there be other passengers?"

He laughed lightly. "Of course. The roster is not yet

231

full, but there will be others. Let's see . . . an older couple, the Westons, a young French family by the name of Jemeaux, an American called Duff Green, and his companion, whom I've not yet met. And then, when we call at Antigua, we'll be taking on more. So you see, Miss Mulvane, you'll have plenty of company." St. James wet his sensual lips.

"It is my good fortune that you are the first to come aboard. We'll have the chance for some uninterrupted conversation this evening." He clapped his booted heels together smartly and left.

Shiloh looked after him quizzically. She wasn't sure what to make of the dashing seaman. He behaved decently enough; he'd been most obliging. Yet there was something about the man, an air of mystery, a sensual kind of danger in the dark eyes and the curling lip below a pencil-thin mustache.

She shook her head to clear it of her vaguely disturbing imaginings about Christopher St. James, and went to see about her trunk.

She chose her lavender dress with its modest high collar for supper that night. St. James's steward came to fetch her. He gave her an odd, assessing look.

"Is something wrong?" Shiloh asked. Her hand went to her tight red curls. Lacking Ina's adept hand, she'd only been able to pull it into some sort of order with a pair of ivory combs.

"No," the man said quickly. But he directed another strange look at her before leading her to the captain's cabin.

Christopher St. James had dressed quite formally. In black velvet with tails and tall, highly polished boots, his almost unreal handsomeness was enhanced. He swept Shiloh's hand to his lips, tickling her palm slightly.

"I was rather distressed, Miss Mulvane, that this voyage would be tedious. Yet now, I've your company to look forward to. Come, shall we eat?"

It was a meal such as Shiloh had never seen before. Delicate boiled shrimp was served cold on bone china plates, garnished with tiny, fresh limes. Then there were generous portions of gulf trout bathed in a rich sauce of butter and wine, with green peas on the side. Finally a tray of mille-feuilles pastry, fruit, and cheese. St. James insisted that she sample at least three different wines.

"You live quite well, captain," Shiloh commented, plucking a grape from the bowl on the table.

"No doubt you've heard stories of rough life at sea, men dying of thirst and starvation . . . well, that doesn't happen on my ship. I take good care of my men—" he licked a crumb from the corner of his mouth "—and they, in turn, take care of my needs."

"Very admirable," Shiloh commented. She hid a small yawn behind her hand. "Excuse me," she said. "I'd like to retire now."

St. James placed his lips around a ripe plum and bit down, his flicking tongue catching a droplet of juice before it coursed down his chin. All the while, his indolent eyes held hers, seeming to give his actions a double meaning as he slowly devoured the plum.

"So soon?" he asked, raising a black eyebrow.

"I'm very tired. . . ."

"Of course, I wouldn't dream of keeping you from your much-needed rest. But I have one question, Miss Mulvane."

"Yes?"

"That ring. Is there something you're not telling me?"

Shiloh blushed and cast her eyes downward. "I'm

233

afraid I may have misled you, captain. I'm married."

"Oh?"

"But my husband and I are—we've decided to live apart for a time."

"I see," he replied with great interest. "In that case, it will be my pleasure to take care of you."

"Really, captain, it's not necessary—"

"Of course, it is."

Shiloh rose quickly. "I can find my way back to my cabin," she said. "Goodnight, captain." She fled before he could escort her.

Through the small, misted portal of her cabin, Shiloh watched the roll and tilt of the white-capped open water. The ship listed sickeningly to one side and she clutched the edge of her berth, leaning over the chamber pot.

In the first eight days at sea, Shiloh had suffered untold miseries. Nothing could have prepared her for the unrelenting, inescapable sickness that plagued her day and night. After the first day, she hadn't bothered to get dressed or so much as poke her head out the door. A steward came several times a day to bring her fresh water and food and to empty her chamber pot. Shiloh looked and felt too wretched to respond to Christopher St. James's frequent invitations. From time to time she was vaguely aware of voices in the passageway outside, but she was so ill that she didn't care to see if Justin was aboard.

Then, on the ninth day, the sun pushed away the billowing storm clouds. With them went Shiloh's sickness, leaving her weak but full of elation, as if she'd been reborn.

At first she couldn't believe the churning nausea was gone, but her breakfast tasted wonderful and miraculously stayed put. When the steward came, offering St. James's supper invitation, she accepted. She was more than ready to leave the cramped confines of her cabin.

She wore one of her favorite dresses, a gown of cotton shot through with green thread, and smiled broadly across the elegant table at Christopher St. James.

"Never, my dear, have I seen a person emerge from the *mal de mer* so triumphantly. You look positively radiant. A bit thinner, perhaps, but absolutely glowing."

"Thank you," Shiloh said, flushing at the elaborate compliment.

After dessert, he insisted she stay on. He plied her with wine, keeping her from protesting with a steady stream of conversation.

"I was born to the sea," he said, his lazy eyes reflective, hands caressing his glass. "It is the one place where a man is his own, not bound by society's rules. That is important to me."

"Why?" Shiloh asked, intrigued.

"Because of my parentage. I carry the name of St. James, but it was given me only as a courtesy. You see, my father, an Englishman, was not married to my mother." His eyes darkened. "I was given a fine education, but I was never allowed to forget that my mother was a Mexican courtesan in Vera Cruz."

Shiloh looked at him with sympathy. Her own childhood had been painful at times, and she understood.

"But here," St. James gestured grandly, "I do as I please, and no one disapproves."

They talked on, and when the hour of eleven was called out, Shiloh didn't know where the time had gone.

"I'd like to share something with you," said St.

James. "Something very special." He took a pipe from a drawer, along with a small, tarlike substance. Loading the pipe with it, he lit it and inhaled deeply.

"Opium" he said, almost reverently. "Here, I think you'll find it most agreeable."

Shiloh had heard of opium's being used for medicinal purposes, but never like this.

"Captain, I don't think—"

"There now, love, you must call me Christopher. Take it. I think you'll enjoy the pleasurable effects." He held it to her lips, pressing close, putting a match to the pipe. Without quite knowing what she was doing, Shiloh inhaled. The slightly sweetish smoke blended with Christopher's musk scent, filling her head with decadent sensations. He had her pressed against the gleaming walnut paneling and made her inhale several more times.

A warm, floating feeling took over. Shiloh's limbs went loose; her eyelids could barely hold themselves open. Although Christopher had promised her ecstasy, she was aware only of a creeping lassitude that sapped her of her will. When he led her to his bed and pressed her down upon it, she could offer only the weakest of protests.

He began stroking her back, his hands traveling the length of her with great intimacy.

"And now," he said, working open her buttons, "I've another surprise." He reached up and pulled a small, tingling bell, keeping her in his lazy-eyed, hypnotic gaze. Almost immediately, a slender youth appeared, clad only in trousers. He was as beautiful as St. James, tall and lithe, his chest and shoulders glistening.

"This is Antoine," said Christopher. "He is well versed in the arts of pleasure. I think the three of us are about to embark on a rare journey together."

At that, Shiloh's eyes flew open. Antoine's appearance had the effect of a bucket of cold water's being thrown in her face. Suddenly the illicitness and the decadence of what was happening hit her like a blow.

"No!" she cried, pushing Christopher away and lunging for the door. He blocked her escape, his smiling red lips twisting beneath the mustache in a sneer of cruelty.

"Come now," he said, "don't disappoint us, Shiloh. Don't run away from this—"

She landed a sharp, bone-crunching kick on his booted shin, pulled the door open, and ran out onto the deck. The canopy of stars lit her way, but she was unfamiliar with the upper decks and promptly tripped over a coil of rope. Behind her, footfalls grew louder. Frantic now, Shiloh righted herself and fled to the middle of the ship. But her flight was hindered by her billowing skirts and a network of railings and grates. A pair of strong arms grasped her from behind, and she felt herself crushed against Antoine's bare chest.

In front of her loomed Christopher St. James. He leered, his perfect features transformed into a visage of ugly hunger.

He laughed lightly. "There is something to be said for the thrill of the chase, Shiloh, but this has gone far enough." He leaned down and grasped her face, holding it still to deliver a punishing kiss. Shiloh bit at his lips and screamed when he pulled away.

"I'd always heard pioneer women liked it rough," he laughed, daubing at the blood with a musk-scented handkerchief. "Very well—"

Without warning, he cracked his open palm against her cheek, causing her head to snap to the side. Then, as Shiloh spat insults of terror and rage, his hands were on her, viciously pinching her breasts, her arms. He leaned down and reached under her dress, working her thighs apart. Shiloh's vision swam. As the rough assault continued, the stars spun and swirled overhead.

Things were beyond her control. She felt tears well up in her eyes. A sob was dragged from her throat. She wished with every fiber of her being that this was some awful nightmare. But the grasping hands, the smacking lips, the sharp, biting teeth, were all too real.

Just as she dared open her eyes, she became aware of a shadowy form approaching. Oh God, she thought, not another—

Like a great cat, the figure dropped onto the deck. There was a sickening sound of flesh against flesh. The force of the blow lifted St. James from his feet and sent him sprawling to the deck. Antoine's hold loosened.

"Get lost, pretty boy," growled a voice, and the scantily clad youth scuttled off into the night.

"Justin!" Shiloh spoke his name with an exploding gasp of relief and hurled herself into his arms.

"My God, Shiloh," he murmured, stroking her hair. "What the hell—"

There was a quiet snarl from behind. Justin set Shiloh aside and spun about to face St. James. The flash of a knife blade glinted in the starlight.

Her heart in her mouth, Shiloh watched the two men. They were nearly the same size, Justin having the advantage of a few inches and pounds. But there the similarity ended. While St. James's face was set in an ugly sneer, Justin's was transformed into a visage of magnificent wrath. He was brilliant light while the captain was a dark threat. Justin's eyes followed his slowly circling adversary with intense vigilance.

Several times, St. James stabbed out and Justin jumped back. Then the Englishman grew bolder with his blade and gave a mighty thrust. Shiloh's scream died in her throat. Lightning quick, Justin's booted foot swept upward and sent the knife clattering down to the deck. The two came together in a vicious mêlée of tangling limbs and curses.

Shiloh allowed herself to relax against the wooden rail. Now that St. James had been disarmed, he didn't have a chance against her husband's towering strength. In seconds, Justin had slammed the captain down to the planks.

St. James began thrashing and whimpering like a whipped dog.

"Mercy!" he cried in his high-pitched voice. "Please, no more. . . ."

Justin looked at him in disgust. "Don't worry, St. James, I'm going to let you sail this bucket to England." He leaned down, his voice a deadly whisper that Shiloh could barely hear above the swishing of the shifting seas.

"But if you ever come near my wife again, if you so much as look at her, I'll make you wish you'd never been born, my friend."

"I—I promise. Please, *please*. . . ."

Justin rose and watched the Englishman run wildly to his cabin. Shiloh faced her husband, words of gratitude on her lips. But he never gave her a chance to speak. Grabbing her by the arm, he took her below.

A lamp swinging gently from a rafter illuminated his cabin. He sat her roughly on the berth and thrust a mug of lukewarm coffee into her hands.

"Drink," he commanded, and she dared not disobey. When she'd had a few swallows, he spoke again. "When will it end, Shiloh? The lies, the deceit—"

"I couldn't help it, Justin. I couldn't stand to live with my aunt, stuck out there with nothing to do. Besides, I'm your wife."

"I believe you decided we shouldn't be together."

"But that was before I learned you were going to England!"

His jaw clenched. "It's all been a game to you, hasn't

it, Shiloh? A way to alleviate your boredom. Damn it, this time you've gone too far. I've tried so many times to protect you, yet you persist in getting yourself into one scrape after another. What would've happened tonight if I hadn't heard your screams?"

Shiloh swallowed hard as a shudder rippled through her. "I had no idea St. James would try something like that."

"That's because you're so damned ignorant," he railed. "If you'd known the first thing about the *Falcon*, you'd never have dared to set foot on this ship. Slaves, contraband, stolen goods . . . St. James is notorious. His reputation is known—and feared—in a hundred ports. Good God, even the wharf urchins could have told you about his bizarre appetite for young boys and opium. Of course, few women have lived to tell the rest of the story. St. James keeps them or discards them according to his whim. It's said he keeps a pirate's retreat off Mexico somewhere."

Shiloh began trembling in earnest now, chilled to the bone by Justin's tale and the remembered warning of the woman called Sylvie. Her head was fuzzy and aching with the effects of the drug. Justin reached out and thrust her head back, using his thumb to raise one of her eyelids.

"He drugged you," he said curtly.

Shiloh winced away from his harsh touch. "I didn't know what he was offering me. I thought he was just trying to be hospitable."

Justin gave a dry laugh. "This," he said sarcastically, "from a woman who fancies herself a spy. I wonder what your father will say when he hears what happened this time."

That was too much for Shiloh. A sob was wrenched from her throat and she flung herself onto the bunk, quaking with bitterness. She cried because the truth of what Justin said knifed through her like a hot, lethal blade. She *was* a failure. She was incapable of becoming what she wanted so badly to be. Although she'd harbored dreams of glory, the miserable reality was that she'd proven herself to be a naive, inept bungler. Perhaps her father had known that all along. Perhaps that was why he — and Justin — couldn't love her. . . .

She wept on, heedless of Justin's stolid, silent presence. Finally, the sobs abated to hiccoughs of misery and she went limp upon the berth.

"Do you want to stay here tonight?" Justin asked. His voice was unbearably cold.

Shiloh forced herself to face him, knowing he was disgusted by her childish tears, her red nose and swollen eyes.

"No, thank you," she said. She couldn't stand to spend another minute in the presence of his disapproving scrutiny.

He escorted her to her cabin. "I guess you'll be safe enough. St. James is a cowardly son of a bitch. But latch the door anyway."

She nodded and looked up at him with wide, reddened eyes. Something flickered in his face and he seemed about to say more. But he only thrust her into the cabin and closed the door firmly.

Justin looked contemplatively at the stub of his cheroot and then flicked it over the rail into the clear, aqua-colored water. As the *Falcon* maneuvered its way into Falmouth Harbor at Antigua, he thought again of Shiloh.

She'd spent the remainder of the voyage sequestered like a nun in her cabin. He couldn't be sure who she was avoiding — St. James, or himself. Grimacing, he recalled how hard he'd been on her the night she was attacked. But, damn it, she deserved every word. She had no business sneaking to England, walking with unbelievable innocence into the hands of Christopher St. James. She had to hear those things before she let something else happen. If she hated him for what he'd said, at least he had the consolation of knowing she wouldn't be so damned blind about people in the future.

He might have gone too far, though. He'd glimpsed Shiloh once when she'd opened her door to a steward. Her face was pale, frightened, and her eyes had the dull look of defeat in them.

Justin caught himself wishing she'd come above, just for these last few minutes. He knew her eyes would grow bright with pleasure at the exotic island scenery. Antigua was a matchless jewel in the necklace of the leeward islands. Towering Boggy Peak stood above lush tropical forests and cane fields of impossible greenness. Even from a distance, the brightness of huge colorful blossoms could be discerned. Justin wanted Shiloh to share the moment with him, to smell the flowers and feast her eyes on the curling silk-cotton trees, to hear the wild calls of the colored birds.

He was joined instead by Duff Green, who came to stand among the passengers at the rail.

"I figure we'll be here two days at the most," said Green. "Looks like all that cargo over there is meant for us."

Justin nodded and looked over at the enormous bundles of cane and crates of rum. There was more than enough to fill the *Falcon*'s hold to capacity.

"I'm glad there won't be much of a delay," he said. "I'm eager to find out exactly what Lord Aberdeen's up to now."

"Nothing good," Green said darkly. "But I doubt you'll find much to pin on him."

They stood and talked while the ship felled some of its sails and crept carefully amid the rocky shoals, finally fitting snugly into harbor and dropping anchor.

Lighting a cigar, Green made his way to one of several gangplanks that had been laid.

"What do you say, Justin? Shall we hit the grog shops, maybe try to find a little entertainment?"

"No, thanks."

Duff looked apologetic. "Sorry. I forgot about Shiloh. What's ailing the two of you, anyway?"

Justin was about to growl that it was none of his business but, seeing genuine concern on Duff's face, he only shook his head. "She came along without my knowledge. She should've known I thought it was too damned dangerous for her. And after that run-in with St. James, she's pretty gun-shy."

"It might make her feel better if she knew St. James's been hiding in the shadows like a scared rabbit ever since you caught him messing with her."

"Shiloh's not about to let me tell her anything," Justin said darkly. "I said some pretty harsh things to her."

Duff looked concerned. "Maybe this island will coax her out. Closest thing to paradise I ever saw. If you don't mind my saying so, Justin, she's sure as hell worth a try."

Those words echoed in Justin's mind as he continued to sit on deck, watching the port scene. Beyond the white roads of the small settlement, fat goats grazed on a hill. Ancient stone sugar mills stood about. To one side were banana trees, called figs by the natives, and orchards of strange, exotic fruit. And all around were the flowers, growing wild or cultivated near the snug cottages, to be tucked into the hair of dark-skinned native girls.

It was time, he decided, to coax Shiloh out of her self-imposed isolation. Tucking his white broadcloth shirt into his trousers, he descended to her cabin.

"Shiloh, open up. It's me."

She let him in, keeping her eyes downcast. Never had she looked so small, so vulnerable. Justin had a strange urge to reach out and tuck a stray tendril of her hair back into its comb. He cleared his throat.

"We ought to go ashore. Antigua looks like quite a place."

"No, thank you," she said softly. "But you go ahead. I'll just stay here."

He felt like he was talking to a stranger. Where was the fire, the ambition, the hunger for adventure she'd always had?

"Damn it, Shiloh," he said, taking her by the shoulders and forcing her to face him. "You went to a lot of trouble to make this trip. You might as well make the most of it."

"I can't. I—"

"Then there's no point in going on, is there?" Justin challenged. "You may as well stay in Falmouth Harbor for the first boat back to New Orleans or Galveston. You could be back with your aunt in a few weeks."

"No!" she cried, some of the glint of defiance returning to her eyes. "I—you're right, Justin. I'll get my things."

The evening light bathed the port city in a shimmer of pink-gold. Trading was still in full swing. Women with brightly painted handcarts hawked trinkets and fruit, and malodorous fish stalls were laden with odd-looking creatures, freshly caught. Justin bought Shiloh a large yellow mango and sliced it with his knife. He watched with pleasure as Shiloh devoured her portion, marveling at how delicious it tasted. Already he could tell her zest for life was returning.

They stopped at an open-air cantina and dined on fried blue marlin steaks, yams seasoned with molasses, and more fruit, and something called goat water washed down with swigs of raw rum. Overhead, a balmy breeze rustled through the palm-thatched canopy of their table. Justin overpaid the smiling, dark-skinned boy who served them.

"Where's the best place for my wife and me to take a walk on the beach?" he asked.

"I know a very good place, sir, Pigeon's Point. Sand white and still warm from the sun. Very private, very quiet. Walk to the end of the road and circle round that large rock. You will pass a glade on your right with a cold spring and then there will be a wide beach."

Justin offered Shiloh his arm. They strolled at a leisurely pace, inhaling the heavy perfume of flowers and watching the graceful swaying of tall palms. The beach was everything the boy had promised: waves lapped up on a wide, pristine stretch of sand, and a cooling, salt-scented breeze blew in.

"Oh," said Shiloh, "oh, it's beautiful!" She bent and removed her shoes and stockings and ran down to the water's edge. Drawing her skirts up above her knees, she waded, in, sighing with pleasure. As she felt the fineness of the sand under her feet, she realized that her old vigor was returning. She was filled with excitement at being in this wild, exotic place so different from anything she'd ever known.

Justin, too, had taken off his boots, and he joined her in the clear water. The rising moon and a spray of stars illuminated the breaking waves, making them glow as they rolled in.

"It's breathtaking," Shiloh whispered. She was talking about the scenery, but her eyes were fastened on Justin's handsome face, on his fine golden hair as the breeze blew through it. "Thank you," she said softly.

He smiled. "For what?"

"For making me get off that ship. I hid there too long."

"I was surprised at you, Shiloh. You've never been one to give up."

"But you made everything clear to me. The things you said—"

"—should never have been said, Shiloh. I realize that now. I had no business judging you. Look, could we forget all that for now?"

She couldn't help smiling. "Gladly," she breathed. Just then, a wave rolled up and propelled her forward. With a small cry, she fell against Justin's chest and grasped his arms for support.

"Sorry," she said quickly, feeling clumsy.

"Not at all," Justin laughed. He reached behind her and began unbuttoning her dress.

Her heart leaped. "What are you doing?"

"It seems a shame," he said, continuing to work at the buttons, "not to take advantage of this private beach. Surely you must be wanting to swim."

"Swim? Why, I—" Suddenly it seemed like she'd been thinking it all along. Laughing, she went back to the dry sand and began removing her clothes. When she was clad only in her shift, she started back toward the water.

"Not so fast," Justin said, placing himself in front of her. "What's this?" He plucked at the ribbons of her shift. Without further ado, he swept it off and raked his eyes over her slim body.

With a cry of alarm, Shiloh ran down to the water, modestly burying herself in the moon-glowing waves. She would never get used to Justin's behavior. He wasn't far behind her. As she swam through waist-deep water, she felt him lunge at her and grasp her about the middle. He laughed at her cry of alarm and turned her easily.

His kiss was deep, throbbing with sensuality. As the water swirled up between them, Shiloh thought she would burst with the sudden longing that flowed through her. Justin's hands worked their magic over her, finding her tightly drawn nipples and caressing them until she thought she would drown in a sea of longing. The silky water surged up between her breasts in a compelling rhythm.

"Justin," she whispered into the dampness of his hair.

He must have heard the longing in her voice. He smiled and dipped his head to her bosom. Shiloh was suffused by heat, and her trembling body welcomed it. She wrapped her arms around Justin, never thinking to deny him now.

He raised his head. Soft moonlight played over his features and flooded his eyes with a silvery gleam. He took one of Shiloh's hands and brought it to his lips, kissing the fingers one by one.

"You're lovely," he told her between kisses. "I'm almost glad you decided to follow me on this trip."

She splashed him. "Almost, Justin?" She grew bold, allowing her hands to descend beneath the warm water to caress him intimately.

"You're determined to make a liar of me, Mrs. McCord," he growled, and then he, too, dipped his hands underwater. He sipped the sweetness from her mouth as his fingers, moving secretly, found the small bud of sensation between her legs.

Shiloh inhaled and held her breath. The stars above spun before her dizzy eyes, turning from bright points of light into long, livid streaks. The unending rhythm of the sea thundered in her ears, relentless, compelling, urging her toward Justin.

"Please . . ." she begged, her voice ragged with emotion.

Justin mistook her meaning. He ceased his sensuous caresses and took her by the shoulders, cursing himself for not being more sensitive to her. The last man who had tried to touch her had been Christopher St. James, and he'd scared the daylights out of her. No wonder Shiloh was begging him to stop.

"Sorry, sweetheart," he said gruffly, battling his own frustrated desire. "I should have known you weren't ready so soon after that scare with St. James."

She shook her head, spraying droplets of water. "You don't understand, Justin. I'm not so stupid that I'd mistake you for St. James. I—I wasn't asking you to stop."

His teeth gleamed in the moonlight as he grinned at her. "Just what were you asking for, Mrs. McCord?"

She remained serious. "I want you, Justin. What St. James tried to do to me was evil, and only you can erase that memory for me. Only you—"

He cut her off with a triumphant kiss that took her breath away. Now there was no hesitation, no teasing. Shiloh gloried in the pure ecstasy of his touch, and she reached out to him. Shifting water eddied between them like a small, warm gulf. A wave lifted Shiloh and pushed her gently against Justin.

She brought her legs up and wrapped them around his torso, amazed at how much the unfamiliar position aroused her. Justin must have felt likewise, for he reached around and cupped her buttocks and lifted her onto him. Shiloh gasped as they came together. When he began to move she clung to him and placed her mouth on his salty-tasting shoulder. The lapping of the water, the undulating of their hips, Justin's breath in her ear, all combined in an erotic symphony that rose to a breathless crescendo and then crashed down as Shiloh cried out her ecstasy. She felt as if she were drowning in a pool of exquisite sensations.

She heard Justin's low laugh. "How do you feel, Mrs. McCord?"

She smiled. She'd heard that question before and she'd never been able to answer it with words. "Mmm . . ." she said, dragging her lips along his shoulder and up his neck. "I must be possessed by voodoo magic."

He traced the curves of her torso. "Is that right?"

She brushed a tendril from her cheek. "I don't know what else it could be." A troubled shadow crossed her face. "Justin, I wasn't brought up to be a religious person, but sometimes the things we do . . ." Her voice trailed off as her face grew warm.

"Tell me, Shiloh," he prompted.

She looked up at him, her eyes wide and bathed in moonglow. "Justin, what we do—could it be wrong?"

He smiled and pulled her through the water against him. "Is that what's bothering you? Listen, my girl, you've got to forget whatever missish notions you have. There is nothing wrong with the pleasure a husband and wife bring to each other. Just because we didn't make love in a proper bed doesn't mean we've committed any crime." As he spoke gently, his hands moved discreetly under her and he brought them together again. At her soft sigh of pleasure, he whispered, "How can this be wrong, Shiloh?"

She moaned and wrapped herself around him again, knowing in her heart how right she felt with him.

They enjoyed the interlude at Antigua for another day, and then it was time to set sail again. Justin and Shiloh stood together on deck, along with Duff Green. The port bustled with activity.

"Ah, a man could get used to this life," Duff declared, patting his generous middle and puffing on his cigar. "All it takes is a little money, and you get the

249

royal treatment. Perhaps I was hasty in throwing in my entire lot for Texas."

"It seems you're not the only one who thinks that way," Justin remarked. He gestured at a gleaming, overloaded coach that had stopped on the wharf. A liveried footman handed down an elaborately gowned and bonneted woman.

She raised her head and Shiloh found herself staring into the china-blue eyes of Jessamine West.

Eleven

"What are they doing here?" Shiloh asked that night. By unspoken agreement, Justin had moved into her cabin, and they lay crowded together in the small bunk.

"Harmon West is overseeing his sugar plantation, no doubt. And it appears that Captain Elliot has some interest in it, as well. From what the *Falcon* took on, they should make a tidy profit."

"Is that why Judge West is so dead-set against annexation?"

"That's one of the reasons. If Texas becomes part of the United States, he'd have some pretty tough competition in the Gulf."

"What are you going to do about it, Justin?"

He allowed himself a satisfied smile. "I'll hardly need to lift a finger. When President Houston learns how thick West and Elliot are, the judge will be stripped of his appointment. Duff's going to take care of Elliot. This might finish him as a diplomat. The English can't have their representatives getting rich off their policies.

251

It looks too bad."

"Are you sure, Justin? It could just be a coincidence."

"It doesn't matter. They wouldn't survive the rumors. And don't forget whose ship we're on."

"What do you mean by that?"

"By now you must know that St. James doesn't limit his trade to sugar, cotton, and rum."

"The opium?" Shiloh shivered, recalling the mind-numbing effects of the drug the captain had given her.

Justin nodded. "I'd be willing to bet that there's a connection there. Elliot was in China during the opium wars. And Harmon West has never been one to turn his back on a big-money deal like that. I think we've got him up against the wall now."

Shiloh yawned and snuggled against him, savoring the feel of his warm chest beneath her cheek. "I'm glad," she murmured. "I hope we've seen the last of the Wests."

"McCord needs to be silenced," Harmon West muttered. "For good." He crossed the deck where he, Jessamine, and Elliot were standing, jaw twitching in agitation.

"Any ideas?" Elliot asked.

"I'd like to feed the meddling son of a bitch to the sharks," West blustered. "Sorry, Jessamine," he added, apologizing for his language.

"Never mind, Father," she trilled. "I'm a big girl now; I've done a lot of growing up since I found out why you wanted Justin to marry me. By now you should know it's best to include me in your plans." She finished the pastry she was eating and delicately licked the crumbs from her fingers.

"Now," she continued, primping, "I think you two

gentlemen should use a little imagination. You don't want Justin to let on that he knows of the plantation—" she glanced over at Elliot, "—or the other business. All you have to do is blackmail him, just as you're doing to Mr. Green about his Del Norte land company."

"My dear," said Harmon, "you've proven yourself to be most shrewd. But unfortunately our Mr. McCord is utterly devoid of any taint, unlike his friend Duff Green. What could we possibly reveal about him that would prevent him from revealing us in turn? He has a spotless record. His reputation in Texas and Washington is pure sterling."

Jessamine grimaced. "It wouldn't have been if he'd married me instead of that appalling bit of riff-raff—" She stopped as a smile spread slowly across her face. "Now there's something," she said.

"Tell us," Elliot and the judge said at once.

"We all know that Justin's marriage to me would have thoroughly discredited him by showing that he was willing to be bought by you. But what if he did something worse? What if he was caught in a clandestine affair with the daughter of the very man he's supposedly investigating?"

"Jessamine, really, that's too—"

"No, you mustn't object. It's perfect. Not only would people think that Justin had sold out; they'd also condemn him for cheating on his poor little wife. Now, all we've got to do is arrange for someone—Mr. Green would do nicely; he is published in many newspapers, isn't he?—to find us together, and then we could offer Justin a choice. Either he keeps quiet about our business, or we allow Mr. Green to carry his tale to Justin's superiors." She smiled tightly. "And I wouldn't object if dear Shiloh found out. She deserves it."

Harmon West smiled at his daughter. "If your mother had lived to hear how deviously your mind

253

works, my dear, she'd send you to a nunnery."

"I think my plan is rather ingenious, don't you, Captain Elliot?"

His cold, pale eyes gleamed. "It certainly is. That is, if you don't mind compromising yourself. After all, you, too have a reputation to maintain."

She gave him a haughty look. "My position in Houston is secure. No one would dare look askance at me."

"Of course," the Englishman replied apologetically.

"You go on to your cabin now, captain. I'll take care of everything." Jessamine licked her lips in anticipation of the furor she would cause.

Justin was penning a letter in his cabin, where he no longer slept but kept his baggage and papers. Reaching into his pocket, he checked his watch. It was nearly midnight. Shiloh would be asleep by now.

A smile curved his lips. His wife wasn't ever averse to being awakened, not if he did it gently.

The sound of a knock startled him out of his reverie. Opening the door, he was amazed to see Jessamine West.

She was clad in an impossibly thin dressing gown and nothing else. Her generous curves had once been familiar, but now he saw her as a stranger who meant nothing to him.

"Justin, I must speak to you," she whispered. Not waiting to be invited, she stepped inside the cabin and closed the door behind her. "I've been waiting to find you alone." She pressed close, her heavy gardenia perfume filling the room.

"What is it, Jessamine?" he asked curtly.

"I know you think the worst of Father's being in Antigua, and now bound for England. But I must ask

254

you to say nothing of having seen us. There are many people who wouldn't understand."

"I think it's the other way around, Jessamine. Most people will understand perfectly that your father sympathizes with the English against annexation."

She glowered at him. "So you will slander my father, a public figure—"

"Not at all," said Justin with a dry laugh. "His actions will speak for themselves."

He saw her anger flare and then she mastered it. She looked up at him through lidded eyes and moistened her lips.

"Really, Justin," she said in a husky whisper, "you're not being fair to us. But we're prepared to be more than fair to you. There's a nice reward waiting for you if you agree to forget about this."

"You know better than that, Jessamine."

"And then," she went on as if she hadn't heard him, "there is me." Boldly grasping him about the waist, she hugged him to her soft body. "Remember how it was with us, Justin, in the spring?"

Even as he was extracting himself from her embrace, she shrugged her gown off one shoulder and leaned up to kiss him.

Shiloh was awakened by the ship's bell ringing midnight. She blinked into the darkness of the cabin, immediately sensing Justin's absence. She pulled on her robe and went to look for him. A sliver of lamplight glowed under the door to his cabin down the passageway. Shaking her head, she made her way toward it. She knew of no man who worked harder and slept less than Justin.

She nearly collided with Duff Green, who approached from the opposite direction.

"Good evening, Mrs. McCord," Duff said. "You'll pardon my bed gown and cap; I was sound asleep when a steward summoned me to your husband's cabin."

"Summoned you, Mr. Green?"

"Yes, ma'am. What could he want at this hour?" He knocked at the door. There was no answer; only a strange bumping sound and muffled voices, one of them unmistakably female.

Duff gave Shiloh a dubious look. "Perhaps we'd better leave."

A chill gripped her heart and squeezed tight. "Open it," she said.

When he hesitated, she pushed the door open. Jessamine West, naked to the waist, was in Justin's arms. The girl's mouth formed a surprised O, and then gave Shiloh a knowing smile.

Shiloh fled, unwilling to subject herself to the humiliating scene. She latched her cabin securely before flinging herself onto the bunk, pounding her rage into the pillows.

Duff Green was not so hasty. Carefully averting his gaze, he stood just outside the room.

"Miss West was just leaving," Justin growled. Roughly, he pulled her gown back into place and propelled her out of the cabin.

"Goodnight, Justin," she called sweetly, trilling her voice loudly enough for anyone to hear.

"That wasn't what it looked like," Duff said mildly.

"Of course not," Justin almost shouted. "The woman threw herself at me."

"Fully intending, no doubt, that you'd be discovered together. Obviously she wanted something to hold over you, so you'd keep quiet about her father."

"She did just the opposite," Justin said darkly. "She just sealed Harmon's fate."

"Foolish woman," Duff snorted. "Imagine her believing I'd carry some scandalous tale to your superiors in Washington." He pulled his nightcap back in place. "I'll leave you now, Justin. I know you'll want to set things straight with your wife."

But for the remainder of the voyage, Shiloh kept to her cabin, refusing to let Justin enter. She ventured out on deck only in the company of the Jemeaux, the French family on board. Upon arrival in Bristol and on the subsequent journey to London, she kept herself coldly distant from him.

Only when they reached the huge, smoky city and registered at a hotel in Portman Square was she forced to confront Justin in private. Although she tried to secure a room for herself, the proprietor told her there were no more vacancies. She suspected Justin had lined the man's pockets to compel him to say that, but she didn't want to cause a scene.

And so, stiff-backed and still smarting from his behavior, she allowed herself to be installed in a high-windowed suite overlooking the fashionable square.

"I hope this is to your liking," Justin said mildly.

Her eyes swept the delightful green and yellow decor, the slim, elegant lines of the furniture, the ornate plaster molding around the hearth and ceiling.

"The room is fine," she said, deliberately understating her admiration. In reality, she'd only ever dreamed of such luxury.

Justin paid the porters who brought their trunks and ordered up a bath.

"Wear something pretty tonight," he instructed. "We're invited to a reception at the home of Lord and

Lady Henry Parsons. Expect a lot of flattery. Texans are mighty popular in England these days." He turned on his heel and left.

Shiloh breathed a sigh of relief. Just being near him was painful. His very presence made a mockery of all she'd given him, all she'd foolishly felt for him. The bath arrived and she scrubbed herself with a vengeance as if trying to cleanse herself of the voyage she wanted so badly to forget.

A young maid helped her dress, speaking rapidly with a pronounced accent.

"So it's to the Parsons', is it? Terribly grand, I'm told. But of course you'll be treated to such things every day. Right friendly we are to Texans, ma'am. 'Tis Lord Aberdeen himself started the whole bit. What's it like, ma'am?"

"Texas?" Shiloh couldn't help smiling. "If you were to go there, you'd probably think you'd landed on the moon. It's nothing like London."

"Oh, do tell," said the maid excitedly.

"It's hot and dusty, mostly, but almost like a jungle in other places. The towns are few and small, with simple frame houses or log cabins. You can go for miles in certain areas and never meet a soul."

"And the savages, ma'am, have you seen them?"

Shiloh nodded. "Many times. They trade with the settlers for flannel and trinkets. The peaceful ones, that is."

"And the others, ma'am?"

"There's a whole area beyond the settled regions called the Comancheria. The tribes of the Comanche hunt buffalo and make war on the settlers. I've never been in an attack, thank God, but I've heard stories that would make your blood run cold. The Comanches are brutal and usually without mercy."

"Oh . . ." breathed the maid.

"Are you ready, Shiloh?" Justin stood outside the dressing room, clad for the evening in an elegant gray frock coat and white trousers tucked into his gleaming boots.

"Oh sir," the maid said, "how handsome you look, and how striking you and your beautiful wife will be together."

Justin looked slightly uncomfortable. "Yes, well, finish up, will you?" He went back to the sitting room of the suite to wait.

Because of the chilly London weather, Shiloh had the opportunity to wear her newest gown. It was of lavender velvet, with sleeves and bodice banded by wide black ribbons. The generous hem was drawn up at intervals and fastened with black bows, and the exquisite lace of a dressy petticoat peeped out.

"Lord, now, ma'am," the maid sighed as Shiloh pivoted before a free-standing mirror. "You didn't say you'd been to Paris. Surely that is one of Mr. Dumalier's designs."

Shiloh smiled widely, her face glowing with pleasure. "Actually, it was made by a Mexican woman who works on our ranch."

"No," breathed the maid. "Then a genius, she is."

"I'll be glad to tell her that." Shiloh gave herself one last look. The maid had done her hair nicely, swept up on the sides with a long cascade of tight curls down the back. Last spring Shiloh never would have thought it possible that she could look so good.

She was determined not to let Justin spoil the evening. She meant to show the Londoners that Texas women were not the backwoods pioneers that many believed them to be. And above all, she would not allow herself to be outshone by Jessamine West.

Justin's reaction satisfied her. He couldn't seem to keep from staring at the wide, plunging neckline of her gown or the beautifully worked bodice. Shiloh only wished that she was not so affected by her husband's looks. Handsome as a prince and smelling faintly of soap and tobacco, he was undeniably appealing.

And he was determined to clear the air with her. As a hired coach bore them to the tall, ornately facaded house of Lord Henry Parsons, he brought up the subject of Jessamine.

"It's taken me a damned long time to get you alone to talk, Shiloh, but I know we've both been thinking about it. It wasn't what you've obviously conjured up in your mind."

"I know what I saw. Don't insult me by trying to deny it."

He ground his fist into his hand. "Damn it, *I* should be the offended one. How the hell can you think I'd have anything to do with Jessamine?"

"She's very beautiful, and sophisticated, and you kept company with her before."

"You know why. But Christ, Shiloh, I was through with that long ago. Hell, I married you just to avoid the woman."

Hurt knifed through her. "I see," she said coldly. "It's comforting to know I am the lesser of two evils."

"You know I didn't mean it like that."

"It doesn't matter," Shiloh claimed. She erected a silent wall around herself to protect herself from his lies, from the hurtful things he said. Perhaps Jessamine had thrown herself at him, as had the Mexican woman back in Houston, but it was too much. Justin was a grown man, after all. He had no right to be angry at her, but he was. She could tell by the way he sat, stiffly, not looking at her.

When they arrived, they were presented to a circle of smiling, titled people who extended solicitous hands of welcome. Rather than being nervous, Shiloh was relieved to be away from Justin. Despite the formality of the occasion, she found herself responding easily even to the most daunting aristocrats.

She caught sight of Jessamine, whose yellow, multi-tiered gown seemed rather flamboyant for the occasion. The girl had been cornered by a middle-aged gentleman who leaned toward her, studying her through a quizzing-glass as though she were some rare specimen. No one, it seemed, was going to rescue Jessamine from him. Shiloh smiled, satisfied, and turned her attention to a dashing young man who'd been introduced as the Viscount St. Amberly.

Although slight in build, he joined numerous toasts robustly, and offered a tribute of his own to Shiloh.

"The belle of the Texas Republic," he proclaimed grandly, "May we ever be grateful that she has graced our shores."

Others murmured agreement as they lifted their glasses. Shiloh blushed happily as Jessamine seethed before the gentleman's quizzing-glass and Justin smiled indulgently from another corner of the ballroom.

When the dancing began, Shiloh waltzed with the eager young viscount.

"Thank you for the toast," she murmured.

"It wasn't nearly eloquent enough for you."

"Certainly it was, your . . ." Shiloh cocked her head in puzzlement. "Is it 'your lordship'? I'm afraid I'm quite ignorant of titles."

He grinned delightedly. "Then call me Andrew. It's much simpler."

Shiloh didn't leave the dance floor for hours. Gentlemen of all ages claimed her, and she was exhilarated rather than fatigued. She enjoyed most of her partners, with the glaring exception of Krieger Wilkes, who was some sort of aide to Lord Aberdeen. The odious little man leered unabashedly, and even invited Shiloh to his flat later.

"Out of the question, Mr. Wilkes," she said firmly. "Excuse me."

His hand gripped her arm. "I'm not sure you appreciate my position, Mrs. McCord. It would behoove you to treat me well."

"I think not," she retorted. She disengaged herself and walked away.

Inevitably, she found herself in Justin's arms.

"A last dance with your husband?" he inquired.

She only nodded and followed him woodenly through the steps.

"You handled Wilkes quite well," he commented. "The man is a notorious lecher, but he's tolerated because of his connection to Aberdeen. Aside from him, you've captivated the peerage of England."

Shiloh glanced up and was amazed to see that he was angry. She tossed her head.

"I noticed that you never lacked for a partner." Indeed, she'd seen him dance with any number of ladies, some of them quite beautiful.

Justin was grim as he took her back to the hotel. Nothing was said, but when Shiloh closed the door to the bedroom he stayed in the sitting room, unwilling to breech the wall of silence between them.

The following two months were a whirlwind of activity. There were many more balls and dinner parties, picnics in Hyde Park when the winter mist let up, shooting contests, and horse races. Often, Justin was absent from such events. He attended many meetings with British officials, who were cautious with him. Charles Elliot had obviously warned them that Justin was a proponent of annexation.

At one such meeting, George Hamilton Gordon, the

fourth Earl of Aberdeen, was expounding on the various evils of slavery.

"It is the scourge of the American South, and we fervently wish that it not be extended to Texas," he said, thick eyebrows lowering accusingly at his listeners.

"That's commendable, your lordship," Justin said. "But what about your own colonies in the Caribbean, which thrive by virtue of slave labor?"

"I'll ignore that comment," Aberdeen replied imperiously. "What we really want, gentlemen, is for your fledgling republic to make peace with Mexico, settle its frontier disputes, and achieve success independently. And England is prepared to help in any way."

Justin ingratiated himself to no one during the many discussions. He probed and questioned relentlessly, trying to force an admission from Aberdeen that England's real motive was to protect its interests in the Gulf of Mexico and to extend its influence to yet another part of the world.

"You're treading on delicate ground," Duff Green commented one day shortly after the new year.

"I'm not here to ingratiate myself like Harmon West. I just want something concrete to prove to the United States that they'd damn well better get moving on annexation."

"What are you going to do?"

"I intend to find out what Aberdeen is planning. I'm going to start by searching his ministerial chambers."

Duff gave a low whistle. "You're a braver man than I. Aberdeen'll have your tail if you're caught."

Justin shrugged. "There's no other way. And I'm running out of time. I think tonight's as good a time as any to pay a visit to his lordship's chambers."

They stopped at an alehouse and went over the details of his plan. "I believe I'll make a good thief," Justin said, grinning. "I just hope I can make it out of the country before Aberdeen realizes what hit him."

Green nodded. "Leave that to me. I'll make all the arrangements."

Justin set down his tankard and leaned forward. "Listen, Duff, I need a favor from you. If something should go wrong, if anything happens to me, I want you to look after Shiloh. See that she gets back to Texas. And if times get hard, write to my father in Virginia. Even though I'm not in his good graces, I'm sure he wouldn't turn his back on my wife."

"Sure, Justin. Whatever you say. But I've got to admit, it makes me nervous as hell to hear you talk like that."

Justin sipped his ale. Over the rim of his tankard, he noticed a fleeting figure, the flash of a cloak, leaving the alehouse. The skin prickled on the back of his neck, but he ignored it. He was too edgy, too ready to read danger in every little thing.

"Don't worry," he said, setting down his drink. "Everything will be fine."

That night, Justin's stealthy efforts were richly rewarded. Alone in Aberdeen's chambers, he managed to locate a small packet of papers in a locked drawer. The papers were written in cipher, but it wasn't a very good one. Scratching with the stub of a pencil, Justin uncovered a plot that was so heinous that even the anti-Texas faction in Washington would not fail to move for annexation when they heard about it.

Aberdeen's plan was to move British warships into the Gulf of Mexico, ostensibly to force Mexico to recognize the sovereignty of Texas. But of course, the fleet would have an obvious secondary effect. Not only Mexico, but the United States would be intimidated. And Texas, too impoverished to defend itself adequately, would become an outpost of English imperialism.

"Not if I can help it," Justin muttered, replacing the papers. He blew out the stub of his candle and prepared to leave.

The quiet dark of the office was shattered suddenly. Justin heard the thud of boots and lunged toward the second-story window through which he'd entered. The steeply slanting tiled roof was slick with nighttime mist and he nearly lost his hold. His pursuers climbed out after him, but they balked at the sheer drop to the cobbled courtyard below.

Justin showed no such hesitation. Clinging desperately to the rough edge of the roof, he traversed hand-over-hand to a drain pipe at the corner of the building. This, too, was slick with moisture, and his every limb shook as he made his descent. At last he dropped to the cobbles.

And was promptly seized from behind by two burly men. Although he bucked and struggled in their grasp, they held fast and dragged him, cursing, to a public wagon.

Shiloh dined alone in her suite at the hotel in Portman Square, after a hectic day of shopping and sightseeing with some of her self-appointed hostesses. Surprisingly enough, she seemed to be in great demand in London society. Her outspokenness was admired, as were her tales of life in Texas. She, in turn, found the Londoners well educated and interesting. Only the rift between her and Justin marred the visit.

His absence tonight wasn't unusual; he'd been so busy that she'd seen almost nothing of him. Sighing discontentedly, she pushed aside her plate of stewed chicken. She told herself that it was better this way, that being with Justin would only compound the hurt. But the hours alone were tedious.

When a knock sounded, she jumped to answer it. Her eyes opened wide at the sight of Duff Green and a very unhappy Jessamine West.

"Forgive the intrusion, Mrs. McCord. I should have done this long ago," said Duff. "Miss West has something to say to you."

Shiloh's face hardened into a cold mask. "Yes?"

"Mr. Green," said Jessamine angrily, "I resent this. You are being ridiculously—"

"Never mind that, Miss West. Just say what you came here to say."

"Oh, very well," she snapped.

Shiloh had never seen Jessamine so agitated. "I'm listening," she said with growing interest.

"What you saw between Justin and me on board the *Falcon* was only play-acting. I—I forced myself on him and arranged for us to be discovered."

Shiloh's head began to pound. "But—*why*?"

"Because your meddling husband won't stop hounding my father. He won't stop until he ruins us."

"And so you decided to have your revenge on him," Shiloh said, her voice trembling. "Jessamine, how could you—"

She tossed her yellow ringlets. "You're in no position to judge me, Shiloh. Before you got your claws into Justin you were nothing but a no-account drunkard's daughter—"

Fury exploding, Shiloh leaped at her, scratching at the sneering, haughty face. Falling to the floor, they became a tangle of billowing skirts and petticoats.

"Get this madwoman off me!" Jessamine screeched.

Duff took his time lifting Shiloh from her. He held her firmly about the waist as she calmed herself.

"You can leave now, Jessamine," she said hotly. "But

if I ever hear you insult my father again, if you dare go near my husband again, I'll make sure there's no gentleman around to protect you from me."

Jessamine righted herself with an effort, arranging her skirts around her.

"I was foolish to think you'd accept my explanation gracefully," she said, sweeping with great relief from the room.

Shiloh faced Duff Green, regarding him quizzically. "Would you mind telling me what that was all about?" she asked.

"I apologize for meddling, but I felt you deserved an explanation. The strain between you and Justin has been pretty obvious, and I thought this might help."

"I see. Well, I guess I'm going to have to humble myself now."

"Justin would never let you do that."

"Mr. Green?"

"Yes?"

"I'm curious. How did you get Jessamine to admit the truth to me?"

He smiled. "There are few people in Texas who know more about the illustrious Miss West than I. There are a number of things I was able to forget in exchange for her confession."

"Thank you, Mr. Green." She closed the door with a quiet click and turned back to the room. It wouldn't be easy to face Justin now that she knew the truth, but she owed him an apology.

How many times had he tried to explain, and she'd refused to listen? How could she ever find the words to tell him that she should have trusted him?

She sat before the lowering fire in the hearth, pondering long into the night. Finally she dozed off into a fitful sleep, and didn't awaken until the light of late morning slanted across her face.

She squinted, and slowly stretched. Pouring herself a glass of water, she went to the bedroom door. Perhaps Justin had slept there, not wishing to disturb her. But the bed was perfectly made, the counterpane drawn tightly, as it had been the previous day.

A cold prickle touched the base of Shiloh's neck. As she gulped her water and put on a fresh gown, all manner of grim imaginings plagued her.

Justin's enemies, and there were many lurking behind congenial aristocratic masks, might have finally gotten the better of him. Shiloh swallowed hard. Perhaps he'd finally grown impatient with her constant accusations and sought the solace of someone else's arms. Lord knew, there were enough willing ladies about, practically panting over Justin's tall handsomeness.

Heart pounding, she hurried down to Duff Green's room one floor below.

"Where is Justin?" she demanded.

He wiped a bit of coddled egg from his mouth. "He didn't return last night?" Duff leaned against the door frame as if in sudden need of support.

"He's in some sort of trouble, isn't he?" Shiloh said quietly. When Duff nodded, a strange, unexpected calm crept over her. It was no use going into hysterics. Whatever had happened, she'd need a clear head to face it. She stepped inside the room and pulled the door shut.

"Perhaps you'd better tell me what you know, Mr. Green."

He sighed heavily. "I guess you have a right to know. Justin and I both suspected that Lord Aberdeen has some unscrupulous plans in the making for Texas. Last night he went to the minister's office to try to find out about it. I'm afraid he must have been discovered."

"But where could he be?"

Duff shrugged. "At best, he'll receive a dressing-down from Ashbel Smith at the Texas consulate and be deported."

"And at the worst?"

"Prison. Since he's not an official diplomat, he could be treated like a common thief."

Twelve

Shiloh kept her hands folded in her lap, carefully hiding her nervousness. After an interminable wait, Lord Aberdeen had deigned to see her.

"My husband is missing," she said, not wasting time on niceties.

Aberdeen raised his quizzing-glass. "I'm sorry to hear that, Mrs. McCord. But why do you come to me? Surely the prefect of police—"

"I think you know where he is, your lordship."

"Preposterous," he blustered. "My dear girl, London is a big place. Your husband could be anywhere. Now, if you'll excuse me, I've work to do."

"My husband is a citizen of Texas," she persisted. "And a guest in this country. Lord Aberdeen, I know you do not wish to have this incident become an international affair."

The man's face reddened beneath his powdered wig. "Young lady, if you make unsubstantiated accusations, it will reflect quite poorly on the country you represent."

She raised her chin proudly as she rose to leave. "I can see I'll have to go elsewhere for help, Lord Aberdeen. But you haven't heard the last of me, sir."

Outside his office she slumped, trembling with frustration, against the wall. She squeezed her eyes shut to prevent the flow of hot tears that threatened to erupt.

"Miss . . . ?" Shiloh opened her eyes and saw a clerk staring at her, his pale eyes concerned. "Are you all right?"

"Yes, thank you." Shiloh clutched her reticule and prepared to leave.

"I'll see you out," the clerk offered.

"I can find my own way, thank you."

But the clerk followed her anyway, opening the door to a long corridor. "Never know what you might run up against," he said conversationally. He gave her a meaningful look. "Only last night it was, a thief was discovered right there in his lordship's offices."

Shiloh froze. "What are you telling me, sir?"

He glanced left and right, lowering his voice. "Took him off to Newgate, they did," he murmured.

"Thank you," Shiloh breathed. She fairly flew down the stairs and out into the street, where her hired cab was waiting.

"To Newgate Prison," she told the driver, ignoring his look of astonishment. The ride seemed interminable as they wound through narrow streets among carts and coaches, beneath the overhanging roofs of top-heavy buildings.

Finally they reached to forbidding gates of the prison. Shiloh practically had to force her way into the day warden's office, pushing past clerks and guards.

The warden was a small, whey-faced individual, dressed in soiled finery, looking like a caricature of a gentleman. His watery eyes appraised her and showed approval.

"I am Shiloh McCord, from the Republic of Texas. I believe my husband was brought here last night."

"Is that so?" the warden asked. He shuffled through a stack of papers and located a blotted list. Scanning it with a dirty finger, he nodded.

"Aye, here's a McCord."

Shiloh breathed a grateful sigh. "Please send for him immediately. What is the amount of the fine?"

But the warden only shook his head, looking quite satisfied with himself. "There'll be no release for the prisoner, ma'am. I've a special order here."

Shiloh's heart sank, but she kept her head high. "Suppose, sir," she said softly, touching the strings of her reticule, "that you decided it would be more profitable to ignore that piece of paper. . . ." She let her voice trail off and allowed him to hear the coins falling to and fro.

The warden licked his lips and his hands worked nervously at his sides. But he shook his head regretfully.

"You tempt me, madam, but I couldn't afford the consequences. This order is signed by the secretary of a very highly placed official."

"I understand," said Shiloh. She had no doubt about the identity of the official. "May I see my husband?"

"Alas, no. There's nothing more I can do. Good day, madam.

"You know I wouldn't be here if I weren't desperate." Shiloh said, gripping the sides of the wingback chair she was sitting in.

Harmon West looked across the sitting room of his suite, fairly gloating as she finished her tale. Jessamine sat nearby, looking smug.

"You have a great deal of influence," Shiloh continued, hating herself for having to cowtow to Judge West. "More, probably, than Mr. Ashbel Smith. Lord Aberdeen will listen to you."

"Tell me, Mrs. McCord, why should I lift a finger to help your husband? He's threatened to ruin me."

"Justin is your countryman."

"He's also my enemy."

Shiloh drew a deep breath. "I can't speak for Justin, but if you get him released I'll do everything I can to see that he doesn't mention what he knows to President Houston."

"You have that much influence over your husband?"

"I don't know, Judge West," Shiloh said honestly. Indeed, when had Justin ever trusted anything she'd said? "But surely, once he's released, he'll feel beholden to you."

Harmon West rose slowly and sat down at a small wooden secretary. Dipping a quill into the ink, he scratched out a brief message, signed it, and sealed it with a bit of wax.

"Take this to Lord Aberdeen's secretary, Krieger Wilkes," he said. "And Mrs. McCord, don't make me regret this."

She took the letter. "You won't, Judge West." As she fled from the suite, Jessamine's mocking laughter pursued her.

She remembered Krieger Wilkes all too well from several receptions she'd been to. The tiny eyes, sharp as needles, the thick, perpetually wet lips, the mottled, pock-marked face. But it was not his physical appearance that repulsed her so much as the transparent lust she saw when he looked at her, his moist, chubby hands that seized every opportunity to come in contact with her.

Shiloh almost wished she hadn't rushed to his residence, a tawdry little apartment in Philpen Row, so cramped that he slept on a day bed in the sitting room. The smell of cigar smoke and stewed cabbage hung in the air and in the dark, water-marked drapes that covered the single window.

"Mrs. McCord," Wilkes said in his nasal voice. "What a pleasant surprise. Do sit down." He gestured grandly at a stained, musty-smelling chair as if it were a veritable throne.

Silently, Shiloh handed him Judge West's letter. He broke the seal and squinted at it. "Light's bad," he muttered. "I'll fetch my spectacles." He rifled through a drawer by the day bed. Shiloh's eyes widened at the sight of a small, ill-polished pistol, but she said nothing. Wilkes located his spectacles and read the letter. He laid it down on a table and approached Shiloh, circling her chair like a shark coming in for the kill.

Finally she spoke. "Can you help me, Mr. Wilkes?"

"I can," he said without hesitation. "A release order from me would give your husband immediate freedom."

Shiloh nearly wept with relief. "Thank you, Mr. Wilkes, I —"

"Not so fast, Mrs. McCord," he cautioned, sharp eyes glittering avidly. "I'll have to do no little amount of explaining to Lord Aberdeen if I decide to do this. Surely I'm entitled to some sort of modest payment."

"Certainly," she said quickly, reaching into her reticule. "Name your price."

"Oh no," Wilkes countered. "I wouldn't think of taking your money." His finger circled her shoulder, causing her to recoil against the back of the chair. "What I have in mind, dear lady, will cost you nothing to give."

She knew what he was asking. The idea made her insides roil with revulsion.

"I'm a married woman," she said, absurdly thinking

274

that Wilkes might have some hidden shred of decency.

"And I am a lonely man. A few hours of your company is all I ask. Surely that is not too high a price for your husband's liberty."

Shiloh's mouth was dry as cotton. "I—I can't—"

Wilkes shook his head regretfully. "Then I'm afraid I can't help you, Mrs. McCord."

She stared at the scuffed planks on the bare floor. "I'll stay," she whispered at last.

"I didn't hear you, Mrs. McCord."

She flung her head back, eyes seething with loathing. "I'll stay," she repeated more strongly.

His tongue flicked over his thick lips as they parted into a leering grin. Long yellow teeth gleamed in the lamplight. "Excellent," he said, rubbing his palms together. He extended a hand. "Come and sit on the bed. We'll be more comfortable there."

Shiloh obeyed, her every limb stiff with repugnance. As she seated herself, she noticed a stain on the pillow from the macassar oil Wilkes smeared on his hair.

"I'd like something to drink," she told him.

He seemed pleased at her compliance. "Of course. I've nothing for a delicate palate, but if you'd like some gin—"

"Gin is fine," she said quickly. The moment he turned his back, her hand snaked out, fingers closing around the drawer pull. It began to creak as she eased it open. Gritting her teeth, she forced herself to go more slowly. At last she slipped her hand inside and took out Wilkes's small pistol.

When he turned around from his pouring, she had it pointed squarely at his chest.

"Write the release order, Mr. Wilkes," she commanded.

His face fell. "Come now, Mrs. McCord, surely you wouldn't do murder just to avoid my company."

"It has been a very long, very frustrating day," Shiloh said slowly, her finger caressing the trigger. "I'm just about at my wits' end. Now, you can risk crossing me, and see what happens, or you can do what I say."

Grumbling a curse and something about uncivilized outlaws from Texas, he snatched up paper and quill and wrote out the order. Shiloh didn't lower the gun until he'd placed an official stamp on it. Then she directed a nervous Wilkes to the chair and snatched the paper. She extracted a key from the inside lock and locked Wilkes securely in his tawdry lair. As she fled down a flight of narrow, uneven stairs, she could hear the man's enraged shouts.

The driver who had borne her all day through London's maze of streets was nodding, nearly asleep. Shiloh jostled him roughly and pressed yet another coin into his hand.

"Newgate," she said. "And hurry."

Justin moved away from the dank wall of his cell to avoid the droplets of moisture that formed on the stones. The floor was little better, strewn with moldering straw that provided a haven for lice and other vermin.

Justin's cellmates were a rough assortment of petty gamblers and cutpurses. None of them was willing to challenge the tall, grim-faced Texan, although ordinarily there was a crude initiation to establish a pecking order.

The indolent, unwashed men accepted him with surprising tolerance, giving him his pick of the worm-infested biscuits and brackish water that was brought at intervals during the day. Then they pressed him for stories of Texas, tales of Indian wars and the struggle against the Mexican army.

At nightfall the talk subsided and Justin's thoughts returned to the predicament he'd landed himself in. Someone had betrayed his plan to Lord Aberdeen, that was the only explanation for his seizure. But the only one he'd told of his plan had been Duff Green. And Duff was as close-mouthed as they came. Suddenly he remembered the fleeting figure in the alehouse and grew rigid. That was it. Cursing his own stupidity, he slumped back against the wall.

It didn't matter now. What was important was getting the details of Aberdeen's plan to his superiors. Justin's request to send a message to Duff had been flatly, laughingly denied. The only hope was escape.

One by one, Justin's cellmates dropped off to sleep, curling against the damp chill beneath ragged blankets. Justin went to the heavy locked door. A brief examination told him he wouldn't be able to budge it. Then he went to the drainage grate in the middle of the cell. An unholy stench of sewage and rot arose from it, stinging his eyes. Grasping the iron grate, Justin pulled until his muscles quivered. At last the rusting metal gave. But the hole, too dark to see into by the glimmer of light from the corridor outside, offered no promise. It was too narrow for even a child to fit through, and there was no telling where the drain led.

But the grate itself would be useful. Much as he disliked the idea, Justin knew he must use it as a weapon against the next sentry who came to the cell. The heavy iron would probably kill a person, but he would avoid that if he could. He sat by the door, listening for hours, ready to spring up with the grate at the first sound of a key.

After what seemed like an eternity, he heard the jingle of a key in the lock. He stood, flattening himself against the wall, and raised the heavy grate high.

The door creaked open and a figure stepped into the

cell. Too late, Justin saw the lace of a petticoat and the fringe of a shawl. Unable to stop the downward momentum of the descending grate, he could only throw it aside.

But it wasn't far enough. The grate struck a glancing blow and the woman crumpled with a sigh to the floor.

As Justin dropped to his knees, he saw the mass of tight red-gold curls, so unique that they could only belong to one person.

"Shiloh," he rasped, "Oh my God—"

"A fine way to thank the lady," grumbled the night warden, who had followed Shiloh to the cell. "She went to no little trouble to get you released."

"Released? Oh my God," Justin said again. He cradled her head and felt the warm stickiness of blood on his hand. Feeling a pain like no other, he gathered her up and hastened from the cell.

The hastily summoned doctor rose from the bedside. "It's not grave, sir," he told Justin. "Your wife should come around shortly. And you look as though you could use a rest. Get some sleep; she's resting quietly."

Justin nodded and overpaid the doctor, and stayed beside Shiloh until dawn peeped coldly through the curtains. Finally, catching sight of his grimy, haggard face in the dressing table mirror, he went to clean up.

A few minutes later, a knock sounded at the door. Justin answered it, clad only in his trousers, thinking it was Duff. But Jessamine West sailed in instead, feasting her china-blue eyes on his bare arms and chest.

"So it's true," she said. "Shiloh really did manage to get you out of Newgate."

"I—she's been injured, Jessamine, and I'm tired as hell. Now, would you—"

Jessamine blinked in disbelief. "Injured! Don't tell

278

me that awful Wilkes hurt her!"

Justin's fists clenched. "What does Wilkes have to do with this?"

Her lips drew together in a pout. "Oh dear, perhaps I've said too much. She may not have wanted you to know how low she had to stoop."

"What's that supposed to mean?" Justin asked, but already he had some idea.

"Well, you know what Wilkes is like. But I'll leave it to Shiloh to tell you the details—if she's not too ashamed."

Justin felt himself growing taut with anger. "Jessamine, did you come here just to gloat, or do you have something else to say?"

She shrugged prettily. "I only wanted to remind Shiloh about the promise she made my father. But I'll let her tell you about that, too."

As she swept out, Duff Green entered, garnering a stare of pure loathing from her.

"Nice girl," he said wryly, extending his hand. "Welcome back, my friend."

"Thanks, Duff."

"I was all over London trying to get a release order for you. Should've known Shiloh would beat me to it. Smart lady, your wife. How'd she manage it?"

Justin didn't want to think about that. "I haven't asked her yet, Duff. I knocked her on the head with a drainage grate when she came to my cell."

Duff shook his head. "I won't ask for an explanation of that; I'm sure it would take too long. Is she all right?"

"I think so."

"Good. Because we've got to get the hell out of England. Our hosts might not be so hospitable to us now. There's a ship in Falmouth, the *Cutter's Way,* bound for the States. I'll have to miss that one; I've some business to do. But you and Shiloh had best be aboard it when it sails."

"We can be ready to leave in a few hours," Justin said. "Hire a good coach; I want Shiloh to be comfortable."

Duff nodded. Before he left, he asked, "Was it worth it, Justin?"

For the first time, Justin grinned. "Hell, yes," he said. "Wait till you hear."

As a pair of sleepy-eyed maids worked at packing their things, Justin sat beside Shiloh until she finally gratified him by opening alert, beautifully clear eyes.

"Justin," she breathed.

He pressed a kiss on her forehead. "It's me, sweetheart. How are you feeling?"

"Fine," she said, starting to sit up. Then she sank back down to the pillows. "My head feels terrible," she admitted. "What happened?"

Eyes full of remorse, Justin squeezed her hand. "That was my fault, Shiloh. You caught me in the midst of attempting an escape. I figured the first person through that door would be a guard. I'm sorry sweetheart. You don't know how sorry I am."

Shiloh was touched by his sincerity, the gentleness in his voice when he called her sweetheart. For perhaps the hundredth time, she regretted her recent behavior toward him.

"Justin?"

"Yes?"

"I'm the one who should apologize. I've been horrible to you about—about Jessamine. I know now what really happened that night. Can you forgive me?"

He smiled. "I can forgive anything you do." Even Wilkes, he added silently, vowing that he'd try to forget Jessamine's sly insinuations. "Are you well enough to

280

travel?"

This time she sat up and her head didn't swim. "Of course. Where are we going?"

"To Falmouth, on the Cornish coast. From there, on to Washington, in the District of Columbia."

Shiloh closed her eyes. "Good. I'm more than ready to be away from London."

A private coach, hired by Duff Green at considerable expense, bore them away from the smoky, muddy hive that was London. Reclining on one of the bench seats, Shiloh stared at the receding, hazy skyline dominated by the massive Tower and St. James's. It was a relief to be out on the open moorlands, where brown and green hills were layered on more hills, in a wavy line as far as the eye could see.

She knew she would never forget London's grandness and frivolity, the itinerant street-bands, Punch and Fantoccini, the noisy routs, the daily pageantry of parading guards and races. But there was nothing about the glittering life that called to her. More than anything, she longed for the quiet of the open sky over Texas, the trill of mockingbirds at twilight.

But she said nothing to Justin. He was obviously looking forward to Washington, that American capital on the Potomac. Texas could wait a few months more.

Falmouth was an interesting town, peopled by the ruddy, well-fed Cornish fishermen. It was set in a placid green harbor by gently worn hills. Houses crowded the shoreline, their steps slick with seaweed as the tides washed up to the foundations.

Before boarding the *Cutter's Way,* they dined on rich fish stew and soft bread at a seaside inn. Once again, Justin had his mind on business.

"I hope the London trip was worth it," he mused,

281

almost to himself. "I think it may have been. Nothing can stop annexation now. Any true American would rather die than see British ships blockade the Texas coast."

"You're right," Shiloh said. "I'd hate to think we went through all of this for nothing."

"Don't even think like that," Justin said.

"I won't. I'm proud of you, Justin. You've done the United States and Texas a great service."

Justin smiled in his new, gentle way. "Don't underestimate your own contribution, Shiloh. Not only did you charm the socks off half of London; you also saved me from being eaten alive by critters in Newgate Prison, so I could live to tell my tale."

Shiloh glowed with pleasure. "So you're not sorry I came, after all."

He tried to look severe. "I can't say I approve of your sneaking onto the *Falcon*, but it all worked out for the best."

Amiably, they boarded the *Cutter's Way*, an American ship that offered clean, snug cabins and a friendly crew. Captain Sobol, a middle-aged New Englander, was nothing like the slimy Christopher St. James.

Yet even the comfortable surroundings and the newfound peace with Justin couldn't cure Shiloh of her appalling seasickness. The minute they reached open water, the ship was buffeted by swirling, late-winter storms that tore at the sails and strained the ship's timbers almost to breaking. As days passed, the storms and squalls seemed to blend into one mighty tempest, offering not so much as a single breath of calm.

Shiloh shivered beneath layers of blankets, weak and wan, barely able to keep down the few sips of watery tea and broth that Justin pressed on her. Through a haze of nausea, she tried to show appreciation for his solicitousness, but could only smile weakly and mumble a word of thanks.

Only when the *Cutter's Way* had plowed through the roiling North Atlantic to the high shores of Newfoundland did the weather abate. At last, Shiloh could see the end of the weeks of seafaring torment. Her illness lessened somewhat, although not completely.

Justin made no demands on her whatever, even when she declared herself well enough to eat and have a cordial with some of the other passengers at the captain's table. At times Justin seemed almost too solicitous, still flailing himself for having injured her at Newgate. His attitude, so gentle and caring, puzzled Shiloh.

She found him one evening mending a shirt, his hands large and clumsy, frequently dropping the needle and pulling the thread into a frayed web.

"Really, Justin," she laughed, "I'm not so sick that I can't do that for you."

He raised an eyebrow at her. "Is that so? Seems to me I remember a little girl who stamped her foot at me and swore she'd never lift a finger on my behalf."

Shiloh felt herself blush. Only months ago, but it seemed like another place and time, another person.

"Back then," she said softly, "I had no desire to do any sort of favor for you." As she stood to take the mending from him, the ship lurched and she suddenly found herself in his lap.

Justin laughed, a low sound. "And now, Mrs. Mc-Cord?"

She snatched the shirt from him and tried to still the quaking of her body, the almost-forgotten response to his nearness. Grasping the side of the bunk, she righted herself.

Justin watched with great interest as she began to sew the torn seam. She was as inept as he, pulling the thread too tightly and making a pucker, or leaving it too loose, resulting in a gap. She looked up at him, glowering at his amused stare.

"I never said I was any good at this."

He placed two fingers under her chin and tilted her face upward. 'We're both hopeless. Fortunately, there *is* something we excel at." His eye, brimming with meaning, held hers as he took the mending and set it aside.

Shiloh was mesmerized by the passion etched on his face. All the old bitterness and misunderstanding fell away as Justin took both her hands and raised her to her feet. She whispered his name, softly, yearningly, and reached her lips up for a kiss.

It began gently, mouths brushing at first, and then their tongues meeting in lingering exploration. Shiloh felt herself melting against him, rocked from without by the shifting winter seas, and from within by a warm rush of awakening desire. She moved her hands over Justin's taut, rippling torso, burningly aware that he, too, was caught up in the intensity of the moment.

Swiftly, he unbuttoned her gown and bestowed a possessive caress on her passion-warm skin. Tender yearning flowed from his fingertips as they circled her breasts, finding their taut peaks firm and expectant. Encouraged, Justin sank to his knees in a worshipful stance to finish undressing her. The cool air tingled over her skin. Outside, she heard the sound of waves rising to slap the sides of the ship, curling in from some unknown deep place.

Spellbound by the sensations that rushed over her, Shiloh slid her fingers into the silky gold of Justin's hair, sighing out her restless hunger. Although she was more than ready for him, he made her wait, refusing to set her free until he'd driven her half mad with wanting.

His hands slipped around to cup the smoothness of her hips while his mouth moved covetously over her

284

flat, tightly drawn middle, his tongue flicking out suggestively. Then his hands continued their erotic journey, moving down the backs of her legs, lingering behind her knees until Shiloh gasped with pleasure. Then his fingers returned along a different path, up her inner thighs to her quivering center.

"Justin," she whispered, "It's been so long. . . ."

"Too long," he murmured raggedly, raising his head to the silken undersides of her breasts. Long moments ago, he'd cast aside Jessamine's ugly hints about Shiloh's dealings with Wilkes. Not even that man's sliminess could sully the sensual purity of his slender wife, dim her unflagging spirit, or her ardent response to his lovemaking. He wanted this time to be a cleansing experience for her, to reaffirm the unique, healthy bond that was growing inexorably between them.

His mouth and hands revered her smooth flesh, worshipped her beauty, and brought her shudderingly alive. Justin forced himself to take his time, even when she begged for him to stand and began loosening his shirt and trousers.

"Patience, sweetheart," he told her, grinning, but he found that his hands hurried to assist her.

Shiloh devoured him with her eyes, thrilling at the play of dim light from the portal, which highlighted the hard lines of him. Her hands went out to touch him, running over his large shoulders and down his rib cage, and then lower, until with a groan of male pleasure he drew her against him and settled them both down on the berth.

Crowded together, facing each other, their ardor grew like a gathering wave, moving ever closer to its unfurling. Justin continued to touch her tenderly, yet with searing provocativeness. His hand slid between her legs and she moved against him, her hips taking up the throbbing rhythm that pulsed through her. She wound her fingers into his hair and kissed him in the way she had learned from him, sliding her tongue along his lips and delving it into his mouth to let him know how she ached for him.

Justin accepted her invitation with a deep rumble of longing and pressed her back on the berth, to bestow his passion on her at last. He gathered himself up above her, his flinty eyes raking her reposing form, and then came to her like a great wave of strong maleness. At long last his thrusts set her free, sent her soaring as she cried out her joy.

As the *Cutter's Way* entered American waters, husband and wife were reunited with new tenderness, new understanding. Shiloh fell asleep content that night, her heart so full of hope for the future that she couldn't imagine anything coming between them again.

Shiloh found the town of Washington, rising from the marshes around the Potomac, to be a uniquely interesting place. There was an indolent, somewhat disheveled air about it, an atmosphere of impermanence and unreality, because the town had just one reason for its existence: to house the government of the American people.

Those charged with the task seemed a group of overly serious, self-important men, who loved to argue bombastically and air their grievances to any audience.

Her strolls with Justin through the city revealed an amazingly diverse population. There were many foreign visitors and government officials, stern judges and pious church ladies clutching Bibles to their bosoms, saucy young belles, Indians, and Negroes. Shiloh found all of them fascinating, unaware that she, too, garnered her share of attention.

"It's that flame-red hair," Justin teased as a young

urchin stopped playing at stickball to stare at her. "Or it might be those freckles on your nose."

She slapped him on the arm in mock anger. "He's probably looking at you, Justin, and thinking the town is being overrun by giants."

He left her at their lodgings at Brown's Indian Queen, sometimes called the Wigwam. "You'll have to take dinner alone. I have my first meeting with Mr. Upshur at the State Department."

Shiloh clasped her hands. "He'll be so pleased when you tell him what you found in England."

Justin nodded. "Not to mention what I know about our friend, Judge West."

Shiloh froze, seized by a chill that had nothing to do with the sharp February air. She'd been able to put the nightmare of her last day in London behind her, but now it resurfaced.

"Justin," she said, her whisper making little frozen puffs in the air between them. "You mustn't say anything about Judge West's activities in the Caribbean."

His eyes narrowed slightly, although he was still smiling. "Why not?"

"I promised West that you wouldn't ruin him. Please understand, Justin. You were in prison and I was desperate. The judge only agreed to help me when I made that promise."

Fury leaped to his steel-hard eyes and his jaw twitched dangerously. The mouth that had been smiling twisted into a sneer.

"So you struck a bargain with the judge as well as Krieger Wilkes. Is there anything else I don't know about? How else did you prostitute yourself, Shiloh?"

Before she knew what she was doing, her hand shot out and cracked against his cheek.

Justin didn't flinch; he didn't even move. As the

imprint of her hand formed on his skin, he gave her a last look of disgust and walked away.

Eyes smarting, Shiloh stared after him. A bleak February wind whipped up, scattering the scraps of an old broadside across the road. Shivering, Shiloh tore her eyes away from Justin's tall receding form and went into Brown's. Her appetite gone, she fled to the room they shared and flung herself onto the bed where they had lain so close every day for a week.

The bedding still held Justin's scent, mingling with her own. Punching the pillows, Shiloh cursed. She should have known that her contentment wouldn't last. How could it, with a man as pig-headed and insensitive as Justin? Instead of being grateful to her for getting him out of prison, he was angry at her for the methods she'd used. Of course she would have preferred not to deal with West and Wilkes, but what choice did she—

Wilkes. Shiloh frowned at the pillow. How had Justin known about that? No matter, she decided as she began flinging her things onto the bed. The sooner she got back to Texas, back to a life of her own, the better.

She was interrupted by a knock at the door. A young liveried black boy stood at attention.

"Miz Justin McCord?"

"Yes?"

He extended an envelope, clicked his heels, and left. Shiloh closed the door and looked at it. It was addressed to Mr. and Mrs. Justin McCord. Perhaps she should wait. . . .

"Nonsense," she said aloud, breaking the seal. It was for both of them. As she stared at the small engraved invitation, her eyes widened. She could hardly believe what she saw.

It was issued by Captain Robert F. Stockton, inviting them to a reception aboard the Navy's newest steam warship, the *Princeton*.

Shiloh clasped the card to her bosom. She'd read about the much-touted sloop-of-war, and knew that the reception would be no ordinary occasion. President Tyler would be in attendance, along with many of his cabinet. Dolley Madison, aging, but still the town's undisputed social arbiter, would surely make an appearance.

Suddenly, it didn't seem so important to flee to Texas. Shiloh would wait a day, for not even Justin's malice could stop her from pleading Texas's cause to the president in person.

Thirteen

Justin's meeting lasted the entire night. He cat-napped in Upshur's office and arrived back at the Wigwam in the early morning chill. He found Shiloh in her robe, sitting at the dressing table while she brushed her hair. With a pang, he saw her narrow back stiffen when she heard him come in. That, and the obstinate set of her jaw, told him that she hadn't softened.

During a break in his meetings, Justin had spent a long time wandering along the riverside, sorting out his feelings. His initial anger at Shiloh had dissipated. Anything she'd done had been for him, to win his freedom. She had subjected herself to West's manipula-tion and the grasping, slimy Wilkes, compromising herself in his interest

"I was wrong, Shiloh," he said in a low voice. He stood behind her and watched her reflection in the mirror. Her eyes were hard, like two emeralds. "I shouldn't have gotten angry at you; I should thank you for getting me out of that scrape."

Still she said nothing. He saw her grip tighten around her hairbrush. Kneeling, Justin pulled her around to face him. "I had no business getting angry," he continued. "But hearing what you promised West, coupled with what you had to go through with Wilkes, just set me off. I never considered myself a jealous man, but when I think of that bastard's hands on you—"

"What?" Shiloh broke her silence with loud disbelief.

"You don't have to feel badly about anything you did—"

Amazingly, she started to laugh. "Is that what you think, Justin? That I shamed myself with Wilkes to buy your freedom?"

Now he was confused. "I'm sorry I reminded you of it."

Shiloh shook her head. "You really don't know me, do you, Justin? How could you think for a minute that I'd let that unwashed lout lay a hand on me?"

"Then what—"

"Oh, he tried. But I don't think he counted on my finding his pistol and turning it on him."

As Justin digested this information, he pictured the scene in his mind. Shiloh, small and fierce as a wildcat, intimidating the hell out of Wilkes.

"I didn't know," he said, more regretful than ever now. "I thought it was something else." Shiloh lowered her eyes, but not before he saw the hurt he had put there.

"Why didn't you ask me? Better yet, why didn't you trust me?"

"I—"

"Never mind, Justin. Do you know about the reception today?"

He nodded. "Abel Upshur told me to expect an invitation. I hope you'll be wearing that gown you had for the Parsons' party."

"As a matter of fact, I am. Why?"

He placed an oblong velvet box in front of her. "I

291

thought these would go well with it."

She glanced up at him and then lifted the lid. An array of amethysts, shaped like teardrops, winked out from settings of black onyx.

"Oh . . ." Shiloh breathed, holding up the necklace to admire it. Justin fastened it around her neck and enjoyed her pleasure as she put on the matching bracelet and earrings.

She smiled up at him and his heart lurched. "Where did you find such beautiful things?"

"I found a clever jeweler, Levi Manning. These are one of a kind."

She looked troubled. "This must have cost you a fortune."

He leaned down and kissed her temple, savoring the light scent of honeysuckle that emanated from her hair and skin.

"Didn't you know? I'm a wealthy rancher from Texas."

Her face glowed. "Thank you, Justin. I had no idea you ever noticed any of my dresses." Then, suddenly, her lips trembled and he realized that the sparkle in her eyes was put there by tears.

"What's wrong, Shiloh?"

"You're making it very hard for me to say this, Justin."

He felt himself grow tense. "What is it?"

"I'm going back to Texas as soon as it can be arranged."

"Damn it, Shiloh, I told you how sorry I was."

"It's not just that. It—it's everything. We simply aren't compatible, Justin. Oh, we have our moments, of course, but there's no trust between us. I think it's best if we stay out of each other's way."

"The last time you said that, you ended up following me to London."

"I won't do anything like that again. I promise. I'll leave you alone, Justin."

At that moment, Justin knew he felt something for Shiloh, because his heart emptied out, leaving a great gulf of emptiness. Somehow, she had crept inside him through a back door and made herself part of him. The smart-mouthed little girl who had seized him last summer was now the woman who ruled his heart.

A curse erupted from him as Justin pulled Shiloh to her feet and crushed her against him, kissing her in the way he knew ignited her senses. With his probing tongue and insistent, roving hands, he didn't relent until he felt her weaken.

Just as she began to respond, he lifted his lips from hers. "I dare you, Shiloh," he growled, "to deny the power of what we have."

"I—"

"Don't leave, sweetheart. Things were just getting good."

"It won't last. It never does. We'll only hurt each other again."

"That's just the nature of—" Justin stopped, searching her face.

"Of what?"

Seeing the shadows of distrust still in her eyes, he shook his head. "This isn't a good time to talk about it. I've got a carriage coming around for us in a few minutes."

Heads turned to admire the striking young couple as they stepped aboard the *Princeton*. The steam warship was festooned with evergreens and ribbons for the tour up the Potomac. Every inch of wood and steel gleamed with polish. Glancing over at Justin, Shiloh saw none of the strain of their previous conversation on his

293

handsome, smiling face. She hoped that her attempt to conceal her jumbled feelings were as successful.

Apparently it was, for when she was presented to President Tyler, the little Virginian complimented Justin on his lovely wife. And many others, including Secretary of State Upshur, were lavish in their admiration of Justin himself.

"Finest agent we've got down in Texas," Upshur proclaimed, lifting his glass. "Your husband, Mrs. McCord, hasn't let a thing slip by. Thanks to him, we'll have an annexation treaty by year's end."

Shiloh leaned forward eagerly. "Do you really think so, Mr. Upshur?"

"Why, sure. And I'm not ashamed to admit it's been a dream of mine for many years. I'm just thankful that I'll live to see this nation made even greater by the addition of Texas."

"Hear, hear," murmured a few of his listeners, though not too loudly, for the Texas issue was not universally popular.

Miss Julia Gardiner, who was the widowed president's eager companion, took Shiloh's arm and steered her toward a circle of ladies.

"Are you enjoying your stay in Washington, dear?"

"Yes. This is my first visit here. I'm a native Texan."

Julia clasped her plump hands. "How interesting. Come, my dear, you must tell us all about it."

Shiloh would have preferred to tour the ship with the gentlemen, for she'd heard the *Princeton* was the best new fighting ship in the world, but she followed the lady docilely. She made a concerted effort to keep track of names and faces, but there were so many that she had to be content with a great deal of smiling and nodding. She found Dolley Madison utterly delightful, and readily answered a barrage of questions about the Texas frontier. She was sure that if she extolled her land's virtues well enough, Texas would win the ladies' favor. After a while, she escaped to the rail for a breath of fresh cold air and to listen to the band of musicians who had come aboard at Alexandria. It was a flawlessly bright, chilly day, the sky a scintillating blue. Along the shore, tenuous masses of ice were breaking away, being pulled round and round by a lazy current as they drifted downstream.

Every so often, a sailor would yell out, cautioning the illustrious guests to open their mouths and cover their ears in anticipation of the ship's guns firing. Shiloh felt a huge concussion of air as one of the long guns shattered a distant ice floe, which Captain Robert Stockton claimed was three miles away. It was an awesome spectacle as the ice was shattered into a cloud of flurries.

"Amazing, isn't it?" murmured a soft, cultured voice.

Shiloh turned to see a tall, striking woman of middle years, swathed in a fur cape, her silvering blond hair glinting with diamond pins. The woman smiled. She had, Shiloh noticed, extraordinary nostrils that flared expressively as she said, "I don't believe we've been introduced."

"Shiloh McCord," she said quickly, extending her hand.

"Why, how very intriguing. I, too, am a McCord. Perhaps you're from the South Carolina branch of my husband's family."

"No, ma'am. I come from Texas."

"I say, this really is odd. I have a son who—" The woman stopped abruptly, her eyes falling to Shiloh's hand, where Justin's crest ring glinted in the sunlight.

"You're Justin's wife," she said, her voice suddenly flat and toneless, her nostrils working.

"I am. And you are . . . ?"

"Caroline McCord. Justin's mother."

Shiloh didn't know what to say. She considered embracing the woman, but Caroline's eyes had grown cold as they studied her.

"I think—Shiloh, is it?—that we had best get to know each other."

"Justin's here. Don't you want to see him?"

Caroline's nostrils flared. "I haven't made up mind about that yet. Why don't the two of us talk?"

"Of course." Shiloh began to feel uncomfortable beneath the probing gaze.

"You said you're from Texas. When did your family migrate there?"

"Before I was born. My father was one of the earliest followers of Moses and Stephen Austin."

Caroline appeared to relax slightly. "Ah, so he was part of a select group."

Shiloh looked at her sharply. It was fast becoming obvious that Caroline McCord was groping for something respectable about the woman her son had married.

She was not about to color the truth to appease the woman. "Actually, Mrs. McCord, my father left Tennessee because he'd been convicted of drunken brawling. He didn't want to serve time and couldn't afford to pay for his freedom."

The older lady was genuinely flustered now. "Oh, my. Well, I suppose gentlemen do tend to overdo—"

"Mrs. McCord, my father isn't a gentleman; he never was. I wish I could tell you that I come from a fine, wealthy family, but I can't. My father was born to a sod farmer in Ireland. He came here as a boy because his family couldn't afford to feed him. And my mother was born to a serving girl and unfortunately had no father to give her a name. She died when I was a child."

Caroline staggered back against the rail, her nostrils working in earnest now. She had gone quite pale.

Shiloh knew she hadn't been touched by her description of her parents' poverty, but by the appalling fact that her well-bred son had actually married the spawn of such people.

"I don't mean to shock you," Shiloh said quickly. "But neither will I hide the truth about myself. I'm not ashamed of who I am. Now, don't you think it's time you said hello to your son?"

Caroline drew herself up. Although she was still breathing rapidly, she managed to weave her way through the milling crowd with an air of stateliness.

Angus McCord greeted Justin simply.

"Hello, son."

Justin turned from his inspection of the ship's great gun, called the Peacemaker. He was flooded by tidal waves of memories at the sound of his father's voice.

"How are you, Father?" he said, masking all emotion.

But as they shook hands, something very warm passed between them and they embraced, briefly, awkwardly.

"By God, it's good to see you, lad," Angus said. "It's been too damned long."

Justin nodded. "That it has."

There was still a strain between them, the remembered tension of harsh words and bitter arguments. But Justin could tell that the years had mellowed his father, just as they had tempered his own feelings.

"Your name is on everyone's lips today," said Angus, his chest rising with obvious approval. "You've done damned well for yourself in Texas."

"I get along."

"I should have known you would. You were a gawky lad of nineteen when you took off to fight the Mexicans. I figured you'd be killed in your first battle, you were so hotheaded and defiant of all authority. Maybe that was why I did everything in my power to keep you at the Willows."

Justin smiled at his father for the first time in nearly ten years. "I found out there wasn't room in Texas for hotheaded boys, so I grew up in a hurry."

"Well, I'm proud of the man you've become. I'd be prouder still if you'd forget what passed between us before."

Justin nodded, although secretly he wondered if his father would have welcomed him back if he'd been an utter failure in Texas. But now was not the time to probe those feelings. The two men found a quiet corner below deck to have a cigar and a glass of Stockton's free-flowing champagne.

"How are things at the Willows?" Justin asked.

"The last years have been excellent. The tobacco yield just gets better and better, in spite of the depletion problems most folks have had. Your mother has redecorated at least three times."

"Is she here today?"

"Yes. But let's talk a bit before we find her. I'm sure she's trading fashion secrets with the other ladies, and gossiping about the delectable Miss Gardiner. Tell me about Texas, son."

Justin sipped his champagne, savoring the taste as it moved down his throat. "Best thing that ever happened to me."

Angus laughed. "Maybe so, but staying on at the Willows wouldn't have given you those scars." He indicated the crescent-shaped mark on Justin's cheekbone and the more recent one on his temple.

"I've had a few scrapes."

"Indians?"

He nodded. "Comanches, Mexicans . . ." He

touched the small line on his temple. "And one hell of an ornery filly. I've got a horse ranch near Houston. It's not much of anything yet, but I mean to turn it into something big someday, when my work for the government is done."

"Any chance you'll come back to Virginia?"

"No. I have a new home now. Hell, I even got married."

"Married!" Angus roared, his rugged face alight with surprise and pleasure. "That's fine, lad. That's just fine. My God, tell me about her. You had every belle in Loudoun County at your feet, including, I might add, a perfectly charming young lady I myself selected for you. What sort of woman finally snared you?"

Justin grinned. "You'll see for yourself. She's with me today." He refused to think of what tomorrow would bring. "She's not like anyone you've ever met."

Angus slapped his thigh. "By God, what are we waiting for?"

They met on the lower deck. Caroline McCord, ever mindful of propriety, kissed Justin lightly on both cheeks, although her eyes were bright with tears.

"What a man you've become, my son," she murmured, marveling at his great height and the breadth of his shoulders.

"I see you two have met," Justin said. He took Shiloh's hand, missing her strained look, and drew her closer. "Shiloh, this is my father, Angus."

"How do you do, sir?" Shiloh found herself staring at an older replica of her husband. She saw the same handsome, sculpted cheekbones, the gunmetal eyes, the arresting smile and intriguing dimple. Angus's hair fell like Justin's in a straight blond shock over his forehead, although his was streaked with gray.

"Justin told me you were something special," Angus said, appreciatively eyeing her soft skin, the play of light over her curls, her narrow waist outlined snugly by the bodice of her gown. "I'm inclined to agree."

Shiloh felt her color rise. "Thank you," she murmured.

Angus turned to his wife. "I think this calls for a celebration." He signaled a steward, who was passing a tray of sweet whiskey punch.

Raising his cup, he said, "To all the McCords."

Shiloh looked from father to son. They both seemed so happy. She guessed that they had finally patched up their differences, and her heart swelled. Justin had rarely talked of his family, but now she knew it was because the estrangement had been painful.

Caroline then began speaking as if Shiloh weren't there. She spoke of neighbors, people Shiloh had never heard of, and expounded on the merits of a certain family in particular.

"The Grangers bought an adjacent plantation, so they're even bigger than us now. Do you remember young Conrad, Justin? He's at the university now. The boy always looked up to you. It was the greatest disappointment of his life that you didn't marry his sister Ivy."

Justin gave his mother a sharp look, which she ignored. "And speaking of Ivy, she never married. It broke her heart when you left. She went to Paris to study art, to try and forget."

"Mother—"

Now Caroline addressed Shiloh. "Have you ever been to Paris, dear? No, of course you haven't. I imagine your farm life keeps you quite busy. But a trip abroad is *de riguer* for every young lady of quality. Dear Ivy is *so* accomplished. Since her mother is ailing, she runs the house all on her own, and does it beautifully, I

300

might add. Why, even when she and Justin were courting—"

"That's enough, Mother," Justin snapped.

"No, Justin," Shiloh interjected. "Let her finish."

Only the slight flaring of nostrils betrayed Caroline's agitation. "All I'm saying, my dear, is that Ivy Granger was the perfect mate for Justin. She adored him, saw to his every need. And," Caroline gave her a meaningful look, "she was of his class."

"And I'm not," Shiloh finished for her. She placed her hand on Justin's sleeve and gave him a look that said she wanted to handle this on her own.

"You mustn't say that, my dear. But as Justin's mother, I'm naturally concerned about his happiness. I want to know that he has married wisely, and not just as an act of defiance against us."

"How very interesting," Shiloh said coldly, mimicking Caroline's genteel Virginia accent. "Justin married a woman who is the complete opposite of your Miss Granger, just to rebel against you."

Caroline made no attempt to deny it. "He always was a headstrong boy, wasn't he, Angus?"

"You're making everyone most uncomfortable, Caroline," said the older man. "Let's talk of something else."

As Angus was speaking, Shiloh moved away. She knew exactly what Caroline McCord was doing, and she wasn't about to allow herself to be ripped to shreds by the lady's velvet-sheathed claws.

"Excuse me," she said, tossing her head. "I'm sure you all have a lot of reminiscing to do. I think I'll go learn more about that big gun they call the Peacemaker. I believe they'll be demonstrating its firing power one last time."

Justin came after her, took her arm. "Shiloh—"

She shook her head and looked directly into his eyes.

"Go to your parents, Justin. Talk to them. Ten years is a long time."

Before he could reply, she hurried up to the deck.

Justin returned to his parents instead of following Shiloh, only because he wanted to set things straight with them.

"Shocking," Caroline McCord was saying. "Imagine, a woman going to a cannon firing. She'll be the only one there."

Justin stood stiffly before her, his limbs taut with rage. "What the hell do you think you're doing, Mother?" he asked, his voice deadly quiet.

She opened her fan and flipped it rapidly in front of her face. "Such language!" she scolded. "But I'll forgive you, son. I'm sure you've been under a lot of strain lately. It can't be easy living with a woman like that." She gave him a sorrowful look. "How could you, Justin? How could you marry that impudent little nobody—"

"You will apologize to Shiloh," he commanded, refraining from raising his voice.

Caroline's carefully pruned eyebrows shot up. "I shall do no such thing. Why, didn't you hear the way she spoke to me?"

Justin's icy stare never wavered. "Then we have nothing more to say to each other." He extended his hand to his father. "It was good to see you again. I'll write." He turned to stride away.

"Justin, wait!" Caroline called. Her eyes pleaded. "I didn't know you felt so strongly about it." For the first time, he saw his mother's haughty mask fall away, saw the vulnerable sad woman beneath.

"I wanted so much for you, Justin," she whispered, unmindful for once that there were many people around to witness her distress. "Perhaps that was where I went wrong. I tried to put my own ambitions before yours. I was so certain that I knew what was best for you that I never paused to consider what was in your heart."

Caroline hung her head. A strand of hair fell down along her cheek, but she ignored it. "When I learned about Shiloh, it was like the final blow, the final realization that you were your own person, and not what I tried to make you. Before that, I always clung to the hope that you'd come back to us, and settle down like we wanted you to."

She was weeping openly now, her pain naked. "There is another thing I must confess. I suppose it is the sin of all mothers that they do not want their love for their sons to be displaced. I knew you didn't love Ivy, and deep down, I was pleased. She was no threat to me."

Stunned by these revelations, Justin handed his mother a handkerchief and waited while she daubed at her face.

"Ah," she sighed, "but your Shiloh is a different story, is she not? You've found the one woman who can take my place. You love her deeply, and that is why I attacked her so maliciously."

Justin tensed. It was the first time anyone had given a name to what he felt for Shiloh. He gathered his weeping mother against him.

"There is room in my heart for both of you," he said hoarsely.

Angus approached, his voice gruff with emotion. "Well said, by both of you. Now, shall we go up and find Shiloh, and give her a proper welcome into the family?"

Although the *Princeton*'s master gunner was taking great pains to explain the power of the Peacemaker to his august audience, few were listening. The men clustered around the great cannon had gotten into a political discussion, as those in Washington were wont to do.

"It's a southern plot, I tell you," said Peter Shane, a congressman from New England. "They only want Texas to enter their immoral fold as yet another slave state. It's a well-known fact that Texans favor the disgusting institution."

"I beg your pardon, Mr. Shane," Shiloh said hotly, entering the knot of gesturing men, "but pray, where do you get your 'facts'?"

He turned to her disdainfully. "Young lady, this discussion is between knowledgeable men. I don't think—"

"Answer the lady, Shane," said Abel Upshur, smiling delightedly at Shiloh's boldness.

"He doesn't need to," Shiloh replied. "I wouldn't want him to make more of a jackass out of himself than he already has."

Her comment was greeted by a mixture of shocked gasps and appreciative laughter.

"I suggest you consider Texas a little more deeply, Mr. Shane," Shiloh continued. "Instead of worrying about the various states of the Union taking sides against one another, why not see how the addition of Texas would benefit all of you?"

"The question of slavery overshadows all other considerations," Shane maintained. "But of course, that is not an issue with you, is it, Mrs. McCord? You undoubtedly think human bondage is a way of life. Why don't you tell these gentlemen just how many slaves you own."

Spots of furious color appeared on her cheeks. "Mr.

Shane, I would no more own a slave than you would."
Then, remembering something she'd read in a Washington paper, she smiled coldly. "But perhaps that is not quite true. I understand that in your state you work children in clothmaking factories until they drop from exhaustion in front of their looms."

"Those people are not slaves," the congressman answered heatedly. "They are not forced to—"

"Of course, they are," Shiloh shot back. "They're slaves to the pittance they're paid for laboring under appalling conditions. Don't go spouting your accusations about Texans, Mr. Shane, unless you can defend your own brand of bondage."

She saw Mr. Thomas Gilmer, the secretary of the Navy, lean over to Upshur and quip, "If this is a Texas woman, what are the men like?"

Upshur laughed to diffuse the tension of the moment. "I think we'd best put this argument aside for now, and give our attention to this excellent officer and his fine gun."

"Hear, hear," someone murmured. Even Peter Shane seemed unwilling to tangle further with Shiloh. He backed off sullenly as the master gunner and his men prepared to fire the long gun.

Shiloh felt many eyes on her, and when she turned, she saw Justin and his parents some yards away, at the stern. From their faces, she could tell they'd heard the argument. Justin raised his glass in tribute, grinning broadly. His father had a look of amused devilment in his eyes. Although Shiloh expected righteous indignation from Caroline, she was amazed to see a softness in the lady's look, tenderness almost. She started toward them.

"You don't want to miss this, Mrs. McCord," said Thomas Gilmer, taking her arm. "It's a historic event."

She nodded. The McCords could wait. With a great

flourish, the master gunner gave the order and the cannon was loaded, powder and sulphur tamped in place.

"Stand ready to fire!"

"Ready, sir!"

"Fire!"

Sparks flew and the burn of sulphur filled the deck.

Justin was still thinking about what his mother had said. Love . . . was it possible? As he looked down at Shiloh, her face flushed and expectant as she clasped her hands, something touched him. What a beauty she was, she, who once had disdained herself as hopelessly plain. Her spirit shone through like a beacon, glowing, transforming that small, intriguing face into a visage of loveliness.

Suddenly his view was blocked by billows of acrid smoke. A blinding explosion followed, splintering wood and metal, filling the deck with flames.

Justin tore across the planks, instantly aware that the cannon had misfired. He waded through utter chaos to get to Shiloh. Men were screaming, cursing, begging for mercy as sailors rushed to douse the fire. A man ran past, his back in flames.

"The president!" someone shouted. "Where is the president?"

"He's all right; he was below."

Through thick, eye-stinging smoke, Justin stepped around unspeakable carnage. Bodies lay all around, riddled with debris, some torn and burned beyond recognition. Justin saw Abel Upshur, his friend, his mentor, left with only half his skull, most of it blown to pieces. He pressed on, eyes streaming and smarting, his fear growing with each passing second.

Finally he saw Gilmer's body, face down, a gaping,

bloody hole in his back. And beneath, a slim wrist, the onyx and amethyst bracelet gleaming.

A cry of anguish tore from his throat as he heaved aside the lifeless body of Thomas Gilmer, who apparently had thrown himself in front of her.

Shiloh's face, still and blackened by soot, had been burned and cut by debris. There were several places where fire and hot metal had seared through her gown, and a bloody stain, widening like a macabre blossom, on her skirt.

Heart hammering, Justin gathered up the limp form and bore her away, past a dazed and injured Captain Stockton, adding his bellows for help to the cacophony on the deck. The thunderstruck onlookers who had come up from below, including the shaken president, cleared a path for him to the stern. His parents, their faces drawn with worry, followed him.

As the *Princeton* steamed back to Alexandria, from where the injured would be ferried to the hospital in Washington, the agonized screams rose above the churn and hiss of the great engines. But Shiloh lay still, her faint pulse throbbing beneath the thin, blackened skin of her temple.

The ship's surgeon worked feverishly, applying bandages and tourniquets, shaking his head at several limbs which had to be amputated. At Angus's insistence, he hastened to Shiloh's side. Quickly, he assessed the burns.

"Superficial," he said curtly. "They'll heal." Then he removed the torn petticoats that Justin was pressing against the wound on her thigh.

The surgeon let his breath out with a quiet hiss. The gash was wide and long, a piece of metal having ripped through the flesh of Shiloh's leg. Blood seeped continually from deep within, soaking Justin's cloth.

"It'll have to be sewn," the doctor mumbled, "or she'll

bleed to death." He thrust a pile of clean linens into Justin's hands. "Here. Staunch the flow as best you can. I'll be around as soon as I can."

"Do it now," Justin snapped. "Good God, can't you see she's—"

"I've got to attend to the worst cases first, sir. Perhaps you can find someone else to cleanse and close the wound. It's a simple operation." The doctor moved away, leaving Justin gritting his teeth in frustration.

Shiloh moaned and moved her head from side to side. Justin soothed her brow with his hand.

"Hang on, sweetheart. Hang on. . . ."

Tears squeezed from her eyes. "It—it hurts—"

"Shh. Please, darling, don't try to talk."

She bit her lip and clung to his hand, her grip appallingly weak.

Suddenly Justin's mother was at his side. "We can't wait for the doctor," she said, flinging aside her elegant cape. "I'll do it."

Angus commandeered a cart of medical supplies as Caroline plucked off her gloves and rolled up the sleeves of her gown. She placed several thicknesses of toweling beneath Shiloh's leg and dipped a bandage into a basin of water. As she daubed gingerly at the torn flesh, she removed several tiny splinters from the wound.

Shiloh moaned again and began to thrash.

"Hold her still, Justin," Caroline said. "That bottle there, it's chloroform."

He held a cloth soaked with the stuff above Shiloh's nose until her lids fluttered shut and she lay still.

There was none of the glittering socialite in Caroline McCord as she began to work in earnest. Justin was confident of her skills; as the mistress of a huge plantation, she'd done more than her share of doctoring, from delivering babies to tending field hands who had been injured. With swift, deft fingers she threaded a small curved needle and began closing the flesh. With every stitch Justin winced, watching Shiloh closely to assure himself that she remained unconscious. The ooze of blood was slowing as a result of his pressing on the artery above the wound, and by the time Caroline was finished, it stopped. The jagged but neatly sewn cut stood out like an ugly black line on the pale perfection of Shiloh's thigh.

Caroline, who had worked steadily and with great concentration and precision, stood up slowly and collapsed against her husband.

"Well done, my dear," he said. "What's this? You're shaking."

Caroline gave Justin an agonized look. "I'm so sorry," she whispered. "So very sorry."

He frowned. "I'm sure you did an excellent job," he assured her.

Tears squeezed from her eyes. "No, it's not that. I just feel so responsible for this. Shiloh never would have gone to the gun deck if I hadn't been so monstrous to her." She crossed to Justin and took his hand. "You must let me make it up to her. Let me bring her to the Willows. I'll tend her myself."

A man approached. "Mrs. McCord?"

She raised her tear-stained face. "Yes?"

"I've been watching you. You closed that wound with great skill. I wonder, could you help me? My brother was injured in the explosion, and—"

Caroline drew herself up and wiped the tears from her cheeks. "Of course. I'd be happy to. Show me to him."

Angus and Justin watched her go. "She's a fine woman, your mother," Angus remarked.

Justin nodded. "I don't think I ever really understood her until today." He sat down beside Shiloh, pulling a blanket up around her. The voyage back to harbor lacked all of the frivolity that had characterized the trip upriver. Silence hung like a pall over the shocked passengers. President Tyler moved solicitously among the wounded and the grieving friends of the dead, offering comfort. Women wept quietly and the engines hissed on, until finally the warship, with twenty feet of its bulwark torn away, bumped and jostled its way home.

Shiloh opened her eyes and looked at Justin.

He dropped a kiss on her forehead. "You're going to be fine, sweetheart."

She gave him a thin smile and closed her eyes again.

Angus McCord's light-draught sailboat was an elegant microcosm of the opulence in which he lived. Shiloh was installed in a tiny sleeping area deep in the bow, surrounded by eiderdown pillows and comforters, her every need attended to by a silent, smiling black girl called Molly. A tiny portal gave her a shifting view of the tree-fringed shores of the river. Molly brought her a second cup of sweetened tea and she settled back, letting her mind go over the events of the previous day.

She barely remembered the explosion. Vague images of carnage, bloodied tufts of hair on a jagged piece of wood, blood crawling from an open mouth, Justin's agonized face as he came to her . . . it was like a waking nightmare, haunting her.

And it had changed her fate, like the shifting winds in the sails above. Instead of being aboard the southbound packet, on her way to Texas, Shiloh was couched in luxury as the sailboat bore her to the Willows.

At first, she had resisted going. There was something dreadful about having to face Justin's past, a past she was fast learning about in small snatches. Shiloh knew the differences would be glaring. His had been a pampered boyhood of tutors and well-bred belles, of elegant hunts and parties. In no way would Shiloh fit into that sort of life, even as a visitor. Her own rough-and-tumble upbringing simply didn't compare.

The curtain that separated Shiloh's tiny, cocoonlike bunk from the sitting area parted. Caroline McCord peeked in.

"Molly said you were awake. Did you sleep well?"

Shiloh's eyes took on a guarded look. She expected Caroline to pounce on her again with a few scathing comments. But then she realized that this was a different woman she was facing now. No longer haughty, Caroline's eyes were soft with concern, her features slightly drawn and fatigued.

"I feel fine," she said slowly.

"Shiloh," Caroline said, coming to her side. "I can't tell you how sorry I am about all that happened."

Shiloh nodded, fingering a tuft of eiderdown. "I'm sorry too . . . for Mr. Upshur, Mr. Gilmer . . . all those people who were killed."

"It was a great tragedy. But my dear, I want to apologize for the things I said. I had no call to attack you the way I did."

Shiloh searched the handsome face, and saw sincerity. "I'm sure it was a great shock to see Justin again," she said.

"I admit it was. And when I realized he'd married, I—I didn't stop to think. I felt so—so *betrayed*—"

Shiloh gave her a questioning look.

"I'm a foolish, sentimental old woman," Caroline continued. "When Justin left, I felt my world had ended. And then, in you, I found an outlet for all my anger. I was so afraid."

Shiloh couldn't imagine the commanding woman

being afraid of anything. "I don't understand."

"I know it's ridiculous, but I saw you as the person who took my son away from me, even though he went to Texas with no notion of marrying. In my mind, I saw you as a calculating seductress, after Justin for his wealth. But now I realize nothing could be further from the truth."

She took Shiloh's hand, smoothed a curl away from her cheek. "You wouldn't have recognized Justin when he left The Willows. He was so young, so terribly restless. He had a reputation for recklessness and was fast becoming notorious in Loudoun County. It was as if he were seeking something and couldn't find it. When he learned an expedition to Texas was being organized, he jumped on it.

"My dear, you, and the country you call Texas, have accomplished all that I could not. Justin is a fine man, a responsible person, and he seems very happy. Someday, perhaps, you'll understand how hard it is for a mother to face her own failure."

Shiloh felt a wave of sympathy for the older woman. She squeezed her hand. "You haven't failed, Caroline. It was your influence that made Justin the man he is. You gave him the strength and courage to strike out on his own, to make a successful life for himself."

Tears filled Caroline's eyes. "I don't deserve to hear these things from you, Shiloh. You're far too kind." She hugged the girl gently. "No wonder Justin loves you so."

Shiloh pulled back, stiff with shock. Never, in her deepest imaginings, had she ever dared think that Justin might feel something like love for her.

"What is it, dear?" Caroline asked. "Is your leg—"

"No, it's not that. Caroline, did Justin explain to you the circumstances under which we were married?"

"Why, no. Surely it's all legal."

Shiloh nodded. "But Caroline, I think you should

know that Justin and I were virtual strangers when we wed. I don't want to disappoint you, but love never figured in it at all." She smiled ruefully, remembering how she'd fought him.

"That's not so uncommon," Caroline insisted. "It's often the case. It takes time, and great patience, for love to grow. It needs to be nurtured, like a fragile seedling."

Shiloh grew pensive. Although her relationship with Justin had had its glorious moments, she knew that she had never done a single thing to foster tenderness. On the contrary, she'd deliberately tried to drive a wedge of bitterness between them more than once.

"Thank you, Caroline," she said softly, "for explaining things to me. I said Justin and I were strangers when we married. We still are, in many ways, but I feel I know him better now."

"I'm proud, Shiloh. Proud to have you as a daughter-in-law." Caroline touched the bandaged burn on her face. "When I think how close we came to losing you, I just want to die."

"I'll be fine, thanks to you. Justin told me what you did."

There was movement above, a few shouted commands. Caroline's face brightened.

"We're home," she said, clasping her hands. She spoke the word like a prayer.

Shiloh sat forward, trying to catch a glimpse of Justin's boyhood home. But all she saw was a stand of leafless gray poplars, the wooden stilts of a dock, and beyond, perhaps, a manicured lawn.

"The view from the river is so grand." Caroline left the bunk. "Just a moment."

Seconds later, Justin arrived. He was grinning broadly, and looked incredibly handsome. His color was high from the chill February air, his hair tousled

313

about his head.

"My mother thought you'd like to come above for the landing," he explained. As he spoke, he swept her up into his arms, feather comforter and all, wrapping her securely against him.

Shiloh gasped at the shock of his nearness.

"Did I hurt you?" he asked, his brow knitting with concern.

"No," she said, trying to collect herself. "And I can walk on my own."

"I won't hear of it," Justin said good-naturedly. "Besides, my mother would probably take a lilac switch to me."

Laughing, Shiloh gave in and fastened her arms around his neck. She smelled the wind in his hair, and suddenly she had a feeling of such sublime contentment that it was almost frightening. She felt as if nothing could befall her so long as she was in Justin's arms.

A crystalline sky greeted them as they emerged from the cabin.

"There it is, Shiloh," Justin murmured, his voice husky with emotion. "The Willows."

Fourteen

She couldn't take it all in at once. Never had she seen anything so grand. Willow trees, the hallmark of the plantation, were in evidence everywhere, dipping their slender branches into the river, standing protectively above a large, stone springhouse, bending over a small, high meadow. Higher up, evergreen holly bushes led the way to a white gazebo and along paths to dozens of neat, regular outbuildings. In the distance were the fields, brown corduroy-plowed earth stretching for what seemed like miles.

At the center of it all was the house. Shiloh had known to expect some measure of wealth from the McCords, but nothing could have prepared her for what she saw.

White columns rose majestically in front of a long, railed verandah. Dozens of windows, covering three stories, looked out over the lawn. The gabled roof made the single structure look endless, like a many-faceted jewel. Even in winter, devoid of the color of flowers, the house sat in stately serenity.

"Justin," Shiloh breathed. "It's magnificent."

"You like it?"

"Why—" Did she? Or was she merely overwhelmed by the grandeur of The Willows? No, there was definitely something about the place that drew her to it, even if it was only curiosity.

"Yes, Justin," she said. "I do."

"You can stay as long as you like."

Shiloh laid her head upon his shoulder and watched as the sailboat was greeted by a half-dozen black men who scrambled down to help with the mooring.

Both Angus and Caroline were watching Shiloh expectantly. Noticing them, she smiled.

"You have a lovely home," she told them, raising her voice above the babble of the scurrying men.

"You're welcome here," Caroline said. "This is your home, as well."

Shiloh looked again at the plantation house, and wondered if she could ever call such a place her home.

Justin insisted on carrying her, even when she protested that surely she should be allowed to walk on dry land.

"I'm not about to let you undo some of my mother's best stitchery," he laughed. On a more serious note, he added, "Don't underestimate that gash on your leg, Shiloh. I've seen men die of lesser wounds."

"I'll take care," she said, not at all reluctant to remain safe in his arms.

The house servants had lined up in the grand entranceway to welcome the family. They stood, smiling but decorous, obviously trying to hide their amazement at seeing Justin again.

But he would have none of it. Setting Shiloh gently on the black and white marble floor, he faced them, arms akimbo, trying—and failing—to look stern.

"Nine years," he boomed, "and this is the welcome I get?" He opened his arms to the slender, graying black woman at the head of the line, scooping her up and twirling her about.

"Miranda, my love, you're still a beauty, and I'll bet you've still got the sharpest tongue in Loudoun County!"

They embraced, and were quickly joined by the others. There was a great deal of laughter, dozens of questions, sincere embraces.

And then Justin presented Shiloh to the staff. "Ladies and gentlemen," he said grandly, "my wife, Shiloh, from Texas."

Shiloh flushed with the unabashed warmth of their greeting, and also from self-consciousness. She was sure she looked wretched, with her face bandaged and her hair singed, her clothes rumpled from travel. She knew that the maids and cooks and houseboys were slaves, but at this moment she felt herself part of a great, extended family, a feeling that was alien to her.

Gradually, the entranceway emptied as the servants went back about their duties. Caroline insisted that Shiloh was to go to bed at once, and showed her up a long, wide staircase.

"Justin's room is just as he left it," she explained on the way up. Shiloh followed slowly, gazing at a series of portraits of still, stern-faced McCord men and women. At the top, she hesitated, staring in wonderment at the last painting.

There was no mistaking Caroline, who had been tall and aristocratic even in her youth. Posing before a blooming garden, graced by willow trees, she stood with her hands upon the shoulders of a young boy.

Justin. Shiloh didn't know why she was surprised by his appearance, but she was. He had been a child of unutterable beauty. A face that was now hard and sculpted had once been sweetly rounded. The piercing eyes of steel had been, in younger years, soft, almost dreamy. The one feature that hadn't changed was

317

Justin's hair. The artist had caught it in a moment when the breeze had lifted silken strands that gleamed in the muted light. It looked so real that Shiloh had the urge to stroke it, to put the strands back in place.

"That's a great favorite of mine," Caroline said, noticing Shiloh's interest. "Justin was eight at the time it was done."

"He was beautiful. You both were."

Caroline nodded. "You can see why I was so possessive of him." They went down a long paneled hallway and stepped into a bright room.

Again, Shiloh was transfixed by the remnants of Justin's past. The wide alcove bed where he'd slept in his youth, had perhaps lain dreaming about the man he would become. The double-doored clerk's desk where perhaps he'd labored with his tutor over his studies. A shelf of books, from schoolboy's primers to agrarian manuals. And on a small seat at the recessed window sat a frayed and faded skin horse, missing one of its button eyes.

Caroline mistook Shiloh's silence as she moved about the room, touching a wooden chest, gazing out the window at a spectacular view of the lawn and river.

"There are other guest rooms, if you'd prefer," she suggested.

"Oh no," Shiloh said quickly. "This will be quite comfortable."

"It will be time for dinner soon. Shall I have something sent up?"

"I'd rather come down, Caroline. Really."

"Very well. Ah, here's Molly. She'll be your maid."

As Caroline left the room, Shiloh smiled at the shy-looking, pretty little maid. She was dressed crisply in a dove-gray dress with white apron and cap, and had enormous, doelike eyes.

"I'll just be unpacking your things, Miz Shiloh," she

said in a soft, musical voice. Shiloh was immediately charmed by her. As Molly worked, she went into the dressing room and found a small table with a hand mirror on it.

As she'd suspected, her appearance was appalling. She loosened the bodice of her dress and gingerly lifted a bandage. The burn on her shoulder was worse than the one on her face, livid and blistered, beginning to ooze. There was a small cut on her chin, still more on her arms. Finally, Shiloh raised the hem of her skirt and pulled aside the dressing on her thigh. The wound looked horrid, puckered around the macabre black stitches. Shiloh buried her face in her hands, feeling as if she'd been through a great battle.

"Miz Shiloh?" Molly's voice intruded softly.

"Yes?"

"This here's Bethany. She does some doctoring. She brought some of her things."

Shiloh looked up to see a ponderous woman with large strong hands and bright white teeth. She smoothed down her skirt. "I—I was just looking at myself. I'm a horrible sight."

"Now, you never mind that, missy," Bethany said briskly, bringing in a tray of bandages and a fragrant-smelling potion in a tin cup, some potted salves and poultices. "Don't worry 'bout being modest with me. Let's get you cleaned up."

Shiloh surrendered to Bethany's deft but tender ministrations, trying not to wince as her burns and cuts were cleansed and dressed. Bethany ended by giving her a cup of strong chamomile tea, which Shiloh drank as Molly helped her dress for dinner.

She chose a simple, soft gown of gray merino, one that didn't chafe her wounds. Molly worked patiently with her curls, artfully tucking away the singed strands and concealing them with combs.

Shiloh thanked her sincerely, admitting that she looked and felt much better. She heard a bell ring somewhere in the house.

"That'll be dinner," Molly said. "Wait here. I think Mr. Justin'll be up to fetch you."

Shiloh seated herself at the window ledge, watching the play of evening light across the river's slow-moving water. A movement off to the side caught her eye. It was Angus and Justin, galloping up the lane on two of the finest-looking horses she'd ever seen. Their black flanks gleamed in the amber light, their hooves thudding on the packed-earth track.

There was something about the two men that touched a tender note in her heart, a deep cameraderie that, even from a distance, she could see. They were so alike, they of the flashing grins and dimpled cheeks, the careless grace with which they moved. Shiloh knew there was real love between them and felt a wave of satisfaction at their reconciliation. As they slowed their horses and came up the curving drive, she couldn't help thinking of her own father.

After an absence of many years, Justin and Angus were closer than she and Nate had ever been. She tried to swallow the lump that rose in her throat, a sharp pain born of all the years of unloved and unloving emptiness she'd shared with her father.

Perhaps if she'd been different, a better daughter to him, he would have shown her some affection. *Affection.* It was something Shiloh hadn't even known she'd craved until she had experienced it with Justin.

He'd taught her so much, so many painful lessons. It was no wonder she fought him; every time they got close, she learned more about her own inadequacies. Yet she couldn't hate Justin for what he showed her.

In the drive below, he dismounted and, smiling, tossed the reins to a waiting groom. As Angus did likewise, Justin looked up and saw her in the window. His grin widened as he waved. Shiloh raised her hand to the cold windowpane, and waited in pensive silence for him to come to her.

As February slid into March, Shiloh spent her days at the Willows couched in luxury. The languorous passage of time was marked by lazy hours of bed rest, with a book from Angus's vast library in hand, gentle pampering by Molly, delectable meals created by the talented kitchen staff.

Bethany's daily visits were something Shiloh looked forward to. The friendly woman was full of stories and earthy good humor, always ready with her big-toothed smile.

The day came when Bethany announced the leg wound clean and free of infection. "The worst is over, missy. I was looking for the bad fluids, but they never came."

"You and Caroline have taken such good care of me."

Bethany nodded and took out a tiny pair of scissors. Frowning as she worked, she carefully removed the black stitches one by one. Shiloh gripped the bolster she was resting against and gritted her teeth. The sight of her own flesh being tugged this way and that, the tiny pricks of needle-sharp pain, caused her to close her eyes.

"Not so different from your husband, are you, missy?" said Bethany without looking up.

"What do you mean?"

The large shoulders shrugged. "Sitting there, grinding your teeth, when you really want to cuss me to high heaven. Mr. Justin was the same way. He wasn't but twelve years old when he broke his arm falling out of a tree, that big willow down yonder. Didn't make a sound as I was setting the dad-blamed thing, squeezed his eyes shut so tight that nothing could come out."

"I'm sure this doesn't compare to having a broken arm set."

"He was a good boy," Bethany reminisced, cleansing the cut after she'd finished removing the stitches. "Not a mean streak in him, but jackass stubborn and so dad-blamed honest he'd put a preacher to shame. That was the one thing that got him mad, when he saw an injustice being done. Boy was just fourteen when he punched out the overseer for whipping a field hand. I guess that's why he went to fight the Mexicans down in Texas."

"He hasn't changed," Shiloh said softly, seeing yet another facet of her husband.

He appeared just as Bethany finished her visit, giving a last satisfied look at the fast-fading burn on Shiloh's face.

Shiloh raised her hands to his, feeling the dry chill of the March air on his rough skin. His color was high with vigor, his smile natural and appreciative of the new silk bed gown Caroline had given her.

"You're amazing," he said, sitting on the edge of the bed.

She cocked her head. "How so?"

"You're mending so fast. But I guess that shouldn't surprise me. You're too damned bull-headed to sit still for long."

Shiloh smiled at his speech. More than once, Caroline had lamented Justin's adopted Texas mannerisms, although she was more amused than offended.

"This is all so foreign to me," Shiloh said, "being waited on hand and foot. I haven't lifted a finger since I arrived at the Willows."

Justin sat forward, searching her eyes. "Do you like it here, Shiloh?"

322

"I—It's lovely. But I feel so useless."

Again he gave her that heart-melting smile. "Idle, maybe, but not useless. Besides, I'd say you earned a rest."

Shiloh found herself wishing, as she had many times lately, that he would pull her into that familiar rough embrace, the one that excited her beyond measure and made her feel wanted and whole. But Justin had been unusually tender with her, his infrequent touches light, almost impersonal. Even when he slept beside her at night she was aware of a certain restraint.

It was because of her injuries, Shiloh told herself. Or was it? Looking down at his broad, well-shaped hands, she wondered. Before the fateful day on the *Princeton*, things had been strained between them. She'd had plans to leave; he was still smarting over her promise to Judge West. Perhaps, slipping back with incredible ease into the role of gentleman planter, Justin had become aware of the glaring differences that separated them.

"What are you thinking?" he asked gently.

"I . . ." A dozen questions popped into her mind, but Shiloh wasn't ready to hear the answers. "I was just thinking I'd like to go out for a walk."

He jumped up, pleased with the notion. "I'll send Molly to get you dressed."

There was a narrow, winding path along the river, where the tight-budded trees bent over in a natural arch. Squirrels trilled and scolded as Justin and Shiloh strolled beneath, savoring the sharp air and sensing, only faintly, the promise of the coming spring. A duck shot up from the reeds at the water's edge, its wings bearing it westward, toward the setting sun.

"Are you glad to be home, Justin?" Shiloh asked,

watching the duck's graceful flight.

"This place was my whole life, my whole world once upon a time. I feel like I'm a part of it, or maybe it's a part of me."

"Everything is so perfect here, so well-ordered and neat." Shiloh smiled slightly. "No flooding bayous or Indian raids, no foreigners peddling their influence."

"We're a long way from all that, Shiloh."

She studied his profile, the play of dappled golden light in his hair. "Yes," she said. "We are."

They walked on in silence for a while. Justin showed her a tiny, bubbling spring and a pool so clear that the rounded, colorful pebbles were visible in sharp focus. They doubled back past a glade of alders and took a higher path back to the house.

Caroline hurried in from the front parlor to meet them. "It's good to see the roses in your cheeks again," she declared, taking Shiloh's cloak and handing it to a maid. "Did you enjoy your walk? You were gone nearly two hours; I was beginning to worry."

"Was it really that long?" Shiloh asked. "It didn't seem like it." Time with Justin always flew by.

Caroline led the way back to the parlor. "Come sit by the fire, where it's warm." She poured sherry from a crystal decanter for Shiloh and herself and handed Justin a small glass of whiskey.

"We've had an invitation," she said excitedly. "Several, in fact. It seems the news of your homecoming has spread quickly." Caroline gave Shiloh an apologetic look. "I've declined most of them, of course, not wanting you to be under a strain. But you seem so well now, I thought we might go calling next week."

"That would be fine," Shiloh assured her.

"I thought so," the older lady said, clasping her hands. "I'm sure you're used to much more activity." She turned to Justin. "The Fairfaxes are hosting a hunt, complete with breakfast and races later."

"The Fairfaxes?" Justin frowned slightly. "I don't know, mother. I'm not sure I want everybody gawking at Shiloh all day."

"Don't be silly," Shiloh chided. "Of course people will gawk. After all, I'm your new wife from Texas. We'd be happy to go, Caroline," she finished, ignoring Justin's dubious look.

An early morning frost clung whitely to the meadow grasses and hedgerows along the river road. Justin took Shiloh's hand and tucked it into the crook of his elbow as the carriage bounced northward to the Fairfax plantation, a good-sized farm.

The side of her face that had been burned was turned to him, and he was gratified to see that her skin had returned to its usual perfection. She wore a high-necked blouse with her riding habit, which concealed the still-visible scars on her neck, shoulders, and arms.

To the casual eye, she looked very delicate, a fragile little thing, but Justin knew better. The dainty exterior concealed a will of pure steel. A lesser woman would be eaten alive by the honey-voiced planters' wives today, but Justin had no such fears for Shiloh. Still, he wished she hadn't agreed to this outing. He knew firsthand that the youngest Fairfax daughter, Virginia, had a mean streak in her a mile wide. Years ago, Virginia had made life miserable for Ivy Granger, and she probably hadn't changed.

A half-dozen coaches were already in the circular drive in front of the house. As Justin handed Shiloh down, he caught a waft of her honeysuckle scent. He'd dispatched a rider all the way to Alexandria for that soap, although Shiloh wasn't aware of it. She was a hard woman to buy gifts for, appreciative of jewels and ornaments and clothes, but not sentimental about them. The soap was the only thing Justin knew that she craved, and her pleasure was well worth the trouble of getting it.

The hunt was being organized around the back of the house. Hounds bayed and strained at their leashes, and were subdued by a pair of heavy-handed slaves. Justin didn't care much for the useless sport, but didn't mind a lively morning ride. He hailed his groom, who'd brought his horse from the Willows.

Shiloh looked around at all the activity. "So many people," she breathed, and then laughed. "You'd think an army was being mustered, all for the sake of pursuing a little fox."

Justin squeezed her hand. "It's a way to pass the idle winter months, I suppose. Come. Let's get the introductions over with." He hesitated for a moment. "Maybe you'd better avoid the topic of politics today, Shiloh. People — even the women — tend to be easily offended around here."

He felt Shiloh stiffen slightly. "I'll do my best to behave," she said, a distinct chill in her voice.

Cursing his careless choice of words, Justin said, "Damn it, Shiloh, I didn't mean — "

But there was no time to finish. Like a flock of chattering birds, the company descended on them, full of hearty greetings and curious stares. Justin's hand was shaken, his back slapped, his cheek kissed by several women. He tried to keep Shiloh at his side, but she was swept away by the women, already speaking animatedly to a rapt audience.

Angus caught his eye and winked broadly, and Justin had to grin. They both had the same opinion of Shiloh. She'd hold her own in any crowd.

The hung began with much fanfare, the blowing of horns, the singing of "John Peel." Before he spurred his horse after the frantic hounds, Justin looked back at Shiloh. Seeing him, she tossed her head impudently and turned away.

It was like London all over again. Insulated on their elegant plantations from the outside world, the ladies begged for tales of wild Indians, Mexican desperados, the rough frontier life of Texas. Shiloh complied, hoping to temper the women's view of her country without detracting from the decided mystique of it. As she spoke of the wild land, trying to find words to describe the dusty plains, the endless prairies, the wide starry sky at night, she was amazed at the longing she heard in her own voice. It had been nearly five months since she'd left the shores of Texas. For all its ruggedness and discomfort, she found herself wishing for the buzzing of cicadas, the sight of a buffalo herd grazing amid bluebonnets in the hill country.

"Imagine," breathed a girl called Helen, clutching her bodice with exaggerated drama, "living on the very fringe of the civilized world. You must be constantly fearful."

"Not really," said Shiloh, trying to hide her displeasure at the girl's remark. "I'm usually too busy to worry about things I can't do anything about."

"Besides," said another, the Fairfax girl called Virginia. "Shiloh is Justin's wife. What better protection could she ask for?"

Shiloh had taken an immediately dislike to the raven-haired beauty. Just before they were introduced, Virginia had been berating a houseboy, twisting his ear until the lad cried out.

Coolly, she said, "I don't need a protector; I never have."

Virginia pursed her pretty lips and swept her eyes

disdainfully over Shiloh. "I don't guess you would," she said smoothly. "But tell me, my dear, how *did* you come to marry Justin?" She directed a scathing glance at pretty, shy little Ivy Granger. "Lord knows, a number of us tried to snare him."

Shiloh couldn't help laughing. "If I told you how we wed, you'd never believe me. We were introduced — sort of — by a judge. Soon after, it was apparent that marriage was inevitable." She allowed her listeners to draw whatever titillating conclusions they would from that, and deftly turned the subject.

"These pumpkin cakes are wonderful, Mrs. Fairfax. You must tell me how they are made." She was, of course, a complete stranger to kitchens and cooking, but she listened carefully and let the attention ebb away from herself. Justin would probably be pleased to hear her speak of domestic things, she thought ruefully.

Some time later, the hunters returned on winded, steaming mounts. They had not even a small field mouse to show for all their efforts, but they were in high spirits, nonetheless. Coffee laced with brandy was served, and the company sat down to the lavish hunt breakfast.

The meal was a delicious profusion of local specialties. Tender biscuits slathered with fresh white butter, thick slabs of cured ham, mountains of fluffy eggs, and trays of sweets graced every table and were consumed with ravenous good cheer.

Justin and Shiloh were seated at an oval table with an elderly couple, the Boyds, a timid young solicitor called Hamilton Pruitt, Virginia Fairfax Holmes and her stodgy-looking husband, Emory, and the quiet Ivy Granger. Shiloh guessed that it was no accident that Ivy was included in the group. Virginia tried her best to dredge up old memories.

"It was that ball in Richmond, surely you remember

it, Ivy dear. You were so afraid that Justin wouldn't ask you to dance, and then when he did, you ran off with a sudden fit of the vapors!"

Ivy blushed down at her plate and Shiloh directed a look of pure venom at Virginia. Then, pointedly, she turned to Mr. Boyd and asked him about his fine yacht, which was sitting down at the docks. His long-winded explanation of the craft's virtues dispelled the tension Virginia had tried to create. Under the table, Shiloh felt Justin's knee press against her. When Mr. Boyd had exhausted the subject of boating, she asked Ivy about fashion, complimenting her on the lovely, understated style of her pink dress. By the time the meal ended, the small group was relaxed. Even the fearful Pruitt did his share of talking, and showed unmistakable interest in Ivy.

As the gentlemen went to retire for a while with their pipes and cigars, Justin ran his hand across Shiloh's shoulder.

"Well done," he murmured. "You left Virginia flat on her face. But I think she's gone to the powder room to sharpen her claws."

Still rankled by his earlier remark, Shiloh moved away. "I'm glad I haven't shamed you, Justin. But remember, we've the rest of the day ahead of us."

There was a long period of lazy rest after breakfast, the men at their smoking and the ladies discussing needlework in the morning room. Shiloh grew restless and bored, and was more than happy to don her cloak and follow the company outside for the races.

A pavilion had been set up and a track marked off in a field. The betting was lively, and Shiloh quickly surmised that Justin, on his excellent midnight stallion, was the clear favorite. No one was surprised when the expertly handled horse won by a length and a half.

"Do the Texans favor racing?" Ivy asked, watching as

Justin claimed his prize, a silver cup overflowing with champagne.

Shiloh nodded. "Most holidays are celebrated with riding. There are a lot of stunts and rough games on horseback. The Mexicans have one in which the riders try to capture a greased rooster."

"How positively barbaric," said Virginia. "And silly."

Shiloh shrugged, refusing to be nettled. "No sillier than chasing all morning after a single small fox."

Virginia tossed her raven head. "That is a time-honored sport. A sport of kings and nobles. There is simply no comparison."

Shiloh and Ivy, who stayed close to her newfound ally, ignored Virginia as the races continued. There was more eating and drinking afterward, and then a shooting match. Markers were set up at various distances, and shot at with dueling pistols. The wagering became more outlandish as more champagne was imbibed.

Finally Malcolm Boyd, a son of Shiloh's breakfast partner, declared that he would destroy six champagne bottles in a row, and defied anyone to dispatch the targets more quickly.

Shiloh couldn't stand sitting by and watching any longer. She sought out Justin's groom and whispered a request. The lad appeared shortly with a stout case. Taking it, Shiloh approached the open-air gallery. Her color was high, and a breeze lifted her curls as she faced the cocky Malcolm.

"I'll take you up on your challenge, Mr. Boyd," she said, catching sight of Justin's devilish grin in the background.

"Ah, our little guest from Texas. Will your husband be your champion?"

"I'll do my own shooting." A murmur rippled through the crowd, and then more wagering started

330

up. The odds were lopsided, favoring Malcolm heavily. Six more bottles were set up on the fence.

Malcolm steadied his two pistols and watched while Shiloh drew hers out.

"What the devil is that?" he demanded, staring.

Shiloh lifted the heavy pistol, loading it as she spoke. "It's a Walker Colt," she explained. "Very new. I believe my husband brought it along to show you gentlemen. I hope he'll forgive me for upstaging him."

Justin nodded and leaned indolently against the back of a chair. Shiloh had almost hoped he'd be angry, but he gave her a wink of encouragement.

"This chamber allows for six shots," she continued. "Useful for fighting Indians on horseback, I'm told."

"Just a minute now," Malcolm began, but a barrage of catcalls silenced his protests.

"Let the lady shoot!" "You gave the challenge, Boyd!" "Get on with it!"

Even before Malcolm got off his second shot, Shiloh had laid waste to all six of her targets. A cheer went up, and her victory was vigorously celebrated. A number of women expressed indignation at Shiloh's performance, but for the most part, she was feted as a heroine.

"You've taken them all by storm," Justin said, coming to her side. "I'm proud of you, Shiloh."

She turned to stare at him. There was an arresting timbre in his voice that gave her pause.

"Are you, Justin?" she asked softly.

"Absolutely." He bent and brushed his lips against hers, causing her to flush and smile. All day, she'd nursed her anger at him, but he'd charmed it away with a smile and a kiss.

When the Virginians had a celebration, Shiloh

learned, they squeezed every bit of amusement they could out of the day. After the shooting there was a light buffet and then an enforced rest period before the evening's festivities.

Shiloh was shown, along with the rest of the ladies, to a large, dim guest room where cots and trundle beds had been set up. She wasn't at all sleepy, but she allowed a maid to help her undress to her shift and reclined on a bed next to Ivy.

The girl was staring, open-mouthed, at the scars on her shoulders and arms.

"Oh Shiloh . . . is that from the *Princeton?*"

Shiloh nodded. "I guess I found myself in the wrong place at the wrong time."

"How awful for you—"

"Hmph," Virginia sniffed, arranging herself on a pillow. "From what I heard, your whole ordeal could have been avoided. Mrs. Benton, who was at the reception, said you behaved outrageously, joining a gentlemen's discussion about politics."

Shiloh gave her a cool stare. "Is there something wrong with that?"

"Well of course! You had no place—"

"Virginia, the discussion was about Texas, my home. I wasn't about to stand by and listen to lies about it."

"I don't know why everyone's so keen on Texas, anyway. Who needs a great wilderness overrun by savages and Mexicans?"

Suddenly Ivy spoke, more forcefully than Shiloh would have thought her capable of. "It's thinking like that, Virginia, that will hold our country back. We'll never achieve supremacy over England if we don't allow Texas into the Union. Besides, I'd be proud to have Shiloh as a fellow citizen."

Virginia gave them both a scathing look and turned her back, pulling the covers up. Shiloh took Ivy's hand

and squeezed it, surprised and pleased with her un-likely ally.

"I'm so happy that Justin found you," Ivy confessed in a whisper. "I knew he needed more than I could give him."

"I'm not so sure that's true, Ivy. I seem to infuriate Justin more than I please him."

"If that's so, at least he feels something for you. With me, it was a great nothingness. I was always a little afraid of him. He was so intense, so driven. I was relieved—for both of us—when he struck out for Texas. You and Justin have something very rare."

"Rare . . ." Shiloh said wryly. "It is that. But I can't help but wonder if it's right."

The formal ballroom had been festooned with greenery and slender beeswax candles, gleaming silver gracing the sideboards, and a small ensemble playing at one end. In her emerald-green satin, Shiloh was whirled this way and that, changing partners often. She was as much in demand as the lovely Virginia, who clearly resented the competition.

The raven-haired beauty managed to claim Justin for several rounds, and made a great show of speaking intimately into his ear and filling the air with her musical, exaggerated laughter. Shiloh did her best to ignore it, although she recognized the twinge of jeal-ousy when it came.

Toward the end of the evening, she found herself in Justin's arms.

"You've managed to cause quite a stir," he said, smiling down at her. "But then, a beautiful woman usually does, especially when it's discovered she has a good head on her shoulders, as well."

"Why, sir," Shiloh said, imitating the honeyed Virginia drawl, "are you flattering me?"

"Just stating the truth, my dear." His hands moved discreetly down her back, fanning a flame of desire. Shiloh found herself hoping that his careful treatment of her was coming to an end.

She stared up at him, saying with her eyes that she wanted him.

He misread the message. "We'd best be on our way. I don't want you getting overtired."

Shiloh wasn't sorry to leave the Fairfax party, but she resented Justin's mistaken impression. They left after a barrage of invitations, sufficient to fill half a year with frivolity, was issued.

In the coach, Angus and Caroline dozed while Shiloh and Justin spoke of the day.

"I've never done anything quite like that," Shiloh admitted. "To simply play all day, without a care . . . It's so strange to me."

His eyes gleamed in the dim interior of the coach. "It seems to agree with you. You've never been lovelier."

Shiloh didn't answer. She was thinking how meaningless it all was, the frivolity, the odd standards for women, the total insulation from the larger world. She couldn't understand a world in which the pursuit of pleasure was the foremost goal. She moved restlessly until Justin pressed her head against his shoulder, inviting sleep.

The upper veranda offered a spectacular view of the Willows, now starting to bloom with the coming spring. Crocuses were in full blossom, hundreds of small purple and golden heads bursting through rich brown soil. A waft of lilac scent rose as Shiloh turned the page of the newspaper she was reading.

She heard hoofbeats and looked up, spying Justin

and Angus as they rode in from the fields, where the spring planting was beginning. Not for the first time, she was struck by how effortlessly Justin had slid back into the role of gentleman planter, fitting in perfectly with his well-bred peers.

She shouldn't have been surprised. It was the life he was born to, steeped in long tradition. According to what Angus had told her, the Willows had been founded by a Scottish adventurer four generations before. It was only natural that Justin would follow in his ancestors' footsteps.

More and more, Shiloh was beginning to think that Justin's nine-year odyssey to Texas had purged him of his restlessness, and now he was ready to settle down. Here, where he belonged and fit in. No mention had been made of returning to Houston.

A maid appeared with a cup of mint tea and a silver tray of biscuits. Shiloh murmured her thanks and sipped the tea. The lazy luxury in which she lived was seductive, but still she wasn't completely comfortable being waited on by slaves, or having nothing better to do than while away the hours.

She glanced down at the paper and an article caught her eye. "Letter from Texas" was the title of the piece. It was a rather wordy, pastoral thing by a German called Beckendorff, but Shiloh savored every phrase praising the stark beauty of the land, the tenacious, hard-working settlers, the untold thousands of fertile, flower-painted acres.

An intense wave of longing swept over her. Texas, for all its unrelenting heat and dust and wildness, was the only place she could truly call home. She was but a visitor at the Willows, an outsider. The sense of belonging she lacked created a great void in her life, a sadness she was finding harder and harder to conceal.

Looking back down at Justin, who was speaking

with his father and the overseer, she felt herself being pulled in two different directions. She had to tell him, but how? How could she explain her burning need to be back in Texas, away from this plantation splendor? Was there a way to explain to him that this life wasn't for her?

She bit her lip. There was only one solution. She had to free him—they had to free each other—and go back to Texas alone. She couldn't bear to ask him to come with her, knowing that he'd long for the Willows every day. She didn't want to be responsible for his unhappiness. Because eventually he'd come to blame her, to hate her for taking him away from his beloved home. And that was something she couldn't face.

Justin's mind strayed from the discussion with his father and the overseer, who were talking of the spring planting as if it were a matter of life and death. At first, he'd enjoyed working alongside his father. They were equals now, not adversaries, and their feelings ran deep.

But the gratification Justin found in this new relationship with his parents didn't extend itself to other things. He couldn't stop thinking about Texas. With Upshur's untimely death and the Whigs' pushing against annexation, statehood was no longer a foregone conclusion. There was still much to be done, and Justin wanted to be part of it, even though he'd been given an indefinite leave because of Shiloh's accident.

In his mind, he contrasted the Willows with his own property, Post Oaks. While the plantation shone like a polished gem, the ranch was as rough as an uncut diamond, but just as valuable, waiting to be carved into its potential. Justin wanted his hand to be the one that did it. Because although the Willows was the home of his birth, Post Oaks was the home of his heart.

His eyes scanned the upper veranda, where Shiloh sat, reading and sipping tea as she warmed herself in a shaft of golden afternoon sun. By now he knew that the stirring he felt each time he saw her was love, as pure and light and glorious as the sun itself. He also knew that was why he had been holding himself back from her. Justin had never been afraid of anything until now. But if he allowed himself to love her and she betrayed him, as other women had, as Shiloh herself had, he didn't think he could stand it.

He wondered how long he could sustain the facade of contentment for her sake. Although Texas called to him, he could see it was the opposite for Shiloh. Her life at the Willows was effortless, and she deserved every last bit of comfort she got. Was it fair to ask her to go back to Texas with him, to a harsh life and an uncertain future? Or should he stay here for her, and let her live like the lady she was?

Justin was stirred from his musings by a sudden silence. The overseer had left and Angus was looking at him, a question in his eyes. Then he followed Justin's gaze to the upper veranda.

"I've said it before, Justin. She's a beautiful woman, and spirited, too. Yet she's settled down here at the Willows like she was born to this life."

Justin nodded.

"But you haven't, have you, son?"

Justin started to deny it, but finally he had to agree. "Am I that transparent?"

Angus smiled. "All the signs I saw years ago are coming back. Something down in Texas must've gotten into your blood. You're like a young stallion chomping at the bit."

"It means a hell of a lot to me, all the work I've done, the ranch . . . but I don't want to disappoint Shiloh.

No woman in her right mind would give all this up for the rough frontier."

"Is that the only thing you're worried about, son?" When Justin didn't answer, Angus said, "Damn it, boy don't you think I haven't noticed how you've been treating her? You've been walking on eggshells for weeks. She's not some fragile butterfly, so easily crushed. And she's not a mindreader, either."

Angus put a hand on Justin's shoulder. "Go to her, son. Tell her what's in your heart."

Fifteen

Shiloh would never forget the view of the placid river slipping by, as she and Justin sat together that evening in the garden gazebo. The scent of new growth was in the air, the call of the returning birds celebrating spring's arrival. All was soft and new, gilt-edged by the setting sun, unspeakably lovely. The setting contrasted sharply with the feeling in her heart as she contemplated what she had to say.

"I'm glad you asked me out here," she began. "It seems like a long time since we really talked."

"Too long," said Justin, exhaling loudly. "That's my fault, I'm afraid. I guess your accident scared me so damned bad that I didn't want to jeopardize things by upsetting you."

"What could you possibly say that would upset me?"

He had to laugh. "Come on, Shiloh, I don't have to answer that. Used to be, a word or two got your dander up."

She smiled a little, remembering all the bitter clashes and heated arguments. The smile faded when Justin suddenly captured her hands in his.

"Shiloh, I have something to tell you. Something

that's been on my mind for a long time. I should have said it a long time ago, but I kept fighting it, almost hoping things would change. . . ."

Dread curled in her stomach. She already knew what Justin was going to say and she couldn't bear to hear it. He was going to ask her to stay permanently at the Willows, never to return to Texas again.

"Please, Justin," she said, her voice a faint whisper on the spring breeze. "I, too, have something to say." She ran her fingers over his hand, choosing her words. "The Willows is a beautiful place, and I couldn't be happier about you and your parents. They've been wonderful, like a real family to me. I never knew the importance of family. And I want to thank you, too." She looked up into his questioning eyes. "You've taken me so many places, shown me so many things. But . . ."

"What, Shiloh? Say it."

"I don't belong here, Justin. I want to go home to Texas. Of course," she added quickly, plunging on, "I wouldn't ask you to come with me, not after you've found your way home after such a long time. I'd like to leave as soon as it can be arranged."

"Alone." His voice was dull and flat, slightly tinged with restrained anger. She winced at the look in his eyes.

"Yes. I'm sure there's no danger in it, if we find a reputable ship."

He sat so long in brooding silence that she grew nervous. "Justin," she said at last, "I'm sorry. I know you wanted me to be happy here, but I can't help myself. I have to go."

"And so you will, since that's what you want."

She breathed a sigh of relief. Yet there was no happiness, only a leaden feeling in the pit of her stomach. "Thank you," she said, "for understanding.

Now, you were going to say something to me . . . ?"
She looked up expectantly.

Justin regarded her intently, tasting the bitter irony
of it all. What he'd planned to say was that he loved
her, that he wanted to take her back to Texas and make
a life for them there. Had she protested leaving, he
would have agreed to stay on at The Willows, just to
please her.

But none of that mattered now. She didn't care about
him, only about Texas. She was willing to forget all
they had been together and go off on her own. His
head pounded with self-deprecation. Like a fool, he'd
allowed himself to love this woman, to open himself up
to the hurt that only she had the power to impart.
Thank God she'd spoken before he had committed the
cardinal sin of confessing his love to her. At least, he
thought bitterly, she'd given him that, left him his
pride.

"Justin?" Her soft voice broke the silence. "What was
it you were going to tell me?"

"Never mind," he said quickly. "It wasn't important.
Now, I know you'd prefer I stayed here, but you won't
be going to Texas alone. I'm taking you there."

"Please, you don't have to do that. Not if it makes
you so angry —"

"Damn, it, Shiloh," he cut in, "you don't know me at
all, do you? Do you really think I spent the last decade
fighting for Texas just so I could come back here and
farm tobacco for the rest of my days? Am I just
supposed to forget all about the ranch I left behind, let
it fall to squatters?"

She stared, eyes wide and luminous, in amazement.
"Justin, are you saying you *want* to go back to Texas?"

"Hell yes, I want to go back. I just had a letter from
Calhoun, the new secretary of state in Washington. He
wants me down there again."

341

"So you want to go because of your work, and the ranch," Shiloh said slowly. Wild hope leaped in her heart. She had to know if she, too, figured in his plans. "Justin, are those your only reasons?" she asked softly, hardly daring to breathe.

He looked at her coldly, his eyes hard as granite. "Of course," he said curtly. "What other reason would there be?"

"I—none. None that I can think of," she replied quietly, lowering her eyes to hide her pain.

"We'll sail down to Washington in the morning, if you can be ready that soon."

Shiloh knew, from the chill in the bed and the absence of a certain unique scent, that Justin hadn't slept with her that night. She'd spent the evening packing and retired alone, tossing restlessly without the protective circle of his arms. She went to the dressing room and poured water into the basin, shaking her head. She didn't understand why he was so angry. It seemed they both wanted to go back to Texas and make their home there. So why did he seem so bitter toward her?

As Molly helped her dress, she looked down and saw their things being loaded into the sailboat. She barely touched the excellent breakfast that had been sent up, and hurried down to say good-bye to Justin's parents. This, she knew, would be the hardest step of all.

They were already on the porch, waiting for her. Caroline turned a tear-dampened face to her and the two women embraced.

"I can't say I'm surprised," Caroline said softly. "I think I knew, deep down, that the two of you had a different road to travel."

Shiloh nodded, a lump in her throat. "You've been

lovely to me. I've never really had a family before."

Caroline stroked her cheek. "Make one of your own, dear, down in Texas. I was blessed with only one child, but even that one made my life so full. You and Justin have so much to give. . . ."

Shiloh looked away, unable to listen anymore. This talk of her and Justin, and having babies, was all so ludicrous, since her husband could barely tolerate her.

Angus came to kiss her, brushing his lips across her forehead. Then, flinging decorum aside, the big man gathered her against him in a great bear hug.

"You're quite a girl, Shiloh. A man would be a fool not to follow you to the ends of the earth."

She gave him a tremulous smile. Justin was following his own goals, and she wasn't included in that. But she said nothing as she held fast to Angus, feeling more fatherly affection from him than Nate had ever shown her.

Her last impression of the Willows was poignantly sweet. As the sails filled and drew the boat downriver, Angus and Caroline stood before the grand house, amid all the spring color, their hands raised in farewell. She would miss them, but she couldn't deny the surge of excitement she felt at the prospect of going home.

It was a long but restful journey to Texas. A packet bore them from Washington to Savannah, and from there an American trader sailed down into the warm, balmy Florida seas, around to New Orleans. Finally, a big steamer called the *Starlight* took them toward Galveston.

Shiloh found herself alone during most of the voyage. Justin spent a good deal of time with other traveling men, drinking and laughing far into the night, to collapse on the bunk below Shiloh after she'd

343

already fallen asleep. They were like two wary strangers, watching each other, yet seeming not to watch, or care. Shiloh found it nearly impossible to talk to him. His long, brooding silences grew more forbidding with each passing day.

But what, really, could she expect from a marriage such as theirs? It was a union forged by necessity, based on utility rather than trust. The times they'd made love together began to seem like a gilded dream. And a relationship could not be sustained on dreams alone.

By the time they were installed in their stateroom aboard the steamer, tension was taut between them. That evening, as Justin prepared to join a game of cards, he brushed past Shiloh.

Something in her snapped at his inadvertent touch. All the weeks of watching him, longing for him in spite of his coldness, had built to this moment.

"Justin," she said. "Don't go."

He gave her an angry look. "Isn't it a little late to ask me to start acting the husband?"

"I—I just think we should settle things between us. I don't understand what's happening."

"What is happening, Shiloh," he sneered, "is that you are getting exactly what you want. In a few days' time you'll be back in Texas. If you want to stay with your aunt, that's fine. Or you can return to Post Oaks. The choice is yours to make."

"I'll be coming to Post Oaks. If you'll have me."

"Why wouldn't I?" he asked coldly. "After all, you're my wife."

At that, she seized his arm, looking fiercely up at him.

"Then treat me like a wife, damn you," she hissed.

He plucked her hand from his sleeve. "I don't think that would be wise. You were badly hurt in the explosion—"

344

"That was almost three months ago," she said heatedly. "How long are you going to use that excuse? We both know I'm perfectly all right."

He grasped her roughly by the shoulders. "What do you want from me, Shiloh?"

She gasped at the ferocity of his demand. How could she tell this raging giant that she only wanted him to hold her, to stroke her hair as he used to do, to kiss her in the way that made her feel she was the only woman in the world, and he the only man?

"I—I want . . ." She bit her lip, searching for the words.

Justin made a sound, a groan of mingling anguish and rage, and crushed her against him, capturing her mouth with his. It was a brutal kiss, one that punished her for daring to challenge him. Even so, Shiloh's body began to throb with all the weeks of unrequited desire, and she molded herself to him. If this was all he had to give her, then she would content herself with it. His rough touch sapped her of her pride.

Then, abruptly, he released her. "This isn't any good, Shiloh," he growled. "We'd best stay out of each other's way." He strode across the room. Shiloh stared for a pain-filled moment at the door, her insides roiling, and then flung herself on the bed.

Justin drank too much that night and played his cards foolishly. He couldn't wrench his thoughts away from the scene with Shiloh. Again and again he went over the angry words they'd spoken, searching for what it all meant.

Shiloh had asked—demanded—to be treated like a wife. He had no idea whether she wanted his love, or merely for him to satisfy her lust. Bitterly, he suspected it was the latter. She was a passionate woman, with a woman's needs. Justin had half a mind to accommodate her. God knew, he wanted her badly enough. But even his whiskey-numbed mind heard the voice of reason. It was too risky. In the heat of lovemaking, he might lose himself in her, he might say or do something that would let her guess what was in his heart. And then he'd be soft and pliant as clay in her hands. He couldn't trust her to respect that.

It was his own doing, this entire mess. It was he who'd taken her as an innocent, untried girl, and initiated her into the world of love. She was what he'd made her. Who could have guessed that he'd lose his heart in the making?

He played until his pockets were empty, and then stumbled back to the stateroom. The faint scent of honeysuckle hung in the air, seductively taunting. Muttering a curse, Justin kicked off his boots and tossed back the rest of his whiskey, letting it lull him into oblivion.

Post Oaks, it seemed, had fared well over the months of their absence. An able manager, Wylie Stokes had augmented the herd with more mares, and fenced a bigger range. With obvious pride, he told Justin how well the newly broken horses had done at auction, how cheaply he'd bought a number of new wild horses from the valley.

"You've done a wonderful job," Shiloh said, her eyes devouring the longed-for sea of grass and the plump, gleaming herd in the distance.

"I hope you paid yourself well," Justin added. "If not, you've got a bonus coming."

Wylie colored slightly and his grin widened. "Matter of fact, Justin, I did draw a little extra pay. Needed to. Done got myself hitched, and there's a little one on the

346

way."

Laughing heartily, Justin clapped him on the back. "Why you slippery old horse thief. So your bachelor days are over."

"Come on," Wylie said, so full of pride he seemed about to burst. "I want you to meet her."

They crossed the stableyard to the bunkhouse. That building, once a sorry little clapboard structure, had been transformed into a neat whitewashed cottage, complete with picket fence and rows of sunny marigolds in the front.

"The hands have been sleeping up over the stables," Wylie explained. "I told them they didn't have to, but they insisted. Besides, Prairie Flower feeds them better than they could ever do for themselves." He leaped to the door and called inside.

"Honey? Come on out. There's some folks I want you to meet."

The woman appeared in the doorway. Both Justin and Shiloh froze, recognizing her. Shiloh staggered back against Justin; his hand steadied her.

"This here's Isabella," Wylie said proudly.

She was as beautiful as ever, even with swelling belly and ponderous breasts. Her moist red mouth curved into a smile of malicious triumph as she extended her hand, first to Shiloh and then to Justin.

"Welcome to Post Oaks," Shiloh said quietly, remembering her manners.

"And welcome back to you, Shiloh," said Isabella in her husky voice. "You have been away a long while."

"You've got yourself a fine man," Justin said tightly. "Wylie's the best there is."

"Of course," Isabella replied, although the look she gave her grinning husband was tinged with distaste. "Please, you must excuse me. I cannot take the strong sun." She drifted back into the house.

Justin congratulated Wylie again, though not as heartily as before. As they walked up to the main house, his jaw ticked in irritation.

"What's *she* doing here?" Shiloh asked. "She's obviously not in love with Wylie."

"You noticed it too," Justin growled. "I was hoping I'd only imagined it."

"What does she want?"

He shrugged. "I've got a few ideas. But let's worry about that later."

Ina rushed out to greet them, hugging them both together, not noticing how they stiffened at each other's nearness.

"Shame on you for leaving us so long," she scolded happily. "I hope you are home to stay."

"Looks that way," Justin assured her, and they went inside together.

Ina hadn't been idle during their absence. She had cleaned and polished and added touches of her own, creating an inviting, homelike environment.

"You're a rare one," Justin said, grinning. But his mind was clearly on other things. He went up to change into his work clothes and join the hands at their work.

Ina and Shiloh went to the kitchen to see Prairie Flower. The Indian woman cracked a gap-toothed smile and immediately set to preparing an elaborate homecoming supper. She chased Shiloh and Ina out onto the back porch, to sit in the shade and go over all that had happened in the months of separation.

"It was many weeks before we realized you were missing," Ina said disapprovingly. "Your father asked after you, so I decided to visit you at your aunt's. Imagine what an awkward moment that was."

"Ina, I'm sorry. I really was planning on going to Aunt Sharon's, but then I heard about Justin's trip. He was going to England, Ina. How could I sit by and let him do that? I just couldn't resist."

"We guessed what had happened. A man who knows your father, Lamar Coulter, told him Justin had gone, so we assumed he took you along."

"He didn't exactly take me," Shiloh admitted. "He wouldn't have allowed it. But I think, after all, he was glad I was there." She pushed aside the wistful memory of the wild night of love on Antigua, and all that had come after it.

"So tell me," Ina prompted. "What was England like?"

"I can hardly describe it. The countryside is beautiful, but London is old and smoky, so crowded you'd hardly believe it. At first we were treated like honored guests. Parties in houses like palaces, opera, the theater, every sort of entertainment. Every street corner, it seemed, had its own little amusement. A dancing dog, a fiddler, a mouse in a small spinning cage . . ."

"What were the people like?"

Shiloh shrugged. "Like people everywhere: good, evil, greedy, giving . . . unfortunately we got mixed up with some of the worst sort. We had to leave the country suddenly, to avoid the wrath of a very powerful man. We went to Washington, in the District of Columbia."

Ina nodded. "I know of the American capital. Did Justin have business there?"

"Yes. But our stay was brief. Did you hear about the explosion on the steam warship *Princeton*?"

"Of course. It was in all the papers. *Dios*, were you there?"

Shiloh closed her eyes, remembering. "It was horrible. A terrible tragedy. I was injured in the blast, and went to the home of Justin's parents in Virginia to recuperate. It was a lovely stay, Ina. Justin's parents

349

are wonderful. And everywhere I went, London, Washington, and all the other places, people complimented me on your dresses. I had as fine a wardrobe as anyone. A number of ladies demanded to know the name of my *couturier*."

Ina clasped her hands in delight. "And what did the ladies say when you told them it was an old Mexican woman on a farm in Texas?"

"They declared you must be a genius, and they were right."

Ina flushed with pleasure. "I think, Shiloh, that it is not the dress so much as the wearer that makes an ensemble beautiful. You have been good advertisement for me, though. Mrs. Allen and Mrs. Hanks both wanted me to sew for them after they saw you at the auction house."

"Good for you, Ina." Shiloh sipped her lemonade and gazed out at the wavy green prairie, the wide cloudless sky above. "It's so good to be home," she sighed.

"You have been to the capitals of the world, and you still like it best here?"

Shiloh nodded. "It's the only place where I feel like I truly belong."

They sat in amiable silence for a while, listening to the bees buzzing in the ligostrum hedge and savoring the sweet, warm air.

Then Shiloh turned to Ina again. "Have you seen my father?"

Spots of color appeared in the handsome woman's cheeks. "I did as you asked. I checked on him from time to time, brought him a meal or two and did his mending."

"How is he, Ina?"

"Quite well, I think. I know there were some lean times for him, but then things picked up. Some of the new arrivals had him searching for their relatives."

"Did—did he ask about me?" Shiloh didn't know why she was doing this to herself. Nate didn't care what she did; when had he ever?

But Ina's answer surprised her. "What kind of question is that? Ask about you, indeed! When it appeared you were missing, he was like a madman. Mr. Coulter didn't want to say where Justin had gone, but Nate—er, your father forced it from him. Even then, he didn't just guess about you. He went to Galveston and practically tore the town apart until he found a Creole woman—one with a shocking reputation, I might add—who confirmed you'd gone aboard the *Falcon*. Why are you looking at me like that, Shiloh? It is only natural that a father would be so frantic about his daughter."

"He really searched for me?" Shiloh could hardly believe her ears. "I wonder why?"

"What is to wonder about? He cares about you very much, Shiloh."

She gave Ina a dubious look. Long ago, she'd learned not to hope for much from Nate.

"Perhaps he needed money. Of course, that's it. He was broke after that cattle raid. Oh, why didn't I leave him some?"

Ina grew terribly stern. "Listen to yourself, Shiloh. Listen to what you are saying about your own father. Why do you not admit the truth, that the man loves you, and was worried about you? You do him a great disservice—"

"My father loves his work, and his whiskey bottle. But he's never loved me," Shiloh said. Her matter-of-fact voice concealed the hurt she felt.

"You are wrong," said Ina stubbornly. "Your father loves you very much. He just never knew how to show you. Raising children is women's work, and he felt inadequate."

351

"How do you know all this, Ina?"

Again the woman flushed. "We talked some. He spoke of you constantly. He is very proud of you, Shiloh. I hope you will see him very soon."

"I will," Shiloh promised. "But it seems he speaks to me better through you."

Justin galloped into town, trying out one of the new horses. She handled well, had a smooth gait, but a bit of a hard mouth. He'd have to speak to the hands about that. But overall, in the week he'd been back, he'd been greatly pleased with the ranch, although there were things that troubled him.

He and Shiloh had come to a sort of fragile truce, working, eating, even sleeping side by side, but they always seemed to be miles apart. Nights were sheer torture, lying so close he could feel her soft warmth, the beating of her heart, but at least he was safe. There were no hotheaded arguments, only cautious conversation here and there. It was better that way, Justin told himself for the hundreth time.

And then there was Isabella. She was like a dark shadow, ever present, but hard as hell to figure. She'd made herself scarce in the past week, yet Justin knew she was watching him. He hoped Lamar Coulter could shed some light on the problem.

He strode into the solicitor's log cabin office, extending his hand to the lanky man.

"Glad to see you, Justin," Lamar said. "Damn, I thought you'd be back a lot sooner."

"I thought so, too. But we got bogged down in London and then again in the East."

"It was worth the time, my friend. What you found out in England, about Aberdeen's plan to station British ships in the Gulf, has put us in the catbird seat.

352

I heard not long ago that the U.S. Senate voted in favor of a treaty. Houston's being mighty coy about it, though. He's not giving an inch, wants the States to beg for Texas."

"That's not such a bad idea. We'll get all the concessions we want if Houston plays his cards right. Still, there are a few things bothering me. I don't think the Accord will give in too easily."

Coulter nodded. "I'm sure they've got a few cards to turn yet."

"Have you heard from Duff Green?"

Lamar frowned a little. "Hard man to figure. A bit of an opportunist, I think. He's got this Del Norte land company and hopes to make a bundle off it when Texas is annexed. Will Murphy doesn't like the way Green does business, so there's some tension there."

"Too bad. What's Harmon West up to?"

"He's been laying mighty low, Justin. I don't know what you've got on him, but he's running scared. I'd say our main worry is Captain Elliot."

"I think so too, Lamar. I've got a feeling he's put a spy out on my ranch. I came home to find that Isabella Hernandez had married Wylie Stokes."

Coulter whistled. "You don't say. The woman's a viper, but I don't have to tell you that. Be careful, my friend."

Nodding, Justin strode outside and remounted, and headed for Nate Mulvane's house off Main Street. He wasn't sure what he was going to say to his father-in-law. Shiloh hadn't been to see him, and he'd been thinking about that a lot lately. Sometimes, when she grew pensive and wistful, Justin suspected she was suffering from a lack of love from her father. Perhaps that was at the root of the enigma that Shiloh was. No one had ever taught her to love, so how could she, in turn, love anyone else?

It was ridiculous, sentimental, but it was a lesson Justin had recently learned from his own parents. It was probably too late, but he had to try.

"We've been back for a week," Justin said to Nate, leaning on the door frame. "Why haven't you been up to the ranch?"

Nate ignored the question and countered with one of his own. "How's my girl?"

"Why don't you see for yourself?"

"Just answer the question, McCord."

"She's fine."

Nate exhaled loudly and chewed on his cigar. "I thought as much. She always was one to look out for herself. Did she have a good time?"

Justin strode into the room. "Christ, Nate, I didn't come here as a message boy. I think Shiloh'd like to see you."

"I'm available most days," he answered indolently. "I assume Shiloh has everything she needs at your ranch. If she has anything to say to me, she'll say it in her own good time. Besides, what's it to you? Why the hell are you so all-fired eager to get us together?"

"Because you're family, Nate. I never put much store by that until this spring, when Shiloh and I were staying with my folks. I learned something, Nate. I learned that there's nothing like being close to your family. It gives a man something to hold on to."

Nate shook his head. "Take a good look at me, Justin. I'm an old warhorse, and a drunk one at that. I got nothing to offer Shiloh; never have. She's better off without me."

"You'll never convince her of that. She looks up to you, Nate, no matter what you think of yourself."

Mulvane's meaty fist pounded the table. "Looks up to me? Is that what you think?" He laughed harshly. "Last I saw of Shiloh, she was trying to give me money."

"Because you wouldn't take anything else from her."

"Leave me be, Justin. You know better than I how to keep Shiloh happy. I'll let you —"

"She's not happy, Nate. Maybe that's why I'm here. Things aren't good between us."

Nate rose, green eyes snapping fiercely. "If you hurt my girl, McCord, I'll —"

Justin raised a placating hand. "It's nothing like that, Nate. Shiloh's put up a wall around herself and there isn't anything I can do about it." He didn't tell Nate the rest, that he'd erected a barrier of his own.

Nate picked up a bit of whittled wood from the mantel and turned it over in his hand. "Sam Houston taught Shiloh how to whittle, back when she was a bright-eyed little firecracker of a girl. Houston was always carving something. Shiloh made this for my birthday one year. She was just about ten years old at the time." He handed the piece to Justin.

It was a small horse, roughly done by a childish hand, but the overall shape was good; it almost looked like it was in motion. A lot of patience and care had gone into the carving.

"I was drunk when she gave it to me," Nate said, a faraway look on his face. "I remember laughing, saying it looked like a deformed armadillo, when I knew it was meant to be a horse." He clenched his fist. "God, I'll never forget the look she gave me, those big green eyes and her mouth all pressed together so she wouldn't bawl. . . ." He choked out the words and buried his face in his hands.

Nate's description of that one scene from Shiloh's childhood told Justin volumes. No wonder she never talked about the past. No wonder she hadn't accepted the love he'd come so close to offering her. She didn't know what love was; no one had ever taught her.

Nate raised his head and took the carved figure.

"How can I ever make up for this, for everything?"

"It's not too late," Justin said, thinking of his own father. "Believe me, I know."

"I'll get cleaned up," Nate said quietly, and left the room.

The heat of the afternoon sun beat down on Shiloh's bare head as she led one of the new mares around the corral, speaking soft words of encouragement to the skittish animal. This was a part of ranching Shiloh loved, working with the horses, helping to transform them from wild, nervously snorting beasts into tractable animals.

She had been adamant about changing the ranch hands' breaking methods. Their way was to blindfold a horse and jam a huge bit into its mouth, and jump onto the bare back wearing six-inch spurs with knife-edged rowels. As the frantic horse was run to utter exhaustion, the bit tore its mouth to shreds. The end result was a disappointing animal. The wildness had been punished out of it, but it was replaced by malice. The ill-treated beast could—and often did—turn on a rider.

The ranch hands listened to Shiloh and gave her a chance to prove that her methods would work. This mare, whom Shiloh had dubbed Belle because of her well-formed shape and beautiful long-lashed eyes, was to be her example. So far, the gentle treatment was working. After she and the mare had done several more turns about the corral, she stopped beneath the branches of a spreading oak for a rest. She gave Belle corn from her own hand and a bucket of water.

Tomas came to sit in the shade with them, chewing on a long strand of Indian grass.

"She is a real lady, this one," he said, indicating the

356

mare.

"That's because I treat her like one. Whatever kindness and respect I show her, I'll get back tenfold when I'm finished."

"But it is so much faster," the boy said, "to ride them to their knees. Leonicio can break a horse in one hour."

"There will be no more of that, Tomas. Leonicio can only turn a horse into a resentful beast that hates and fears all men. My way is better. You'll see."

"I think you're right," Tomas confessed, watching the mare nuzzle Shiloh for more corn. "So does your husband," he added.

Shiloh looked up sharply. "How do you know that?"

"Because he came to the stables to speak to us about it. He said we were to do exactly as you told us."

Shiloh frowned. No wonder the men had been so agreeable. Justin's intervention had been helpful, to be sure, but she felt a prickle of resentment at his meddling.

"He also said," Tomas went on, cocking his head as he recalled the words, "that we should feel privileged to work for the finest woman in Texas."

Shiloh sat forward. "He said that?"

"*Sí.* And he is right, Shiloh." Tomas blushed to his ears and scampered off, embarrassed by his own admission.

She leaned against the tree, shaking her head. She didn't understand Justin at all. Most of the time he treated her as if she didn't exist, yet he'd praised her to the ranch hands. It was all so maddening, especially since she had no one to confide in. Ina was a good listener, but as an unmarried woman she couldn't explain a husband's foibles. And she was busy lately, tending the house and making dresses for a fast-growing clientele.

"I need someone to talk to, or I'll go crazy," Shiloh

357

said to the mare. The animal grunted and raised its head, ears pricking. A few seconds later, Shiloh heard the noise, too.

She ran to the gate to see who was coming up the road. Her hands tightened around a fencepost as she recognized the riders.

Nate spurred his horse and galloped up to her. His eyes seemed to devour her and his fingers worked restlessly over the reins.

"Shiloh," he said. "Shiloh, my girl."

Without quite realizing what was happening, Shiloh leaped the gate as Nate dismounted. Then she found herself wrapped in his embrace for the first time in her life.

Sixteen

For a long moment, neither of them spoke. Feelings long suppressed passed between them, and Shiloh felt her eyes fill with tears. Stepping back, she saw her own astonished joy reflected in her father's eyes.

"Hello, Papa," she said finally.

"Papa . . ." he echoed. "I haven't heard you call me that since you were two years old. I guess I haven't been much of a father to you."

"You did your best. And I was a contrary child."

"And now you're a beautiful woman and a fine person. I wish I could say I had something to do with that."

They embraced again as the years of estrangement fell away. Over her father's shoulder, Shiloh saw Justin watching them. He gave her a slight nod and then turned away to walk his horse to the stables.

"It's getting on toward suppertime," Shiloh said. "Let's go up to the house."

As they walked together, Nate's arm slung about her shoulders, he said, "That's quite a man you married. He really opened my eyes today. Shiloh, I can't make up for all the years I neglected you, but I want to try.

I'm an irresponsible man, and no one knows that better than you. I guess I couldn't face the responsibility of raising a daughter. I hid behind my work and my bottle and left you to figure things out for yourself."

She smiled. "You weren't that bad, Papa. You taught me things no other girl ever learned. Riding, shooting, tracking—"

"That was easy. I didn't have to put myself at risk to do that."

Shiloh had never seen such honest emotion in her father. And it was all Justin's doing. She wondered what he had said to Nate to bring them together like this. And she wondered why he'd done it.

Supper was a festive affair, a big meal of cornbread and snap beans, a big ham from the spring house. Shiloh watched her father closely, noting with great satisfaction that he didn't touch his wine and declined the whiskey Justin offered. She saw, too, an interesting thing between Nate and Ina. The woman seemed to know exactly what portions of food to put on his plate, and that he loved plenty of butter on his wedge of cornbread.

It seemed impossible, perhaps she was imagining things, but she was sure she saw a secret smile pass between the two. Maybe, just maybe, Ina had finally found the man she was looking for in the unlikely personage of her father. Smiling down at her place, Shiloh decided it was well worth pondering.

Justin, too, was a quiet observer. But tonight he wasn't the usual brooding presence across the table. He seemed to derive real pleasure from Nate's new affection for his daughter. A few times, Shiloh caught his eye and gave him a questioning look, but he only smiled vaguely.

Afterward, they watched the sunset from the porch, enjoying the beauty of the long mare's tail clouds as they streaked evening color across the sky. They spoke of the ranch and the influx of settlers into Houston and the coming elections in the fall. This was a matter of great concern, for Texas was at a pivotal point.

"Sam Houston appears to favor Dr. Anson Jones as his successor," Nate said.

Justin shook his head. "A vacillator. And a good friend of Charles Elliot."

"Which means he's against annexation," Shiloh added.

"That's hard to say. If he gets elected, it might be a blessing in disguise. It might put the entire issue into the hands of Congress."

"But we need a strong negotiator," Shiloh insisted. "How else will we get the best terms in the treaty?"

"We'll get them," Justin assured her.

"You can't be certain, Justin. We've a debt of ten million dollars that the United States will have to assume, and the Mexicans ready to pounce at the first sign of a treaty. I think—"

"Excuse me," Nate said suddenly. "I'm going to see if Ina could use some help in the kitchen."

Shiloh watched him go, smiling after him.

"You were saying . . . ?" Justin reminded her.

She looked at him blankly. "I forgot. Oh Justin, do you think my father is courting Ina?"

He grinned. "If you could call washing dishes courting. Would you like them to be?"

"I—yes, I would. Ina has always wanted to marry, and my father needs someone like her. I know they seem an unlikely pair, but I think it would be lovely."

"Why?" he asked suddenly.

The question threw her. "I don't know. I guess it's because they both need someone to love. Doesn't everybody?"

His stare grew intense. "Maybe. But I'm surprised to hear you say it, Shiloh."

"Surprised? Why?"

"Because you're a direct contradiction of it. You don't seem to need anyone."

She almost told him how wrong he was, but stopped herself. Instead, she countered his claim. "Neither do you, Justin. In fact, you get along better when no one is in your way."

"Do you really think that, Shiloh?"

"Of course."

"Maybe I don't know any other way," he mused. His gaze had grown so intense that Shiloh had to force her eyes away, fearful that he'd discover her longing. She was treading on very shaky ground with this conversation. She watched the breeze stirring the top of distant oak.

"We were talking about my father," she said, anxious to turn the subject. "How did you get him to come here today?"

He shrugged. "I just figured you'd like to see him, and I knew both of you were too damned stubborn to make the first more."

"But it's more than that, Justin. My father is a different man now. He said some things I never dreamed of hearing from him."

"We had a bit of a talk," Justin admitted. "He showed me a little carving you made for him when you were a child."

She smiled, remembering. "The first time I saw General Houston, he was sitting on a fallen tree, whittling a piece of driftwood. I was so fascinated that he showed me how to carve. I made my father a horse, spent hours doing it. Thank goodness it was the last whittling I ever did. It was a disaster, as you probably saw."

"It was a damned good effort for a ten-year-old," he said, but he knew she'd never believe it. Not with Nate reacting as he had.

"What does that carving have to do with tonight anyway?" she asked.

"I think he finally saw it for what it really was. A gift from the heart. A gift of love."

"This is all very confusing to me, Justin. I still don't see—"

Suddenly she was in his arms. He had stood and pulled her from her chair and wrapped her against him, holding her so tightly that she gasped.

"You really can't stand the thought that someone could love you, Shiloh," he said against her hair. "Long ago you must have convinced yourself of that."

"Justin—" His closeness was overwhelming. She had to pull away to gather her wits about her.

"You haven't changed at all, Shiloh. You're still that frightened little girl who jumped me at Washington-on-the-Brazos."

That hurt. He was saying she hadn't grown at all, that she was still the child he'd disliked so intensely at their first meeting. She twisted away and went to the porch railing, clutching it tightly.

"I'm sorry you're so disappointed in me, Justin. But I never asked for your approval."

"No," he said quietly, keeping his distance. "No, you didn't."

They stood in tense silence, not speaking, not looking at each other. Laughter drifted out from the kitchen, mingling with the rising night sounds.

Finally Shiloh turned around. "Why did you bring my father here tonight, Justin?"

"Because you both had some things to say to each other. In Virginia, I learned that family is important, even to you and Nate. You're two fine people, but you needed a little prodding to get together."

"Thank you," she said, her voice softly sincere. She started to reach for his hand.

Just then, a shadow crossed the yard between the porch and the side of the house. Leaping down the steps, Justin captured the dark figure.

"Evening, Isabella," he drawled, searching her beautiful face. "Is there something I can do for you?"

Her eyes were fierce and searching in the evening light. "No, Justin. I was just out taking some air." She passed on and headed for the cottage.

"What do you suppose that was all about?" Shiloh asked.

"I'm not sure. But she's up to something."

"Justin, you'd better tell me everything you know about Isabella. I can't deal with her unless I know what I'm up against."

He nodded, pulling out a cheroot and rolling it between his fingers. "I met her back in March of '43. I was scouting down along the border near Mier. I'd been following Ampudia's contingent, which sidetracked me a little. There was a Texan expedition there, poorly organized, and the Mexicans laid waste to them. I took a ball in the shoulder while trying to get down to the river."

Shiloh recalled his crescent-shaped scar and shivered a little.

"Isabella took me in and got a doctor for me. She took excellent care of me and I started to trust her. Then she turned me over to the Mexicans. It was only then that I realized she was with the Accord, and knew who I was. I wasn't able to escape until the Mier executions took place in Saltillo." He lit his cheroot and inhaled deeply. "Later, she turned up in Galveston, and now here. I'm sure she married Wylie because Elliot wanted her out here. She's mighty thick with the captain."

"I thought the Accord was finished."

He shook his head. "They're not giving up yet. We'd best watch Isabella as closely as she's watching us. She may give us a clue about their next move."

Nate came out, interrupting them. "I'd best get on my way if I want to make town before dark." He shook hands with Justin and hugged Shiloh close. "I'll see you again, girl. We'll talk some more."

"Good-bye, Papa."

They watched him ride away in the deepening twilight, and then they went their separate ways: Justin to his study and Shiloh to the comfortable little parlor, to sit and think. So much had happened, so much had been said. It was impossible to make sense of it all. The only thing she was certain of was that the two men in her life, Justin and Nate, needed something from her. And she wasn't sure she had the capacity to give it.

Summer passed with all its heat and dust, baking the clay banks of the bayous and searing the long yellow prairie grasses. Despite a long dry spell, Post Oaks flourished under Justin's expert management. He was constantly supervising new building and adding selectively to the herd. His day began at sunup and didn't finish until after dark. He was away a lot, too, making frequent trips to Galveston and San Antonio, Washington-on-the-Brazos, and the new capital in the hill country called Austin.

Shiloh worked tirelessly with the horses. Her method of saddle-breaking proved successful, and soon the ranch hands adopted her approach of patience and restraint. McCord horses were in great demand that summer, and profits were good.

One September day, as Shiloh was walking a newly tamed young stallion, she reflected on their good fortune. She rode to a small ridge on the eastern boundary of the ranch and looked back at the house. It sat neatly amid the trees and outbuildings, a symbol of the ranch's success.

Everything was perfect, on the surface. The promise of the land had been fulfilled. But Shiloh stirred discontentedly on the stallion. The great gulf still existed between her and Justin, and she was beginning to think it would always be there. He held himself aloof and she responded with a distance of her own. Neither was willing to make the first move to span the gulf.

It was ironic, really. In Houston, they were feted as the golden young couple, a symbol of the bounty of Texas. At the auction house, at parties, they garnered admiring stares and wistful sighs from people who thought them deeply in love.

Shiloh wondered bitterly what those same people would think if they knew of the coldness between her and Justin, the long, restless nights when even an accidental touch was studiously avoided. And every day, the pattern became more set, more impossible to stray away from.

Shiloh looked down again at the ranch, which had become her sole source of gratification. Her thoughts were interrupted when a movement caught her eye.

Isabella. Her ponderous figure, clothed in crimson, was visible even from a distance. She was in the small garden plot behind the cottage she shared with Wylie, bending down over a pumpkin vine. There was something not quite right about her movements, or about the fact that she was outside in the full blaze of the afternoon heat. As Shiloh watched, Isabella doubled over and fell to the ground.

Forgetting to be cautious with the newly broken

366

stallion, Shiloh dug her heels into its flanks and sent him galloping toward the house. Even before the horse came to a sliding stop, Shiloh was on the ground, running toward Isabella.

She lay awkwardly upon the ground amid the ripening pumpkins and squash. Her lovely face was contorted by intense pain.

"Is it the baby?" Shiloh asked urgently.

"*Sí*. I think so. I—I had such a craving for some squash, and then—*madre de Dios!*" Isabella screeched out her agony, clutching at her middle.

Shiloh waited for the pain to pass and then placed her hands under Isabella's arms, hauling her to her feet. "We'll get you into bed, and I'll fetch Prairie Flower." Isabella gave her a wild-eyed look of terror and Shiloh felt, for the first time, a soft sympathy for the woman.

"Everything will be fine, Isabella. You'll see." Calmly, she helped her into the cottage and to the bed, arranging pillows comfortably around her. She left quickly, with another word of encouragement. But once she was outside, she ran as fast as she could to the kitchen.

"Isabella's baby is coming!" she shouted at Prairie Flower.

The woman nodded, showing no surprise. With infuriating slowness, she donned a fresh apron and washed her hands in the basin. She gathered herbs and salves from the cupboard and placed them in a basket.

"Prairie Flower—" Shiloh said urgently.

The Indian woman shook her head. "There is time. Babies do not appear so suddenly."

They found Isabella huddled miserably on the bed, her knees drawn up and her fists clenched.

"Do not fight it," Prairie Flower instructed as she went about preparing a calming pot of tea. She nodded at Shiloh and made a gesture.

Shiloh knelt beside the bed and took Isabella's tightly closed hands, gently stroking them until they opened. She helped Isabella relax her legs and arms, and spoke softly, encouragingly, as a pain rose and then passed.

So it went for the rest of the afternoon and on into evening. Prairie Flower administered her medicines and draughts while Shiloh bathed Isabella's brow and tried to help her through the agony of childbirth.

Her small efforts were useless. Isabella slid in and out of moods ranging from pitiful whining to outright hostility. She screamed, she swore, she cried, she babbled Spanish prayers. Several times, Shiloh heard her curse her husband and the baby, who were the cause of her pain.

When several hours had passed, Shiloh began to worry. She wasn't alone. She could hear Wylie's voice outside, and Ina's as she placated him and barred him from the cottage.

"Can't you do something about the pain?" Shiloh asked Prairie Flower. "She's suffering so."

The Indian woman shook her head. "It is the way of nature. It will not be much longer now."

The pains came harder and faster, and suddenly Isabella shot up from the bed, her eyes wild, unseeing. As she screamed, Prairie Flower drew back the hem of her dress.

"Bear down," she hissed. "Bear down."

Something like relief appeared in Isabella's eyes. She gripped the side of the bed and did as she was told. Her face grew red and then purple, veins standing out at her temples. It was terrifying to watch, but fascinating, too. There was something elemental about Isabella's struggle that filled Shiloh with wonder.

Acting on Prairie Flower's instructions, she fetched a pile of linens and stood ready. The birth happened quickly. First the crown of a tiny head appeared, followed by a wizened face. Then, with a final push, Isabella delivered herself of the child, a girl.

Prairie Flower swaddled the minute thing and daubed at its face until a thin wail pierced the air.

Shiloh's heart was in her mouth as she took the precious bundle from Prairie Flower. She brought it to Isabella, tilting the baby toward her mother.

"A girl," she told Isabella. "A perfect little girl."

Isabella rolled her eyes and turned her head away. "I need some water," she gasped. "And then I'm going to sleep."

Although Shiloh was astounded that Isabella had so little interest in her child, Prairie Flower only shrugged.

"I will get her the water. You clean the child off."

Shiloh had never seen anything so tiny, so beautiful. The baby suffered her hesitant ministrations quietly, gazing up at her with squinting eyes. The little mouth opened and closed, as did the hands. Shiloh was utterly enchanted.

She called Wylie in, assured him that Isabella was fine, and handed him the baby. Cradling it awkwardly, Wylie grinned from ear to ear.

" 'Bella said I could name her. I'm calling her Cassandra, for my mother."

"That's beautiful," Shiloh said. "Congratulations, Wylie." Eagerly, she took the baby from him while he went to see his wife.

Shiloh's enchantment with Cassandra grew with each passing week. At first she'd excused her daily visits by bringing meals to Isabella, but as time went on, she didn't bother to hide her desire to be with the child.

Isabella was more than willing to hand Cassandra over to Shiloh. She was a singularly disinterested mother, suffering the periodic nursings and looking forward to the day when the child was weaned. Shiloh couldn't understand the woman's apathy, although she suspected it had something to do with the fact that Isabella did not love her husband.

Cassandra had her mother's dark beauty, right from the start, with a rosebud mouth and lovely olive skin. But she had her father's quiet, pleasant disposition, and by six weeks of age, would smile readily.

The days of November were warm, almost balmy, and Shiloh loved to take the baby walking. Justin had made a small bench beneath one of the post oaks, and Shiloh often went there, to sit in dappled shade and hold Cassandra.

Justin found her there one afternoon as he was coming in from the fields.

"Come and see," Shiloh invited. "She's found her hands."

Justin sat beside them and watched, amused, as the baby gummed her little fists, obviously thrilled with her discovery. Cassandra stopped, though, when this new face loomed above her.

"I think she likes you," Shiloh declared. "Here, take her." She laughed when Justin recoiled. "Go on, she won't break."

"I'm covered with dust and sweat," he protested.

"She's not fussy." Without further ado, Shiloh placed the baby in Justin's arms. The tiny face contorted and Justin waited for a wail of terror, but it never came. Cassandra gave him a miraculous smile and made a soft cooing noise.

"Well, I'll be," Justin said, absurdly pleased. "Little lady, I do believe we're going to be friends." He relaxed and watched, fascinated, as the baby continued to smile and coo.

"I was right," Shiloh said, smiling. "She does like you."

Justin lifted the baby to kiss the dark fuzz on her head, savoring the warm, milky scent of her. He gave her back to Shiloh reluctantly.

"You spend a lot of time with the little mite," he commented.

"I think she needs me. Isabella doesn't seem to want to have anything to do with her."

"I know. It's got Wylie a little worried."

"I won't let anything happen to Cassandra. She's very precious to me, Justin. I never thought much of children, I guess because I was never around them."

"You're doing just fine with this one, Shiloh. But don't let yourself get too attached."

She looked at him sharply. "What do you mean by that?"

"She's not yours, Shiloh. And she's going away."

Dread curled within her. Unconsciously, she clutched the baby closer.

"Wylie told me this morning he's thinking of leaving. He wants a place of his own, and the money he's made this summer is more than enough to buy a good spread. He mentioned Bastrop, some hundred miles northwest of here. They'll probably go in the spring, when Isabella is stronger."

"No . . ." Shiloh breathed, shaking her head. "I couldn't stand it."

Justin looked at her, real sympathy in his eyes. "You'll get used to the idea. In the meantime, I'd say that's one lucky little girl. You're the best friend she's got." He left, and Shiloh's tears dampened the baby's soft blanket.

Houston festooned itself grandly for election day. Banners were strung across the streets and bunting hung from the Capitol Hotel, and speakers shouted from raised platforms that had been set up along the bayou landings. Excitement vibrated through the air as men clamored to cast their votes.

The results surprised no one. Sam Houston, the hero of San Jacinto and a veteran of two terms, had placed Anson Jones, his secretary of state, in office.

There was a Christmas reception for the victor at the home of Harmon West, who had wasted no time ingratiating himself to the president. Jessamine played the hostess well, moving amid the guests with the stately air of a queen. She fancied herself the social equal of Mrs. Allen, and made a great show of ordering her servants about.

Captain Charles Elliot was much in evidence at the reception. Shiloh wasn't surprised to see him, as he was a personal friend of Dr. Jones, but his presence made her nervous. He was still in a position to jeopardize annexation.

She acknowledged his greeting with a nod.

"The belle of Post Oaks," he said smoothly, eyes pale and chilly. "You've made quite a reputation for yourself, Mrs. McCord."

"Have I?"

"Indeed. And your husband is considered one of Houston's leading citizens. Very impressive."

"If you say so," she answered vaguely, and started to move away.

"Mrs. McCord, wait. There is no reason why we can't be civil to each other. I've finally come to realize that my work in Texas is nearly over. I still think it's ill advised, but it seems that Texas will soon join the United States, keep its Negroes in bondage, and go to war with Mexico."

372

"You paint a dark picture, captain."

"But it's accurate."

"Why are you telling me this?"

"Because I've seen the way you've been looking at me all evening. You don't trust me."

"Not in the least," she stated. "And I've been wondering what your friend Isabella is doing at my ranch."

He shrugged. "I can't answer that." He bowed slightly and said, "Goodnight, Mrs. McCord. I wish you all the best."

She watched him move across the room, to strike up a conversation with Harmon West.

"What was that all about?" asked Justin, coming to her side.

"I don't know. I think he wants me — and everyone else — to believe that he's through meddling with Texas. But he's not, Justin. There's something going on, I know it."

He grew suddenly tense. "How do you know it? Shiloh, have you been —"

"No," she snapped, angry that he would become instantly suspicious. "I haven't been snooping around. It's just a feeling I have. But what about you, Justin? I think you know something, and you're not telling me."

He pressed his lips together. "All I have are a few ideas. Not worth mentioning."

"Why not? I think the president should be told that Elliot is up to something."

"Let me handle this in my own way, would you, Shiloh?"

She folded her arms. "Of course." As he moved away, she frowned. She had a few ideas of her own, and unlike Justin, she wasn't going to keep quiet about them.

Her first impression of the new president was that he seemed a little in awe of his position. His great jowls quivered and his eyes darted nervously. He kept looking to his predecessor, Sam Houston, as if to gather some of the man's forcefulness to himself.

"Mr. President?" Shiloh said.

He looked at her with recognition. "Good evening, Mrs. McCord. It's a pleasure to see you."

"I wonder if I could have a word with you, Mr. President?"

"Of course."

They retreated to a quiet corner of the room, away from the crowd and the noise of the musicians.

"Mr. President, it's no secret that my husband and I favor annexation, along with the majority of Texans. I'd hate to see anything stand in the way of statehood."

Although Jones looked a little befuddled, she knew it was a ruse.

"Go on, Mrs. McCord."

"I'm concerned about Captain Elliot, sir. I'm afraid he will try to prevent a treaty from going through."

"Charles is my dear friend, young lady. Just exactly what are you accusing him of?"

"I'm not sure, sir. Huckstering, I guess you'd call it. Trying to turn Texas into a British protectorate."

"I don't like the sound of that, Mrs. McCord. Charles is a forthright, honorable man. I trust him implicitly."

"But—"

He nodded abruptly and moved away, leaving Shiloh to flush in embarrassment. Looking around the room, she saw that a number of people had seen Jones snub her. Gritting her teeth, she went to find Justin. She murmured a vague politeness to the smugly satisfied Jessamine, and made her escape.

"You should've known better than to try that," he snapped once they were on their way home.

She turned on him angrily. "Don't start in on me,

374

Justin. I know I made a mistake."

"Give it up, Shiloh. You'll save yourself a lot of pain." Sensing her coldness, he let her sit in silence for the rest of the drive.

When she went up to retire, however, he followed her instead of going to write letters, as he usually did. Embarrassed, Shiloh went to the window and opened it to the cold night air.

Night sounds filled the silence of the room: the horses nickering and stamping in the stables, the screech of an owl. And, faintly but disturbingly, the small cry of a baby.

"Cassandra . . ." Shiloh said, taking up her shawl. "Maybe I should check on her."

But Justin planted himself in her way, barring the door. "Leave the child be. It's for Wylie and Isabella to quiet her."

Shiloh looked troubled. "Isabella leaves the baby to cry too long. It's not good for her."

Justin went and shut the window, giving her a searching look. "Would it make you happy, Shiloh, to have a child of your own?"

She felt herself begin to tremble. "I . . . Justin, what are you saying?"

He stepped closer, and she became uncomfortably aware of his warmth, his scent.

"You seem so happy when you're around children. There's not much I can give you, Shiloh, that you really want, but I believe I can give you a child."

She was mesmerized by his nearness, his soft, compelling voice. His suggestion conjured up images of unspeakable bliss. A baby of her own, someone to love and be loved by. And Justin would be so fatherly . . . but then she thought further and saw another aspect of his suggestion.

"No, Justin," she said softly. "It would be wrong."

375

"Wrong? I've watched you, Shiloh. You'd be a fine mother—"

"It's not that," she insisted.

"Then what?"

She searched for the words. "I just don't think it would be right for us to make a child. It—it's too much like breeding the horses, putting a mare and a stud together for just one purpose." She looked at him squarely. "I won't lie to you, Justin. I would love to have a child. But when—if—it happens, I want it to be more than mating. I want it to be a celebration of love, conceived by parents who understand and trust each other. It wouldn't be fair to the child otherwise. We can barely get along with each other, much less raise a child together."

He reached out and cupped her chin, his eyes strangely soft, sad, almost. "I'll leave it completely up to you, Shiloh. When you're ready, I'll be there."

He didn't stay with her that night, or for the next several weeks, as he went out of town. Shiloh found herself lonely for his presence, and she was constantly haunted by the idea he'd put into her head.

Seventeen

Justin dropped a creased, blotted letter onto the desk in his study. A March breeze swept it into the lap of the American chargé d'affaires. William Murphy looked up questioningly.

"Where did you get this, Justin?"

He shook his head, thinking about the stunned post rider he'd left sitting in the dust at a distant roadside.

"You know better than to ask me that, Will."

The American chargé cleared his throat. "Of course. Well, tell me what it's all about. The light is bad and I don't have my spectacles."

"Maybe you'd better sit down," Justin said.

Lamar Coulter, who had been reading the letter, grew livid. "I can't believe my eyes. The son of a bitch—"

Handing Murphy a drink of whiskey, Justin said, "It's from Charles Elliot to his superiors in England. Apparently we were right in thinking he'd have a last-ditch effort up his sleeve. He's going to Mexico to see if he can get President Herrera to recognize Texas as a sovereign nation. He'll be traveling incognito to Vera Cruz as soon as he can get a ship out of Galveston."

Murphy tossed back his whiskey and smiled grimly. "Why that slippery British bastard," he said. "He told me he was going on the *Electra* to meet his wife in Charleston. Does President Jones know?"

Lamar went, stone-faced, to the window. "Jones is sending him, he and Saligny. It's all there in the letter. Our president, gentlemen, has been seduced by Elliot's grand illusion, it seems. In a way, I can't blame the man. The presidency of Texas is a mighty powerful position."

"I don't know why we're all worried," Murphy said suddenly. "The legislature is meeting to vote on the issue in late May. There's just not time for Elliot to go to Mexico, negotiate with Herrera, and return by that time."

"If Jones is behind him, he'll see to it that he gets word from Elliot before anything is decided."

"So what are we going to do?" Murphy asked.

"I'm going to Mexico," said Justin. "I have to get proof, and this letter just isn't enough. Elliot, Jones, and Saligny could all declare it a forgery."

Murphy looked troubled as he reached for the whiskey bottle again. "I don't like it. You'd have to be in disguise, too, and that won't be easy. There aren't many around with your height and build."

"I'll figure something out," Justin said. Murphy and Coulter left, and he sat at his desk, hands clasped behind his head. A great weariness swept over him. It was starting all over again, the secrecy, the underhanded dealings. Once, it had been exciting, uncovering plots, manipulating things. But by now it had grown old. Justin had no desire to go capering down to

Mexico, dressed as a padre or an adventurer. He'd do it only to stop Elliot once and for all.

He drew out a sheet of paper and began composing several letters to Washington.

Shiloh sat beneath the awning of the dry goods store, holding little Cassandra Stokes. Isabella was inside, getting some things for their move to Bastrop. Shiloh held the baby close and was rewarded when a little hand reached up and laid itself on her cheek.

"I'll miss you more than I can say," she whispered to the child. "Nothing at Post Oaks will be the same after you're gone."

The baby gurgled and chewed on Shiloh's finger, and Shiloh could feel the tiny sharp ridges of a first tooth. Before long, Cassandra grew restless and cried to be let down, to practice her new skill of crawling.

Shiloh looked down dubiously at the dusty planks of the walkway, but the baby was insistent.

"I guess there's no harm in it," she said at last, and set the child down. Cassandra explored a knot-hole in one of the planks, poking her finger curiously into it. Then she crawled with surprising speed to the edge of the walk, drawn by a shiny porcelain butter crock that sat there.

"No, you don't," Shiloh laughed, hurrying over and scooping the baby up. Out of the corner of her eye she caught a flash of movement. There was a long, narrow alley at the side of the dry goods store and a flight of wooden steps leading to some living quarters above. Shiloh looked up just in time to see Isabella glance this way and that and then disappear into one of the doors.

Her curiosity piqued, Shiloh followed. Isabella had done little in the past few months to arouse suspicion, but there was something decidedly secretive about the way she was behaving now. Giving the baby a corner of her blanket to suck, Shiloh mounted the stairs and stopped, listening.

". . . be found out," Isabella was saying urgently. "They know about your Mexico trip."

"How do you know?" That was Charles Elliot, speaking in his clipped tones.

"That fool Murphy. He drinks too much. When he left the meeting a few days ago, he was all too eager for my company. My lout of a husband was away, so I had plenty of time to feed him more whiskey and get the story from him. He knows all about you and Saligny and the president. And Justin has been writing a lot of letters; he seems to be getting his things in order. Charles, he means to follow you to Mexico."

There was a long silence, and then Elliot laughed. "Don't you see, Isabella, it's perfect! The ship I'm taking is the *Eurydice*. The *Eurydice*! It's a British warship commanded by my cousin George. He'll cooperate with me completely. Once we're on the high seas, we'll be able to get rid of McCord for good."

Isabella said something inaudible as Shiloh's heart skipped a beat. She leaned closer.

". . . can arrange for a fatal accident to befall our friend. These things happen all the time; no one will ask questions."

Shiloh listened a bit longer, but the conversation turned to other things. Isabella demanded money and complained about having to go to Bastrop. The baby began to fuss, so Shiloh ran back down to the walkway.

A few minutes later Isabella came out, laden with parcels. It took every bit of Shiloh's restraint to keep from assaulting the woman with furious accusations. But that would serve nothing. Best to let her believe her secret was safe.

"Did you make a satisfactory transaction?" Shiloh

asked coldly.

Isabella's wide lips parted slowly, smiling. "Oh yes. Several." She moved away with a satisfied air.

Shiloh went over her quandary in the stables. She didn't know what to do. Her first impulse was to tell Justin what she'd heard, to warn him. But that was no good. He would never abandon his plans just because Elliot was plotting his death.

Yet she couldn't let him go. She brushed a horse's side vigorously, frowning. The scent of spring wild-flowers drifted in through the windows, mingling with the smell of hay and horses. Again, she vowed that she couldn't let him walk straight into a trap. He was too precious to her to lose. He was—

Shiloh dropped the curry brush she was holding and ran to the stable window. The greening meadows shifted in the breeze. Clouds were piled high on the horizon against the sharp blue sky. She put a hand to her racing heart.

It was all so clear to her now. So painfully, wonderfully clear. It had taken the possibility of Justin's death to chase away the fog of numbness that had shrouded her for months, but finally it had happened. A mockingbird alighted on a branch in front of her and cocked its shining eye.

"I love him," Shiloh said to the bird and the sun and the sweet-scented wind that rippled through the distant fields. Her voice shook, almost beyond recognition as it came from her heart. "God help me, I *love* him." She didn't know when it had started. Perhaps the feeling had been there right from the beginning, when she'd huddled on the saloon floor in Washington-on-the-Brazos, studying him. Nearly two years had passed since then, and Shiloh had fought her emotions, denied them, refused to let them blossom within her. But it was love she felt now, pure and sweet and aching. That was why her heart leaped each time she saw him, each time he smiled her way. That was why Justin's touch, and only his, ignited in her a flame of passion so intense that the world fell away. And that was why she couldn't bear to lose him.

All the dark shadows in her life were burned away by this new, bright flame of feeling. Her bare feet hardly touched the dusty ground as she rushed out to the stableyard, where Tomas was working.

"Where's Justin?" she asked breathlessly. He pointed down to the western range, where a carpet of bluebonnets rippled up to the tree-fringed bayou. Squinting, Shiloh saw him and his horse as two specks against the cloud-piled horizon.

Lifting the hem of her frock, she ran toward him, her veins pounding with the fever of her newly discovered love. She didn't think; didn't plan. She only knew that Justin was where her heart's destiny lay. She called his name, a shout of gladness, as her feet raced over the field of bluebonnets.

He straightened up from the fallen tree he was hewing with an ax, his bare chest gleaming golden with sweat, a look of astonishment on his face. Shiloh pitched herself into his arms, the force of her small, hurtling body causing him to stagger back and let the ax fall to the ground.

She wrapped her arms about his strong neck and stood on tiptoe to cover his astounded face with kisses.

"Oh Justin," she said, savoring the salty taste of him. "Oh Justin, I've been so foolish. All these months of denying you . . . please, please say you'll forgive me, that you'll give me another chance. . . ." She held his face and placed her mouth upon his, giving him a kiss that spoke her heart for her.

Justin didn't question the merciful gods that had finally sent her to him like a ray of bright sunshine. He didn't allow himself to wonder at her openness, her giving. He merely held her against him, took her tender offering, savored the sweetness of her breath and lips.

She moved intimately, invitingly, against him, begging for his touch. His hands freed the fastenings of her dress and slipped it, along with her shift, to the bed of bluebonnets on the ground. Together they sank upon the spring-soft flowers and meadow grasses, clinging urgently, letting all the pent-up tension of the past months explode in feverish lovemaking.

Shiloh was wild with desire for him. Her hands ran over every beloved inch of his flesh, removing his boots and then his trousers. Her hungry mouth assaulted him with kisses, pressing to his chest, his shoulders, his neck, and finally his mouth again.

He, in turn, availed himself of her silken flesh, holding the small warm globes of her breasts and sipping the honey of her mouth. Shiloh felt alive as never before as he caressed her and moved his lips down to her turgid nipples while his hands found and massaged the aching core of her desire.

Shiloh's love freed her from all modest caution. She moved her hands down over his hips and took his manhood in a grip of passion, eliciting a gasp from him. This ignited her beyond measure, beyond hesitation. She pressed him boldly down to the bed of wildflowers, straddling him, sheathing him in her moist, ready warmth. Her hips began to move in that steady, long-suppressed rhythm, passion building urgently. His hands and lips toyed with her breasts, causing a moan of ecstasy to burst from her. She rose up, gasping, and then seated herself deeply as she reached the scintillating moment and felt him spend himself with a mighty thrust. Slowly, filled with the glow of love, she collapsed onto him.

"Justin," she murmured, nuzzling his neck. "Justin . . ." She felt his flesh grow wet with her own tears.

He held her tenderly, watching the scudding clouds overhead and a pair of martins as they dipped and wheeled through the sky. Only the loud thudding of his own heart in his ears convinced him that he wasn't dreaming, that Shiloh wasn't a golden fairy of springtime, but a flesh-and-blood woman, his at last.

He took up a corner of her dress and dried the tears from her cheeks. "Shiloh? Are you all right?" he whispered.

She gave him a smile that caused his heart to lurch. "Yes, Justin," she replied, the tears starting again. "I've never been so happy in my life." She kissed him deeply and his desire stirred anew. As if she had read his mind, she lifted her mouth and bent to whisper in his ear.

"I want you again," she said, and found her answer as she touched the evidence of his desire. The second coupling was slower, more tender, its sweetness confirming the reality of the first. For hours they lay and loved in the sun, speaking little, but feeling everything, letting mouths and hands say what words could not. Only when the western sky was streaked with evening color did they stop and dress themselves.

Justin gave her a kiss that promised a night of passion, and lifted her onto his horse. Mounting in front of her, he walked the horse slowly back to the house.

Shiloh rode in glowing silence, her hands wrapped about his waist, her cheek against his back, her bare legs dangling. Never had she felt so utterly complete. The rest of her life stretched rosy before her and it seemed nothing could mar her happiness.

Yet the sight of Wylie Stokes's loaded wagon, Isabella sitting proudly in front, shot her through with a shaft of pain. She jumped from the horse and ran across the yard.

"You're leaving?" she asked. "But I thought—"

"Wylie has found a steamer going up the bayou. We leave tonight," Isabella informed her.

Wordlessly, Shiloh reached for the baby. Shrugging, Isabella handed her down. Cassandra had been drowsing, but she came awake and greeted Shiloh with a smile. While Justin and Wylie conferred quietly on the other side of the cart, she held the baby to her cheek as if to stamp herself with the impression for years to come.

Wylie cleared his throat and Shiloh looked up.

"Time to go, ma'am," he said regretfully, taking up the traces. Eyes filling, Shiloh kissed the baby and handed her to Isabella. Only Justin's warm presence behind her kept her from feeling that her world had emptied out.

"It'll be all right, sweetheart," he said quietly. "We'll visit them. When the new capital is built in Austin, we'll be making plenty of trips up that way."

She nodded and turned in his arms, leaning up to kiss his cheek. Hand in hand, they walked to the house.

A snug room in a boardinghouse insulated them from the rollicking noises of the port of Galveston and the rushing sounds of waves on the sandy shore. There had been a bittersweet note in their lovemaking this night, for in the morning they would be separated. Justin expected to be aboard the British *Eurydice*, bound for Vera Cruz. And Shiloh expected to take his place on the vessel.

Shiloh wondered if he'd ever forgive her for what she planned to do. As he slept soundly, she slipped from the bed and went to the window ledge, sitting and hugging her knees to her chest. She told herself that she had to do it, had to stop him from going on this dangerous mission.

During the day, while Justin and Mr. Murphy had held long, secret planning sessions, Shiloh, too, had been busy. She purchased a supply of widow's weeds, a shapeless black bombazine and the all-important concealing bonnet and veil. Then she went to the offices of the Galveston *News*, to confer with its editor. Without being too specific, she promised to send him dispatches from Mexico that would prove, once and for all, the depths that Great Britain would sink to in order to prevent annexation. In turn, the editor pledged to publish her message and send it to Houston and Washington, so that the entire nation would know of England's treachery.

Shiloh's last errand in Galveston that day was the most difficult of all. She searched numerous dark parlors and ten pin alleys at the fringes of town, where foreign sailors went for their amusement. In one shadowy establishment she found the handsome Creole woman called Sylvie, who had cautioned her against Christopher St. James.

After much coaxing and the promise of complete secrecy, Sylvie had sold her a potion, guaranteed to induce a long, heavy sleep. Shiloh was fearful of drugging Justin, but she was more afraid of what would happen if he boarded the *Eurydice*.

She considered not going, but her conscience wouldn't allow it. Elliot must be exposed, and it was she who had to do it. She was the ideal person for it. No one would ever suspect a young widow, traveling alone to her family. Her sleep was troubled that night by accusing ghosts and shadowy things, but when morning came, her resolution hadn't flagged. While Justin was still asleep she sent for coffee and emptied the vial into his cup.

She woke him with soft kisses to his eyelids. With a sleepy smile, he reached for her, opening her robe.

"Let's have coffee first," Shiloh suggested quickly, going to get it.

"I love being waited on by you," he remarked, and sat up to sip the fragrant dark brew. Shiloh watched him from the corner of her eye. He continued to drink, not seeming to notice anything strange about the flavor. He drained his cup quickly, eager for her.

She made love to him as if it were the last time. But she refused to think of it like that. Silently, she promised to return before the end of spring, and the whole ordeal would be over. Justin was tender with her, and there was a languor in his movements that told her the drug was taking effect. They spent themselves sweetly and lay back to hold each other.

"I should be going," Justin said, but lazily, as if he didn't care whether he boarded the ship or not.

"Stay with me a little longer," Shiloh begged, pressing him back against the pillows. "There's plenty of time."

He was only too happy to comply. His hand traced lazy circles on her shoulder and toyed with a pouting nipple. Shiloh shuddered beneath his touch, and before long found herself breathlessly making love to him again. When finally he collapsed, she heard his deep, even breathing.

She raised her head. "Justin?" He didn't respond. "Oh, my God," she breathed, stunned by the enormity of what she had done. But there was no turning back now. She dressed swiftly in the black bombazine, concealing her hair in the pleated bonnet and her face with the black veil. Her bag was packed. She found

Justin's billet among his things and looked it over quickly. The name he'd given was J. Willows. Very well, she would be Justine Willows, a young widow returning, after the tragic death of her husband, to her family, who resided in Mexico City.

She gave one last regretful look at Justin, who hadn't stirred. Her heart filled with love for him. Lifting her veil to kiss the slack lips, she said, "Good-bye, my love. Please forgive me."

Justin was dreaming of floating on a warm, shifting sea. The smell of brine was strong; the waves swishing gently as they lapped over him. He heard his name called by a faraway voice, faint at first and then growing louder. Finally he dragged himself awake and reached for Shiloh.

"Best be going, sweetheart," he mumbled. "Don't want to miss—"

"Justin! Are you there?"

He suddenly recognized Will Murphy's voice. The pounding on the door thudded in his aching head. It felt as heavy as iron when he raised it from the pillow.

He pulled on his trousers and stumbled toward the door, reeling slightly.

Murphy stormed in. "What the hell is going on?"

Justin rubbed a hand across his stubbled face. "Calm down, Will. It's barely sunup. I've got plenty of time to—"

"My God, you look terrible. Have you been drinking?"

Justin shook his head. "You shouldn't be here, Will. We don't want anyone to suspect a connection between us."

"What does it matter now? We've lost the *Eurydice*, and the *Electra* as well."

"Damn! But I was told the *Eurydice* wasn't leaving until the twenty-ninth."

"Clever of you," Murphy said wryly. "But today's the thirtieth."

"What?"

"You heard me. What have you been doing since the day before yesterday? Everything was all arranged—"

Justin snapped out a curse and grabbed his empty coffee cup. Sniffing it, he could smell nothing unusual, but he knew still, with cold certainty, what had happened.

"I was drugged," he said dully setting the cup down so hard that it shattered.

Murphy looked a little afraid. "That means someone knew about your plans. But who . . . ?" He drove his fist into his hand. "The Mexican woman! Isabella. The night you showed me Elliot's letter, she started acting real friendly. I didn't think anything of it at the time, but . . . oh, Christ!"

"It couldn't have been Isabella. She left for Bastrop days ago. No, Will, the person who stopped me from going aboard the *Eurydice* was my wife."

"Shiloh? Why would she do a fool thing like that?"

"I don't know. But she'd better have a damned good explanation."

"I guess what's done is done," Murphy sighed. "Maybe it'll work out anyway. We've still got Elliot's letter. I'll see what I can do."

Justin sat down on the bed and held his throbbing head in his hands. A storm was whipping up in the Gulf, the wind shivering the windowpanes. What was Shiloh up to this time? he wondered. Moving sluggishly, he washed and shaved and finished dressing. As he was putting his things away, he noticed that Shiloh's carpet bag was missing. Searching further, he discovered that not one of her possessions remained in the room.

With a growing sense of alarm, he went through his own belongings. They were all there, with one notable exception. His billet was missing.

He closed his eyes. "Sweet Christ . . ." he whispered. It all fell together. Shiloh had drugged him to go in his place. The reason was obvious. Apparently, she'd never gotten over her passion for detective work, and wanted to make a name for herself by exposing Elliot's excursion to Mexico.

And that, Justin realized with dull misery, was the reason for her sudden change toward him. Fool that he was, he'd wanted to believe that she loved him. Although she'd never actually said it, her words and actions had conveyed the feeling so convincingly that Justin had trusted her. Now he knew that it had all been a charade, a ploy to get him to bring her to Galveston "for one last night together under the Texas sky," as she'd put it.

He wasn't surprised that he'd swallowed her falseness. He was still crazy in love with her.

But no more, came the hard-edged thought. At least she'd freed him of the damnable burden of loving her. This would be her final gift to him. When she returned, she'd find herself a divorced woman. Lamar Coulter could probably arrange something in a hurry. It was, after all, abandonment, pure and simple.

Yet Justin didn't dash back to Houston. He tried to tell himself that Shiloh deserved whatever she got in Mexico, but he couldn't stand the thought of her making the trip alone and unprotected. The Gulf between Galveston and Vera Cruz was a pirate's haven; the ships that passed through were loaded with Mexican gold and silver, even goods from China, via Acapulco. And the Mexican interior was rife with bandits and brigands, desperados hiding in the rocky hills. Elliot himself was a threat, too. There was no telling what the Englishman would do if he found out Shiloh was watching him.

Sighing heavily, Justin pulled on his boots. He'd have to go after her. He collected his things, hoping that there would be a ship bound for Vera Cruz in the harbor. Although even if he found one, the incoming gale would have to pass before they could sail. He opened the door to leave.

And found himself staring down the barrel of a pistol.

"Apparently," said Harmon West, "Captain Elliot's information wasn't quite accurate. I was supposed to come after your wife, Justin. Where is she?"

"Gone to stay with relatives," he said quickly, gauging the distance between himself and the pistol. There was too much leeway to risk jumping West.

The judge shrugged. "You'll do, I guess. Let's go. And don't get any crazy notions. I wouldn't mind pulling this trigger. Not at all."

"What do you want with me, Harmon?" Justin demanded.

"Captain Elliot has gone on a matter of delicate business. I don't want you interfering. You'll be spending some time at that burned-out warehouse on the bayou, the one you blew up. Well away from civilization."

Harmon kept the gun pressed to Justin's side as they went out to the street, down to a small landing where Houston-bound steamers started up the bayou. West had a small sailboat there. Looking down the slippery mud bank, Justin saw that Murphy was already in the boat, guarded by Harmon's strong-armed Negroes.

"Yes, I have the letter," West said, his voice ringing with triumph. "I intend to be very thorough about this."

He still pointed the pistol at Justin, his other hand gripping a tree root that rose up out of the mud. "Now, I'll stand here, and you get into the boat, nice and easy."

Justin started down the bank, but he stopped when a dark, slithering shadow crept down the tree just behind Harmon. He had no reason to try to save the judge, but it was beyond him to stand by and watch a man be killed.

"A moccasin," he whispered. "Behind you, Harmon."

The judge only laughed. "Nice try, Justin, but I'm not buying it. No, I don't believe I'll take my eyes off you."

"Damn it, Harmon, I'm not bluffing—"

The next all happened in a blur. West lost his footing in the mud and groped wildly with his hand. The snake struck like a bolt of black lightning, fastening its disjointed jaws around his wrist. With a scream of terror and agony, Harmon dropped his pistol and slid down the bank, the snake whipping wildly, still locked to his wrist. He stopped halfway into the silty water.

While the guards quailed in the boat, Justin and Murphy went to the judge. The snake had slithered off into the water, but the bite mark on Harmon's wrist was growing livid. Already, the deadly venom was coursing through his veins.

"Get him in the boat," Justin ordered the guards. "I'll go see if I can find a doctor."

"It's too late, Justin," Murphy said quietly. They both looked down at Harmon. His eyes had glazed over and his breathing had become rapid and shallow. Beads of sweat mingled with the rain on his ashen face. He made no sound, no movement. And then the breathing simply stopped. The eyes stared sightlessly, the mouth gaped. Harmon West had met an inglorious death on the muddy banks of the bayou, his days of treachery and ambition ended by a water moccasin.

Justin felt nothing as he scaled to the top of the bank, followed by Murphy.

"Where are you going?" Murphy asked as he ambled toward the landings.

"To Mexico," Justin said curtly. "To get my wife."

"He hides beneath the wide brim of a white hat," Shiloh wrote, "his features obscured and in shadows. Yet there is no doubt as to the identity of this mysterious stranger. He is none other than Captain Charles Elliot, the British chargé d'affaires in Texas. He boarded the British warship *Eurydice* with utmost secrecy. Although he left Galveston on the *Electra*, that was but a ploy to defray suspicion. Once both ships were out of sight of land, the Englishman came aboard the *Eurydice*, bound for Vera Cruz. The warship is, incidentally, commanded by the chargé's cousin, Captain George Elliot. The two have formed a league of secrecy and will doubtless work together in Mexico."

Shiloh ended her dispatch with a few remarks and folded it away, putting it in a packet that she intended to send to the Galveston *News* as soon as they reached Vera Cruz.

The thirteen-day voyage had been abominable, as all sea travel seemed to be for Shiloh. She kept to the cramped mustiness of her cabin, alternately shivering and sweating, tormented by nausea. This did have one fortunate effect, however. She was left completely alone by the crew and passengers. She ventured out only to seek more information about Charles Elliot, and spent the rest of the time writing or lying stiffly in her bunk.

Relief washed over her when the *Eurydice* made port at Vera Cruz. Shiloh made note of the fact that the warship was reported under another name, so she could include that in her dispatches. A packet going to New Orleans took her first set of reports, and she felt proud of her accomplishment.

She also added a personal letter to the mail. In just two weeks, she'd grown accustomed to putting her thoughts on paper, and she'd written a brief but eloquent message to Justin. In it, she'd explained why she'd had to trick him. It was so much easier to say "I love you," on paper than to his face. There was no danger of rejection from the paper.

Vera Cruz was a colorful melange of humanity, busy and restless, never sleeping. Dark-skinned girls hung out of flower-laden balconies along a narrow street called Independencia, watching the stream of burros and carts below. The town was dominated by the cathedral in the Plaza de la Constitución, and by a fort with rough, flattened battlements called San Juan de Ulúa, but its true appeal was the vibrancy and energy of the people themselves.

Shiloh rode with Captain George Elliot and Charles in his ridiculous white hat, and a few others crowded into a poor conveyance. They squeezed through a crowded marketplace, where dark-gold-colored, loud-voiced vendors stood behind their mounds of fruit. There were coconuts, mamey, *zapote*, oranges, and a dozen other varieties that Shiloh didn't recognize. She nearly swooned at the smell in the fish area, declining the concoction of lime-seasoned raw *huachinango*, called *ceviche*, which the others availed themselves of.

They spent the night in a small *posada*, none too clean, lorded over by an ingratiating proprietor. While the others went out to tour the city, Shiloh stayed in her dank, cell-like room, unable to go because of her guise of mourning. The room's one redeeming quality was that it had an iron-rimmed balcony, which gave out onto the busy *zócalo*. From that vantage point, she sipped a glass of hot, sweet coffee and watched the action in the plaza below. The open-air, palm-roofed cantinas overflowed with people. Somewhere a small harp strummed, exhaling sweet sounds in a rippling, roundabout rhythm.

Shiloh sighed, longing for Justin. The dulcet song of the harp touched a chord in her heart. She wanted nothing more than to feel his arms about her, his breath in her ear as he whispered to her.

What was he thinking now? Did he miss her as badly as she did him? She hoped so. She dared to think it was so. Since she'd discovered her love for him, she hadn't asked him if he reciprocated her feeling. But in his tender caresses, in the silvery depths of his eyes, she'd read a clear message of caring. Even if he didn't love her, he had accepted her freely, and that was all she asked. Perhaps the day would come when he would tell her what he felt, but she could wait. In the meantime, she hoped he got her honest letter and forgave her.

It was a rough three-day journey to Mexico City. The small contingent lumbered through the dusty highlands, which were dominated by the maguey plant standing in straight, gray-green rows. The driver offered Shiloh a flask of *pulque*, which, he explained in broken English, was made from the maguey's *aguamiel*. The sweet-sour taste of the whitish liquid was surprisingly pleasant.

Through her veil, she watched Charles Elliot closely. He conversed in low tones with his cousin, and neither man took any notice of her. The journey passed uncomfortably, through tiny, hill-clinging pueblas, past a few opulent haciendas, until they reached the outskirts of Mexico City.

Evening was coming on, orange against the hills, but the driver promised they could reach their lodgings by nightfall. For the first time, Shiloh was at a loss. Her traveling companions expected to escort her directly to her family, and she had no idea what to tell them. She moved forward in the cart and seated herself next to the driver. He gave her a mustachioed grin and offered her more *pulque*, which she drank sparingly, as it was potent stuff.

"Please, I need your help," she said quietly, not looking at the driver. She pressed a gold coin into his hand.

"*Qué?*" He spoke softly too, respecting her desire for secrecy, and her coin.

"I do not know where to go in Mexico City. But I have told these gentlemen that I have family there. Do you understand?"

"*Sí.*"

"I don't want them to question anything I do."

The driver gave the slightest of nods. Looking straight ahead, he said, "I know of a place. Quiet, clean, very safe. No one will question you."

Shiloh breathed a sigh of relief and settled back as they entered the teeming, cramped city. As they wound through narrow, flower-hung streets, she looked in wonder at the sights. Lamplit gardens, airy saloons, poverty hidden behind ancient, crumbling walls, and a steady stream of people walking in high-spirited, laughing groups past dozens of beggars who huddled in doorways.

Shiloh assured Captain Elliot and his white-hatted companion that they didn't need to see her to the end of her journey. They were left at the British consulate, and she went on with the driver.

He took her a few blocks away to a small hotel and

396

carried her bag in for her. The proprietor and his wife listened closely as the driver gave a quick, staccato explanation. Shiloh was shown to a little room in the back of the second floor and served a meal of *pozole*, which she ate with good appetite. She spent the remainder of the evening on the terrace, which overlooked a tiled patio. A small fountain surrounded by dahlias and hyacinths bubbled in the middle. Holding her writing in her lap, she wrote out a description of the journey from Vera Cruz, again emphasizing Charles Elliot's amateurish guise and his easy assurance that the Mexican president would prove instantly compliant.

She also started a private journal. In it, she unabashedly wrote everything that was in her heart, including all she felt when she and Justin made love. Somehow, it soothed the ache in her to put the words on paper. The explicitness of what she wrote shocked her, but she knew that no eyes but her own would ever see it.

For the next two weeks, she was like a shadow in Mexico City's streets, moving discreetly through crowds as she delivered her letters for mailing, then went as close as she dared to the British consulate. She caught several glimpses of Charles Elliot and the British minister, always conferring, ever secretive, even when they ventured out onto the plaza for a meal at one of the cantinas.

One April day, she saw them leave on horseback, their bags stuffed with papers. She entered the consulate and struck up a conversation with one of the clerks, questioning him casually until he mentioned that Mr. Packenham, the British minister, had a meeting at the president's palace in Tacubaya, four miles distant.

Shiloh knew that the negotiations had reached a pivotal point. The British were undoubtedly going to offer all manner of concessions to Mexico in order to get that nation to recognize Texas. Elliot would return from Tacubaya loaded with damning evidence.

And Shiloh meant to get her hands on it. She spent the day in a seedy, rough district, buying a new disguise. If she was to get to Elliot's lodgings, it would have to be as someone quite different from the shy young widow.

Elliot was ridiculously easy to dupe. When Shiloh appeared that evening at his favorite cantina, her head tightly wrapped by a colorful scarf, her face heavily painted, her body clad in a snug-fitting crimson dress, he was only too pleased with her company. He celebrated what appeared to be a victory with Herrera by imbibing many glasses of fiery tequila and mescal and groping lustily at the lady who laughed and teased him in her thickly-accented English.

He reeled a little as he held the door to his room open for her.

"This way, señorita. We won't be disturbed here. . . ."

He lunged for her, reaching for her slim body. At the same moment, Shiloh stepped away, and he fell to the floor. As he spluttered and cursed, she grabbed a heavy clay doorstop and brought it down on his head.

Back in her hotel room, Shiloh hugged herself with glee. The papers she'd found in Elliot's quarters were as damning as a smoking gun. Lord Aberdeen had offered all sorts of concessions to the Mexicans in exchange for a treaty of recognition of the Texas Republic. The British believed that when the Texans learned that Mexico would live peaceably beside them, they'd abandon all plans for statehood.

Shiloh sighed happily. At last her work was done. At last she could go home, to Texas, to Justin.

Eighteen

Shiloh thanked all the stars of heaven the next day that she'd resisted the temptation to shed her widow's garb. Because among the passengers in the coach to Vera Cruz was a white-hatted Englishman.

"Mrs. Willows, I'm surprised to see you," he said. "I thought you'd planned to stay on in Mexico City."

"It doesn't suit me," she said, her voice studiedly soft and lower in pitch than it normally was. "I'm going back to Texas. And what about you, sir? Your trip was quite short also."

"Mexico City is an abominable place," he said darkly, his hand reaching gingerly under his white hat to touch the lump on his head. "I'm only too happy to leave it. I was robbed last night, most brutally. Besides, my business is concluded. I shall spend a little time at Jalapa, awaiting the results. The climate is quite pleasant there."

She stayed clear of him during the uneventful journey. Outside Mexico City, the road climbed back up to the maguey fields and pine forests, through the broad lands and clear air of ranch country, and then higher still, to whitish hills that embraced flower-fringed lakes.

Finally the road descended again into pueblas huddled beneath the ice-capped Pico de Orizaba and the brooding extinct volcano called Perote.

The coach stopped to allow a herd of sturdy goats to pass. Shiloh noticed the tattoo of hoofbeats as they waited, but thought nothing of it until the driver, a lad of about fifteen, gave a shout of alarm.

"Brigands!" he cried, and raised his hands in supplication. He was armed with a rusty pistol, but didn't think to avail himself of it.

As the other passengers began to shout and scream, Shiloh watched the robbers approach. Having spent most of her money, she had little to fear. She did twist Justin's willow ring off her finger and drop it into the bodice of her dress.

The two brigands rode up on tired-looking mounts. Only one of them was armed. Although he barked an order in Spanish, Shiloh saw through the facade of bravado the man tried to affect. He and his companion were both painfully thin, trembling from drink, or perhaps the lack of it. In their frayed serapes and ancient boots, they were a sorry sight.

The other passengers didn't seem to notice the weakness of their assailants. They began removing jewelry, taking out money and valuables. With a snort of disgust, Shiloh bent and took up the driver's pistol. The weapon was unfamiliar and rusty, but loaded. Aiming carefully, Shiloh fired off a shot that knocked the gun from the brigand's hand.

His scream was high and thin, a sound more of fright than pain. His horse reared, then bolted down into the valley. The other followed close at his heels.

A wondering silence ensued. The driver and passengers stared in disbelief at the little Tejana widow who had defended them so coolly. Shiloh grew uncomfortable under their stares and returned the pistol to the driver.

"Let's go," she said quietly as she set the gun down. She suffered their gratitude in silence, looking down at her hands. When one of the passengers insisted on treating her to a meal in Jalapa, she could hardly refuse. They ate a hearty *comida*, served by a barefoot girl in a wide skirt, near the town's ancient public washing place.

At the end of the meal, Shiloh went to avail herself of the facilities, such as they were. As she was returning through the dusty back dooryard, the girl who had served the meal hailed her.

She seemed to be agitated, although Shiloh didn't understand a word she said. She spoke rapidly, animatedly, gesturing in the air. Shiloh shrugged helplessly and gave her an apologetic look. The girl stopped speaking and passed on.

Shiloh felt herself being gripped from behind. It all happened so quickly that she forgot to cry out. A foul-smelling sack, stiff with dust, was placed over her head, her hands bound behind her back.

Her protests were muffled by the sack as she felt herself being lifted up and tossed onto the bed of a cart. Helpless and furious, she was taken a short distance away. Again strong arms lifted her and carried her up a flight of stairs. She was placed upon a mat of some sort, and then her hands were unbound. She clawed the filthy sack from her head, removing her bonnet and veil with it.

The door closed after two fleeing men, but there was still a presence in the room. Charles Elliot stood against a long, iron-barred window, eyes cold and pale, smiling at her.

"It frightens me," he said conversationally, "when I think how close you came to getting back to Texas."

With a cry of fury, Shiloh lunged for him. He

stopped her when he produced a small, deadly-looking knife.

"Your disguise had me fooled right to the end, Mrs. McCord. And I assume that was you in my room the last night in Mexico City. I didn't suspect a thing, though, until you shot at those brigands. Very few women can shoot like that. Naturally you were the first who came to mind."

Shiloh wiped a hand across her sweat-stained face. "Let me go, captain. Holding me here will serve nothing."

"Don't be ridiculous," he snapped, suddenly angry. "Do you think I'm going to let you carry tales back to Texas?"

She smiled in bitter triumph. "You're through, Captain Elliot. By now, all of Texas and the United States know of the underhanded dealings of the man in the white hat. Your story is in all the papers. I sent off the last dispatch the day we left Mexico City."

"I don't believe you," he growled, growing pale.

She shrugged. "You'll find out soon enough. I'm afraid your career is over. Of course, this sort of thing goes on all the time in diplomatic circles. But you've committed the cardinal error of being found out."

A snarl of pure rage came from him. For a heart-stopping moment, Shiloh thought he was going to stab her with his knife.

"Don't add to your crimes, captain," she said quickly, backing away. "It's one thing to blunder in a deal with the Mexicans, but if you murder me, you'll hang. The editor of the Galveston *News* has a sealed letter, which is to be opened if I don't return to Texas by June first. I'm sure you can imagine what's in it."

"Damnably clever," he remarked, calming a bit. "But the letter will be opened, because you won't ever get back to your beloved Texas." He turned on his heel and left the room, bolting the stout door from the outside.

There was no hope of escape. The one window had close-set bars and looked out over a small yard where hens scratched in the dust. Shiloh waited out the night and through the next day, watching for someone to call to, but no one crossed the yard.

Finally, when the second twilight fell and blue fog settled on the mossy mountains, she heard voices outside the door. Fear prickled at her as she heard something familiar in one of the voices. The bolt slid and the door opened.

Shiloh looked up, her head tossed back defiantly. Then her face drained of color.

"*St. James . . .*"

The strikingly handsome man with his lazy, glittering eyes and thin mustache strode into the room. His sensual lips parted, revealing twin rows of ivory teeth.

"So you remember me," he said, seemingly delighted. "But here I do not go by Christopher St. James. I am known as Cristobal Santiago."

Shiloh tried not to cringe as he circled her slowly, his lazy eyes assessing her. Suddenly, his hand grasped the bodice of her gown and pulled roughly, tearing the garment from neck to hem. St. James, or Santiago, studied the scars Shiloh had received on the *Princeton*, but said nothing.

His cold inspection made Shiloh furious. "How bold you are," she sneered, "now that my husband is not around to lay waste to you."

Santiago looked over at Elliot and laughed. "You did not underestimate her charms, *mi amigo.*"

Elliot nodded grimly as Shiloh clutched the shreds of her gown about her. "I think you'll find she's well worth the price. But I should warn you, she is not as fragile as

404

she looks. She's a wildcat, Santiago. Don't turn your back on her."

The man called Santiago took Elliot's advice and bound Shiloh's wrists behind her. She gave him a venomous look as he took out a length of cloth to use as a gag. She stopped to glare at Charles Elliot.

"When Justin finds you," she whispered, "you'll wish you'd never set foot in Texas."

"I shall only be too glad to wash my hands of your dirty little republic, Mrs. McCord," he sneered, and watched as Santiago secured the gag in place.

They traveled the night through, winding down the hills around Jalapa to the outskirts of Vera Cruz. Santiago kept his cart away from town, going down to a rocky cove where the waves rushed in. He freed the mule, sending it on its way with a slap to the rump.

He gripped her arm and thrust her down a jagged incline. A small boat waited at the shore, bobbing patiently. Santiago settled Shiloh in the bow and cast off, raising a pair of sails with an expert hand. He set them on an easterly course, secured the rigging, and came toward Shiloh, a knife held between his teeth.

She shrank back. He looked exactly like a pirate, eyes full of fierce greed.

He laughed at her. "Did I pay for you in gold just so I can kill you?" he asked. "No, my beauty. I think we are sufficiently far from civilization. I will relieve you of your bonds now. But let me remind you, these waters are full of hungry sharks. You wouldn't want to try to escape by swimming." He knifed through the ropes on her wrists and removed the gag.

Shiloh chafed her raw flesh and worked her aching jaw, accepting a canteen of fresh water to relieve the appalling dryness of her mouth.

"I am a citizen of Texas. What you're doing is a violation of international law."

Santiago threw back his head and laughed richly. "I am bound by no law, *cara mia*. I am a citizen of the high seas."

She shuddered. She recalled all that Justin had told her about him, something about a pirate's retreat off Mexico.

"How did Captain Elliot find you?" she asked.

"We are old friends. We knew each other in China, and had a very profitable relationship there. As it happened, he found me in Vera Cruz, looking for an *Indio* girl to replace one of my servants. Imagine my pleasure when I learned he had an available woman."

Shiloh went weak with relief. If she was only to be a servant, that was bearable.

Santiago grinned at her, his next words shattering her relief. "But I paid far too high a price for a mere servant. You, I think, will serve me in other ways."

"Where are you taking me?"

"To Sacrificios. A small island not far from here. I have a fine house there, very private. No one ever comes to Sacrificios, so-named because of the offerings the Old Ones made to their gods there."

"My husband is a wealthy man," Shiloh said, her voice rising in desperation. "He'll reward you handsomely for my safe return."

"Come now, my dear. What kind of man would reward me for buying his wife from an Englishman?"

Dawn broke in the east as they approached the tiny island. It rose up out of the dark blue water like a forbidding castle. Anchored some distance away, safe from the jagged shoals, was a tri-masted ship. The *Falcon*.

"Ah, Sacrificios," Santiago said happily. "And that," he added, pointing to the ship, "used to be known as the *Falcon*. But she is my real mistress. She is called *Angelica*."

He moored the boat in a narrow cove and lifted Shiloh from the bow, carrying her to dry land.

"Tiny as the *mitla* bird," he said delightedly as he held her. "I think you will make me very happy, my love."

Shiloh bit the inside of her lip until she tasted blood. Then she coughed, convulsing violently, spitting blood onto the rocks.

"What is this?" Santiago demanded. "Are you ill?"

She nodded slowly, spasms still lifting her chest. "Consumption. My mother died of it."

He dropped her so quickly that she fell to the rocks. "*Puta!*" he raged. "Do not come near me with your killing sickness." But then he hesitated. "This is a trick, is it not? You are not really sick."

"I wish that were so," Shiloh said.

"Why did I not see you cough blood before?"

She shrugged, improvising quickly. "The mountain air of Jalapa agrees with me. But here, at sea level, I am weak."

"I do not believe you."

"Why do you think Captain Elliot was so eager to be rid of me?" Shiloh had another fit of coughing and brought up more blood.

Santiago uttered what sounded like a curse in Spanish. "Get away from me," he ordered. "If you cannot earn the price I paid for you by warming my bed, Shiloh, you will repay me by doing the lowliest jobs imaginable at Casa Santiago. You will be a slave to slaves, a servant to scullery maids. And if I find that you are lying to me about this wasting disease . . ." He let his voice trail off and his long-fingered hand move caressingly down to the knife in his belt.

407

Shiloh stared, unflinching, at her captor. It was far too soon to despair. Santiago was fierce, yes, and darkly dangerous. But she, too, was a fighter.

Justin slowed his horse to a walk as he entered the dark labyrinth of Mexico City. He patted the lathered beast's neck encouragingly. The horse, a sturdy little broom-tailed mare he'd bought in Vera Cruz, had more than proven her value on the fast ride in from the coast. With incredible stamina, she had covered the distance in two days.

Still, Justin was at least two weeks behind Shiloh. Fate, it seemed, was working against him. He'd waited nine days at Galveston for a vessel. Finally, the *Prospect* came in from New Orleans, bound for Vera Cruz. A storm from the tropics buffeted them through the Gulf waters, throwing the clumsy *Prospect* several days off course. There were more delays as repairs were made. Finally, in the last week of April, the *Prospect* had limped into port at Vera Cruz. According to port officials, the British warship *Eurydice* had never landed there. Justin didn't believe that for a minute. Charles Elliot's cousin had undoubtedly given his vessel another name.

Now, in Mexico City, he searched every face he passed, looked through iron grilles into flower-decked patios, and scanned dozens of markets for a glimpse of Shiloh's fiery curls, the creamy fairness of her skin. But it was useless. He didn't know how she'd disguised herself or where she might have stayed. The only thing he knew with any certainty was that she'd used the alias on his billet, J. Willows. The name meant nothing to the numerous innkeepers he'd asked.

At nightfall he found a good livery for his horse and went to the house of his friend and associate, Hamilton

Coffey. Coffey worked for the American consul and had been instrumental in getting the Mier survivors released after a long imprisonment.

The intense, agitated little man gave Justin a cordial welcome, but his concern was evident.

"Are you sure you haven't been recognized, Justin? Your description was widely circulated after you escaped from Saltillo."

"That was two years ago, Ham. Anyway, I'm keeping my head down."

A barefoot servant brought food and a bottle of fiery mescal.

"What can I do for you?" Hamilton asked, biting into a tortilla-wrapped *carne asada*.

"I'm looking for my wife. She came here under the name of J. Willows."

"Alone?" Hamilton gasped. It was unthinkable for an Anglo woman to do such a thing in Mexico.

Justin nodded as demons of fear entered his mind. "She—Shiloh—is an unusual woman. She's done some detective work in the past and is damned good at it. She followed Charles Elliot here."

Coffey's astonishment increased. "Elliot is here? What the hell are the English up to now?"

"It's a last-ditch effort to keep Texas independent. I believe he made some offers to President Herrera in order to pursuade him to recognize Texas's sovereignty."

"Damn! Do you think Herrara'll go for it?"

Justin nodded darkly. "England can be pretty generous when it comes to protecting her interests."

"So what's your wife's part in it?"

"She wanted to catch Elliot in the act, discredit him. Hamilton, have you heard anything about her? Anything at all?"

He shook his head apologetically. "We don't know

every American in the city. But I'll ask around. I think your best bet is to find Elliot."

Justin nodded again. "I intend to do that first thing in the morning." He sipped his mescal, savoring the burn of it.

"Why don't you tell me a little about your wife so I can spread the word?"

Justin ran his hand idly over the carved arm of his chair, thinking. "If you saw her, you'd never forget her. She's petite, I guess you'd call it, with the brightest head of red hair you ever saw. Pretty as a Texas wildflower." He nearly choked on the words as he experienced a gut-wrenching sense of loss, in spite of his anger at her. "Shiloh's a talkative woman," he continued, "but not what you'd call frivolous. Mighty outspoken, especially when she feels strongly about something. She's got a stubborn streak a mile wide, too, and more courage in her than most men."

"Not your typical retiring homebody, is she, Justin?" Hamilton said wryly.

"Far from it."

Hamilton looked at him squarely. "She sounds like she's worth the trouble of finding, Justin."

He nodded, wishing like hell that it weren't so. He'd almost managed to convince himself that she was nothing to him . . . almost. But he could no more deny how he felt about her than he could deny the rising of the sun each morning. Shiloh, with all her maddening foibles and faults, was as much a part of him as his right arm.

Lewis Packenham, the British minister, was a harried-looking, sloppy man. He looked up from his papers at the tall blond American who had entered his office.

"Yes? What is it?"

"I'm Stephen Turner," Justin said, extending his hand. He hoped like sin that Packenham had never met the real Turner, one of Anson Jones's aides.

"President Jones sent me," he lied. "It's a matter of mutual concern to both our countries."

"Do you have a dispatch for me?"

Justin shook his head. "I must see Captain Elliot. Can you tell me where he is?"

Packenham looked at him sharply. "How would I know a thing like that? He's assigned to Texas. There was something about his going to South Carolina. . . ."

"Come on, Mr. Packenham. We both know he's in Mexico."

But the man wouldn't budge. Justin fought the urge to lunge across the desk and choke an admission out of the Englishman.

"I'm sorry, but I can't help you. If you had a dispatch, something in writing, I might be able to tell you something useful, Mr. Turner."

Their gazes locked and held for a moment, Justin's fierce and steely, Packenham's stubborn.

"Good day, Mr. Turner," he said quietly.

Justin strode from the office, tense with anger. He brushed past a Mexican clerk who was bent over a ledger.

"Jalapa," the clerk mumbled.

Justin froze. "What did you say?"

The clerk's pen scratched across the book. Without looking up, he said, "I was just thinking the weather is fine in Jalapa this time of year."

"Thank you," Justin breathed.

"Vaya con dios, amigo."

For two days he climbed toward the hilly, high region

411

of Jalapa, stopping only to give his horse a rest and a drink in one of the icy mountain pools. Finally the chalk-white hills came into view, shrouded by a thin fog that rose up from the valley.

It was time for caution. If the Mexican clerk's information was reliable, Elliot was down somewhere in the town. Justin stopped at the outskirts and removed his hat. From his saddlebag he took a jar of lampblack mixed with saddle soap, usually used for polishing his boots. He used this to dye his hair and the thick blond mustache he'd been cultivating. The image that stared out of a nearby mountain pool was quite satisfactory. The newly blackened hair hung in oily hanks, the locks falling to conceal Justin's facial scars. Unfortunately, there was nothing he could do about his size. The Mexicans, in general, were a diminutive race, and his height would probably draw attention.

But he had to take the chance. Pulling down the brim of his black hat, Justin slouched in the saddle and walked his horse into town.

He selected a small, dirt-floored cantina near the *zócalo* to sit and assess the town. A fine, needlelike rain began to fall, stinging droplets coming through a tear in the canvas awning over the table. Justin moved away from the rain to prevent it from removing the coloring in his hair.

"*Chipi-chipi*, we call this rain," said a quiet voice behind him. "Penetrates like surgery."

Justin raised his head cautiously. The speaker was a stocky little man with several teeth missing and a large silver hunk of a ring on one hand. He was speaking English. Justin tensed, disappointed that his disguise was so inadequate.

He squinted at the stocky man, saying nothing.

"You like our little town, Jalapa?" the man asked.

"Just passing through," Justin said quietly.

412

The Mexican eyed his saddlebag. "You have some money? There is much to be had in Jalapa, for a little sum."

Cautiously, Justin took a double eagle from his pocket and turned it over in his hand, toying with it idly.

"A woman, perhaps?" the man suggested, "or maybe a potion to soothe the soul. . . ."

"Just some answers."

"I will do my best, señor."

"I'm looking for an Anglo, an Englishman. Middle-aged, well-fed. Probably has plenty of money."

The serving girl, barefoot and wearing a wide skirt, approached and said something to the man in rapid Spanish.

The man stroked his grizzled face and eyed Justin's coin. "Hmm . . . I am not sure. It is possible that I have seen such a man. . . ."

Reaching the end of his patience, Justin shot to his feet and grabbed the man by his filthy collar. "Look my friend," he growled, "I don't have time to play games with you. Just name your price and tell me what you know."

Squirming under the tall Anglo's steely gaze, the Mexican babbled out his information. "The man you seek calls himself Marshall. He is at a villa in the Calle Morelos, a house with a brass snake on the door."

Justin set the man down and strode away, leaving his coin on the table. He walked his horse up a network of narrow, cobbled alleys, studying the doors of a series of pastel-painted facades. Near the top of the hill, he found the brass snake knocker. It was the hour of siesta, and the stinging *chipi-chipi* still fell steadily, so no one was about. Justin brought his horse across the alley and tethered it under the shelter of a tiled eave.

Loose plaster crumbled under his fingers as he

scaled the wall, pulling himself up with a handhold on the iron grille of a second-story window. From the top of the wall he looked down into a tiny patio, surrounded by open hallways on the ground and upper floors. He dropped soundlessly to the tiles and scanned the three windows, two of them dark. The third glowed dimly with lamplight. He stole toward this one. Through a gap in the fringed curtains he saw a small stove with a fire glowing inside. And the bulky form of Charles Elliot, sitting at a table, writing.

Hatred rose in Justin's throat at seeing the Englishman so comfortably settled, when Shiloh was God knew where, alone in a strange country. He swallowed the bitter feeling, knowing he'd have to remain calm.

He stood in front of the arched wooden door and drew both pistols. His boot splintered the wood as he opened the door with a mighty kick.

Elliot shot to his feet, upsetting the table. His heavy face drained of color, his mouth working soundlessly. He backed away from Justin, toward the glowing stove. Clearly, he saw through the disguise.

"Where is she, Elliot?" Justin demanded, his eyes narrowing to deadly slits.

"I—I don't know what you're talking about," Elliot began. Justin almost believed him until his nervous eyes flicked to the papers that had fallen from the upended table. The glance was so subtle that it might not have happened at all, but Justin knew his questions would be answered by Elliot's letters.

Slowly, eyes never leaving the panting Englishman, Justin holstered one of his pistols. He kept the other trained on Elliot as he stooped to gather up the fallen papers.

"Don't move," he warned Elliot, and studied the florid scrawl, glancing up frequently. The first page appeared to be a self-congratulatory summation of the meetings with Herrera, the second a brief letter to Mrs. Elliot. Finally Justin found the passage he was looking for. His eyes darted over the phrases.

". . . was but a small annoyance, easily dispensed with, and quite profitably, I might add." The sheer arrogance, the smugness of the statement enraged Justin. He crumpled the letter and raised hate-filled eyes to the Englishman.

Elliot panicked. His terror lent swiftness to his movements. He reached for the oil lamp and hurled it at Justin's head. Justin ducked and nearly pulled the trigger on Elliot. But not yet. The captain still had something to say.

Lamp oil formed a burning pool on the tile floor. Justin advanced on Elliot, who backed closer still to the hot stove. Sweat appeared on his throbbing temples as the heat grew more intense.

"It's getting mighty warm in here," Justin drawled. "You'd better talk fast, Elliot. Now. What have you done with Shiloh?"

"I—she was kidnapped. I had nothing to do with it!"

Justin shook his head. "Try again, Elliot. The more you lie, the hotter this stove's going to get."

"She was taken by a man called Santiago. He has some sort of pirate's lair on an island called Sacrificios, off Vera Cruz."

Justin had to fight the urge to leave immediately. Elliot was too terrified of being roasted alive to be lying now, but he was holding something back.

"What was your part in it?"

"Nothing! I did nothing, I—" Elliot screamed as his backside touched the hot iron. Dissolving into tears, he sobbed out his confession. "I had to do it. She was going to ruin me! I—I sold her to St. James—Santiago—ah!"

Justin shoved him against the stove. "You're scum,

415

Elliot. You don't deserve to be spared, but you're not worth the lead in a single bullet. I'll leave you here to lick your wounds. But if I don't find Shiloh, alive and whole, I'll find you again."

Elliot moaned and dropped heavily to the floor, fainting with pain and dread.

Justin gave him a brief, contemptuous look and left the way he had come, dropping to the street and running to his horse. Ignoring the sting of the mountain drizzle, he spurred the animal toward the coast, not allowing himself to imagine what Shiloh was suffering at the hands of the man called Santiago, also known as Christopher St. James.

Shiloh glanced down at her filthy hand, which held a scrub brush. The fingers that clutched it had grown bony, birdlike from lack of nourishment, the skin chapped and scabbed. Shiloh ached in places she hadn't known she had. From the time she was kicked roughly from her pallet at sunup until she collapsed again after cleaning up from the late dinner hour, she worked. The winding stone halls and stairways of Casa Santiago were spotless from her ceaseless enforced labor. Every wall, every tiny window ledge and nook was cleaned daily. The dark, heavy furniture gleamed.

Shiloh was given every odious task that existed, from emptying chamber pots and spitoons to mucking out the small dog run at the side of the strange, pieced-together house.

Her reward for all of this was that she was left alone by Santiago and his bizarre crew of seasoned pirates and lithe young men. She could stand the taunts and little cruelties of the other maids, but she knew she couldn't have stood being Santiago's whore.

416

"Get to work," ordered a flat-faced *Indio* woman, stopping to prod Shiloh with her broom.

Shiloh dropped to her bruised knees and resumed her scrubbing. A cough rattled in her throat. She smiled grimly at the wet stones. She no longer had to pretend illness. The cold windy nights on a thin pallet, coupled with a poor diet and exhaustion, had weakened her, opened her up to sickness.

Still, Shiloh had not been beaten and worked into submission, even though she let it appear that way. While she scrubbed and polished, her mind roamed free, dreaming and planning. She would soon be away from Casa Santiago. She would escape, she vowed to the stones, or die trying.

When the house settled down for afternoon siesta, Shiloh stole out every day to the beaches, slipping barefoot across the sand and scaling the sharp crags to a hidden, secret cove. Coming and going was easy; Santiago was confident of the security of his sea-moated lair.

Shiloh had spent days gathering driftwood, lashing the smooth white pieces together with the ropelike grass that grew in profusion on the isle. Now her crude raft was finished, and tonight she would leave.

In her mind, she went over the plan. The night sentry, who walked the high wall at the top of the house, was an indolent, careless man who waited until the moon rose and then settled in a corner to snore the night away. Shiloh would climb the wall, dropping to the forbidding, ancient ruins of an Aztec sacrificial altar, darting down to the tiny cove. Her raft wasn't sturdy, but with luck, the ingoing tide would carry her to the mainland.

Shiloh did her usual work and ate every bit of her rancid, watery *pozole* that evening. It tasted abominable, but she would need all her strength. She stole some

417

corncakes from the detached baking house and ate some of those too, tying a few others into her ragged apron.

Finally she settled down on her pallet to wait. A small, high window displayed the openness of the night sky, and freedom whispered in on the waves as they crashed against the rocks. By the time the moon rose, Shiloh's nerves were wound taut. She ventured out into the hall, leaning against its cool dampness to will away the trembling of her limbs.

She groped her way along the dark hall and left by a narrow window. A small ledge led up to the walk. Shiloh didn't allow herself to look down; it was a sheer, deadly drop to the crags below. But she had made the climb plenty of times before. Her toughened bare feet knew every foothold and tuft of vegetation to help her along the way.

She reached the upper wall, and as expected, found the watchman snoring under a full moon. She hoisted herself up with a final heave.

Suddenly part of the wall crumbled and several rocks catapulted fifty feet down. Shiloh froze and hung, legs dangling, watching the guard. Her breathing returned to normal when he didn't stir. She slung her leg over the wall.

Frenzied barking filled the air. The dogs. Shiloh had forgotten about the dogs. As she scrambled over the wall, the watchman awoke, befuddled and cursing. Before he could right himself, Shiloh hurled her body against him, gaining precious seconds as she ran the length of the narrow walkway.

The guard shouted to alert the household and dashed after Shiloh. She heard his heavy breathing as he came at her. But the end of the walk loomed close. The blood pounded in her veins when she reached the wall, barely touching the jagged stone as she leaped over.

It was a ten-foot drop to the hard-packed ground. Shiloh fell clumsily, pain shooting up her leg. She ignored it and stumbled on, toward the darkly forbidding shapes of the Aztec ruins.

The footfalls from behind grew closer. Shiloh ducked her head and ran, cutting her feet on the rocks, piercing them as she trod over needle-fine stinging prickly pear. The moon cast an otherworldly, eerie glow on the ancient ruins. But to Shiloh, the crudely-cut monoliths offered safe haven from her pursuer, a place to hide.

She delved into the scattered carvings, darting amid huge faces with thick, leering lips rolled back over pronounced jaguar fangs. The creatures from another time, animals given distorted human features, glared in the moonlight. Shiloh crouched behind the jutting chin of some age-old deity, not daring to breathe.

The underbrush rustled nearby. Finally the footsteps receded and Shiloh dared to move, looking cautiously about before she began to creep, slowly and soundlessly, to the far edge of the cliffs. Like a shadow, she stooped low and scuttled from one rock to the next.

In front of the cliff was a grassy slope, open to the night and the silvery moonglow. Twenty yards, twenty-five, perhaps, to the edge, where she could drop down to the safety of her cove.

Shiloh hugged the rock and drew a deep breath, holding it, listening. The waves rushed ceaselessly, the salt-scented wind rustled the grass. There was no human sound.

She burst from her hiding place, astounding herself at her own speed. Never had she run so fast, so desperately. The brink loomed closer, closer. . . .

And then it was all over. Her ankles were grabbed by a diving, cursing figure. She hit the ground with a jarring thud that knocked the breath from her. Even as she gasped for air, Shiloh writhed and fought, scratching and kicking like a wild thing. Through a haze of panic and rage, she became aware that it was not the lumbering guard who had caught her, but Santiago himself. She smelled the scent of tequila on his breath and felt the hardness of his lean, wiry body as he struggled to subdue her.

Shiloh fought as if possessed by demons. She raked her broken, uneven nails across Santiago's sneering face, bit savagely at the hand that pressed down on her mouth. Her foot found a long, hard shin. Santiago's hand landed in a scintillating blow across her face. She countered with another vicious swipe, laying open the flesh above and below his eye, scratching at the moist orb.

Santiago bellowed a curse, clutching at his eye. "Blind!" he screamed. "I'm blinded!"

Shiloh scrambled, half crawling, away from him. But despite his screams, Santiago's wound was superficial and he recovered in time to catch her again. Now he beat her in earnest, no longer enjoying the struggle. Twin blows to the head, one which split her lip and the other raising bells of agony in her ear, pushed Shiloh to the brink of unconsciousness.

Her vision swam as she felt herself being picked up and slung over his shoulder. She pounded at his back and writhed, but his arms held her fast. His breath came quickly; he'd exerted himself in the struggle.

He didn't take her immediately back to the house. He went back to the Aztec ruins, to a central stone that had been crudely cut into a wide-based, bowl-shaped altar. He lay Shiloh on the rough, unyielding rock, straddling her, placing his knees upon her hands, grinding them into the stone.

Santiago smiled wickedly, teeth glittering, eyes hard

420

and bright. "At last, the wildcat is subdued. If you have half as much vigor when I take you — here, now — I will be pleased."

Shiloh struggled helplessly, beating her bare feet against the stone. "But the consumption —" she protested.

"No more lies!" he shouted. "A woman who is wasting away could never run like you did, fight like *el diablo* himself. You are no more ill than I am." Roughly, he grabbed a handful of her matted, long-neglected curls, holding her head still.

"Do you know what this place is, *diabla tejana*? It is the place where the ancients fed their hungry gods, just as you will satisfy my appetite." He jerked her head to one side and she found herself staring at an obscene goddess, with breasts jutting, the tip of her tongue pointing maliciously.

"Look well to her, *cara*. She is the love goddess. You find her repulsive, but she is the elemental woman: frank, lustful. You will be my love goddess, Shiloh. Tonight we will become one."

She knew then that he was mad, and this frightened her more than any of his cruelties. His dagger gleamed. Shiloh felt the cords of her neck tighten in anticipation of the first bite of metal. Santiago was a madman, spouting his talk of the ancients and feeding their gods. She squeezed her eyes shut. To die, like this, at the hands of a maniac. . . .

But the knife didn't touch her. Santiago slipped the point under first one button, and then the next, slicing them from the cloth of her dress. As he cut, he spoke again.

"The ancients had many ways of offering sacrifice. Some victims had their throats slit; others had their hearts cut out before their living eyes."

Shiloh almost begged him to kill her and be done

with it, but she knew he would take his time with her. He finished with her bodice, pushing it aside with the tip of his knife. She shivered, feeling the wind on her bare breasts.

She turned her head away from his avid face. She found herself looking at a jaguar deity with slanting cats' eyes and long sharp teeth, the very image of strength and ferocity. Strangely, she took heart from this mythical beast. Santiago was mad enough to be incautious; perhaps there was yet hope, if she could just remain as strong and unyielding as this stone cat.

She arched her back with a mighty thrust. Although Santiago kept his seat, one of his knees gave a little and Shiloh tore her hand free. She caught his wrist and dug her nails in.

"So the fight is not gone from you yet, *diabla*," he said angrily. "Do not push me too far. . . ."

He slapped her with one hand while the other fumbled at the top of his trousers. "The time has come," he muttered. "The Old Ones will wait no longer."

"No!" Shiloh screamed, writhing beneath him. "Oh God, no—"

She stopped suddenly, sure that terror played a cruel trick with her mind. As graceful and catlike as the jaguar deity, a tall form dropped into view. Dripping wet, the moonlight carving shadows in the muscles of his bare chest, he was himself a god, as strong and fierce as the feline sculpture.

She breathed his name like a prayer.

"Justin . . ."

Nineteen

With a snarl of animal rage, Justin leapt at Santiago, the two falling to the ground beside the altar. The pirate had a madman's strength, but the power of Justin's fury was awesome. Shiloh jumped down, ready to help, but she could do no more than pound Santiago's heaving back. She looked about for a loose stone to dash against his head, but the rocks were too large, embedded in the ground.

The bodies twisted. Santiago was beneath Justin, cursing and struggling. The hand that held the dagger was locked between them, quivering in mid-air, edging first toward one man, then the other. Veins stood out on Justin's arms as he strained to conquer the pirate.

A bitter, incomprehensible curse leaped from Santiago's mouth. His muscles gave out and the knife, held by his own hand, drove down into his neck.

Shiloh screamed at the sight of the short hilt sticking out of the flesh. Blood flowed, pulsated from the wound. Incredibly, Santiago dragged himself up, holding the edge of the stone altar. He collapsed onto it, gurgling his life out into the bowl, adding his blood to the blood of the victims of the ancients he had so revered.

Shiloh turned to Justin, unable to speak. She was filled with such a profusion of emotions: horror, relief,

423

love, disbelief, that no words could say what she felt. Justin stood, tall and straight with the moon at his back. Shiloh took a step toward him, then another, and then tumbled into his arms.

"Justin. I thought I would die tonight. I—"

"Shh. Don't talk. Are you all right?"

Her feet were raw and bleeding, her hands scraped, her jaw already beginning to swell from Santiago's blows. She tried to smile when she looked up at Justin.

"I'm all right," she said.

He took her hand and led her down to the water. "I left my boat about a hundred yards out," he said. "Can you swim it?"

Shiloh didn't hesitate. More than anything she wanted to be away from the horror of Sacrificios. She shed the ragged remains of her dress and walked down the sandy beach, wearing only her shift. The salt water stung her myriad small wounds, but it was a cleansing sensation and she welcomed it.

They struck out together, Justin staying close in case Shiloh weakened. Both were aware that sharks circulated in the inky night waters, but neither voiced the fear. They reached the boat without incident.

Justin pulled himself into the small shallop and helped Shiloh up after him. He settled in the stern and began rowing swiftly toward the distant winking lights of the harbor of Vera Cruz.

"Put that blanket around you," he said, indicating it with his head.

Gratefully, Shiloh wrapped herself in the thickly woven wool. She wiped a strand of wet hair from her cheek. She looked at Justin, watching his sinewy arms as they pulled rhythmically at the oars. She was elated to see him again, yet she felt awkward in his presence. Questions hung in the air between them.

"How did you find me?" she asked.

"Elliot told me where you were."

She shuddered to think how Justin had induced the Englishman to talk.

"Justin, I'm sorry for everything you had to go through. And—and thank you. I would have died tonight if it hadn't been for you."

"Never mind. It's over now."

An hour later, they boarded a French brig of war, called the *Céline*. Justin shielded Shiloh from the stares of the crew and passengers, taking her to a private cabin. A young boy brought fresh water and towels and a meal on a tray.

"Shall I get the ship's doctor?" Justin asked.

"No. I just need to get cleaned up." She felt the color rise to her cheeks. "I haven't bathed in weeks."

Justin was about to leave her alone. But then he looked at her, small and forlorn, wrapped in the shapeless gray blanket. A bit of seaweed clung to her cheek, beside the swelling jaw. Something knotted in his gut.

"Sit down," he said, indicating the bunk.

Like an overtired child, she complied. She didn't protest when Justin removed the blanket and wet shift. Looking at her thin, battered body, he felt a wave of pity.

"How long were you on the island?" he asked. As he spoke, he wetted a towel and began daubing at the lacerations on Shiloh's legs and feet.

She shrugged vaguely. "I don't know. Maybe three weeks. I lost track of the time."

He worked slowly, cleansing every inch of her skin and hair. There were bruises everywhere in various stages of healing. Her ribs showed plainly and there were shadows beneath her eyes, giving her face an ethereal, hollowed-out look.

"My God," he hissed. "What the hell did he do to you?"

"It wasn't Santiago so much as his servants. I guess they were trying to work me to death."

Justin frowned at a swelling knee. "So I see." His jaw worked tensely as he fought his next question. But he had to know.

"Shiloh."

"Yes?"

"Did he—did Santiago violate you?"

She stared at him. "He certainly did. He violated me, and every human conscience. He was a madman. You saw for yourself what he was like."

"That's not quite what I meant, Shiloh."

Realization dawned suddenly. He saw her eyes narrow. "He didn't take me to his bed. I convinced him I had a disease. But he must have been watching me, because tonight he guessed I was lying."

Justin looked down to hide the relief that washed over him. He was glad, not so much for himself as for Shiloh. She was too young and innocent to learn that carnal love had a dark side to it. He finished bathing her and gave her one of his white broadcloth shirts to wear as a bed gown.

She ate ravenously, devouring the thick fish soup and a quantity of white cheese and bread. Then, as abruptly as a candle flame going out, her eyes closed.

Justin washed himself and lay down, exhausted beyond measure. But sleep would not come. As Shiloh snuggled against him, Justin began to tremble. He couldn't stop thinking about how close he'd come to losing her.

The usual sickness plagued Shiloh during the voyage home. Yet it was somehow even worse this time, the nausea so intense that she couldn't see straight. A

426

constant, incessant hunger induced her to eat, although most of it was rejected by her protesting body.

Justin was gentle and solicitous, yet strangely distant. While she was in Mexico, Shiloh had imagined their reunion a hundred times, creating a golden, happy scene in her mind. The reality was a far cry from that daydream.

By the time they reached Houston, weary and tense, Shiloh could stand it no more. With the relief of being back on dry land, her strength returned and she was ready to face Justin's strange mood.

After a brief reunion with her father, who was now installed in the cottage at Post Oaks to take Wylie's place, they shared a meal and went up to retire for the night. Shiloh bathed in the dressing room, glorying in the feeling of being completely clean for the first time in weeks. She slipped on a white cotton gown and went out to the bedroom. Justin was gone.

Pursing her lips, she went to find him. She'd looked forward to this night, which would be their real reunion. The hunger in her was strong now that she wasn't being churned about on shipboard.

He was in his study, standing at the open window, looking at the spray of stars across the sky. Shiloh padded over to him on bare feet and wrapped her arms about his waist. She laid her cheek against his back.

"You feel so good to me," she murmured, breathing his scent.

Incredibly, he removed her hands and set her away from him. "You've had a long ordeal, Shiloh. Go upstairs and get some rest."

Her spirits plummeted. "But Justin, we're home at last. Don't you at least want to—"

"No. I have work to do."

A coldness formed around her heart. The pain of his rejection was too much for her to bear.

427

"Justin, why are you treating me like this?" She had a sudden, ugly thought. "It's Santiago, isn't it?"

He frowned. "Santiago?"

"You didn't believe me when I told you he never bedded me. You think I've been soiled. . . ." She turned away, hurt that he hadn't trusted her.

"You're wrong, Shiloh."

"Then what is it?" she demanded, growing angry.

His eyes were steel-cold. "I'm surprised you have to ask. Perhaps you've had a lapse of memory. Don't you recall drugging me and stealing my billet in Galveston?"

Shiloh swallowed. So that was it. His damned pride had been wounded.

"Justin, I had to do it. It was the only way."

"I'm sure it was." He shook his head. "You never give up, do you, Shiloh? You had to do it all on your own, to prove to the world your worth as an international spy."

She froze. "Is that what you think, Justin?"

"Of course. There's no other explanation. I'm tired of it, Shiloh. All your tricks, your lies . . ." He laughed bitterly. "You really had me fooled back in March when you threw yourself at me. I thought we finally had a chance together. But it was all part of your game, wasn't it? Just a way to follow me to Galveston and take my place on the Mexico mission."

Her head pounded. She couldn't believe what she was hearing. The accusations were like a knife, slicing through to her very soul.

Slowly, she backed away, moving her head from side to side in denial. "You're so wrong, Justin," she whispered.

"Go to bed, Shiloh. I've got things to do."

She fled, slamming the door behind her.

Justin went slowly to his desk and sat down. God, but Shiloh was becoming an accomplished little actress. Waltzing in as if nothing had happened, expecting him to welcome her back with open arms. He couldn't deny that he'd been tempted by the soft invitation of her touch, the seductive timbre of her voice in his ear . . . but she was asking too much this time. She'd pushed him too far. Coldly, the idea of divorce pushed its way back into his mind again. He'd ask Lamar Coulter about it in the morning.

For now, he needed something else to occupy his mind. Nearly two months' worth of correspondence was stacked on his desk. The night might not seem so long and lonely with the mail to occupy him.

He shuffled through letters from various places: Washington, the new capital of Austin, a thick envelope from the Willows, copies of newspapers. Justin grimaced when he noticed several pieces about the "man in the white hat" by S. Mulvane. Naturally she wouldn't want to credit her married name with the articles. . . . He picked up one of the letters. Creased and smudged, with Mexican markings and his name penned in Shiloh's tight, neat hand.

He turned it over a few times before unfolding it. In spite of himself, his eyes devoured the page.

"My dearest Justin," he read, his hands tightening on the paper. "By the time you read this I shall be in Mexico in pursuit of our acquaintance Capt. E_____. I know you consider it your place to be here but I had to come in your stead. You see, your careful plans were discovered by Mrs. S_____, who relayed them to your enemies. You would not have been allowed to reach Mexico alive. It was a cruel deception I played on you, my darling, but a necessary one. Having so recently discovered my great love for you, I could not bear the

429

thought of losing you. So forgive me, my heart, and look to the day when this business is concluded and we are reunited. Until then, and forever after, I remain your loving wife, S."

The words swam before his disbelieving eyes. The blood surged and pounded in his temples. He reread the letter, again and again, searching for a flaw in her sincerity. He found none.

Suddenly it all made sense to him. She loved him. She *loved* him. Everything she had endured in Mexico had been for his sake. His heart filled as he jumped up and climbed the stairs, taking them two at a time.

He threw open the bedroom door and stood, clutching the letter in his hand.

Shiloh was at the window. In the moonlight tears gleamed wetly on her cheeks. She turned her bleak face to him.

There was so much to be said, yet Justin couldn't find the words. He lifted the letter a little.

"I didn't know," he said, his voice rough with emotion.

"What didn't you know, Justin?" she asked softly. "I thought you had all the answers."

He winced at her subtle, angry tone. "I never knew how you felt about me, sweetheart. I thought you went to Mexico just to prove how clever you are."

She shook her head sadly. "You're a fool, Justin. A blind, proud fool. Didn't you understand what I was saying to you last March? I was giving myself to you; I don't know how I could have made myself any clearer."

"But you never said it, Shiloh. How could I have guessed, after all that had gone between us?"

"I was afraid you'd reject me. Besides, you should have trusted me."

The space between them was wide. The moonlight slid across the floor, emphasizing the distance.

"Is it too late now, Shiloh?" he asked softly.

She studied his face for a long, searching moment. "No, Justin. I can no more stop loving you than I can stop my heart from beating."

Suddenly the distance closed. Justin dropped the letter and strode to her. She opened her arms, reaching for him. They came together in an embrace so achingly sweet that it was akin to physical pain. Justin kissed her tears away, dissolving all the bitterness.

"God, I love you, Shiloh," he rasped. "You're everything to me."

"Justin, I've waited so long to hear you say that, so very long. . . "

He swept her up into his arms, gathering her so close that he could feel the wild beating of her heart and smell the lovely honeysuckle scent of her hair. Gazing down into the melting depths of her eyes, he lifted her up and placed her on the bed. Slowly, wonderingly, he removed her clothes, sliding the bed gown away from her silken skin, marveling at the thought that she was finally, completely, his. Shiloh heard the hiss of his indrawn breath, her name whispered in a voice she barely recognized. He slipped out of his own clothes and placed himself at her side. Eyes brimming with adoration, she raised her lips to him.

He made love to her tenderly, every kiss a reverence, every touch a tribute to their love. His fingers wound through her curls and stroked her face, her lips, the soft throbbing pulse at her throat. His mouth rained butterfly-soft kisses over her eyes and brow, then skimmed her neck and delved to the valley between her breasts, circling, teeth nipping lightly at the dusky-rose peaks.

Shiloh made a sweet offering of herself, arching upward to meet his caresses, feeling his love in every sensitive nerve ending. Then she returned the gift of his touch, gliding her hands down his sinewy back to his rigid flanks and ready maleness. Never had her emotions been so tightly strung, her senses so full of Justin. She realized that the element of love, discovered at last and admitted to by both of them, had changed everything.

There was no holding back, no shadow looming over them as in times past. They were now free to merge their souls together, unhindered by doubt. Shiloh knew that Justin felt the same way. They were closer than ever before, completely in tune with each other.

Justin took her lips again in a deep kiss, his tongue probing and his hand exploring her female warmth. Shiloh surged against him, feeling as if she were about to explode with her need to love and be loved by him. Whispering endearments that touched her to her very core, Justin answered her need, and she his, and their bodies and hearts were one.

They lay together afterwards, limbs tangled, breathing in tandem, in quiet awe of what had happened.

"I'm so happy," Shiloh said, softly, as if she almost didn't dare to believe it.

He propped himself up on one elbow and smiled down at her.

"I'm only sorry it took you two years to feel that."

She leaned up and kissed him sweetly. "You've been so patient with me."

"It wasn't hard. You're fascinating. But I admit I thought I'd lost you more than once. I thought it was all over in Virginia, when you said you wanted to come back to Texas without me."

She shuddered. "I remember that day. It was awful."

"I was going to tell you then, that very night, that I loved you, Shiloh."

"Oh God, Justin. I'm so sorry—"

"Never mind. It doesn't matter now. You weren't

ready to hear it at that point."

She pondered for a moment. "I don't suppose I was. I guess I didn't know how to love, or accept love. Only after you helped me straighten things out with my father could I really understand what I was feeling." She wrapped her arms around him joyously. "Everything is perfect now, isn't it, Justin?"

She told him with a kiss that she wanted him again, now, and for all time.

"Girl, you're glowing like the Texas sun," Nate proclaimed, opening the door to his cottage. "Never saw the likes of it before."

Shiloh smiled. She always seemed to be smiling these days. She leaned up and kissed her father's cheek. His face was tanned and healthy looking, a great contrast with the dissipated way he used to look.

"Ranch life seem to agree with you," she commented.

"Oh, it does, believe me. Come on into the kitchen and have something to eat."

She was surprised to see Ina there, frying bacon and setting out a plate of biscuits.

Shiloh was suddenly ravenous. Eagerly, she accepted a mug of coffee and sat down. Nate brought an extra stool and seated himself across from her.

"Have I told you how proud I am of you?" he asked, covering her hand with his.

She felt a little thrill of pleasure. "No, Papa."

"Well, I am. You pulled off that bit in Mexico like nothing I've ever seen before. Those articles you wrote were the talk of the town. Elliot didn't have a prayer."

She sipped her coffee. "I'm just glad it's over. The legislature has voted for annexation and now it's just a matter of time. Thank God."

"We'll be at war with Mexico soon," Nate said,

tempering her gladness. "Both the United States and Mexico seem ripe for it."

Shiloh nodded. She, too, had sensed the feeling in the papers she read, the speeches and debates of politicians.

Ina set down plates heaped with food. Shiloh stared at the bacon and fluffy eggs, her appetite leaving as abruptly as it had come. The smell reviled her and she turned her head away. Not wanting to offend Ina, she nibbled at a biscuit and sipped her coffee. But she saw the bright dark eyes looking pointedly at her plate.

Nate seemed preoccupied as he ate. Shiloh looked at him quizzically. "Are you still thinking about war?" she asked, her tone slightly chiding.

Nate glanced up, and then at Ina, and burst out laughing. "No, my girl," he chuckled. "It's something much closer to home." One of his broad hands reached for hers; the other closed around Ina's, and the Mexican woman blushed.

"You're not going to believe this, Shiloh, but this lovely lady has agreed to be my wife."

Shiloh was stunned. "Papa . . ." she breathed. "Ina . . ."

The older woman looked slightly apologetic. "I know I can never replace the mother you lost, Shiloh, but we can be friends if you will allow it."

"Allow it!" Shiloh cried, jumping up. She threw her arms around Ina, her heart bursting with happiness. "Nothing could please me more. Both of you are so dear to me."

Together, Nate and Ina breathed a sigh of relief. Their faces glowed with love.

"When are you getting married?" Shiloh asked eagerly.

"As soon as it can be arranged. Telling you was the last formality."

Shiloh laughed, feeling light and airy. "You have my every blessing," she told them. "Let's do it this month. June is a lovely time for a wedding."

Ina stood up and began clearing the table, but Shiloh stopped her. "Let Papa do that," she insisted, ignoring his look of exaggerated outrage. "We've got to start planning your wedding!"

In the two weeks that followed, the days were filled with the fun and anticipation of preparing for the great day, and the nights were soft with tender lovemaking. It was a golden time, aglow with love and kinship.

The weather was perfect on the day of the wedding. The ranch hands had hastily raised an octagonal gazebo in the yard. Shiloh and Prairie Flower festooned it with ribbons and golden marigolds, dark pink crape myrtle, and the laceweed that grew wild in the meadows.

Nate and Justin were setting up benches for the guests as Shiloh arrived with still more wildflowers. Nate gestured to her and she came to his side.

"I wanted to tell you together," he said, looking from one to the other. "Ina and I will be making a wedding trip. We're leaving tonight on the late steamer. I'm taking her to Mexico to find her family."

"Are you sure that's wise, Nate?" Justin asked.

"We'll be all right. War's still a long way off." His eyes took on a thoughtful, faraway look. "She's been so good to me, that woman. Given me everything and never asked a thing for herself. But I know she's missed the brothers and sisters she was separated from years ago. I want to do something for her for a change."

Shiloh kissed his cheek. "I think it's a lovely idea. How long will you be gone?"

"Months. Maybe a year." He turned to Justin. "I've

435

asked Eb to take my place around here while I'm gone. He's an old coot, but he works damned hard."

"Thank you, Nate." Justin shook his father-in-law's hand. "And good luck."

Shiloh placed her flowers in a large crock and went upstairs to find Ina. At Shiloh's insistence, Ina had agreed to dress in an upper guest room, her own quarters off the kitchen being far too small.

"All this fuss," Ina scolded. "*Dios*, I am not a young bride of eighteen."

Shiloh laughed and hugged her. "Every bride is special, Ina."

The handsome face softened. "What a dear you are. Come, I have a present for you."

"But this is *your* day," Shiloh protested. She broke off and gasped when Ina opened a box and moved aside the tissue. Proudly, she held up the most beautiful dress Shiloh had ever seen.

It was a gown of muslin, its lines simple, but it was embroidered so lavishly that it stunned the senses. Tiny, varicolored stitches depicted every field flower known in Texas: the intense color of spring bluebonnets, the deep reds of Indian paintbrush, lavender wisteria, and yellow jessamine, all united by twining green vines.

"You did this for me?" Shiloh breathed. "But how . . . When did you have the time?"

"I started it a long time ago, when you left. It was for your birthday in May, so it's a little late."

Shiloh hugged the gown to her, savoring the feel of the fabric against her. Digging deeper into the box, Ina took out a circlet of dried flowers, woven together.

"For your hair," Ina said.

Shiloh thanked her. "But it's your wedding day, not mine, Ina."

"Don't worry," Ina said, smiling. "I managed to make

436

something quite acceptable for myself from that yellow silk you insisted on buying me."

The minute Ina held up the dress of her to see, Shiloh knew she wouldn't outshine the bride. The yellow dress had been cunningly pleated and gathered, the skirt drawn up on one side with a subtly Latin flare.

"It's beautiful," Shiloh declared, "and so are you."

Prairie Flower arrived with a tray of food to tide them over until the barbecue after the wedding. Shiloh attacked the cornbread and pickle-preserved vegetables.

Almost immediately, she regretted it. The now-familiar nausea rose. She swallowed hard, putting her hand to her mouth.

"Excuse me," she mumbled, and ran for the chamber pot. When she returned, she looked slightly sheepish.

"I guess I've had a nervous stomach lately," she said. "I don't understand it, I've always been so —" She broke off, seeing the curious way the other two women were looking at her.

"What is it?" she demanded. "Why are you laughing?"

Ina took both her hands. "Sit down, Shiloh. Tell us when this 'nervous stomach' started bothering you."

"I really can't say. I thought it was seasickness, but it never went away. Ina, do you think I should see a doctor about it?"

"No, Shiloh. At least, not for several months."

The tears that began to roll down Ina's cheeks frightened Shiloh. She began to dread some fatal disease.

"Ina, *what is it*?"

"You poor child. Poor, motherless child, with no one to confide in, to tell you about being a woman."

Shiloh stood up, at her wits' end. "Ina!"

"We spoke of this before, dear. Remember—"

Prairie Flower snorted in disgust at the Mexican woman's emotional outburst. She circled Shiloh slowly, speculatively, lifting her chin, frankly examining the lines of her torso from breasts to hips.

"Six moons," she grunted. "Maybe five and a half. Then the baby comes."

"A *baby?*" Shiloh whispered, hardly daring to breathe the word. Then she gave an overjoyed whoop, hugging Prairie Flower and then Ina, babbling excitedly all the while.

"A baby of my very own! I can hardly believe it, I—" She broke off and ran for the door. "I've got to tell Justin!"

She leaped down the stairs and out into the garden. Justin and the ranch hands were hauling wood for the barbecue and stacking it beside the great pits.

"Justin!" she cried, running across the lawn to him. "Justin, I have something to tell you!" She collided with him.

Laughing, he caught her in his arms and pulled her against his sweat-damp chest.

"Slow down, sweetheart. Now, what's on your mind?"

"Justin," she panted, "I—I'm" She broke off, looking around. The ranch hands were watching her, openly amused by her display. Suddenly she knew the time wasn't right. Something so important demanded privacy, intimacy, a special moment.

"Well?" Justin asked, grinning.

"I love you," she said simply, and leaned up to kiss him. Then she was gone, leaving him to smile, bemused, behind her.

Birdsongs and the gentle strumming of Leonicio's

guitar provided wedding music of incomparable sweetness. Rows of smiling guests from Houston—the Allens and the Hankses, Lamar Coulter and Mr. Murphy, even two Texas Rangers—graced the benches beneath a spreading oak tree. Nate Mulvane stood, stiff and nervous and glowing with pride, awaiting his bride. Shiloh caught his eye and smiled encouragingly.

Ina arrived shortly, blushing, clutching Justin's arm. They walked slowly to the gazebo. Justin placed Ina's hand in Nate's, bent and kissed her, and stepped back to stand beside Shiloh as the ceremony began.

His hand stole out and found hers, squeezing it as Nate and Ina repeated their vows. Shiloh looked up at him. The two of them had never spoken such words to each other, but now, hearing them, it was as if they had. Silently, they promised a lifetime of love and faithfulness, erasing all the bitterness that had gone before.

When Nate leaned down to kiss his bride, Justin did likewise. Shiloh had never felt so full. Tears of happiness rolled down her cheeks as she contemplated their bright future, with her loving husband, her father and Ina nearby, and soon, a baby . . . she almost sobbed for joy.

The wedding celebration was glorious. A fiddler from town scratched out happy melodies, and food was consumed in huge quantities. Everyone was full of good wishes, toasting the newlyweds until shadows crept long and the sun began to set.

Shiloh was thrilled with the perfection of the day. The guests began to trickle homeward, and she and Justin stood beneath the flower-decked gazebo, smiling at each other.

"People say there's nothing more beautiful than a bride," he murmured, "but I think I've found someone who is. That dress is stunning."

Shiloh fingered the embroidered wildflowers. "Ina has been so wonderful to me. I'm glad you insisted on paying for their wedding trip as a gift from us."

A warm breeze lifted his golden hair and amber shafts of evening light played across the lines of his face. He'd never looked so dear to her.

It was time to tell him about the baby. The moment was perfect, shining with rose-gold light, alive with the sounds of birds and fragrant with the perfume of flowers.

Shiloh brought both of Justin's hands to her lips and kissed them.

"Justin—"

"Oh my," interrupted an unpleasantly familiar voice. "Aren't they the happy couple?"

Justin and Shiloh whirled to see Jessamine West, escorted by Charles Elliot, coming up the walk.

"You're not welcome here," Justin growled. "Either of you."

Jessamine blithely ignored him. "This silly little wedding has turned out to be the social event of the summer," she said. "I'm quite miffed that I wasn't included. And poor Charles, here, has been treated like an outcast ever since those terrible articles came out in the paper. It's all terribly unfair."

"You both got what you deserved," Shiloh said stonily.

Jessamine grew hot with anger. Yellow ringlets bobbed in agitation as she began to pace. "Nothing in my life has been right since you came into it, Shiloh," she stormed. "First you robbed me of the man I was supposed to marry, and then you ruined my father with your meddling . . . he was killed because of you, too. Both of you!"

Shiloh felt an unexpected wave of pity for the girl. She had a twisted sense of logic, but beneath the anger she was truly agonizing.

"Jessamine, I'm sorry about your father. We both are, we—"

"Shut up! I don't want your sympathy. I just want you to pay for what you did." She grew sly, malicious. "Charles's career is ruined because of you. He's too much of a gentleman to call you to task for it, but I have no such compunction. I think it's time Justin learned exactly what went on down in Mexico."

"He already knows everything," Shiloh snapped. But there was something wild and fearsome in the china blue eyes.

Jessamine's malice was infectious. Charles Elliot stepped forward and spoke for the first time.

"If that's true, then I'm sorry to say you're not the person I thought you were, Justin. Have you no pride, man?"

"What the hell are you saying, Elliot?"

He raised an eyebrow above an ice-cold eye. Shiloh noticed that the eye was shot through with red, bleary from drink.

"Perhaps, then," the Englishman sneered, "she has kept it a secret."

"Shiloh and I have no secrets from each other. Say what you came to say, Elliot, and then get the hell off my land."

Jessamine stepped forward. "My life has been ruined, and I certainly don't think Shiloh has the right to be happy. The captain and I think it's only fair that you know that he and Shiloh were lovers in Mexico."

Justin's face hardened; Shiloh's hand went to her mouth. "Oh my God," she whispered, shaking her head in denial. "Oh my God."

Justin had gone rigid. He spoke in a deadly calm voice to Charles Elliot.

"Is this true?"

The Englishman savored the moment. "I'm afraid so, old boy. She came right to my room, brazen as can be. Now, if this unfortunate incident should result in a child, of course I'd assume full responsibility—"

"No!" Shiloh yelled. "He's lying, Justin! Don't listen to him!"

Jessamine's smiled glittered. "We knew she'd deny everything, of course. But we have proof. Show him, Charles."

He produced a crumpled sheet of paper, holding it out as if it were a distasteful thing.

Shiloh gasped as she recognized a page from the journal she'd kept in Mexico, where she'd recorded her most private and intimate thoughts.

"You have no right," she stormed. "That journal is private!"

"Private?" Elliot asked. "But I thought you gave it to me as a memento."

Justin snatched the paper and scanned it with his eyes. Shiloh knew with one glance that it was the page she'd written about their lovemaking, one soft night when the music of harps had set her to longing. She saw a small flower which she'd idly drawn in the margin.

"Justin, he stole that from me in Jalapa," she cried.

"I can tell you other things about your wife that only a lover would know," Elliot suggested slyly. "The scar, for instance. Pity such a lovely thigh had to be marred like that."

Justin's fist shot out and smashed into the leering face. Elliot reeled and fell, blood spurting from his nose.

"Get out of here," Justin said, threatening quietly. "If I ever see you again, I'll kill you."

Elliot took out a handkerchief and dabbed at his nose before getting to his feet.

442

Jessamine tossed her ringlets. "Come on, Charles. We don't have to tolerate any more of this uncivilized behavior." Her blue eyes gleamed with triumph as she gave Shiloh a last, haughty look.

When they had gone, Shiloh collapsed against Justin's chest.

"Thank God they're gone," she breathed. "I hope we've seen the last of them." She put her arms around him to try to recapture the tender moment that had been so unpleasantly interrupted. But his body was stiff and unyielding and his arms hung at his sides.

She looked up. "Justin?"

His fist crumpled the page he was holding. "Is it true?"

She took a step back. "I can't believe you're asking me that. Doesn't my word mean anything to you?"

"You didn't give me your word about anything. Did you go to his room?"

White-hot anger rose in her. "How dare you interrogate me!"

"Just answer the question, Shiloh."

She snatched the paper away. "Yes, damn it, I did go to Elliot's room. But it was to get evidence!"

"And did you show him your scar while you performed your patriotic duty? How far did you go to prove yourself a master spy, Shiloh?"

Fury burst from her and she slapped his face, all the rage she felt putting great force into the blow.

Justin gave her a last hard look and turned sharply. He strode off into the evening light.

Twenty

Houston swarmed with new immigrants eager to settle the nation's newest state. Cotton factors, jubilant after sending off a record crop, celebrated in the grog shops and hotels. There was an air of newness about the town, anticipation of good things to come.

Justin hunched over his beer in a saloon, listening to the talk and laughter around him. Now and then a woman sidled up, her painted face issuing a clear invitation. Justin only shook his head and looked away, and signaled the barkeep for more beer.

A pair of Indian traders came in, their fringed and beaded buckskins greasy and stained, probably from weeks on the trail. One of them had a copy of the *Morning Star*.

"What month is this, Jake?" one of them asked.

Jake laughed. "You kind of lose track out on the frontier, don't you, Mason?" He glanced down at the papers. "October ninth."

"What's been going on?"

"One of these days I'm going to learn you to read, Mason. Let's see here . . . seems we'll be joining the Union officially early next year. Oh, and here's another

444

article by S. Mulvane."

"Read that one, Jake. I like that fellow's writing."

"Fellow?" Jake laughed. "Don't you know about her? She's the woman who blew the whistle on the British when they were huckstering for terms from the Mexicans."

"Yeah, now I remember. Brave woman, wasn't she?"

"I don't know about that. I hear tell she coaxed the secrets out of Captain Elliot in the boudoir, so to speak."

Justin's chair scraped viciously as he shot to his feet. Slamming his beer down, he stalked out of the saloon. At first, he'd challenged everyone who dared speak of the rumor, laying the men flat and leaving the women gasping at his language. But now, four months later, he realized that there was little he could do to stop the gossip that had been perpetuated by Jessamine West.

He didn't go to town much. He couldn't stand the knowing looks, the pitying glances. Thanks to Jessamine, half of Houston knew his wife had left him after a confrontation with Charles Elliot. The Englishman had fled north, pleading ill health, and Shiloh was away at her aunt's, so Justin alone bore the brunt of the rumors.

He went to the auction house and did some horse trading, making a good profit for himself. He got no satisfaction from the deal; he never did anymore. His life was hollow, joyless. He lived haphazardly from day to day, trying—and failing—to forget the red-haired girl who had, for one golden, fleeting moment, captured his heart.

He stopped on the rise in front of Post Oaks. The ranch was the picture of prosperity, a land tamed. Horses grazed peacefully on autumn grasses, drinking from a placid, newly dug tank. The fencing was finished, straight outlines stretching for miles across the acres. Tomas, growing tall and straight into adolescence, was working with a horse in the corral.

Browning leaves blew across the path as Justin rode up to the house. He tried to ignore the gnawing at his gut. This should have been a triumphal year for him and Shiloh. Statehood was imminent, the ranch was a success. The culmination of all they'd worked for should have made their happiness complete.

But her final deception had been the killing blow. She hadn't even tried to defend herself. She'd left without speaking another word to him that night in June.

Months later, he was still haunted by her, hearing her laughter in the rustle of the wind, seeing her smile in the opening flowers in the morning. And then there were those articles, dozens of them, published by the *Morning Star*. She wrote political things, supported abolition, or merely described a pastoral Texas scene. Justin tortured himself by reading all that she wrote. It was like hearing her speak again: impassioned, witty, full of conviction.

He knew that something would give soon. Perhaps he'd sell the ranch, hook up with the Texas Rangers, and leave for the frontier. But for the moment, it was all he could do to endure the numb aftermath of losing Shiloh.

A flock of geese wheeled overhead, flying to the sun-warmed regions below Matagorda. Shiloh watched them from her rocking chair on the porch, feeling as bleak as the iron-gray November sky. There was a pronounced stirring in her belly. The tiny, secret presence there was as restless as Shiloh herself.

Sharon appeared with a tray. She poured two cups of tea and leaned on the railing, the strands of her graying hair lifted by a cool breeze.

"I finished putting up the late squash."

"You should have let me help you."

"Nonsense. I enjoy the work, the warm smells of the spices. Besides, you were busy with your writing. Did you finish with the piece?"

Shiloh nodded. "I wrote about a barn cat making a nest in the hay for her kittens." She smiled slightly. "I seem to be preoccupied with nest-making these days."

"It's only natural. Your time's getting close."

"The weeks seem to drag by. I can't wait to make this little person's acquaintance."

Remembering something, Sharon reached into her apron pocket. "A letter from your father. He tells me they've located Ina's family in San Miguel de Allende."

Shiloh smiled broadly now. "That's wonderful. I'll read it later."

"Nate's not going to like it when he finds out you're here, Shiloh."

She scowled. "I'll deal with that when he gets back from Mexico. Was there anything else in the post?"

Sharon produced another envelope, pursing her lips. Shiloh immediately recognized the scrawling handwriting. As always, she peered inside. And as always, there was a sum of money without a word of explanation.

"Send it back," she said tightly, handing Sharon the envelope.

"Shiloh, he wants to help."

"I won't accept a penny from him. I'm surprised he hasn't gotten the message by now. I must have sent back a dozen of these." She winced slightly as the baby moved.

Noticing, Sharon shook her head. "We're going to be so helpless, you and I. Neither of us has ever been a mother before."

"We'll manage," Shiloh assured her. "There was a

447

baby at Post Oaks for a while. Cassandra. I think we all fell a little bit in love with her. Even Justin used to—" She broke off and swallowed, angry at herself for blundering into the unwelcome thought of him.

Sharon looked at her, at the soft green eyes blinking hard against tears. "Shiloh," she said gently, "hasn't this gone on long enough?"

"I'm not going back there."

"But you need him. And the baby needs a father."

"That's not true, Aunt Sharon. I can provide for the baby. And the child will be better off without the likes of Justin. The paper pays me little enough, but we'll get by."

"The man has a right to know about the baby," Sharon maintained.

"No. He's not to know about it. I won't have him pitying me, or trying to reconcile with me for the sake of the baby."

"You're not being fair, Shiloh. This is all just an awful misunderstanding. If you simply went to him and explained, I know he'd forgive you."

"Forgive me?" Shiloh asked incredulously. "There's nothing to forgive. Don't you see, Aunt Sharon, he didn't trust me. He believed all those lies—"

"Only because you allowed him to."

"I wasn't about to dignify that filth with an explanation. And even if I had done those things, he should have forgiven me. If he truly loved me, he should be able to forgive anything."

Sharon shook her head sadly. "You're two proud, stubborn people. Foolish people. Living in misery when, with a word or two, you could be happy together."

"I could never be happy with a man who doesn't trust me."

"But you love him. And I know he loves you. What

448

about all the money he sends?"

Shiloh smiled bitterly. "In a plain packet, with not so much as a word of explanation. I want nothing from him, Aunt Sharon."

"Shiloh—" Sharon looked up, spying a small figure coming up the path in a mulecart. "Here's Mrs. Mimms, come to check on the baby."

Mrs. Mimms was a "granny lady," an ex-slave who claimed to have delivered some three hundred babies. She lived with a family a few miles distant. She had bright eyes and a wizened, nut-brown face, and delicate hands.

Sharon brought her some tea and she examined Shiloh and questioned her closely about her diet and activities.

"Four weeks, girl," she proclaimed. "Not a day more."

Shiloh felt a thrill of excitement. "Thank you, Mrs. Mimms." She pressed a silver coin into the woman's hand.

Afterward she stood on the porch, watching the evening color streak the horizon and the first winking star in the sky. Her hand strayed to her middle

"It won't be long now," she whispered.

A chill wind rolled in off the plains. Shivering, Shiloh turned and went into the house.

"Are you sure you want to do this, Justin?" Lamar Coulter asked, looking across his paper-strewn desk.

He shrugged. "It won't raise any more of a scandal than we already have."

"I've never handled a divorcing before."

Justin indicated a shelf that sagged with numerous fat tomes. "You've got all those law books. You should be able to figure it out."

Lamar sighed. "I just don't feel right about this.

Christ, the two of you really had something together."

"It's over, Lamar."

The solicitor looked dubious, but promised to get the papers ready and present them to Shiloh.

Justin walked out into the muddy street. The penetrating, bone-chilling iciness of a blue norther whipped down the alleys of Houston. The weather matched his mood. It was raw an inhumanly cold. An appropriate setting in which to end a chapter of his life.

Shiloh could have the ranch; with Nate's help, she'd do all right. Justin would satisfy his bitter restlessness somewhere on the frontier, riding with the Rangers. He'd already had a letter from Captain Jesse Hampton, inviting him to join a company in Comancheria, on the very fringes of civilized society.

The cruelness of the rough life would suit him, just as scouting had suited him when he'd first come to Texas. He'd come full circle, experiencing many things before learning where he belonged. Yet in spite of all the pain and bitterness, he wouldn't have traded a minute of it.

Sleet lashed against the window panes of Sharon Bledsoe's house and the wind penetrated even the smallest cracks in the walls. Shiloh shifted her position on the settee where she lay before a large, crackling fire. She couldn't seem to get comfortable today; nor could she concentrate on her writing. The baby, too, was restless, writhing within its increasingly cramped space.

Mrs. Mimms had been staying with them, since the weather had been bad and Shiloh was so close to her time. Shiloh caught the bright, darting eyes watching her frequently since the baby had dropped two days earlier. It was the week before Christmas, and Mrs.

450

Mimms clearly expected the birth soon.

Above the hiss of the wind and the rattle of the windows, an insistent rapping sounded.

"My goodness," Sharon murmured, "who can that be?"

The voice Shiloh heard was vaguely familiar. Frowning, she tried to remember. And then it came to her: Lamar Coulter. In sudden alarm she drew her knees up and pulled the quilt up to her chin, concealing the rounded swell of her pregnancy. She didn't want Coulter to go running to Justin with her secret.

"Sit down, Mr. Coulter," Sharon was saying. "I'll bring you something warm to drink."

His eyes took in the small cozy room and the aging black woman sitting in the corner with a bit of knitting to occupy her well-shaped hands. Shiloh held her breath as he looked about. There wasn't a proper cradle for the baby, but Sharon had lined a small wooden crate with blankets. It stood near the hearth. Shiloh prayed that Coulter would not guess its intended use.

"What brings you here, Lamar?" she asked, trying not to wince as the baby protested her cramped position.

He hung his hat and cape by the fire to dry out and pulled a stool up next to her. Looking distinctly uncomfortable, he drew out a sheaf of folded papers.

"Justin asked me to go over this with you."

"Oh? Is it something concerning the ranch? I figured it would be clear that I lay no claim to Post Oaks."

"It's not that, Shiloh, it's . . ." he swallowed.

"Just tell me, Lamar."

He handed her the papers. "This is a bill of divorcement. Believe me, I tried to get the marriage annulled, but couldn't come up with sufficient cause. However, we've managed to avoid any mention of you and El—

er — that is, it's a simple case of abandonment."

Shiloh's heart turned to stone. "My God . . ." she breathed incredulously. Only when she felt a light snuffed out within her did she realize that, all these months, she'd harbored and nourished a very faint flicker of hope that Justin would come for her. The papers she held in her hand dealt that tiny flame a suffocating blow. She knew she shouldn't be surprised. Justin was a young man. He could marry again . . . she forced aside the agonizing thought and took a deep breath.

She picked up a pen from the table beside the settee. "Where do I sign?" she asked faintly.

Lamar suddenly took the papers from her. "Shiloh, maybe you shouldn't. This is all a big mistake. You and Justin need to talk —"

"No," she said more forcefully, reclaiming the papers. "If this is what he wants, I'll sign."

"It's not what he wants," Lamar cried. "He — he asked me to do it, but the man doesn't even know himself anymore. You should see him; he's like a hollowed-out shell. He needs you, Shiloh."

Her pen scratched resolutely across the bottom of the paper. "He should have thought of that when he accused me of — never mind; if Justin's confused, I'm not. I'm sure we're doing the right thing." The baby kicked in protest and she lowered here head, hiding a grimace.

"Will you stay for dinner, Mr. Coulter?" Sharon asked.

He shook his head as he pocketed the documents. "I'd best be getting back to town." He gave Shiloh a last, searching look and went out into the storm.

Out of sight of the small farm, Lamar slowed his

horse. All through his visit, he'd had a niggling sense of doubt, and the distinct impression that Shiloh was hiding something. But now he knew her secret. All the pieces fell into place: the old woman, the nestlike box on the hearth, Shiloh's guarded huddling under the quilt.

He wanted Justin to know, but he couldn't go that far. Clearly, Shiloh wanted her secret kept, and Lamar would have to respect that.

But there was one thing he could do, if not for Justin and Shiloh, then for the child. He took out the bill of divorcement and watched as the falling sleet caused the ink to smear and run beyond recognition. When all that remained was a limp, stained piece of paper, Lamar cast it to the northerly wind and rode on.

"Breathe out, girl. Don't be holding your breath," said Mrs. Mimms, allowing Shiloh to clutch desperately at her hand. "You've got to send that baby some air."

Shiloh let out her breath in a huge puff. Her labor, started shortly after Lamar Coulter's visit, was passing in a thick haze of pain, punctuated by the sharp iron-banded agony of her contractions. She endured it in silence, concentrating on the star pattern of a quilt that hung from a rack at the end of the bed.

But now the pains were coming fast, thundering through her, battering her spirit.

"I can't—go—on—" she gasped. "Can't—"

"Hush now," said Mrs. Mimms.

"Think of the baby," Sharon said encouragingly.

"I—oh my God—" A pressure began building deep within her, pounding, demanding release. Shiloh heard herself calling Justin's name, but she was in too much pain to chide herself for it.

"Bear down," said Mrs. Mimms, hissing into her ear. "Bear down, girl!"

Shiloh strained with all her might, until her ears rang, and her hands grew raw as she clutched at the bed frame. Mrs. Mimms and Sharon were saying something, which she didn't hear and couldn't have heeded if she had. She could only respond to the pain and the pressure and the overwhelming need of her body.

The baby burst from her in a great rush. Sharon sobbed and Shiloh grew rigid. Then a high wail filled the room.

"A boy," Mrs. Mimms said, trying to understate her satisfaction. "A fine boy-child."

There was one last convulsing pain, the afterbirth, and Shiloh's body returned to her control. She reached for the hastily swaddled bundle.

He was a miracle, pure and simple. Blotched and wizened, dark colorless eyes unseeing, tiny mouth opening to cry, yet he was the most awesomely beautiful thing Shiloh had ever beheld.

"Hello, baby," she whispered, already full of love for the tiny creature. At the sound of her voice the child quieted and seemed to stare into his mother's face. He grimaced slightly, appearing to smile.

Shiloh's heart caught in her throat. The little red cheek was creased with a dimple, one that echoed his father's so precisely that she began to cry.

"Damn it, Lamar, it's been eight weeks since Shiloh signed that paper."

"Be patient, Justin," said Lamar Coulter. "These things take time. All the legal cases have been slowed down by the transition from republic to statehood."

Justin had the distinct impression that Lamar was

454

evading him, sidestepping his inquiries about the divorce. But he couldn't refute his friend's logic.

He turned to watch Tomas in the corral. The boy was working with Dawn, the little filly he and Shiloh had brought into the world together nearly three years ago.

God, was it really three years? It seemed like only yesterday when a young girl, feisty and full of bravado, had accosted him in Washington-on-the-Brazos. Every memory was crystal clear, as if it had only just happened. Justin had hoped that the years would dim the remembrances, but it hadn't worked that way. He wouldn't rest until it was all over, and he was deep into the open grasslands of Comancheria.

A dog barked in the distance, a little cur pup Justin had given Tomas at Christmastime. He looked up to see the dog running down the road toward an approaching wagon.

A grizzled reddish head beside a gleaming dark one. Justin recognized Nate and Ina Mulvane, returning at last from their wedding trip.

Nate jumped down from the cart, hugging Justin heartily and slapping him on the back.

"Damn, but it's good to see you," he said loudly. "And the ranch looking so fine. Here, I think my wife needs a little help getting down."

Justin grinned from ear to ear as he beheld Ina. The woman blushed furiously under his delighted scrutiny of her pregnant belly. He kissed the flaming cheek and turned to Nate.

"Why you old coot," he said, pumping Nate's hand. "Who'd have ever thought you'd be a papa again?"

Nate swelled visibly with pride. "This time, there'll be no mistakes, no foolishness."

Ina found her voice and said, "Now we must hear all about your own—"

But Prairie Flower, who had come out to greet them, hissed something and placed her hand on Ina's arm. Nate saw this, and suddenly grew concerned.

"Where's Shiloh?" he asked. "Where's my girl?"

One by one, the ranch hands and all the others withdrew, seeming to dissolve into the background. Nate's green eyes flared wildly in fear.

"What is it, Justin? What the hell is going on?"

Justin sent him a quelling look. "She's all right, Nate. But she isn't here. She left the night of your wedding, and I haven't seen her since. She's staying with your sister." Keeping his voice flat, holding back all emotion, Justin explained.

"You ought to be horsewhipped," Nate growled when he'd finished.

"Damn it, Nate, haven't you heard a word I've said? For Christ's sake, she lied to me."

"Only because she loved you, you dad-blamed fool. She wanted to protect you from knowing about something that couldn't be helped and can't be changed. Have you bothered to think about what it was like for her in Mexico? She was alone, desperate. She did the best she could. And you threw her out because of it."

"I didn't throw her out, Nate. She left of her own accord. I think she was secretly glad that we ended it. I've been sending her money regularly, but she always returns it. Apparently the paper's paying her enough to get by on."

Nate shot him a hard look. Then he called over his shoulder to Tomas.

"Saddle me a horse, lad. I'm going to see my girl."

"I'm glad we decided to make this trip to Austin," Shiloh declared. The big coach bounced and she clutched the sleeping baby more firmly to her bosom.

456

"I think it's important for little Nathaniel to witness the birth of his state."

Sharon laughed. "The child's barely two months old, dear. I doubt he'll be very impressed by a great historical event."

"But in later years I'll tell him all about it, so he can be a proud son of Texas."

"Don't forget to tell him of your part in all this. Texas owes you a debt of gratitude."

Shiloh lifted the leather flap over a window and looked out to hide her face from Sharon. She knew she'd never be able to speak of those years of her life, for those were the years she'd spent with Justin.

She glanced down at the baby. He was the center of her life now. So sweet, so beautiful. Nathaniel almost filled the cold emptiness in her heart. Almost.

When he grew older and inevitably noticed the absence of a father, she didn't know what she would tell him. She'd given him the McCord name, even though she wasn't sure whether or not she was divorced at the time of his birth. But it was the only thing she'd allow Justin to give, unknowingly, to the boy.

One of the riders ahead of the coach shouted. Leaning out, Shiloh saw the new capital city far in the distance. A cluster of log buildings, and little more. But she'd already decided that this would be her home.

She hadn't told Sharon yet, but her mind was made up. Her editor at the *Morning Star* had agreed to let her be the Austin correspondent, and had generously given her enough money to set up housekeeping. In Austin she wouldn't have to hide. Her son would be a hundred miles away from the father he'd never know.

Shiloh tried hard to feel a thrill of excitement at the prospect of a new home, a new life. But the sadness that tinged her days and tormented her nights remained, a poignant, constant presence. It would always be there.

"Look, we're not too late," Nate said, pointing to the crowd in the distant capital city. He made sure that Justin spurred his horse faster, and then followed.

Nate had convinced Justin that this February day in 1846 was not to be missed. That was the first hurdle. His next task was much more difficult, but the rewards would make it all worthwhile.

He thought back on the last few days, when his scheming had begun. He had gone to Sharon's place and found it deserted. A neighbor had shown up, however, to see to the animals, and had told him where the women had gone.

Nate knew that the reunion he was forcing on the unsuspecting Justin and Shiloh might end in disaster. But better that than never to know. He would merely bring them together; the rest was up to them.

It was for Justin to decide if he could forgive his wife, and for Shiloh to tell him about the baby.

They tethered their horses at the foot of newly cleared Congress Avenue and made their way through a noisy, celebrating throng clustered around the pine-timbered capitol building. President Anson Jones was on the porch, surrounded by other officials, including Mr. Henderson, who would become the new state's first governor. Overhead, the lone star flag flapped its farewell to the wind.

"Come on, Nate," Justin chided. "You don't have to push."

"I just want to get a closer look. There. There's a space, just to the right of the steps." He urged Justin toward the spot.

Justin looked up to show Nate his annoyance, and then froze, standing stock still while the crowd around

458

him surged and swayed.

There was Shiloh, not ten feet away, her red-gold curls blowing against her beautiful face, her eyes contemplative as she lifted them to the flag.

Justin groped for his voice. "Damn you, Nate," he growled. "You knew all along—"

"Go to her, Justin."

His eyes left Shiloh for a fraction of a second. He noticed Sharon Bledsoe, a few paces back. Seeing him, the woman smiled and tears rolled down her cheeks. She lifted a swaddled bundle to reveal the serenely sleeping face of a blond-headed baby—*his* baby.

His guts roiled and twisted within him. His heart began to race. But he stood rooted to the spot.

And then Shiloh's soft eyes left the flag. Her gaze locked with Justin's. He could see from the rapid rise and fall of her chest that she was as shocked as he.

The crowd blurred into the background. Everything except Shiloh ceased to exist.

"Go on, you son of a bitch," Nate hissed urgently, somewhere behind him. "Can't you see she's about to turn tail and run?"

It was true. There was a frightened, almost hunted look in the moss-green eyes.

All around, the crowd hushed and Anson Jones began to speak. A few of his words penetrated the thundering in Justin's ears.

"The lone star of Texas, which rose . . ."

"God *damn* you," Nate hissed. "Get on with it!"

". . . over fields of carnage, and obscurely shone for a while, has culminated . . ."

Shiloh took a tiny step backward. Justin's fists clenched and sweat broke out on his brow.

". . . and become fixed forever in that glorious constellation—"

The baby woke and whimpered a little, the sound a

miracle to Justin's ears.

Finally his leaden feet began to come to life. He took one step, slowly. He wouldn't be able to stand it if she ran away.

". . . the American Union. The final act in this great drama is now performed," Jones continued. "The Republic of Texas is no more."

The crowd stamped and hooted wildly, mostly for joy, although there were a few protesting catcalls. Then silence reigned as the lone star flag was lowered and the Union banner rose in its place.

Justin seized the moment and crossed the distance between him and Shiloh, his heart so full of adoration that he almost soared to her.

Suddenly they were in each other's arms, speechless, yet clinging to each other, desperate with love. Caught together in the aching sweetness of their embrace, the small baby in view behind them, their two shattered hearts became whole again, became one. Justin felt the tears on Shiloh's cheeks.

They mingled with his own as he bent to kiss her.

SWEET MEDICINE'S PROPHECY
by Karen A. Bale

#1: SUNDANCER'S PASSION   (1778, $3.95)

Stalking Horse was the strongest and most desirable of the tribe, and Sun Dancer surrounded him with her spell-binding radiance. But the innocence of their love gave way to passion — and passion, to betrayal. Would their relationship ever survive the ultimate sin?

#2: LITTLE FLOWER'S DESIRE   (1779, $3.95)

Taken captive by savage Crows, Little Flower fell in love with the enemy, handsome brave Young Eagle. Though their hearts spoke what they could not say, they could only dream of what could never be. . . .

#3: WINTER'S LOVE SONG   (1780, $3.95)

The dark, willowy Anaeva had always desired just one man: the half-breed Trenton Hawkins. But Trenton belonged to two worlds — and was torn between two women. She had never failed on the fields of war; now she was determined to win on the battle-ground of love!

#4: SAVAGE FURY   (1768, $3.95)

Aeneva's rage knew no bounds when her handsome mate Trent commanded her to tend their tepee as he rode into danger. But under cover of night, she stole away to be with Trent and share whatever perils fate dealt them.

#5: SUN DANCER'S LEGACY   (1878, $3.95)

Aeneva's and Trenton's adopted daughter Anna becomes the light of their lives. As she grows into womanhood, she falls in love with blond Steven Randall. Together they discover the secrets of their passion, the bitterness of betrayal — and fight to fulfill the prophecy that is Anna's birthright.

Available wherever paperbacks are sold, or order direct from the Publisher. Send cover price plus 50¢ per copy for mailing and handling to Zebra Books, Dept. 2054, 475 Park Avenue South, New York, N.Y. 10016. Residents of New York, New Jersey and Pennsylvania must include sales tax. DO NOT SEND CASH.

Now you can get more of HEARTFIRE right at home and $ave.

Preview
Four Brand New
ZEBRA

Heartfire

Romance Novels...

FREE for 10 days.

No Obligation and No Strings Attached!

♥

Enjoy all of the passion and fiery romance as you soar back through history, right in the comfort of your own home.

Now that you have read a Zebra **HEARTFIRE** Romance novel, we're sure you'll agree that **HEARTFIRE** sets new standards of excellence for historical romantic fiction. Each Zebra **HEARTFIRE** novel is the ultimate blend of intimate romance and grand adventure and each takes place in the kinds of historical settings you want most...the American Revolution, the Old West, Civil War and more.

<u>FREE</u> Preview Each Month and $ave

Zebra has made arrangements for you to preview 4 brand new HEARTFIRE novels each month...FREE for 10 days. You'll get them as soon as they are published. If you are not delighted with any of them, just return them with no questions asked. But if you decide these are everything we said they are, you'll pay just $3.25 each— a total of $13.00 (a $15.00 value). **That's a $2.00 saving each month off the regular price.** Plus there is NO shipping or handling charge. These are delivered right to your door absolutely free! There is no obligation and there is no minimum number of books to buy.

TO GET YOUR FIRST MONTH'S PREVIEW... Mail the Coupon Below!